The Taming of Malcolm Grant

Also by Paula Quinn

Lord of Desire

Lord of Temptation

Lord of Seduction

Laird of the Mist

A Highlander Never Surrenders

Ravished by a Highlander

Seduced by a Highlander

Tamed by a Highlander

Conquered by a Highlander

A Highlander for Christmas (e-novella)

The Seduction of Miss Amelia Bell

The Sweet Surrender of Janet Buchanan (e-novella)

The Wicked Ways of Alexander Kidd

The Scandalous Secret of Abigail MacGregor

The
Taming
of Malcolm
Grant

PAULA QUINN

FOREVER

NEW YORK   BOSTON

Copyright © 2015 by Paula Quinn
Excerpt from the next MacGregors: Highland Heirs novel copyright © 2015 by Paula Quinn
All rights reserved. In accordance with the U.S. Copyright Act of 1976, the scanning, uploading, and electronic sharing of any part of this book without the permission of the publisher constitute unlawful piracy and theft of the author's intellectual property. If you would like to use material from the book (other than for review purposes), prior written permission must be obtained by contacting the publisher at permissions@hbgusa.com. Thank you for your support of the author's rights.

Forever
Hachette Book Group
1290 Avenue of the Americas
New York, NY 10104

www.HachetteBookGroup.com

Printed in the United States of America

First Edition: September 2015
10 9 8 7 6 5 4 3 2 1

OPM

Forever is an imprint of Grand Central Publishing.
The Forever name and logo are trademarks of Hachette Book Group, Inc.

The Hachette Speakers Bureau provides a wide range of authors for speaking events. To find out more, go to www.hachettespeakersbureau.com or call (866) 376-6591.

The publisher is not responsible for websites (or their content) that are not owned by the publisher.

MacGregor/Grant
Family Tree

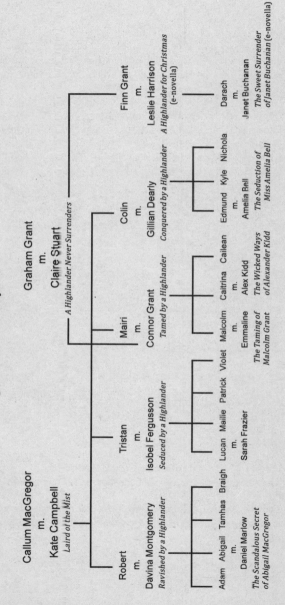

The
Taming
of Malcolm
Grant

Chapter One

I thought travelin' with ye would be different, a bit of an adventure mayhap. But since we entered Hebburn, 'tis been nothin' but ridin' and rain. Where is this brothel ye told me aboot?"

Beneath his hood, Malcolm Grant smiled at his brooding brother riding ahead of him. He didn't bother to look up since, in the downpour, he couldn't see an inch in front of his face anyway.

"We'll be there soon enough, Cailean," he called out, "and then ye'll thank me fer makin' haste and ridin' in the rain."

Malcolm had been to Fortune's Smile before. He'd practically lived there for several months after the proprietor's wife had been killed. He hadn't been back in four years. But now he was here for Cailean. His old friend Harry Grey owned and ran it so Malcolm knew he could expect the best room, the best girl, and the best whisky. Once in a while there was nothing better or more soothing to a man who lived in a hard world than a full belly, a soft bed, and a warm body to share it with. His brother was twenty and one and still a virgin. It was high time he lay with a lass who knew her way around a man's body. Fortune's Smile was the perfect place to go for such pleasures.

"'Tis just up ahead," he said as he guided, knowing how to get there in the pitch black or pouring rain. He caught up with Cailean and they followed the inviting warmth of fire-lit windows to the front of the two-story brothel. "I know how yer passions turn toward cookin'," he said to his brother, "but stay oot of Harry Grey's kitchen if the need to cook strikes ye. His wife died in it and he's verra' sensitive aboot it."

"Not to worry," Cailean drawled quietly.

"Let me do the talkin'," Malcolm continued, dismounting and handing his reins over to a stable boy. "Save fer Harry, the men are no' friendly here. They'll look fer the first excuse to fight."

"So?" Cailean challenged, straightening his shoulders against the pelting rain. "Practice with our kin, nae matter how gruelin' 'twas, has prepared me to stay alive against folks who might someday try to kill me." He slowed and waited for Malcolm to reach him. "Let them look fer a fight and I will give them one."

Malcolm shrugged, quite used to Cailean's bravado, seeing the same in almost every male—and many females—of the Grant/MacGregor ilk. He was, of course, of the same mind. He didn't mind fighting, but he'd like a damn drink first.

He pushed the door open and stepped inside. Familiar scents assailed his nostrils and he closed his eyes for a moment to savor them. The aromas of rose and wine, jasmine and whisky, sex and sweat. The only smell he loved more was early morning in Camlochlin.

Temporarily content, he swept his hood back from his head, releasing a tumble of deep chestnut hair splashed throughout with bolts of gold. He moved his gaze over the patrons, seated at dimly lit tables in the cozy dining hall, and then over a few of the lasses who worked there. He didn't recognize any of them. It didn't matter if he knew them or not. They stopped and waved at him, looking a bit breathless. He personally didn't consider himself handsome, not with his bent nose and mostly disillusioned expression that tainted his grin. But he had dimples, and according to the lasses at Camlochlin, lasses liked dimples, deep ones.

He smiled at them, one by one, wondering who would be best for Cailean's first time. Though Malcolm was infamous for being a heartless rogue, he hadn't come for himself. In fact, he had no intention of taking any one of them to bed. What he wanted was a warm fire, warm whisky, and a warm bed for sleep.

"Close the damned door before I get up and put your head through it!" a patron shouted, spoiling Malcolm's good mood.

Malcolm turned to give the fool a deadly look. Truly? Could a soul not rest for a wee bit before he wet his tongue? What the hell else was new?

Very well then

"Close yer mouth," Cailean called back, taking his time with the door, "before I walk over there and put m' fist in it."

"I doubt you're worthy of such a boast, boy." Rising from his chair, the fool continued, as fools often do.

Malcolm assessed him quickly. Medium height, densely built, slow reflexes. Cailean could handle him.

"But which one of you is going to pay for letting in the rain to soak my clothes?"

Malcolm thought about it while he untied the laces of his cloak from around his neck. "I'll give ye two pence fer yer boots. The rest should have been put to the flame last month." With a flick of his wrist he freed the wool from his broad shoulders and snapped it like a whip, showering the patron with cool droplets.

A true fight would do the youngest Grant good, Malcolm thought, stepping aside and watching the patron go barreling into Cailean. He didn't bother to see how his brother fared against the troublemaker, but turned his restored grin on a long-limbed, extremely lean man limping toward him from the inner parlor. He approached with a cup in one hand and a bonny woman in the other.

"I wasn't sure I'd see ye pass this way again, Malcolm!" Harry Grey let go of the lass and grabbed him in a tight embrace.

"Where would I be, Harry?" Malcolm accepted the cup and tossed his arm around his good friend. "And dinna' say wed or dead. Ye know I'd never fall to either one. Why the hell are ye limpin', old friend?"

"I was stabbed in the leg and didn't care for it soon enough."

Malcolm shook his head, staring at him. "What have I told ye aboot hirin' men to protect ye? Ye dinna' know how to fight."

"I do have a guard, but he's serving another duty presently."

They both watched Cailean make a quick end of his opponent and toss him out the door.

"M' brother," Malcolm said proudly.

"Of course." Harry sighed, sounding worried. "You remember Bess?"

Malcolm sure as hell did remember her. Last time he

was here, he'd stayed for several months and Bess had grown quite fond of him. She was one of the last women he'd been with. A wild cat who jabbed her claws into him and had a hard time letting go.

Harry thanked Cailean for disposing of the man and not leaving him there bleeding on the floor. "I heard yer sister was kidnapped by pirates last year," he told Malcolm as he led him to a table.

"She wasna' kidnapped," Malcolm corrected him, patting his brother's back as Cailean sat.

Harry stopped and turned to him. "She went of her own free will?"

"Aye," Malcolm told him, as if there were absolutely nothing wrong with it. To him, there wasn't. "She's the adventurous kind."

Malcolm smiled indulgently when Bess settled into his lap and proceeded to tell them about her adventure from Ayr to Hebburn last spring. Malcolm didn't think pointing out the difference between her journey and his sister's would do her any good.

They sat together for the next hour, drinking and laughing while Malcolm recalled how he and Harry had met.

"Harry saved m' life," Malcolm told Cailean, "when the Buchanans of Perth were still our enemies, before our cousin Darach wed the Buchanan chief's sister, Janet. A group of them had come upon me on the road and had taken me by surprise. They beat me unconscious and dragged m' body to the brothel, where they celebrated their victory with wine and loose women. Harry discovered me tied to a horse in the stable later that night. He hid me in one of the rooms upstairs and left me alone to recover and live another day. Though Harry is English,"

Malcolm praised, "he didna' throw me oot of the establishment on m' Highland arse."

"That's because"—Harry raised his cup to him—"you kept the men who killed my wife from killing me, as well. Though, sometimes I don't know whether to bless you or curse you."

Malcolm nodded, not understanding why any man would rather be dead with his wife than alive without her.

"You're hard." Bess looked up at Malcolm with dewy blue eyes as vast and empty as the skies. "Like steel," she purred against his neck while she spread her hand over his arm and then down his chest. "I'll wager you're still just as hard all over."

He groaned from somewhere deep in his throat. Bess knew her profession of how to please a man to bursting. But he left her pining after him once. He sure as hell wouldn't do it again.

"Ask Harry for me," she whispered across his ear, "and I'll find out for myself just how hard you can get."

She bit his lobe and settled her narrow hips deeper into his lap.

He wanted what she offered, likely he wanted it more with her than any lass since he stopped sleeping with them. She was good at what she did.

But he was weary of empty embraces.

He shook his head. "I'm payin' fer yer night with m' brother."

She cast him a lecherous smile. "I'll have you both."

He laughed. Hell, she was perfect for Cailean's first. If anyone could suck the demons out of a man, it was Bess.

But Cailean didn't seem interested in Bess at all. Instead, his eyes were fixed on a bonny lass with russet curls and humble breasts. Harry explained that the gel was bought and paid for for the night by Andrew Winther, brother of the Baron of Newcastle. If Cailean wanted her, he would have to wait until tomorrow. Cailean didn't want to wait, but he accepted things the way they were, as he was known to do, and set his sights on someone else—until his fiery-haired interest was flung into a chair by Winther.

Malcolm watched Cailean rush to the lass's side and then turn in time to punch the oncoming culprit clean across the room. Malcolm couldn't have been any prouder.

When Andrew Winther's companions ran toward Cailean next, Malcolm hurried to his brother's side. He swung. It landed a brutal punch to the closest assailant's face. The man swayed, trying to gain his wits. A second punch cracked a bone and knocked the man out.

Malcolm glanced at his brother and found him releasing another man's unconscious body to the neatly swept floor. Malcolm smiled and turned his attention on the third victim, who was coming at him with a dagger raised high.

Malcolm picked up a poker from the large hearth and swung it across the man's belly, breaking two ribs and leaving him squirming on the floor.

The whole thing was over rather quickly, with the four Winthers dumped unconscious outside where the rain washed the blood from their wounds.

A handful less Englishmen in their presence was a good thing. With the place less rowdy, Malcolm and Cailean returned to their table, Cailean with Alison, his russet-haired prize, and toasted the sound of cracking bones.

Harry sat slumped in his chair, his complexion drained of blood. "The Winthers?" he panted at Malcolm. "Why them? You don't know what you've done."

Malcolm hadn't expected Harry to fight with them, he was the proprietor after all, but he did expect Harry to have hired a few strong arms around the brothel to keep the shyt out, the way he used to.

"Harry," Malcolm soothed. "Dinna' fear—"

Harry shook his head. "You don't know the Baron of Newcastle. Oliver Winther is a merciless son of a whore, arresting and hanging or beheading anyone who comes against him. He has the support of his entire family, whose number, it's rumored, is in the thousands. He has a passion for killing that's only exceeded by his lust for women. I don't want him to ever come here—for any reason."

Hell, Harry looked about to shyt his breeches. Malcolm hated that his friend lived in such fear, but this was Harry's home, not Malcolm's. What did it matter what Malcolm thought of the bunch of gangly English who collapsed to the ground after three punches? Why, his sister could have taken them on two at a time. He did all to reassure Harry that the Winthers were nothing to fear. He and Cailean would stay on as long as Harry needed his protection.

"Drink with us, Harry." He pushed another round at Harry and laughed when his friend accepted. "Bess!" he called out to the bonny blonde who'd scurried off during the fight. Where the hell had she gone? He shrugged and smiled at the rest of the girls who worked there.

Here's what he missed—being surrounded by women. What he needed to put away all other thoughts and concerns. What the hell was he doing being celibate? It wasn't his passion in the bedroom that needed taming.

It was the monster biting at his heels, reminding him of what he'd never have.

"Pardon my intrusion."

Malcolm looked up at a lass he hadn't seen before. Then again, would he have remembered her? There was nothing remarkable about her appearance. A slight, wee thing in a gown that was neither colorful nor cut to show off her curves, like the girls' gowns around her. She was rather pale, with large, dark eyes, and even darker circles beneath them, and long, yellow waves. She stood facing Harry, her delicate hand resting in the crook of a brawny arm.

So, Malcolm thought, glancing at the owner of the arm. Here was the seemingly only guard in the brothel and he was too busy rutting to see to his duty.

"I was wondering if I might bring Gascon inside for the night."

Her voice swept across Malcolm's ears like a symphony of tinkling stars. It was light and flimsy, like a veil settling over him, capturing his attention within a web of sensual French inflection.

He liked French lasses.

Why hadn't Harry brought her to him?

" 'Tis still raining—"

"Now, Emmaline." Harry sighed, sounding sincerely regretful.

She lowered her head, displaying the full cut of her mouth and the small slope of her pert nose. Her almost silent sigh of resignation pricked at Malcolm for some annoying reason he didn't know.

"Haven't we discussed this long enough? Dogs don't belong inside, getting everything muddy and wet."

Malcolm laughed, bringing Emmaline's attention to him. "Then ye would hate my home, Harry. We have five wolfhounds, or whatever in blazes they are, roamin' the halls right along with everyone else."

"You're correct," his friend agreed. "I would hate it."

Malcolm thought he caught the lass's slight smile beyond the tilt of her head. He wanted to see it full on.

Who was the escort? Malcolm thought, sizing him up. The brute had no interest in her but to keep her attached to his arm. If he did care for her, he would be trying to comfort her from her obvious distress.

"'Tis a heavy downpour oot there." Malcolm gave it a try, looking toward the door. He might be the worst rogue in Scotland, England, France, but he had a heart. And he liked dogs. He knew firsthand that they perished just like anything else when exposed to the elements. He looked at his brother, remembering Sage, Cailean's faithful hound.

Turning back to Harry, he said more seriously, "Come now. I'll pay fer a room fer the mongrel and a lass to clean him up. I'll count it as a favor," he added when Harry looked about to refuse him, as well.

"As would I," Cailean said, sounding far less friendly.

"Put your coin away," Harry relented, and held up his palms. "Go, Emmaline. Fetch your dog from the rain."

Harry smiled and blushed a tinge of claret when she pulled her hand free of her escort and placed it on his arm. "Thank you."

She turned in a half circle, spinning her long waves over her shoulders and over the smile she aimed just a wee bit to Malcolm's left. Her joy was radiant and infectious. "Thank you, my lord." Without waiting for his reply, she turned again and hurried toward the door.

Malcolm watched her, his smile fading from his lips when she banged into the table in front of her.

"Emmaline!" Harry said harshly. "Wait for Gunter! And what the hell have I told you about not coming down whilst I have guests?"

Gunter with the brawny arms hurried after her and returned her hand to his elbow once again. Harry shook his head, turning back to Malcolm.

"She'll want the beast inside every night now."

"She's blind." It became even more apparent while Malcolm watched her wait for Gunter, who had run out into the rain. She didn't move. She didn't watch the door, but inclined her ear toward it instead.

"Completely," Harry confirmed.

Hence, her need for Gunter, Malcolm thought as her escort returned, soaking wet and not alone.

Gascon, a tall hound of some sort, with flowing brown and tan fur, quite a bit more handsome than the hounds of Camlochlin, galloped into the foyer and sprayed water everywhere. When he saw Emmaline he immediately sat on his haunches, reaching her waist and still dripping all over the floor. The dog's reward for his good behavior was a hug from his mistress.

"Someone's going to have to clean that up!" Harry called out.

The lass nodded, then grasped Gascon by the scruff of his neck and, abandoning Gunter altogether, let the dog lead her away. A dog that helped her see.

Fascinating, Malcolm thought. He wanted to know where Harry found her. "Who is she?"

"My sister," Harry told him, reaching for another cup of wine.

"Yer sister?" Malcolm laughed and shook his head when Bess returned and held a cup to his lips. "Ye never mentioned her before."

"I thought she died ten years ago. She found me last month."

"That's good fortune, friend," Malcolm said.

"'Tis," Harry agreed. "That's why I must ask you to forget her. I know you and love you like a brother. You saved my life."

"As ye saved mine," Malcolm reminded him.

Harry smiled. "Once."

"Once is all it takes to die, Harry."

"Like I said," Harry went on, "I love you like a brother. I know that you've no interest in love. Your reputation with women precedes you. The last time you were here—"

Malcolm forced his best smile but held up his palm to stop where Harry was going. He didn't need reminding.

"You're a rake," his friend continued, granting him less detail. "Quite a notorious one. Stay away from my sister so she doesn't get her heart broken."

Malcolm didn't argue. Harry was correct about him— as far as who he was four years ago. Malcolm didn't bother correcting him. Harry wouldn't believe him.

Malcolm pulled him under his arm and patted his back to reassure his friend of his sincerity. "Ye've nothin' to fret aboot, Harry. I did this fer the dog. No' fer her."

Chapter Two

*E*mmaline Grey rushed up the stairs so that when she came to the next landing, she could drop to her knees and hug her dearest friend in private—or at least in private until Gunter reached them. She'd get Gascon cleaned and dried, but that could wait until after she greeted him.

"Oh, dear Gascon, 'tis good to have you inside again, where you belong." He licked her face and the tears fell from her eyes. "Come, I shall feed you a feast tonight."

She led him down the hall to her room, since he didn't know the way yet. Thanks to Gunter, she didn't bang into anything on the way. But now with Gascon around, she wouldn't need her escort.

She hadn't always been blind. She was struck with a fever that snatched away her sight in her tenth year—the same fever that had killed both her parents and her uncle a fortnight earlier while they visited her uncle's home in France. The fever that had kept her from ever seeing her home in England again. The fever that ultimately drove Harry to leave France and abandon her at the first sign that she was infected. She hadn't blamed her brother for leaving her then, and she still didn't. Harry had been ten and five at the time and afraid of dying.

Emma had been afraid too, and she came much closer to it. An old hag who lived in the woods, a rumored witch who knew how to heal people's ailments, had found her in her bed, deathly ill with the fever. Dying, in fact. Clementine and her faithful hound, Gascon, never left her side and nursed her back to good health. But Emma woke from her delirium into muted light and darkening shadows.

Her world was fading.

Color had gone first, so she fought the hardest to remember the way a ten-year-old would: red, like an apple; green, like treetops in summer; blue, like the beautiful ocean hot under the orange sun. She tried to remember, but after the years, memories faded. Except for one. She remembered seeing the sea when she was on her way with her family to her uncle's home. Those images of sunlight on the water, indistinct as they had become, had often drifted across her thoughts and kept her going while she grew up in the darkness. She'd never see the ocean again, and for her, that was what saddened her most about losing her vision. She wanted to see the water once more.

Clementine never allowed her to wallow in her loss. Instead, she taught Emma to see using the rest of her senses.

Colors had returned to her first, even more vibrant than the ones before. She still thought with her memory of the sky in reference to blue, because she knew it was correct. But blue had become so much more. It was cold like a stream running through a mountain or a brook babbling through a wintry forest.

She had a happy life growing up in Clementine's small

cottage made of stone and winding ivy, surrounded by trees and nature. She was sure her life would have been very different if not for the fever, but she didn't want the life she could have had. She loved learning how to live by a wise old French woman who'd never harmed a fly.

With the help of Gascon, she'd learned to traipse and weave through trees. Under nature, and Clementine's tutelage, she learned what the woods had to offer as food and as medicine. Familiar with every leaf, every petal, every tree, where to find any herb and how to recognize them from touch, scent, and taste. After a decade, she could heal most infirmities as well as her teacher could. But she didn't want to. People didn't deserve it, not after what they'd done to Clementine. So she left her home in the cottage in France before they strung her up next. Finally, she was going home.

But her home was gone, sold by her brother four years ago so he could buy this brothel. She didn't hate him for it. She couldn't. He was all she had left.

It hadn't taken her long to find Harry, since his brothel was famous. When she arrived at Fortune's Smile with Gascon, her brother was suffering with a festering wound in his thigh. She had no choice but to heal him, hoping that Harry would never accuse her of being a witch. She agreed to help his girls too if any of them became ill in exchange for room and board while she and Harry got to know each other.

They still didn't.

She'd realized that coming back to England to find her brother wasn't such a good idea when he cast Gascon out of his establishment. She begged Harry to let her have her dog. He'd agreed, but Gascon had to remain outside. She thought of leaving many nights while she sat by her bedroom window, taking in the scents of jasmine and the sounds of her dog sleeping below her window. Where would she go? She could return to France but she had no coin.

She lifted her hand and ran her fingers over Gascon's muzzle. So happy to have him inside.

She didn't want to think about her past, or what drove her to leave Clementine's cottage in search of Harry. Not now. She wouldn't ruin a grand night with such a memory. She had Gascon back. That's all that mattered. And she had that man—Had she heard his name?—to thank.

Emma didn't know about men, nothing compared to the girls she lived with. But she knew she was forever indebted to this one. She told Gascon about him while she scrubbed him in a large basin carried into her room by three of her brother's servants.

"He's quite tall, and he smells like the rain."

Gascon shook his large frame and splattered her with sudsy water.

"Goodness!" she exclaimed. "You could give a girl warning!"

The dog whined torturously, mollifying her temporary annoyance with him.

"He's the reason you're inside, Gascon. If you see him tomorrow let him pet your head as thanks. Of course, he'll most likely be gone in the morning but I will remember the sound of his voice for a long time to come. It drifted across my ears like the melodic burr of the northern Scots, those they call Highlanders. There was one of them here a pair of weeks ago, but his pitch was different, not weighty and light at the same time like the man downstairs." She sighed happily to herself and continued drying Gascon's coarse coat. When she was done, she hurried off to the kitchen with Gunter to fix her friend a feast, as promised. She didn't care if her escort swore the entire way down to tell her brother that she'd disobeyed his command to remain away from the patrons. Let him tell whatever he wanted. She would have gone alone if she had to.

Gunter led her down the back stairs to the kitchen and left her to her task.

Holding out her arms, she felt everything around her, the sticky surface of the chopping block, an axe, onions. She kept going, feeling her way around the familiar kitchen to a shelf with different sized wooden bowls piled upon it. Emma chose the biggest bowl for Gascon. She gathered carrots and searched for meat, following her nose and using her ears to hone in on the buzzing of a fly. She found some salmon, not too fresh, but not spoiled, a small, defeathered hen, and a slab of deer meat, from which she cut a small piece.

Ready to return to her room, she left the kitchen in search of Gunter. She knew her way to the stairs and up them, but Gascon's bowl was heavy. The thundering collapse of a wooden table just to the left of her head halted the blood in her veins, and her feet. Her ears filled with the sounds of breaking bones and splintering wood. A fight! She whirled around.

"Gunter?"

Men shouted around her. Was that Brianne's scream or Mary's? From above stairs, locked in her room, she could hear Gascon barking. The smells of wine and ale filled the air... sweat, and blood too.

Someone fell into her, just barely, but almost knocked her down. His heart beat hard against her ribs.

This was the reason Harry didn't let her come down

without her escort, and only after the place was empty. He never let her out after dark. She understood that he'd lost his wife and he didn't want the same fate to befall his sister. She didn't want that either. But here she was in the middle of a brawl! Harry would be even more watchful over her now! She had to get to her room. She quelled the rush of fear and anger that boiled up within and gathered up her courage.

She could stand there, or she could keep herself alive. She knew she was bold. She'd already been through the worst kinds of fears anyone, especially a child, could face, and was still alive to think about it. She wasn't frail. Harry didn't know her. Refusing Gascon's entrance into the brothel proved it.

Someone came near. Senses heightened, she smelled wine on his breath and the fragrant aroma of basil coming off the rest of him. She didn't wait to figure out what else she could smell, but lifted Gascon's bowl over her head and brought it down on his with all her might. He fell at her feet. Her heart pumped madly in her chest, making her feel ill. Did she just kill someone? Was he still alive and angrier than ever?

"Miss Grey." The stranger's voice, heavy, urgent, and welcoming behind her. "M' brother Cailean will escort ye upstairs. Go! Now!"

Someone grabbed her elbow and led her out of the path of her victim. He hurried her toward the stairs, making her head spin. Everything was happening so quickly.

Who was pulling her up the stairs? Was he truly the brother of the man who'd saved her dog? "You are Cailean?" she breathed out as they ascended.

"Aye, lass. Ye've nothin' to fear. We'll keep ye and the others safe."

She remembered his voice now. "Ye agreed with your brother about letting Gascon inside. You have my utmost thanks for that."

He didn't speak for two more hurried steps up.

"And your brother?" she asked. "What is he called so that I might properly thank him when this is over?"

"Malcolm...Malcolm Grant," he told her, and then left her on the landing.

Grant. She'd heard the name before. The girls whispered of him every time a patron was dull in bed. Malcolm Grant, who knew how to make a woman lose her wits, her words, and her will to live without more of him.

Emma doubted he was any kind of man who'd ever win her heart. She wasn't fond of his type, the kind who took every woman in a skirt to his bed. But his voice, she would admit, had been sultry and mesmerizing to her ear when he said her name and promised Cailean's help.

Harry had spoken of him too. They were friends, but Harry assured all the girls that Grant broke hearts. He might win them, but he never kept any. He was a silver-tongued rake known throughout Scotland and parts of England. If she remembered correctly, Harry described Malcolm Grant as the snake that tempted Eve in the Garden.

Emma could understand how that could be true. If he went about rescuing animals the way he did for Gascon... Well, how bad could he be? Besides, one thing she learned about Harry since they'd been reunited was that he was overly dramatic.

Mr. Grant didn't seem like a rake, or a cad, or whatever women called men like him these days. But what did she know of such things?

She heard bone snapping against flesh coming from

below—bones or more tables. How would Harry pay for everything to be repaired?

She moved against the wall and returned to her room and to Gascon, where it was safe.

A shot rang out from downstairs. Harry! Where would she go if he were killed? She shook her head. He wasn't fool enough to lose his life. He'd proven that in France.

Another shot, followed by more screams, shattered her nerves and she backed up to her bed and pulled Gascon close to her while she stared toward the door. Would someone come for her? Kill her? Or worse?

She waited until silence resounded through the brothel and made the hairs on her arms rise. Her heart pounded like a drum when she heard someone outside her door. Beside her, Gascon's low growl chilled her blood.

No! If someone was coming in here, they wouldn't find her cowering in a corner waiting for whatever he was bringing. She was made of tougher stuff than that.

Leaping to her feet, she hurried around her bed, snatched up her candle stand, and blew out the flame. Equal ground.

A knock. She held up her bronze weapon and prepared to swing. Gascon's growl grew louder, more menacing. The door opened and her dog lunged.

"Miss Grey!" Gunter shouted behind the door after he slammed it shut again. "Your brother needs you. Call off that beast!"

She swallowed, doing all she could not to panic. "He is hurt?"

"No," he called through the door. "His two friends have been, though, and he wants you to help."

"The Grants?" she asked, opening the door and slipping

out into the hall with him. The desire to help overwhelmed her. She was a healer. She didn't want to be killed because of it, like Clementine had been, but she couldn't stop the need to save someone's life. "Both of them? How badly? Who is responsible for this?"

"They are not moving," he told her. "'Twas the Winthers. There were a dozen of them. Some had pistols. Even so, many are dead down there, so step carefully."

Grasping Gascon's scruff, Emma followed with extra caution. She'd never stepped over dead bodies before and the thought of it made her head spin. Sensing her unease and imbalance, Gascon guided her steadily. Trusting him, she let go of what was around her and focused on what she'd been called to do.

She would save Harry's friends. She owed Malcolm Grant much. He'd brought Gascon back to her, even if just for tonight. She would do her best to make sure her dog stayed . . . and Mr. Grant lived.

"Emmaline." Harry stopped her with a hand to her arm when she moved to pass him. "The Grants, my friends, have been wounded. It is bad enough that they killed Andrew Winther in my brothel. Trouble is coming, I can promise you that. But if the Grants die, it will bring something worse."

"Worse than the Winthers?" she asked. Everyone knew the Winthers. They controlled everything in Newcastle and Hebburn, and parts of Durham. She'd heard rumors of the baron's lust for blood and power.

Her brother nodded to himself. "Malcolm Grant's kin are enemies no one wants to have—most of all, me. Save my guests, Emma. I beg you."

Chapter Three

*E*mma said a silent prayer that she could help them. Of course, she would try, but why not use this as a bit of leverage for Gascon. "Let Gascon stay and I'll do my best—"

"Emmaline—"

"Let him stay, Harry. He's all I have."

"You have me."

She hadn't meant to hurt his feelings, but she barely remembered him, they'd been separated for so long. She was certain they would grow to care for each other in time, but right now, she needed Gascon. "Let him stay."

"Very well," he grumbled, seeming to ignore her enthusiastic thanks.

She would help his friends and began with an examination. She knew what she was doing. Clementine had taught her much and Emma learned how to keep men snoring while she removed a pistol ball or sewed up a wound.

Rather than move the brothers without knowing a bit more about their injuries, she checked them on the ground where they fell. The other girls helped.

With Mary acting as her eyes, Emma discovered that

Malcolm Grant had been shot in the neck, more toward the collarbone than the jaw. The shot had exited from his back so at least Emma wouldn't have to go digging around to find it. She guessed that what had rendered him unconscious though was a blow that, according to Bess, had been inflicted with a loose wooden table leg. It left his skull swollen and dripping blood down his face.

"Emma!" Alison stifled a tight sob from where she waited on her knees beside Mr. Grant's brother. Emma remembered his voice when he told her his name, Cailean, and the name of his brother, his gentle yet firm hand while he'd escorted her up the stairs when the fight began. "He has stopped answering me!" Alison shouted at her.

Emma made her cautious way over and knelt down in a pool of Cailean's blood.

Alison sniffed but there was no time to comfort her. "Where are his wounds?" Emma commanded, skimming her hands over his body.

"He has a shot in his belly. Here." Alison guided Emma's fingers to the bloody wound.

Emma wiped her hands on her skirts, then gently slipped her fingers behind the wound. Her hands returned to her dry. No blood. The metal ball was still in him. With the help of Alison's further examination, she concluded that he had sustained no other wounds. She was glad, since the one he had was bad enough.

"We need to get him upstairs and into bed quickly."

"Whose bed?" Gunter asked, ready to carry him.

"Mine, of course. 'Tis clean. I don't think the ball damaged anything vital according to where it is on his body, but he has lost much blood. I believe by his shallow breath and cool, clammy skin that he's in shock. We need to get him warm. And we need to move him very, very gently. I'll need another bed brought in for his brother. I shall sleep in a chair between them."

"Absolutely not, Emmaline!" Harry refused. "I'll not have you sleeping in the same room with two men."

"They need 'round the clock care, Harry. Would you have them die?"

"Emmaline," her brother lamented, "they cannot die."

She heard the thread of terror in his voice, the rising pitch of panic.

"Oliver Winther has the law to contend with, to some degree, and you and I had nothing to do with his brother's death. We'll be safe. These are the only sons of Connor Grant, and the warrior before him. The Highlanders will come. I don't know what they'll do!"

"I will do my best, Harry," she promised, wanting to soothe him without giving him false hope. "But the younger one's condition is dire. You must send the rest of your patrons away immediately and then help us get them both upstairs, away from the men who will come for these bodies. Then you must let me do my work."

She was grateful that Harry did as she asked without any more questions when he realized that the Winthers were coming back. She would rather move Cailean as little as possible, but if his enemy found him so helpless, she could not save him.

She guided the girls' preparations for her patients and listened while Gunter carried them to her room as carefully as he could. First Cailean was brought to her bed, and after the girls had undressed him she immediately took over. He was slipping in and out of consciousness. She needed to stop his bleeding but she couldn't sew him with the ball still inside. She couldn't remove it now. Any more tampering could kill him.

For now, she packed his wound with ointments and leaves. She smelled every herbal mixture before applying it. One ointment to stop the bleeding, two more to fight infection. She topped it all with leaves and then covered him with many blankets to keep him warm. It was all she could do for now. She must leave the metal where it was until his body recovered.

Next, Gunter brought in Malcolm and laid him in a makeshift bed she'd fashioned on the floor from soft pillows and some of her bed coverings. The pillows would have to do until they could find him an unused bed in the brothel.

Emma wasn't familiar with men's characters, but she knew their bodies. Clementine had often let her assist with her patients while they slept with Clementine's help.

Mr. Grant needed to come out of his shirt, perhaps his entire plaid. She figured she should do it herself, since the girls were too busy arguing about who would do it.

Foolish girls.

Going to her knees, she reached down for his shirt with one hand and produced her dagger with the other. She did her best to ignore the sudden, blessed silence and the slight gasps coming from the girls above as they watched her cut a nick in his collar.

Never mind their reaction.

She was here to help him, perhaps his only hope, depending on the seriousness of his wound. Emboldened by determination, she moved over him to tear the rest of the fabric apart with both hands. She wouldn't fail, because, being on her knees, ripping away his clothes made her feel more senseless than all the others put together.

"He's awake!" Mary shrieked. More gasps.

Emma froze, realizing that if he'd opened his eyes, the first thing he saw was her. Should she smile? She wanted to hide. She didn't like feeling so exposed.

She lowered her eyes but felt his breath on her cheek. His fevered breath. She laid her palm gently on the chest she'd exposed. His skin felt hot over hard, baking muscles. Was he this hard everywhere? She wanted to run her hands over the expanse of his chest, his arms, his belly. She'd never felt any man like this before!

"Emma?" Thankfully Mary interrupted her thoughts and brought her back to her present, real life.

He was developing a fever. She was almost certain she was as well.

She sat up, away from him, and ordered a cup of the tea she had Brianne prepare earlier.

His hand brushed across her thigh and made her hands shake when she reached for the cup.

"There now, you'll be fine," she said softly, hoping he believed her and didn't begin to panic. Was he still looking at her? What if it was her who panicked? She almost laughed at herself. Why would she panic? What did she care if Eden's serpent and the soul who saved her dog tonight was watching her? She couldn't see him. She could ignore it.

"Drink this." She reached for him again, and this time she had to pull him up a little and steady him in the crook of her arm so he could drink. Just beneath her nose, his hair smelled of outdoors, like rain. His closeness and how pleasant it felt unnerved her. It didn't stop her from working though. He'd be asleep in a moment or two and then she could cease this childish whim.

Impatient to be done, she swept her fingers over his shoulder and his neck to closer examine his wound.

She noted the quickening of his pulse while she worked over him.

"Malcolm, dear?" Bess dropped to her knees beside Emma. "Can you hear me?"

"They say hearing is the first to go," Mary lamented over them.

"That's in yer old age, Mary," Alison called out from her station at Cailean's bed. "Not at death."

"Is he going to die?" Jane asked from her place in Mary's arms.

Oh, for heaven's sake!

"He might if you all don't give him some air!" Emma waved her hand but none of the girls moved too far.

"Why doesn't he answer me?" Bess whined at him.

"Because he was shot in the neck." Emma did her best to suppress the sneer Clementine used to warn her would get her whipped, hanged, or burned. She failed. "He won't be able to tell you how magnificent you are for at least a se'nnight."

She was grateful she couldn't see Bess's scowl and returned to her work.

His shot was mostly a serious flesh wound, but nothing more. Thankfully, the pistol ball went straight through the lower side of his throat and came out of his collarbone. He'd be in pain for a while, and he wouldn't be able to lift his sword, but his wound wouldn't kill him. She was more concerned about the blow to his head. By touch, she could tell that blood dripped down above his ear... and that his hair was luxuriously soft in her fingers. It had to come off. He needed sewing and she couldn't do it with flowing locks falling around the wound.

When she used her dagger to begin cutting his hair, the girls collectively gasped yet again.

At least they were stunned enough to keep quiet while she worked. She didn't shear him bald, but left a few inches, so that now, instead of satin, his hair beneath her fingers felt like velvet. When the last lock was loped off, she cut closer around the wound and then cleaned it.

Lizzie and Brianne headed for the door when she began stitching him together. When she was done, she let Bess and Mary tie his head with a clean cloth while she scrubbed her hands again.

She checked her ointments and crushed more herbs into poultices while the girls fussed over her patient.

When she returned to his makeshift bed and knelt before him, Bess scooted closer. "You don't know the story of Samson then, do you?"

Emma could hear the sneer in Bess's voice. For the last month all she heard from the other girls was how pretty Bess was. Emma disagreed.

"I do know the story of Samson, as a matter of fact." She swung an amused smile toward Bess. "Are you suggesting that his hair holds special power from God?"

"Well, no," Bess insisted. "Not at all. I'm not mad in the head."

"Of course not," Emma agreed. "And it will grow back."

"You're correct," Bess conceded, or so it seemed. "His beauty remains, bare and utterly masculine. I wish you could see, just this once, Emma."

Emma's smile remained. She wasn't sure how, but it remained. She could see him if she wanted to. She just had to touch his features, his frame. She remembered what Clementine had told her about building images up in layers of light and shadows, using her fingers as brushes. She'd practiced on the old hag often, learning every line and crease in her weathered skin. Oh, but her face was soft, not leathery and ridden with moles, the way one might expect a witch to look. But then, Clementine was no witch, she simply knew everything about the earth and what it supplied.

She could put her brushes to Malcolm Grant and see for herself what all the girls fussed about. But she didn't want to see him that way. That kind of vision was deceptive.

She didn't care about that part of a person. It meant nothing to her and served no purpose. A man's...or woman's character was how she judged their merit. Still, her hand shook again when she applied her poultice to his neck and every breath in the room paused. No one moved; indeed, it felt like even the air had stopped. At the touch of her fingers to his flesh, they all let out a collective sigh.

Emma had no idea why touching him would be any different from touching any other man. Was it the slow, heavy rhythm of breath, of blood coursing through veins, spreading to her, that made her want to touch more of him? She did, just enough to know he was carved from hard, curved stone. His heart beat beneath her palm and she felt a rush of thankfulness that he lived. She extended the poultice mix down his shoulder, captivated by his solid strength, even in sleep.

"No, Emma." Bess took her wrist and guided her hand back to the wound in his neck.

"We'd all like to touch him," Mary assured her with a delicate pat on the back, understanding a bit more. "You just make sure we all have a chance to, aye?"

Mortified, Emma shook her head. "I didn't mean to...'Tis how I see...and I've never felt a man like him before."

"And you likely never will," Bess muttered.

"Why do you say 'felt' in that way?" Mary asked her, ignoring Bess's insult as Emma did.

"What way?"

"Like you just did more to him than apply that concoction to his skin?"

Emma blinked and burned from her soles to her roots at being caught admiring him at a time like this.

"Are you a virgin, Emma?" Mary asked.

"'Tis all right, gel." Bess's smirk was evident in her voice. "We all want him atop us…or beneath or behind us. 'Tis nothing to be ashamed of."

Emma wished the floor would open up and swallow her. She was certain that the girls could see her unfamiliar and unwanted desire for him creeping red across her face. She wanted to touch him, not make love to him, but since Bess brought it up she could think of nothing but him "behind" her.

When Mary took her hand and laid it on the mound between the Highlander's legs, Emma lifted her free hand to her mouth and gasped so deep and short it made her a little unstable on her feet.

"There's a lot of him to feel," Mary said, her voice dipping low near Emma's ear. "Fix him up and then fuck him until he can't piss for two days."

Mary ignored Emma's burning cheeks and took hold of both Emma's hands. Placing them on his chest, she said, "Feel until your heart's content. We won't tell your brother."

Emma wanted to tell them all that Harry didn't matter. They barely knew each other. But he did matter. He was her brother.

They all waited, some giggling while her breath and

her fingers traversed over the breadth of his shoulders, then stalled over the hills and valleys sculpting his tight belly. She didn't think molesting him while he was helpless to resist was the right thing to do, so she skipped over his groin when she came to it again, despite the girls' disappointed sighs, and continued to his legs. She could feel her breath changing as her fingers trickled over his plaid to his thick, shapely thighs and bare calves, sculpted and strong like the rest of him.

Damn it. They were all correct about him. Malcolm Grant's body was as beautiful as his face was rumored to be.

She shouldn't have looked.

Chapter Four

"He should be in my bed tonight," Bess muttered with deep regret by the door. "I should be beneath him right now, enjoying all that—"

"Honestly, Bess," Alison, who remained at Cailean's side with Emma, complained from the other side of the room beside the bed, "is that all you think about?"

"What else is there?" Bess asked her annoyed friend.

For a moment Alison remained silent, then, "I don't know what it's called, I just know that this one fought for my sake when that Winther bastard struck me, and protected me from being struck again. Whatever that is called, I like it. I like that he would do that for me."

"'Tis called being grateful," Bess said, laughing and heading out the door. "Alison, you're young, a mere babe of what, ten and nine? Don't make more out of it than what it is; you'll only open your heart to being broken, and that's not something we can afford in our position."

Emma continued preparing mixtures and tending to both men while Bess and the others left. Alison stayed, keeping the herb-soaked cloth over Cailean's forehead fresh.

"'Tis called chivalry," Emma said softly while she moved to the other side of the bed to check Cailean's belly.

"That's it," Alison agreed with a smile in her voice. "Chivalry, gallantry, honor. I've heard stories about these traits in men, but I've never seen them at work." She laughed at herself. "Good thing we're alone. Imagine how Bess would react if she heard such words? She'd likely laugh until she lost her wits."

Emma smiled while she tended to Cailean. She liked the girls who lived here, with the exception of Bess. Most were kind to her and appreciated her cures for certain irritations and preventions for pregnancy. But like the villagers in France, they only spoke to her when they needed her and hardly ever the rest of the time. She didn't mind. If Alison wanted to stay with him, Emma wouldn't refuse, but they didn't need to pretend affection until the morning.

"I haven't heard your thoughts on it."

Emma looked up. "On chivalry?"

"Aye. Am I a fool?"

If she was, then Emma was as well. "What did he do, that you offer him such status among men?"

She listened while Alison told her about Andrew Winther throwing her into a chair in a prelude to the next twelve hours that he'd paid for with her, and of Cailean boldly leaping for Andrew and "beating the shyt out of him." She paused for half a breath, then added, "He didn't kill Andrew though."

Emma thought of him for a moment, remembering what he, along with his brother, had done for Gascon. She would do her best to save him.

"Don't let Bess distress you," Alison said, almost as an afterthought.

Emma closed her eyes. She didn't need them to work but oddly, it gave her a sense of privacy. She didn't need friends, especially one who misinterpreted her intentions and assumed she knew what Emma was feeling.

"Bess doesn't bother me."

"She had his attention until you showed up," Alison continued anyway.

Emma dropped the clay cup of oil-coated leaves she was bringing to Cailean's side to the floor. She cursed inwardly, chastising herself for not ending this small talk sooner. "That's a ridiculous thing to say." She bent to pick the leaves off the floor.

"Why is it ridiculous?"

"Because…" Why in damnation hadn't she insisted that Alison leave with the rest of them? "Because Bess is beautiful."

"How the hell do you know that?" Alison persisted. "Was it Bess herself who told you?"

Emma didn't remember where she'd heard it. But what Bess looked like really didn't matter. What Emma looked like did. She didn't know what "gaunt" was or how "washed-out" should look, and it hadn't bothered her that Harry often described her that way. She had foggy images of herself ten years ago and those, along with what she felt when she touched her face, gave her an image of nothing extraordinary.

"I know the rumors about him," she told Alison. "I'm glad I cannot see his face if he is truly so alluring. I don't ever want to pine for a husband and settle on a man who is settling for me, or a cruel sot who thinks he can push me around because I can't see."

"That is not Malcolm Grant, Emma. He helped you bring your dog inside, did he not?"

He did. She owed him everything for that. Had he

truly stopped giving his attention to Bess when Emma appeared at the table? It was a pleasant thought, a passing fancy. Nothing more. She knew about chivalry and courtly love. As a child at her mother's knee, she heard the tales about such noble knights as Sir Gawain, Sir Tristan, and Galahad. She'd never forgotten them. She'd known what Alison was describing to the girls, but that didn't mean she believed it existed. She didn't know, but in this case, she agreed more with Bess on the matter.

These men were either going to die or they were going to recover. Either way, soon she and Alison would be nothing but a memory.

"He should wake up soon," she said of Cailean, and stepped away from him. If he didn't, he'd likely die. She didn't tell Alison that much but called to Gascon and left the room to go hunt for a bed for Malcolm.

In the hall, she stopped to catch her breath. "What's come over me, Gascon? You know me. I'm not easily beguiled, especially by kindness. Aye, we have Malcolm Grant to thank for you spending a warm night by the hearth instead of in the rain, but why should my heart beat so urgently in my chest at the thought of him noticing me? Why should my knees feel shaky simply because I think of him?" So what if he was pleasing to the eye? That meant absolutely nothing to her. The blessing in losing her sight was that she learned to read the heart. So far, Grant had shown her nothing but kindness.

She buried her fingers in her faithful dog's fur. Gascon had never left her, sleeping beneath her window every night for the last month.

"Emmaline," her brother's voice shouted up at her. "What are you doing roaming the hall alone? Are the Grants still with us?"

"Aye, they are," she reassured him. "And I am not alone. Gascon is with me. I am trying to find a bed for Malcolm Grant. The floor, despite its cushions, is no place for recovery."

She heard Harry swear an oath about her being mad followed by a giggle from one of the girls. "How do you intend on finding a bed, my dear?" he asked in utter sincerity. "You are blind."

Emma smiled in the softly lit hall. Harry meant well. He just didn't understand her and her ways yet. He thought of her as being much more fragile and helpless than she actually was. She might trip over obstacles, but she never let them stop her.

"Is Gunter with you, brother? I need him to carry what I find back to my room."

"He's bringing the last of the bodies outside. I'll get him and instruct him to take any bed as long as there isn't a girl already in it and bring it to you."

"I'll need fresh linens, as well."

"Of course," Harry muttered. "Just as long as you agree not to leave your room alone again."

She sighed, but didn't argue with him that she wasn't alone.

"As you wish, Harry. You have my thanks." She gave him a little curtsey, just a slight fold and dip of her head. During her journey from France to England she learned that in order to stay safe in the world, she had to become and always remain unobtrusive. She didn't mind staying in the shadows. Shadows were what she knew. She was comfortable in them.

"I'll be waiting then." She turned, her fingers resting gently on Gascon's head. "Good night, Bess."

"Emmaline," Bess replied through tight lips.

Emma couldn't understand why Bess would be angry with her. It wasn't Emma's fault that Bess's would-be lover was unconscous in her room. So much for trying to be polite and wish a girl good night.

She pushed open the door to her room and was entering when Alison's excited voice stopped her. "Look who is awake!"

Emma assumed it was Cailean since Alison's voice came from her bed. It was good news. He would live.

"Welcome back, Mr. Grant," Emma said. "We are glad you've decided to stay."

"Aye," the younger Grant said, sounding like a groggy bear. "How could I refuse when Alison was waiting here fer me?"

Emma smiled, glad he was awake and glad that Alison was here to greet him.

"Alison told me all the hours ye've put in fer me and m' brother," Cailean told her. "I'll be sure to tell him." He sounded very sleepy and Emma nodded, then checked his wound.

She didn't know what to say really. It was nice of Alison to tell him. The only people who had done nice things for her were Clem and her parents. But Cailean and his brother had rescued Gascon, and now Alison. She wasn't used to it and she didn't know how to respond. She smiled and hoped it was enough.

❖❖❖

Chapter Five

$\mathcal{M}$alcolm came awake in his new bed a half dozen or so times during the next two days. With his eyes hooded and his thoughts clouded, he was mildly aware of a woman standing over him, cleaning his wounds. A veil covered her head. A veil of spun gossamer gold. He smiled at her. At least he thought he did but she didn't even look at him. He was dreaming. Where was his brother? If Cailean had fallen... If his brother was dead, it would be the end of him. "Cai..." His throat burst into flames and he almost passed out from the pain in his neck as he finished calling his brother. "Cailean!"

"Ssh, there now," a woman's soft voice spoke like a foreign whisper against his skin. "Cailean is well. Cailean is well."

She soothed him, getting him to settle down and lay still. She held a cool cloth against his forehead, offering him blessed comfort from the heat. He relaxed, falling back in the deep bliss of sleep.

He dreamed on and off, drifting from consciousness to semi-consciousness, to being out cold. When he dreamed, it was of a lass, an angel wearing a sash around her eyes. He offered his hand to help her when she stumbled, but she refused it and offered hers to him instead. Ah, but he needed an angel's help. So many things in his life had gone to hell.

He'd never call himself extremely political, not like his cousin Edmund and some of his other kin. A few years ago, he'd joined in Edmund's crusade to stop the Union with England Act mostly because there was plenty of fighting to go with it. But he believed in the cause and after coming close to a victory so many times, even trying to stop the treaty by kidnapping the Duke of Queensberry's niece, who ultimately captured Edmund's heart. They had failed and Scotland joined with England to become the United Kingdom.

Edmund also joined with Queensberry's niece, Amelia Bell. Malcolm watched even Lucan MacGregor find love in the arms of a serving wench. The chief's daughter, Abigail, lost her heart to her English escort on the way to meet her aunt, the queen. His own sister had fallen in love with a damned pirate.

Love. He hated it.

He'd heard songs and stories about his parents and his uncles and aunts, his grandparents. The list didn't end. Tales of love, all. That most passionate of emotions was available to everyone in Camlochlin. Except him.

It wasn't that he couldn't find a wife. He'd never looked for one. He didn't have to really. Lasses found him. He'd been with his fair share but none had ever taken his heart. He searched himself for those feelings in his uncle Finn's poems. He never felt a single one. Over the years, he began to believe that he wasn't capable of loving the way a man should love the woman he wants as a wife. Was he lacking in whatever made a man fall in love? Was he unworthy of it? If so, why? What had he done that some of the other men of Camlochlin hadn't? Nevertheless, he tried to fall in love, to find his own happy tale. But he always walked away empty. His lack haunted him and every time one of his cousins fell in love, he took another step toward not wanting it, in hating it because it eluded him. It became what his grandmother would call a dragon. Instead of facing it, fighting it, he avoided any kind of emotional connection so that he wasn't reminded of his deficiency.

He became a rake, infamous at what he did best, fighting or laughing with men, using women, and running from a dragon.

He offered a quick smile to everyone. He lived a seemingly carefree, unconcerned life. People saw what he wanted them to see. But no one truly knew him. Mayhap Edmund knew him best, but even he didn't know all. There was more to Malcolm than people suspected. He lay in bed at night and ached from a void that wouldn't be filled. Like a hunger that would never be satisfied. It had nothing to do with his celibacy, because it was the same before. He was lonely often but he craved no one's company overlong. His inability was always present in his life, no matter how he tried to mask it.

He heard someone speaking and tried to open his eyes. He was tired of sleeping, as well. He wanted to be up and about.

"I knew you'd live. Nothing can keep this body down."

He fought harder to open his eyes and recognized the deep golden tresses around the lass's face, the length of it corded in a thick braid down the back of her emerald gown.

Bess. He tried to say her name, but the livid hot pain in his neck returned. He smiled at her instead.

"Welcome back to the world of the living, Malcolm. I've missed you." She leaned down and planted a kiss on his temple and then one on his eyelid. Both places hurt like hell and he closed his eye again, suddenly realizing that only one had been opened.

"You were shot in the neck, poor dear. And struck in the head with a club of some sort. You're a bit swollen but you'll be as good as new in no time. I've had a terrible time trying to keep the girls from your bedside. We've all been so worried about you. None of us wants to lose our favorite customer."

It didn't bother him that all he was to them was a customer. He was glad Bess had gotten over him. Who wouldn't after so long? He'd never expected to be anything else, especially not in a brothel. Right now, he only cared about one thing.

"Cail…"

"Is recovering well but he's going to need—"

"Bess," another lass's voice, one he'd heard in his dream, light but stern…and French, cut her off. "Mr. Fitzwilliam is expecting you down the hall."

Malcolm studied Harry's sister with his limited gaze. At first glance, she wasn't striking in appearance. But after a moment or two of taking in the elegant curl at the edge of her mouth, the delicate column of her throat, the way light reflected in the curve of her curls, it was clear to see that she was more bonny than he'd first thought. He remembered her and her drooling escort, Gascon, the dog.

He smiled at her and she held a cup to his lower lip. He corrected the rim and obeyed when she bid him to drink and soothe his throat.

"Are ye certain ye aren't interested in going in my place, Emmaline?" Bess asked her in a sticky sweet voice. "Mr. Fitzwilliam has requested ye often. Yer sightless eyes interest him."

Ah, aye, she was blind. He remembered now. He watched her delicate hands feel around for things, her fingers flitting over this surface or that.

Gascon's low growl drew Malcolm's attention. On his haunches, the beast's head reached Malcolm's. What kind of dog saw for the blind? He'd love to know how Miss Grey taught her hound to guide her steps. Dry now, Gascon was more fluff than muscle. His ears pointed straight up with fur flopping down over them. If not for the growling, he would have appeared utterly harmless. Malcolm knew better. He'd grown up with dogs. This one didn't like Bess.

"I'm quite certain, Bess," Harry's sister said softly, her voice shifting an octave in earnest, her hand resting on the dog's head, calming him. "I don't want to give myself to a man I don't love. No one forces me, just as they don't force you."

Her voice held no trace of pride, but still Bess seemed to take offense at her.

"Ha! What is love?" Bess laughed at her. "There is one thing, and one thing alone that men love, and it isn't your good nature. Isn't that right, Malcolm?"

"I believe there's more to love than that," Emma answered before Malcolm could give his voice a try. "That there are men who are capable of giving their heart to a single woman for a lifetime. Men of honor and chivalry."

Malcolm cursed his wounds because they confined him. Why did she bring up love? He wanted to get up and leave the room, the conversation. He didn't know anything about love or why a man would settle down with one lass.

His heart remained perfectly intact in his chest.

"You're a fool, Emma," Bess said, pulling another growl

from Gascon. Before she provoked the dog to tear at her throat, Malcolm rested his palm on Bess's hip and gave her a slight push toward the door.

"I'll return," she promised, proving she wasn't a fool when she moved to leave the room. "Until then, no one else's hands shall feel as good as mine."

Malcolm watched her leave with a flourish and almost laughed at the overdramatic performance. His head hurt. He lifted his hand to it and swallowed his heart. His hair! What the hell happened to his hair? He didn't get a chance to ask when blessed sleep overtook him again.

He woke the next day, feeling a bit stronger. His throat was less raw. He opened his eyes, both of them, and focused on the candlelit room. Where was Cailean? There was another bed on the other side. A bigger bed, bathed in soft golden light, with a single figure upon it and a red-headed lass worrying beside it. He remembered her but not her name.

"Is…" He put his hand to his throat and opened his mouth to try again.

"Here." Emmaline Grey appeared before him in her plain dark gown and pallid complexion and helped him lean up on one elbow. *Her* name, he could remember. Emmaline.

"Drink your tea," she urged. "You are not fully healed yet and mustn't strain your throat."

He did as she bid and downed the concoction. It was a mixture of different teas and oils; lavender among them, making the liquid go down easier. For an instant he prayed she knew what she was doing and didn't poison him.

"Is that…Cailean…in bed?"

"*Oui*, 'tis."

He looked up at her, her face eclipsed behind her

long, loose waves. He couldn't read her expression so he reached for her hand instead. "Cailean?"

Her already large eyes grew larger as she took a seat in the chair by his unadorned bed. "Mr. Grant, your brother regained consciousness the night of his injuries but not again since. He was shot and the bullet had to be removed. His body was in shock and we waited three days before we went in, but today he has a fever."

Malcolm's heart smashed against his ribs. Cailean was the baby. Their mother would perish if he left the earth. They'd already lost Caitrina. Though she wasn't dead, their only daughter spent most of her life on the high seas, a place more dangerous than anywhere else in the world. Losing Cailean would change their family.

Malcolm wasn't too proud to beg for his brother's life.

"Please," he murmured, "save him."

"I'm doing my best," she promised earnestly.

He closed his eyes and tried to regulate his breathing. The Winthers had done this. They'd returned to the brothel with pistols and shot him and his brother. He was going to kill them. If Cailean died, his kin would come and kill them all.

"I want to . . . see him."

She stood up and reached for Gascon. "You'll need to walk."

He nodded.

"Can you?"

"Aye," he answered, forgetting that she couldn't see anything out of those lush, lovely eyes. "I think so."

"Here," she offered her shoulder to lean on and he smiled. If he leaned on her too heavily she'd tip right over. "Alison," she called out to the redhead hovering over his brother.

Ah, yes, Alison.

"Bring the chair please."

She tucked her shoulder under his arm and curled his arm around her neck. "Slowly, now, Mr. Grant."

"Malcolm," he corrected, drawn to the scent of her beneath his nose. She smelled like medicinal herbs. He inhaled and coughed a little.

He remembered something and stopped. He reached his hand up to his head. It wasn't a dream. Someone had chopped off his hair. He asked her who'd done it.

"I did," she admitted easily. "You needed stitching. I couldn't let you die because of some vanity about your hair."

"Why no'?"

"What?"

"Why could ye no' let me die? Ye dinna' know me."

"Because I promised Harry."

That was it then? She promised Harry. And he'd promised Harry.

Alison hurried forward with the chair and placed it beside the bed. He moved slowly, forgetting his hair with Emma pressed close to him.

"Gascon seems to like me."

"He's grateful to you, as am I, for convincing my brother to let him inside."

"Ye trained him well."

She shook her head under his arm. "I didn't train him. He's always known what to do."

Malcolm looked at the dog, admiring the beast's intelligence.

When they reached the bed, she helped him bend and sit, facing his brother. She backed away and went about her business in the room.

Malcolm stared at the lad, pale and lifeless in the bed.

He'd brought Cailean here. Malcolm closed his eyes, unable for a moment to look without tears spilling from him. He'd seen dying and dead men before, but this was his brother.

"Cailean," he said, covering his brother's hand with his own. He recoiled for an instant when the heat from Cailean's flesh ran through him. His fever was high. "Ye can fight this, lad. This is nothin' fer ye. I'll be right here with ye. Ye're doin' just fine."

He looked up at Emmaline stepping around the bed to the other side, and watched her prepare to check his brother's dressing. "Ye think me mad fer talkin' to him like this."

"No." She shook her head. "I think he knows you're here. It could be what he needs to recover."

He didn't know about that, but speaking to him was all he could do, so he did more of it.

When he was done, he turned to her. "Do ye all take turns?"

"Doing what?" she asked from over his brother's body where she freshened his dressing.

"Tendin' to us."

The delicate swirl of her lips made him feel as fevered as his brother. Pity she couldn't see how lovely she was. It was as if she grew a little more bonny every moment.

"Alison is a great help to me."

He was glad she had help. He knew from watching his aunt Davina nearly die of a fever how difficult it was to care for the sick.

He watched her slender fingers at work, tender, fluttering touches that made him wish she was tending to him.

"How d'ye know what ye're doin', lass?"

She tilted her head up and made him wonder how he could think of anything but the beguiling quirk of her brow?

"Do you worry that I don't?" she put to him.

He laughed, liking her boldness. "Nae. I worry that ye dinna' care if ye co or not."

"Mr. Grant, you must rest your throat. If you cannot do that I'll have to drug you again."

He stared at her. Was she jesting? She'd drugged him? It would explain him sleeping so much. He gave her a halfhearted glare but she didn't see it. Instead, she held her index finger to her lips and cautioned him to rest.

He didn't know if he wanted to laugh or argue with her. She hadn't done it, he convinced himself. It was merely a threat to make him obey her. She needn't go to the trouble. He'd be happy to do whatever she commanded.

"I know something about removin' pistol balls from flesh. 'Tis no' easy. Who removed Cailean's?"

"I did," she said without missing a beat as she ground more herbs with her pummel.

"How?" He didn't want to think of the mess she likely made digging around blindly.

"I felt my way around. You can take a look when I'm done. 'Tis quite neat."

How had she done it? He was quite impressed and he must have somehow conveyed the feeling. When she spoke again, she sounded frustrated. "Don't wonder at me, and please don't pity me. I can get along as well as anyone else. Your brother needed help and I did everything I know. The rest is up to him."

He nodded to himself, not really knowing what to say. He'd seen her as less able to help Cailean and he was wrong. He realized how wrong when she lifted Cailean's covering and showed Malcolm his wound. It was small and clean and quite well done.

He commended her work and felt his own wound. She'd saved him. She'd saved Cailean.

"What is your opinion on it, Mr. Grant?"

He turned his attention from Cailean's wound to her and the dainty sweep of her nose. "I think ye are quite the heroine, Miss Grey," he told her thickly, enjoying the blush stealing over her cheeks.

"Not that," she said, her voice breathless when she corrected him. "Not that, Mr. Grant. On love. Is there only one thing that men truly love, as Bess suggests?"

Hell, not love again. He looked around the room like he was planning his escape. He gaze came back to her and he sighed. If his brother lived, it was Emma who saved him. How could he repay her?

By telling her the truth.

"Aye. But I havena' discovered what it is so I canna' tell ye."

※

Chapter Six

E mma kept herself busy for the rest of the night, though there wasn't much to do save mix more poultices and prepare more ointments for her two patients. Mr. Grant refused to get back in bed when the girls began swirling into the room to check on him. The air permeated with various perfumes, but Emma guessed it smelled better for Mr. Grant than medicine.

"I'm fine," he insisted to any female who asked.

"You sure as hell are," was the general response.

Goodness, how they giggled and clung to his every word. She'd heard how they spoke to men—sensual and stimulating their customers into paying for more than just their company.

This was different. They weren't just doing their jobs. They wanted Malcolm Grant. They purred and cooed and flitted around his chair, touching his head, his shoulders, his thighs.

Emma kept herself mostly in the shadows, listening to his laughter and his charming responses to them. She caught every inflection, every dip in the sensuous pulse of his voice. He sounded very at ease with the women, and pleased with himself.

He was a rake, for certain. She didn't doubt any of the stories she'd heard about him. He oozed self-confidence and vitality, even wounded and tired.

She could hear that too. He was exhausted, but he didn't ask his guests to leave. Emma thought about doing it, but he seemed to be enjoying himself.

"Emma," Bess called from where she lounged on Malcolm's empty bed. "When do you think Mr. Grant will be fit enough to leave your gloomy room and come to mine?"

"Is anyone else worried about that mongrel growling at us?" Jane asked concerning Gascon.

"'Tis only Bess he doesn't like." Mary laughed.

"I feel the same about him," Bess told them.

Emma gave her a dark glare but doubted any of the girls saw it, so busy were they primping around Mr. Grant.

"If you wish to leave," Alison said, suddenly appearing beside her, "mayhap take a walk and find your brother, I'll stay and watch over the Grants." Her voice was kind and friendly enough, but Emma shook her head.

"It's just that I know Bess can be cruel," Alison insisted.

Emma let her smile deepen. She could handle Bess. "I've told you already. Bess doesn't bother me. Now, here," she said, and handed Alison a small jar of ointment. "Take this to Cailean and apply it to his wound. I'm fine." She listened to Alison return to her work, sharing words with the rest of the girls as she went.

Emma liked Alison's determination in tending to Cailean since his injury. She barely left his side, begging the other girls to take her customers while she kept her vigil. She was kindhearted and Emma hoped that when

Cailean woke up he proved to be of a different character than his brother.

It wasn't that Malcolm Grant was unlikable. On the contrary, he was too likable. His laughter came easy with the girls. It was low and throaty and filled with wicked intentions that made Emma blush earlier when they were alone.

There was also that disarming lilt that made his words almost musical. She listened while he defied her instruction and spoke to the girls around his chair. She liked the sound of it, a little raw and gravelly.

Hell, he was captivating! She was glad she couldn't see him and completely fall into spasms of giddiness like the rest of them were doing—all except for Alison, of course.

"Miss Grey?"

She blinked, realizing that he'd called her and she was standing smiling like an idiot.

"*Oui*, Mr. Grant?" She stepped out of the shadows with Gascon at her side.

"Come sit with us."

Goodness but his smoky invitation spoken from his unhealed throat was tempting.

"Tell me how ye know so much aboot healin'."

Emma's heart froze. Was he going to accuse her of being a witch? She feared that the girls, so captivated by him, would agree.

"No, I have medicines to mix and—"

"Can it no' wait, lass?"

Despite her misgivings, his query made her knees go soft. He sounded so sincere.

What should she say? What should she do? Was he dangerous? Should she feed him more tea?

She needed to get him well, and get him out of her life.

"Mr. Grant, you must rest." She took another step forward and wiped her hands on her apron. "I think another quarter of an hour should be enough time to bid good eve to your admirers. If you would prefer not to recover, I'll leave you alone."

Immediately there were protests, which she tried to ignore. It was difficult what with him laughing and taking it all in like a beloved prince on his throne.

"Emma just wants him for herself," Mary said, then laughed when the others agreed.

Emma could feel her face go up in flames, but she said nothing and turned away instead. She listened while the girls flirted and offered their bosoms as pillows and their thighs to keep him warm before they left.

She listened while Bess promised him things that made Emma's ears burn—along with her blood.

This was how a rake lived. Did Malcolm Grant love any of the women he took to his bed? He'd said he hadn't found the thing that men loved most in a woman. So it clearly wasn't what Bess suggested.

What did she care? He was her patient. As soon as he was well, he'd be gone.

"Before she left with the others, I was tellin' Alison that Cailean looked better. His color has returned. How did ye do it?"

She tilted her head, inclining her ear. But for Cailean's unconscious body, they were alone.

"Why is *how* so important?"

"'Tis no'." He laughed. "Never mind it then. I'm just glad he's recoverin'. Ye're quite skilled."

"We should get you back into bed, Mr. Grant." Her heart still raced. What was he thinking? Did she want to know? Was he the kind of man who could get her strung up and burned?

"Nae, I want to keep an eye on m' brother."

She went to him and pressed her palm to his forehead. "You're cool, but you could relapse if you don't rest."

"I can rest in this chair, Miss Grey."

He was right. She could work on him better if he was sitting up. The thought of him on his back again set thoughts ablaze about touching his body, all of it. What the hell was wrong with her? Malcolm Grant could end up her worst nightmare. Why did she let him excite her?

She sighed against his neck and he leaped in his skin.

"Are you in pain, Mr. Grant?" she asked, concerned about infection.

"Nae," he told her, but his shoulders were tense and tight. His voice sounded deeper, more throaty than before.

"I do think we should get you into bed now."

"Lass...Miss Grey." He turned just a little, bringing his chin closer to her mouth. "Ye're breathin' on me. Move yer lips away before I'm tempted to kiss them."

She moved away quickly, burning to the soles of her feet. How dare he be so bold with her? What if she didn't want him to kiss her? Did he think he could just do it without her consent and not suffer any consequences? What would he do if she poisoned him?

She tore off another long piece of cloth and wrapped it around his neck. With one last, tight pull, she tied it.

Ignoring his painful cough and mumbled oath, she walked around his chair and leaned down in front of him.

"Mr. Grant, whatever others see in you, I see something different. I'm not blinded by your visage. Your beauty, if you possess any, is here." She poked him in the chest. "You did a kind deed for Gascon. For that, I think of you kindly. But if you believe you can just kiss me whenever the mood strikes you, you will discover you're wrong, and I will discover that I was wrong as well."

"Do I get nae acknowledgment then fer warnin' ye of m' intentions?"

She stood there for a moment, trying to decide if he was serious or not. She couldn't tell, so she stepped away, smiling once she was past him.

Since he wasn't using the bed Gunter had brought to the room, and her feet were aching from standing all night, she sat on the thin mattress and closed her eyes.

The crackle of the hearth fire filled the room for what seemed like a long time before Malcolm broke the silence.

"He canna' die, Miss Grey."

"Mr. Grant," she said softly. She could hear the desperation in his voice, naked and raw. His concern for his brother was genuine. She would be honest with him. "I am trying to make certain that doesn't happen. But ultimately, 'tis not up to me."

"He's verra' passionate aboot life. He was," he said more deeply.

"You speak like he's dead already. He's not. I believe he'll live."

He moved around in his chair, his voice, when he spoke, fell around her like smooth satin. "I'm relieved that ye do."

"He's a damn ferocious warrior," he continued. Emma listened because she sensed he needed to speak of his brother.

"He's a poet too, though no' a verra' good one. Wherever he went, whatever he did, ye could always find ink on his fingers. Or paint."

Emma smiled, imagining a handsome young, passionate man going through life like a storm.

"You love him very much."

"Aye," he told her. "I do. What aboot ye and Harry? He told me ye were reunited last month after a decade. That must be difficult."

"*Oui*," she told him, liking that he wasn't oblivious to the feelings of others. "'Tis."

"How did ye both get separated?"

"He left."

He was quiet for a while, and Emma was sorry she told him if he now thought less of Harry because of it.

"Why did he leave?" he finally spoke again to ask her.

"He was afraid, I suspect."

"Ye've never asked him?"

"No," she said, not wanting to discuss it anymore. "I never asked him. But enough about that. It seems Alison is quite taken with your brother." She didn't think the change of topic was subtle. She didn't care. "Does a prostitute losing her heart to your brother concern you?"

"Nae, and it wouldna' surprise me. Hearts get lost whenever they're around m' kin."

"Then you do believe love is real, Mr. Grant?"

"I never said 'twasn't, lass."

Was it madness that she liked the way he called her lass?

"I know 'tis real," he said. "I just want nae part of it, and it wants nae part of me."

Chapter Seven

*L*ight streamed through the window and cloaked Emma in an almost ethereal luminescence while she crushed some herbs by the table in her room.

From his bed, where he ended up the next morning weak and exhausted after sitting up by Cailean's side all night, Malcolm looked away from Emma when Bess, sitting on the side of his bed, asked him if he was listening.

He wasn't.

He nodded, but his gaze wanted to return to Harry's sister. He remembered her breath on his neck last night, while she tended to him. Hell, he didn't remember anything thrilling him more. She'd fired his blood so much that it actually pained him not to taste her mouth. He liked how she smelled leaning over him. He liked the silhouette of her body through her gown when she stood near the window. He thought about kissing that decadent mouth while she smiled at her dog or Alison, or relaxed it when she looked his way.

He'd promised Harry. His friend had been through too much to be betrayed now as well.

He wondered if liking her company so much could also be considered betrayal. She didn't fawn all over him, giggle at everything he said, amusing or not. He found her knowledge of healing fascinating and admired her fortitude to defy her odds. If he had to be laid up here, he'd prefer her company.

He feared his head was more seriously injured than any of them though.

His gaze returned to her—just a glance to catch the delicacy of her profile, the thick cut of her mouth.

Someone opened the bedroom door and she looked up toward Malcolm in time for him to look into her eyes. He began to smile.

"A group of Winthers just left," Harry informed them as he entered.

Malcolm ignored Bess's slight gasp and stared at Harry's gaunt face, his eyes hard and sharp.

"Did ye tell them I was going to kill them?"

"No, Malcolm," his friend advised with shaking hands. "I told them that you and your brother were dead. Bess," he said, barely looking at her, "I've informed the girls to say the same if asked about our guests. And no one gives out their name." When she nodded, he continued. "I don't think they'll be back as long as they believe you're dead. Just to make certain that you stay dead in their minds I'm having proper English garb sewn for the both of you. Two men lived and likely told the baron that you were Highlanders."

"I'm quite sure I can handle another Winther."

"Oliver Winther is different, Malcolm," Harry insisted. "I don't want that kind of danger here."

"Verra' well, Harry," Malcolm consented. "I'll let them live to save ye from a fight ye canna' win."

"You or Cailean killed Andrew their brother."

"How d'ye know 'twas one of us?"

Harry eyed him like he couldn't be serious. "You're the only two men they were fighting. Now, as I was saying. If the baron knows you're alive, he'll come here and kill you—and me for deceiving him. Eventually, they will leave us alone completely. Or they won't."

"That choice will get them killed," Malcolm vowed. He'd had enough of making promises he likely wouldn't keep.

"Is that so?" Harry asked. "What do you plan to do? Fight a hundred of them in your condition?"

"My condition is improvin'. Is that not so, Miss Grey?" he asked Emmaline while she mixed herbs in a jar by his brother's bed. When he coughed she stopped mixing and poured a cup of tea. When he coughed a second time, still waiting for her answer, she let Gascon lead her to his bed.

"What did I tell you about speaking without soothing your throat first, Mr. Grant?"

"Oh, Emma," Bess whined, piquing Gascon's ears. "Why nag the poor man? Hasn't he been through enough?"

Instead of answering Bess, Emma turned to him. "How does your throat feel, Mr. Grant?"

"Sore," he answered.

"Would you rather I quit 'nagging' you? Or would you prefer the tea?"

"The tea." He was careful not to let Bess see him smile. Bess didn't like Emmaline. He didn't know why. She could be jealous but he had no interest in knowing. It wouldn't make any difference in anything. He did like that Emmaline didn't seem to care one way or the other if Bess liked her or not.

He waited for her to hand him the tea, sipped it, and then asked her his question again.

"You're improving quickly," she assured him. "But you won't be fighting anything anytime soon."

"I'll be ready fer them soon enough," he muttered, turning to Bess's encouraging smile.

"Harry," Miss Grey said to her brother. "Is he normally so prideful and pigheaded?"

Prideful and pigheaded, him? He sipped his tea and turned back to her. "What is pigheaded aboot bein' confident? I know m' strength and m' stamina, fer I practice every day."

She aimed her slightest of smiles at him, and like a thin shard, it pierced his chest and warmed his blood from its source. "I don't doubt your skill or your endurance, Mr. Grant. But has your head ever been smashed in before?"

It was a simple question, and one he should have an easy time answering. She was right. His body wasn't at its peak because of the blow to his head. It would take time to tone his mind, thoughts, and reflexes back to top condition. She wanted him to heal first. She was right.

He should have told her. He should have said something before letting her walk off with her dog, but he didn't.

"Pay her no heed." Bess's voice played like a siren's song against his ear, pulling him back to her. "She has nothing else to do all day but hover around here. Ferget her words and show me how quickly ye can recover."

Aye, Malcolm agreed, forget.

Sleep. He yawned and thought about dreaming. Bess's face was poised over him. Damn, he didn't want to sleep now . . .

His gaze slipped to Emma. He looked at his cup of tea and then closed his eyes. Suddenly relaxed and so sleepy he couldn't open his eyes again. "Och, damn it," he said out loud. "The wench dru..."

He didn't feel Bess's hand on his arm, only the luxurious comfort of his pillow.

She drugged him.

Emma hurried to the other side of the room with Gascon at her heel. She knew the way. She kept herself looking busy though she knew Mr. Grant's sleep wouldn't last much longer. Oh, how did anyone put up with such stubbornness? Did he truly think he could fight the Winthers now? Fool. He needed to understand that he was still too weak. He needed his rest to recover. She hadn't slept a bit, worrying if he would accuse her of witchcraft. All it took was one soul to stir the pot. He had to recover and leave. Emma would see it done even if she had to force him.

She didn't like Bess around him. What red-blooded man could resist her? Bess would work Malcolm up and he would possibly relapse. But not if he was asleep. There was, of course, an added bonus to spiking his tea. Bess had in him a virile, self-proclaimed rogue and a helpless audience. He was bedridden, unable to do anything but lie there and listen to her talk about herself or defy almost all of Emma's instructions.

What Emma did, she did for his good.

She heard him snore and she smiled at Bess's frustration.

"Ye have the look of a wicked angel aboot ye."

Emma tilted her head to the dry voice belonging to Cailean. "You're awake. Thank God."

"Was I doin' that poorly, then?"

"Indeed you were," she replied, checking his dressed wound with the tips of her fingers. Dry and cool, just like the rest of him. Perfect. "But I think you're going to be just fine. You must be starving. You'll have to eat light. I'll have soup brought up."

He stopped her from going with a gentle touch to her wrist. "I take it whatever ye did just now was to m' brother, so he must be well?"

"He will be soon." Emma liked how these brothers asked about each other before anything else. She hoped for the day when she felt things like that for Harry.

"That's good." His deep pitch lightened a bit, but there was no humor in his voice. "How is yer dog?"

She smiled. How kind of him to remember Gascon.

"He's well, sir." She stepped aside to let him see Gascon for himself. "You have my gratitude for speaking up for him your first night here."

He didn't say anything to her but urged her dog forward and then said something softly to him.

"What did ye do to m' brother?" he asked her next. His tone changed just a bit. It wasn't menacing but if she were guilty of causing Malcolm harm, she would have lied.

"I drugged him." she told him honestly.

"Nothing serious I hope?" he asked, sounding neither overly curious nor overly concerned. "Ye're a healer, no' a killer, but I know Malcolm can be...troublesome fer some."

How troublesome was he exactly? If he was that bad, then perhaps she should keep him asleep for another se'nnight, then wake him and send him on his way.

"He'll sleep for a little while," she admitted to Cailean. "I did him a favor. Bess isn't the right girl for him." She pressed down very lightly on his wound.

"M' brother doesna' care aboot the right girl," he told her, shifting his weight beneath her fingers. Emmaline could feel his eyes on her. "But tell me anyway how ye know who is the right lass fer him?"

"I don't, but Bess does not have your brother's best interest at heart. He needs to recover. Just as you do." She let her smile widen, dropping the topic of Malcolm Grant. The less she talked about him, the better. So, he went out of his way for Gascon; that didn't mean he was a saint. She knew after listening to him with the girls last night that he was anything but.

"Ye're French?"

She shook her head. "I spent the last ten years there. I was born in England." What was she doing? She didn't need a friend, someone to confide in. People came and went here. No one stayed. His brother certainly wouldn't be staying.

"In just another se'nnight or two," she told him, back to duty, "you can begin returning to your regular routine and then be on your way with your brother."

"Ah, young Mr. Grant." Harry reached Cailean's bed and greeted him. Emma could hear annoyance in her brother's voice. "Malcolm will be happy to see you awake. That is," he aimed his hardening voice at her, "if he wakes up from his tea."

Damn. How did he know? "'Tis a mild sedative," she admitted. "The same one I gave to you when you were so ill. He'll be awake soon enough."

Harry made little noises, then coughed into his hand before he spoke to Cailean. "You won't mention this to your family, I trust?"

"'Twould make an entertaining story to tell," Cailean answered with amusement lacing his voice. "Malcolm could use a lass in his life who can take control . . . even by force if necessary. But I willna' say a word."

Emma blushed. Was he speaking of her? She could feel the heat burning her cheeks and lowered her head so the others wouldn't see.

Heaven help her, why was she imagining that the lass was her? Mr. Grant would make a full recovery and then leave. Why would he remain in a brothel? After a while, she suspected that even the most voluptuous bosoms would lose their appeal to the memory of home...or to the next adventure. He wouldn't be here long enough for her to become "that lass."

Besides that, his type wouldn't be interested in her humble breasts and plain features.

Alison returned to Cailean's bedside and saw that he'd awakened. She greeted him and the two of them fell into a sea of words and meaningful tones. Harry left soon after that, with Bess close behind.

Emma left Cailean and Alison alone and returned to sit beside Malcolm. She wasn't sure what she thought of him. Why did she have to think anything about him? Who was he but a heart-breaking rogue?

She would stop thinking about him and forget him the instant he left. He certainly was nothing special. Not the kind of man she'd ever choose for a husband.

Tending to him was a burden really, she pointed out to herself while leaving her chair to prepare his medicine. She found little pleasure in touching him to apply her poultice to the wound on his head. His skin felt cool to her touch, his chopped hair, soft in her fingertips. His temples teased and tempted her to traverse down them and feel the contours of his face. She didn't, but moved on to his throat and collarbone next. She could feel previous scars on him and wondered if he was as skilled with his sword as he believed he was. She trickled her fingers over the outline of his corded upper arm. Her breath boomed in her ears while she imagined those arms around her.

Alison's laughter shattered the image, but only for a moment.

Too quickly, she thought of the intimacy of touching his fingers. Were they strong? Would his palm be rough against a softer part of her? Her mouth went dry thinking about it. She'd learned much in a month of living in a brothel. Thank goodness he was asleep and unaware of how bold she was.

She paused and tilted her head just a bit to hear better. His breathing had changed. He was awake.

She pulled her hand away. Oh, damn it all to hell.

Chapter Eight

*M*alcolm knew she was aware that he was no longer asleep. How did she know? He'd been careful not to allow his muscles to twitch while she explored his arm. Hell, he'd never felt anything more sensual than her fingertips gliding over him, lingering on him... here... there, pulling shorter breaths from him

He should be angry with her. He was angry with her! She'd drugged him! But she touched him like she wanted to know him. Did he want her to? What good would it do?

"Cailean is awake." Her soft voice stole across his ears.

"I know," he answered. "And in the good care of Alison, I see. Cailean?" he called out.

"Aye, brother?"

"Are ye well?"

"Aye, Malcolm, are ye?"

Once they assured each other of the other's well-being, Malcolm returned his attention to Harry's sister. She saved Cailean's life. She saved his family. He wanted to offer her a rare, genuine smile but first he had a question to ask her.

"I will leave him to Alison fer another moment or two to ask this of ye instead, Miss Grey." He lowered his voice so that Alison wouldn't hear. He didn't know if she would go to Harry and tell him his sister was drugging folks in his brothel. "D'ye drug all yer brother's patrons?"

Her spine stiffened and she folded her hands together in front of her. "Not all. No."

He wasn't surprised that there had been others.

"Do you often pretend to be asleep so that you could spy?" she countered.

"I wasna' spyin'. I was lookin'. And takin' m' time aboot it too. But enough of ye distractin' me."

Her mouth fell open. "Me? I—"

"I dinna' care aboot yer other victims." He cut her off. "Dinna' drug me again. D'ye understand?"

"I cannot make you any promises," she muttered softly. "I'd like to do it right now."

"What was that, then?"

"Nothing, my lord."

"I'm no' yer lord," he said, a little disinterested. "And dinna' be coy with me. It doesna' suit ye."

"You're correct," she said with a corner of her shapely mouth curling at the edge. "You deserve to hear it."

She repeated what she'd mumbled.

"Mayhap," he mused, liking her sauciness better than her being coy. "Bess should tend to me from now on. Send fer her, please."

"No." Her lips pulled up in a smile that was as exasperated as it was victorious. She didn't give in easily, this one. "Bess is busy in the beds of her customers, Mr. Grant. I have knowledge of herbs." She cut him a suddenly anxious glance. "If you want to recover, your best option is with me."

"Well, if ye're the best option…" He flashed his own

triumphant grin and pushed himself up in bed to a sitting position. He should be angry that she'd drugged him and made him completely powerless, but he was enjoying her too much.

"When can I get oot of bed?" Why the hell was he asking?

"Anytime you wish, as long as there is someone here with you to come get me if you fall."

He laughed. "I doubt I'll fall."

She rolled her eyes. "Of course you doubt it. You're prideful and full of yourself."

"Nae," he corrected. "I'm confident." His smile began to change into one crafted to charm and get him what he wanted from a lass. But what good was it? She wasn't swayed by it.

He much preferred a woman who could see to one who couldn't. "I'd like to leave the bed right now and see m' brother."

"Go right ahead," she allowed.

He scowled at her. He wasn't sure why and swung his legs over the side. He gave himself a moment to stop spinning. He wasn't sure if it was his wound or Emma that unbalanced him. Why was he so confused about how he felt about her? He was angry and grateful and attracted at the same time.

He stood up slowly, straightening to his full height. He gripped the chair in front of him, then reached for her to pull her under his arm. For such a slight woman, she offered much support. She was strong and very, very soft. He hoped to show her that he wasn't too prideful if he admitted to needing her aid. *Why* he hoped to show her anything, he wasn't completely certain. It was all very unsettling.

His eyes fixed on his brother as he grew nearer. Relief at seeing him there, no longer pale but strong, propped against a few lush pillows, filled Malcolm with such relief he paused to keep from tipping over.

"Ye gave me a scare, Cailean," he said, reaching him. "I feared tellin' our mother that ye were lost to her."

"I willna' be taken doun by a pistol ball, Malcolm. The food in this place will kill me before a pistol ball does," Cailean answered, bringing a smile to Malcolm's face.

He felt Alison's eyes on him and he turned that smile on her. Cailean cast him a warning look when she blushed to her russet roots, and Malcolm backed off. But it was good to know he hadn't lost his charm.

Pity Miss Grey didn't see it. Pity for him, that is. If he ever wanted to win a heart like hers, he didn't know how. His appearance usually got him what he wanted from lasses—and it was never their hearts. He'd never wanted to woo or win a woman's heart. He still didn't. He needed to recover quickly so he could be away from Emmaline Grey. She reminded him that his dragon was hot on his arse. She reminded him of love and how incapable he was of it. She was trouble. And Malcolm didn't want any.

He let her go and sat without aid. He was strong. He'd be up on his feet and practicing in a day or two—then gone from here.

"Hell." Cailean grimaced at him from his bed. "Yer face looks like 'tis recoverin' from a memorable poundin'."

"Fortunately fer me," Malcolm replied, pleased to find his brother in good enough spirits to challenge him about his vanity, "I dinna' remember a thing." He turned to Alison. "Do I truly look so hideous?"

Before she answered, Cailean laughed. "Will ye stop at nothin' fer a compliment, then? False as it may be?"

Malcolm didn't answer right away.

Cailean had laughed.

A rare sound of late. Malcolm wanted to thank whoever was responsible for it. He smiled at Alison again while Emma clasped on to Gascon and moved away with Alison to give the brothers time to speak privately.

"Ye were shot in the neck?" Cailean asked him, apparently not knowing what had happened.

"Aye, and ye in the gut," Malcolm told him. "She dug the pistol ball oot." He motioned to Harry's sister on the other side of the room, changing his linens with Alison's help. "But before ye thank her, ye should know that she's been known to drug her patients, even after they recover."

"The stubborn prideful ones I'm told," Cailean said, still smiling!

Malcolm didn't know whether to take offense at his brother or celebrate his return to the living... and more than just in body.

"All who were raised with us are stubborn and prideful, so dinna' drink the tea."

They laughed together, the way they used to, the way brothers do. Malcolm vowed silently to thank Emma for all she'd done for his brother—just before he got the hell out of there.

Emma could hear every word between them. She told herself a hundred times to stop listening and pay attention to Alison, but she failed over and over, drawn toward the sound of his deep, honeyed voice and deep, male laughter.

Why did she even like him? He was just like the folks

in the village who never appreciated what Clementine had done for so many of them.

People were all the same, especially men. There were none alive like the ones her mother used to tell her about from her books. Especially not Malcolm Grant, a rogue who set women talking about him for several months after he left them. And according to her brother, he left every single one. She didn't want to think about him all the time. She didn't want to fall into some deluded fancy about him and have her heart broken—or worse—when he left.

"He has a chill...Emma, you asked me how Cailean looked and then you don't even pay attention when I tell you!"

Oh no! "Forgive me, Alison! I'm listening, I promise!"

Alison held back, probably to cast her a doubtful look but then continued, as if she couldn't wait to describe him.

"He has a look to him that is both chilling and vulnerable. It's his eyes."

"Sad?" Emma guessed.

"Perhaps," Alison allowed, sounding pensive and a bit captivated. Emma suspected she was looking at him while she spoke.

"They are big and deep," Alison continued. "Like oceans and the color of waves in moonlight. But it's his chin that makes my knees weak. It's fashioned with a deep dimple that adds even more fullness to the pout of his lower lip. I think about kissing him all the time. I cannot stop myself."

Emma smiled; better that than let herself blush to her roots, revealing her exact thoughts about Malcolm.

"Then you should kiss him," she said, wishing that if she had the boldness to follow her own advice, Malcolm wouldn't break her heart. But he would.

"That's the odd thing, Emma," Alison said like someone confiding in her dearest friend. "Though I am a…" She paused, struggling to utter what she would say and finally gave up. 'He is different from the others. I…I think I am beginning to care for him."

Emma reached out for her hand. She liked Alison, but she was glad she hadn't fallen for Malcolm the same way. Still, if Alison had the chance of a future with a man who loved her, then Emma would help her. "If your feelings continue to grow you must speak to Harry about finding another duty in the brothel that you can tend to besides the patrons. Perhaps you can cook or clean the rooms."

"Do you think he would let me?" Alison asked hopefully. "I mean, if there turns out to be something with Cailean. Something serious."

Emma nodded. "I will lend my voice to your cause."

They agreed and laughed softly at their silly fancies.

"You would like Malcolm Grant's appearance, Emma," Alison went on to say.

Emma had heard enough. She didn't want to hear how Alison described his visage. She liked letting his character craft it.

"His eyes are blue like the sky and green like a field, blended together."

Hell, Emma knew those colors.

"They are shaped with more of an angle at the edges than Cailean's. His eyes are more playful. I would even say they dance. Or perhaps it's the flash of his twin dimples that give his devil-may-care grin such life."

Emma had heard enough. He was a carefree rogue who'd come here for sex. Nothing more. So, his eyes sounded quite nice. What did any of it matter to her? "I don't care about him," she said to convince herself more than Alison.

"Miss Grey?" Malcolm called to her.

"Mr. Grant?" she called back.

"I'd like to share some whisky with m' brother to celebrate his recovery."

She felt her way back to him. "Mr. Grant, I don't think that getting drunk—"

"Lass," he said, stopping her, sounding weary. "I'd prefer it if ye'd quit denyin' m' every wish and just had the whisky brought to us."

Emma smiled. She wasn't sure how she managed it instead of flinging the nearest, heaviest object at him, but she smiled.

"I deny your wishes because they will cause you harm."

"I appreciate your concern, Miss Grey…" She could hear his smirk in his voice. "…but I'm not a helpless child."

"No, but you're a foolish one," she muttered, and sank her fingers into Gascon's fur. Without another word, she left the room.

In the hall, she dug her hand into a deep pocket in her skirt and pulled out a leather pouch. Inside was a powerful sleeping aid of crushed hops and passionflower mixed with a little bit of Valerian root. She'd scooped up the sachet on her way out of the room.

Heavens, it was tempting.

No. She'd previously drugged Mr. Grant to help him rest and recover without distraction. Drugging him now would be wrong. But it was tempting.

He wanted a senseless twit who did his bidding and kept her mouth shut in the meantime. She sure as hell wasn't that woman, though she wouldn't deny wishing he wasn't a rogue. How could she like him and dislike him at the same time? He was an infuriatingly stubborn warrior who fell weak at the sight of his brother sick in bed, a cad who somehow made her feel as beautiful as Bess.

She wasn't familiar with the ways of men, but this one boiled her blood. He was dangerous to her heart, and perhaps to her life as well. Why didn't she hate him? At least, fear him? She was as daft as the rest of the gels.

He'd get his whisky. The cheapest stuff she could find in the brothel.

Fighting with him was better than desiring him.

But first, she found Gunter, surprisingly exiting a room followed by one of the ladies of the house. Emma smiled as Brianne's favorite rose scent wafted from her.

"Good evening, Brianne," she said as she offered a genuine smile. Though she was Bess's best friend, Brianne had always been kind to her.

"Good evening, Emma."

Gunter groaned when Brianne answered her.

"How are your patients coming along tonight?"

"Quite well, thank you." Emma liked her for asking and then leaving her alone with Gunter.

"Don't tell your brother," her former escort said, knowing it was against the rules for him to have relations with the girls. He was Harry's guardsman, not a paying customer. He was loaned out to be her escort for the last month and now, thanks to Gascon, returned to his first duty: guarding Harry.

"I won't," she promised. She hardly told Harry anything, and after Malcolm's questions to her, she came to the conclusion that she hadn't really cared if she and Harry got to know each other. She wanted to change that now. When she left France, she'd wanted her brother back. A decade had passed and Harry was not who she remembered. But was it any reason to give up on her family? "Where is my brother?"

"In the kitchen, most likely."

She thanked him and continued forward a step before stopping again. "Oh, Gunter, where does Harry keep the cheapest whisky?"

"All the whisky's cheap. But the worst in the buttery is on the second shelf to your right."

She smiled in his direction and waved before continuing on.

She found her brother where she should have suspected he'd be. The kitchen was Harry's sanctuary . . . or his hell. It was the place where, according to Mary, who Emma overheard one night telling Alison, Harry's wife had been killed four years ago by a drunk patron who'd wandered in.

He leaped from his stool when she called out to him and led her to his seat.

"What is it? Are the Grants—"

"They are fine, Harry. I came to speak to you about something else. I have some questions."

"All right." He agreed to the inquiry and dragged another stool closer. "You want to know why I left you."

"No," she told him. "I want to know why you didn't come back to know if I lived or died."

"I did return. I was told you died. Almost everyone in the village died, Emma. I didn't know about Clementine."

Oui, she understood that and forgave him for it.

"Why did you lose our family home?" she brought up next. Damnation she was angry about that. She just now admitted it to herself. "I dreamed of going back many nights. Now I never can. Why did it mean so little to you that you sold it?"

"It meant everything to me." His pitch dipped and his voice broke and cracked. Her fine hearing picked up the shift in his breath. "It was all I had left. Literally, all. I was broke and about to lose the last thing I could call mine. The house was doing me no good. What was a bed if you had to sleep in it each night not knowing if you'd still have it the next day? I paid my debtors and bought this place to try to make a little coin."

She wasn't expecting him to have a good reason for selling their home, but he did. And she forgave him. She smiled at him—the way she'd wanted to for the last month. She had wanted to care for him and she did. He wasn't a thoughtless brute but a man trying to survive. She realized she didn't know about him because she didn't understand his reasons for the things he did and instead of asking, she remained angry.

She asked him about his wife, Lenore. She had asked him about her once before, when she'd first arrived, and found out about her, but Harry had put off speaking about what happened. Now he told her how a drunken patron had stumbled into the kitchen and tried to have his way with Lenore. She'd fought back and was stabbed. The commotion drew Harry's attention and the attention of another patron.

Malcolm Grant couldn't save Lenore. But he'd saved Harry.

She sighed a little while later, reaching for the good whisky in Harry's buttery.

Chapter Nine

*E*mma lay in her makeshift bed of blankets and pillows and listened to Malcolm's and Cailean's steady breaths for another moment before rising to her feet.

Dressed only in her shift and a robe, she tiptoed out of the room with Gascon at her side.

Everyone in the brothel was asleep. All the patrons had left as none were permitted to stay the night. And the night was over. Dawn was about to break and Emma didn't want to miss it. She hardly ever did.

Harry would never approve of her sneaking outside with only Gascon at her side, but Gascon was enough. He'd never led her toward danger, and after walking the same path with him for a month, familiarizing herself with her new environment, she felt confident enough to move without caution.

She walked toward the kitchen, one hand lost in Gascon's fur, the other half raised before her, more out of habit than necessity.

She hurried out the back door and stepped into the world about to come awake. She dragged in a great gulp of the air, smiled, and then moved on. She loved experiencing the birth of the day by herself. It filled her world with color. Like green, but not the green she vaguely remembered. If it were left up to her to describe it, she would speak of the crisp, cool, moisture settling on everything, waking up the fertile earth. Waking her. The dew-scented air flooded her lungs and bathed her in renewal. That was green. Red came moments later with the rising sun and the beguiling heat it washed over her. She danced to the sound of birds squawking for their morning meal and barely missed a tree. Twice. Her own laughter filled her ears and the air around her. She muffled her voice lest someone hear her and think for certain she was a mad witch. They'd never believe what the morning brought her, so she kept silent, smiling as she went.

Until a twig snapped behind her and Gascon began to growl.

Malcolm cursed his footing, which was usually as nimble and graceful as a spider. Did she hear the blasted twig snap? How was he going to explain to her what he was doing following her on her pre-dawn walk alone? She'd either think him odd and dangerous, or pitiful and insulting.

He'd heard her rise from her makeshift bed and leave the room. He followed her because... Because... unbeknownst to her, he'd watched her use caution not to wake him or Cailean before she left. She wasn't making a run to the privy. She was going to do something she shouldn't, and he wanted to know what it was.

He hadn't expected her to leave the brothel, but it afforded him more logic when he wondered why he'd come out after her.

And then the sun rose and bathed her in warm golden shafts of light, and logic sprouted wings and flew off. He'd heard her laughter, watched her frolic like a wood nymph, enchanting him senseless.

He only lost his wits for an instant. That's all it took for him to step on a twig.

"Who's there?" she called out.

Damn! Should he answer? She'd be afraid if he didn't. "'Tis Malcolm," he confessed, and left the cover of the trees. He moved toward her, and every step that brought him closer became easier to take. He stopped a few feet away though, seeing her anxious expression...and Gascon's fangs.

"I heard ye leave the room," he explained, taking in the sight of her long, golden tresses tumbling over her shoulders, her cheeks red, her eyes, so large and haunting. "I just wanted to make certain ye were safe."

"Thank you," she said. She didn't sound angry. "But I'm perfectly fine. Please, go back to bed. The morning air is too chilly for you."

"I'm perfectly fine as well."

"You're stubborn," she argued.

"So are ye."

She stared at him and he smiled at her, even though she couldn't see it. It didn't matter. He wanted to get closer. As close to her as Gascon was. It was going to be more difficult than he thought when she turned on her heel to leave him.

"D'ye want to be alone then?" He picked up his steps and followed her again.

She turned her ear toward the sound of him approaching her and quirked her mouth at him. He thought about kissing it.

"If I answer *oui*, will you leave?"

"Nae," he replied honestly.

"You would deny a lady's wishes?" she asked him.

"Ye can be alone later."

Instead of a number of different reactions she could have had, she smiled at him and then tilted her face to Heaven.

Malcolm couldn't keep his gaze from falling hungrily on her exposed throat. His mouth grew dry and his heart accelerated at the sight of her, so he looked away.

"How is it that your brother's manners are impeccable and you lack even the slightest courtesy? Did you each grow up in a different household?"

Now it was his turn to laugh. "Nae, lass. We grew up together. He had more interest in m' grandmother's tales of Arthur and various other knights."

"I know those stories," she told him. "My mother always read to me. I've forgotten many things, but not her tales of honor and chivalry." She smiled into the past, making him want to be there with her. "I miss those knights."

"They are hard to live up to."

"Which is what makes them heroes."

He laughed, then felt a little sick. He was no hero.

"I leaned more toward other pursuits," he informed her.

She tossed him a knowing smirk. "Women."

"Fightin'," he corrected. "I practiced every day with some of m' cousins."

"Ah, *oui*, I forgot you are the most skilled warrior in all of Scotland."

"One of the most skilled," he corrected.

"Forgive me."

"Ye mock me?"

She turned to laugh at him and tripped over a fallen

branch. Gascon whined but it wasn't the dog's fault she fell. She wasn't paying attention to where Gascon led. She sat in the grass, her hair falling over part of her face, and laughed at herself.

Malcolm watched her, coming more undone with each passing moment. He wasn't sure which he preferred more, the adorable crinkle of her nose when she chuckled, or the sound of her, like a symphony of tiny bells heralding in something wonderful. He wanted to know what that something was.

"I think I tore my stocking."

He dipped his gaze to her hand reaching for her leg. He watched her pull her skirt up over her knee and feel around for the tear. He saw it, but said nothing, ashamed to be staring. She had no idea how beguiling she appeared to him, which was part of her appeal. If he didn't react, she wouldn't know he was a cad.

Why did he even care? That was the question that had begun to prick at him. He'd never been tempted senseless by a woman before. Why now? How hard had he been hit in the head?

"You should go."

Her dulcet voice startled him. His eyes looked away from the shapely curve of her calf. How could she know?

"My brother doesn't like me consorting with the patrons."

Is that what they were doing? Consorting? He couldn't help but smile at her. "I'm not a patron. I havena' paid fer any lass here."

She tilted her chin up at him. Her dark, beguiling eyes searched him deeper than mere sight ever could. "So?"

"So," he answered, bending to sit in the grass with her, "we can consort."

She nodded, then shrugged. "If Harry was the only thing stopping me we could."

There were two questions he could put to her next. He could ask her what the other thing was, or, "Stopping you from what?"

She bit her lower lip and turned a shade more scarlet. But she spoke. It surprised him that she did. "Wanting to kiss you."

Nothing in Malcolm's life had ever tempted him the way Emma's candid confession did. She wanted to kiss him. It made his heart race. It made him forget for a moment why he had stopped being a rogue, and about what he ran from. He leaned in, his mouth inches from hers. He wanted that and much more. Just one night with her...No. He leaned back. He'd fought temptation for a long time. He wouldn't fail now...now, with a lass he admired and to whom he owed his and Cailean's lives. She deserved more than a meaningless tumble.

She laughed again, but this time her nose didn't move. "That's not what I meant to say. I must have hit my head when I fell. *Ou*." She brought her hand to her head. "There, I do feel a bump."

Satan's balls, he'd never wanted to kiss a lass so bad in his life! But he wouldn't force her. And he wouldn't break his word to Harry, or to himself. "We should get ye back then."

She nodded and then stiffened when he stepped in front of her, shoved his hands under her arms, and hauled her to her feet.

"Don't tell Harry I came out alone," she said before he let her go.

"I willna' tell him."

"Give me your word," she demanded.

"How do you know I'll mean it?" he asked.

Her eyes seemed to look at him deeply so that she appeared to be listening to the air. What did she hear? he wondered as she retreated.

"If you say you will," she said, "then 'tis your word. Would you break it?"

"It depends."

Incorrect answer. He knew it when she scowled at him and picked up her pace with Gascon, back to the brothel. What was the correct answer? Didn't it depend on each circumstance? Sometimes, like when your enemy has captured you and you give your word not to kill him if he lets you go, it's perfectly fine to go back. Who the hell would keep his word about that anyway? Should he explain things to her? No. Why bother? He was leaving as soon as he was able. He knew his body needed time to heal fully. So did Cailean's if they intended to take revenge on some Winthers.

"I spoke to Harry last night, before I brought you your whisky."

He turned to her while they walked. He hadn't wanted to drink the spirit, not sure if she had drugged it. She'd given her word that she hadn't. Still, he drank a cup and made Cailean wait a half hour before partaking.

She hadn't done it.

"I put some questions to him that were on my mind," she continued. "And I asked him about Lenore."

Malcolm wasn't sure why she was telling him, but for some reason, he liked that she did.

"Ye never asked about her before?" he asked her.

"No. And he never offered to tell me. Last night though, he told me what happened. He told me you were there."

He nodded, forgetting for a moment that she couldn't

see. He opened his mouth to clarify but was interrupted by Alison coming upon them, out of breath.

Malcolm and Emma both paled in the morning sun. "What is it?" Malcolm asked on a rattled breath, knowing whatever it was, it was about his brother.

"His fever has spiked," Alison told them on the verge of tears.

Malcolm took off after Emma and Gascon. They entered the brothel and hurried up the stairs. When they reached the bed, Emma reached out to Cailean and pressed her palm to his forehead.

"You feel hotter," she confirmed on a shaky voice, leaning down closer to him. She rested her head on his chest and listened intently for a moment or two and then straightened once again.

Behind her, Malcolm was about to ask her what was happening and if she needed his help, when she turned on her heel and walked into him.

He caught her in his hands, close to his body, a hairs-breadth away. The instinct to catch her pained his shoulder, near his collarbone where he'd been shot.

He needed to heal. And so did Cailean.

"What d'ye need? Tell me and I'll fetch it."

She inhaled deep beneath his fingers before she told him. "My jars are all labeled. Can you read?" She didn't sound hopeful.

"Aye, sure as hell, I can. What d'ye need?"

Hours later Malcolm fell into the chair near his brother's bed. His hand shook as he brought it up to his head.

"Malcolm." His brother's voice had grown weaker in an hour. "I'll be fine. Alison's here and she can help Emma. Go. Go and lay down before these poor lasses have two of us to tend to yet again."

"*Oui*, come." Malcolm felt her scrawny but strong arms reach under his arms and give him a tug. "Let's get you back to bed."

If he wasn't already half asleep, he would have smiled because Emma thought she could lift him.

"What is it, lass?" he asked her when she pulled him away from Cailean's bed. "If he's healing, why does he have another fever?"

"Infection, most likely," she told him in a quiet voice. "We've given him remedies for many infections, Mr. Grant. He's strong—"

"Aye, he is."

"He'll be fine," she comforted him. "Better by tonight."

She smiled and damn, but it quickened his slumberous thoughts. He hadn't thanked her yet for working without stopping to prepare and administer all her remedies to Cailean. He wanted to thank her but another thought occurred to him as he yawned. "Did ye drug me again, Miss Grey?"

"Honestly, Mr. Grant," she huffed, and gave him a little push that landed his arse in the bed behind him. "Your body is made of flesh and blood. Like the rest of us. It will rest with or without your approval."

He closed his eyes and nodded. She was right. He felt her moving his blanket up over his belly, caring for him after caring for his brother all morning. He wanted to be standing on his feet when he thanked her but it couldn't wait. He took her hand before she moved away.

"Miss Grey," he whispered. "Emmaline."

"Mr. Grant?"

"I want to . . . kiss ye too."

Chapter Ten

"He must take at least seven sips, Alison."

"Seven yes, Emma."

After six days at Cailean's beside, Alison had earned Emma's trust to tend to him as she herself would. Alison was very fond of the younger Grant. Emma didn't blame her. Cailean was thoughtful and appreciative, unlike his brother.

It wasn't that Malcolm Grant wasn't thoughtful or... Well, in truth, he wasn't. He was charming, and tempting, and he made her want to toss logic, caution, and everything else to the wind. When he had told her that he'd like to kiss her too, every nerve ending in her body ignited and left her burning, her blood boiling.

But he wasn't thoughtful or very courteous. He didn't thank her for anything. Not that she did anything for thanks. She didn't. But no one ever thanked Clementine either. She liked him but he frightened her. People couldn't be trusted. Hadn't the people in her village proved that enough with Clementine?

Bess seemed to like him despite all his imperfections. Yes, she'd returned just in time to greet Malcolm when he woke from his hour sleep.

That was seven hours ago. She had the damn night off, and her voice was driving Emma to the brink of madness.

"Oh, Malcolm," she cooed from her seat at the end of Cailean's bed. "I didn't know you owned your own castle. What do you call it again? Ravenwing?"

"Ravenglade," Malcolm corrected her. He'd only had to correct her three times now. He didn't seem to mind, at least not like Emma did. In fact, he sounded rather amused... a bit too tolerant if someone asked her opinion—which they didn't. But then, this was what Malcolm Grant enjoyed, wasn't it? Painted-faced women dressed in silk and satin, drooling over him and laughing over everything he said?

Emma flashed them both a sour expression. Truly, was Bess that dimwitted and Malcolm that easily captivated?

"I dinna' live there though," he continued, completely missing Emma's scowl.

"Oh, Alison!" Bess laughed and stretched out her ankles from the mattress. "Do you not adore how they speak? He 'dinna'' live there."

"Nae." His laughter did sound a bit practiced and insincere, but he kept the game going because he liked all the attention Bess was giving him. "If ye are the one sayin' it, then 'twould be 'He doesna' live there.'"

"Now, Malcolm." Bess giggled like a fool. "You're confusing me!"

Ugh! Emma nearly retched. Was this what a prostitute did for money? Did men really like simpleminded women? Did Malcolm? She couldn't do it if it meant her life.

"I'd love to go to your Ravenglade and spend some private time with you,' Bess purred like a satisfied kitten. A master of her profession. "I'm sure you could work out a fair price with Harry. Perhaps after our time together you might decide to keep me with you."

So! That's what she wanted! She wanted Malcolm to take her from this life, keep her! Emma felt like screaming. She shook her head instead. She didn't want to be here listening to this, but she refused to leave her patient alone with this seductress. If Bess had her way, she would take him to her bed. What did Emma care? Sadly, she cared a lot. She could pretend that she was concerned about the strain on Malcolm's body if he slept with Bess. But she was certain he'd be just fine. It was more than that. Was she jealous? Did she like him? *Oui*, she did. He'd saved her brother's life. If not for him, Gascon would still be outside. She didn't know if she was jealous, but whatever she felt wasn't pleasant. She had to step in and stop Bess from seducing him. "Mr. Grant," she said in a hushed voice. "'Tis late. Cailean needs sleep."

"Aye, of course," he agreed and rose to his feet.

"Are you permitted out of this room?" Bess's voice grated across Emma's ears.

"I can go where I please," he answered.

He was correct. Emma wouldn't stop him. Let him injure himself further. She didn't care. She turned away.

"Come with me to my room, then," Bess compelled like a sorceress. ' No charge."

Emma fumed. She should just let him go since he

seemed to enjoy Bess's foolishness so much. It would serve him right to have Bess's claws pierce him.

In the month Emma had been here, three patrons had fallen in love with Harry's best girl, but the blond siren had mercilessly rejected them.

"Bess," she said, speaking up for the first time that day. "I think Harry might object to you offering your services at no cost."

A shift of fabric and the equal balance of sound in both her ears revealed that Bess had moved a little closer and turned to face her. "Emmaline." Her voice dragged over Emma's flesh like the edge of a well-sharpened sword as she stood to her feet. "Your brother already offered me to Mr. Grant at no cost. We haven't taken our pleasure in his generosity yet. But I'll see to it that we do. I understand that you ask some of the girls to describe Mr. Grant to you. I've been with him before and let me tell you he—"

"Bess." Malcolm's voice fell like a hammer, stopping Bess momentarily.

In that time, Emma wanted to run. Oh, how she wished she could hide, not from his description, but from her own. She sounded pathetic and desperate, asking others to describe—Oh, she couldn't finish the thought. She wasn't some weak dormouse to be pitied or a groping imbecile. She felt mortified in front of . . . him. *Oui*, his opinion mattered to her. She didn't want it to. She didn't even know if she liked him! But that didn't change anything. She knew her flushed cheeks betrayed her. But if Bess saw her mortification, she didn't spare Emma an ounce of pity.

"When I'm done with him," Bess continued icily, "I'll come to you and describe his body and the way he felt inside me. Would you like that, dear?"

"When ye're done with me?" Malcolm interjected with a laugh just as cold. "Lass, ye speak like I could ever lose m' heart to ye."

Emma closed her mouth and swallowed. Bess had to be fuming, or on the verge of tears—as Emma might have been if Malcolm were speaking to her. Emma knew Malcolm Grant was no knight, shining armor or otherwise, but she didn't expect him to stand up to Bess and especially not at the cost of sleeping with the highest paid prostitute in the brothel. Men didn't argue with Bess. Why was Malcolm doing it?

"Stay out of my affairs, Emmaline," Bess warned her, moving away from the bed. "Especially when they involve him. Or your dog will pay."

Threatening Gascon was going too far. Emma knew her limitations but she'd be damned if she stood by and let someone hurt her dog. She took a step forward, but a pair of huge hands closed around her small waist and stopped her.

"Let her go, lass." Malcolm's breath was warm against her ear. "Let her go."

Malcolm didn't watch Bess leave. His eyes were fastened on Emma when she pulled out of his embrace and stepped away from him. She returned to Cailean's side, but his brother was asleep. She'd done all she could for him. There was nothing else for now.

Malcolm knew Bess had embarrassed her. It had angered him when she taunted Emma about her sight, or lack of it. He didn't give a rat's arse if Bess believed she could make him pant after her. He'd interrupted to keep Emma from going toe to toe with such a viperous tongue as Bess possessed.

It surprised him a little that he cared about Emma's feelings. He wasn't a complete scoundrel, but the people whose feelings he usually concerned himself with were his family. Emma wasn't that. But he cared just the same. It didn't worry him too much. All the talk in Camlochlin about honor was stored somewhere in the back of his head. He'd rarely called upon it. He had no need to—most of the time. He never stayed around long enough to give a damn about anything. But he was here. Now. And he wouldn't stand by and do nothing when someone was being treated poorly.

As for Bess, he had no interest in her whatsoever and he didn't care if she knew it or not. He told himself he felt nothing for Emma either. He liked her but that was all.

"Does his fever linger?" he asked her, eyeing Alison at the same time. Gascon moved between him and Emma, and Malcolm rested his hand on the dog's head.

He'd have a talk with Bess about threatening Gascon and let her know it wouldn't be tolerated. But right now he wanted to get Emma's mind off her.

"He's a bit warm," Emma told him. "Nothing concerning." She took a step toward where her dog should be and rested her hand on top of Malcolm's. She pulled away, but he caught her wrist and held it for a moment.

Tears pooled in her eyes, making them glimmer in the soft light when she tilted her chin to him.

He should have looked away. As much as he hated to admit it, the need to help was obviously ingrained somewhere deep in his head from his grandmother's tales of chivalry.

"Him and Harry are all I have." Her voice trembled along with her hand when she brought it up to swipe a tear from her face. The moment she did, her demeanor changed. Her shoulders straightened as if she were resigning herself to something. "If she intends to harm either one, you will not stop me from dealing with her."

He wanted to smile at the fierceness of her loyalty, but the reason pulled at his heart.

Her life would be so different in Camlochlin, surrounded by laughter and love, and other dogs.

The thought came before he could stop it. He should leave the room. He should leave her. But he couldn't even look away.

"I'll warn her, Emma."

She nodded and offered him a slight smile. He wondered if she'd ever kissed a man before. She had a bonny mouth with plump, naturally coral lips, made for passionate kissing and a life filled with laughter. Pity she seldom smiled.

He placed her hand on Gascon's fur. "Come. Take a walk with me outside."

"But 'tis night."

"Aye, and the moon is full. I wish to get to—"

"No, I cannot." She moved to pass him when he bent to retrieve his boots. "Harry already worries enough about me. If he catches me out at night—"

"I'll be with ye." He caught up with her as she headed for the door with Gascon. "Ye'll be safe." He hopped into his boots and almost collided with her. Gascon growled at him. "Ye'll tell me aboot yer life."

She tried to protest. "I will no—"

"Alison." He turned to her. "We willna' be far."

"We will be apart," Emma corrected. "I'm not leaving here with you in the dark. You're beginning to prove your reputation true."

"I never said 'twasn't." He followed her out of the room and into the hall.

She stopped for a moment to think over what she'd just heard. Gascon looked up at her face and whined.

"Really," she said, continuing on. "I'd feel better if you would stay in bed for now. You're not strong enough yet."

"I'll fergive yer ignorance when it comes to the strength of a Highland warrior because ye— What humors ye aboot that?"

He watched her smile deepen, like sunrise over the moors. He probably should be angry that she found the topic of his strength so amusing. But the sight of her quickened his heart to a maddening pace, and the only thought he indulged was how he could make her smile more often.

"If ye're no' leavin' the brothel with me, then where are ye goin'?" He leaned in close. "A clandestine rendezvous with yer lover, mayhap?"

She turned and almost touched his lips with hers. He basked for an instant in her warm breath before she stepped back and set her fist on her hip. "Oh, so you think I'm a prostitute then?"

"What?" Damn, it was too late. He realized what he said and that the only way out was to deny it. "Nae, not at all—"

"I should slap your face." She cut him off with a silken threat he found utterly captivating.

He smiled. "Then there is no one else."

She tossed back her head, giving him a scintillating view of her throat. "You're insufferable. Did you know that?"

"I've never heard it said before, nae."

Her eyes widened at his teasing and her delightful lips

curled into a smile. "I'll walk with you, Mr. Grant," she finally allowed. "But you'll tell me about your life and how you became so arrogant."

"Confident," he corrected, taking her hand off her hip and leading her to the stairs.

Chapter Eleven

They didn't go too far from the brothel. Emma was surprised when Malcolm stopped a short distance from the door, beside the small brook she'd visited so many times. He sat down and then invited her to do the same.

"I like it here," she told him, sitting next to him and a patch of mushrooms. "I like how it sounds."

"I canna' see much in the wanin' light. Tell me what ye hear?" he asked her on a soft, tender voice.

She smiled and listened. "Gently flowing water and droplets falling into it, the rustle of leaves in the treetops, like the soft chatter of endless voices in the slight breeze. I can hear night creatures scurrying in the underbrush; a hare perhaps, searching for food in the dark."

"Aye." He smiled. "I hear it too. I've spent many nights sleepin' under the stars and I've never paid attention to the natural sounds around me."

"My ears have become my sight," she said. "I can hear the changes in a person's breath, recognize the fall of one's feet, the rhythm of his gait." She knew how

Malcolm breathed: deep and slow, like he had all the time in the world. She knew how he walked: determined and steady. "Sound reveals the things I cannot see."

"That's quite amazin'," he confessed, sounding truly interested.

She didn't tell him about how scent...or touch also helped her see.

She didn't want to talk about her childhood and be reminded that the same thing that happened to Clem could happen to her. He didn't seem the sort to tell her too much about himself, so she asked him about his brother.

"Did he lose someone close to him?"

Malcolm had been looking at her while she'd described the night and its sounds. She could tell by the sound of his voice ringing close to her ear. He didn't turn away when he spoke to her now. "Ye do have a different way of seein', dinna' ye?"

"There's deep sadness in his voice," she told him. "I assumed..."

"Cailean doesna' speak of it." His breathing paused and shifted its rhythm. "His dog, Sage," he told her. "She died after she saved him and our cousins."

Emma pulled Gascon's large head closer to her. "What happened?"

"Cailean, Patrick, and Tamhas went on an adventure in Nairn in search of a few lasses they'd met in Sleat. They found the gels and were caught kissin' them in the family barn. Accordin' to the lads, the gels' faither bound them and whipped them thoroughly. We dinna' know how far he would have gone or if he would have let them live. He didna' believe that his daughters had only been kissed. Sage had been with them. When the lads were captured, she returned to Skye somehow bravin' the rain and hail of the season. She brought m' faither and m' uncles to the lads and saved them."

Emma marveled at such a dog and noted the drop in Malcolm's tone when he spoke of her.

"She grew sick not long after that and died a se'nnight later from exposure."

"Oh, how terrible," Emma said in a low, horrified voice. She gave Gascon a squeeze that made him whine. "I don't know what I'd do."

"Neither did Cailean," Malcolm told her. "The sound of his heart breaking echoed off the braes, and to this day no one in Camlochlin dares speak of her in Cailean's presence. Cailean doesna' speak of her either. 'Twas as if she never existed. But she did exist, and her passin' affected m' brother profoundly."

Emma wiped away a tear hanging from her lid. No wonder Cailean had a melancholy to his demeanor. She hadn't thought he sounded happy until he woke to Alison at his bedside. Her heart broke for Cailean, but Malcolm's reaction to his brother's pain made her heart leap. She'd often wondered whose arms would comfort her at Gascon's death. Her beloved friend was old, at least twelve years. Who would she weep to? Harry? He didn't even like Gascon.

In that, Cailean was fortunate.

"You're a good brother, Mr. Grant."

"Malcolm," he corrected gently, his breath a little shallow.

"Malcolm," she gave in, letting herself enjoy the intimacy of speaking his name. "Cailean is fortunate to have you."

"That's kind of ye to say, lass. But," he said, laughing hollowly, "m' siblings might disagree."

"I don't care if they disagree." She slapped her thigh. "I know what I see."

Disturbed from its resting place, a frog leaped and landed in her lap and startled her. She squeaked, then did a bit of leaping herself. Into Malcolm's arms.

He caught her in his embrace. The feel of his hard slabs of muscle keeping her close—and warm—lit her blood on fire. Heavens, but he was warm. She wanted to giggle. She did. She giggled in his arms like a witless fool and didn't regret it when he pulled her closer.

He had her in his arms. Where he'd been wanting her since he woke up. She fit nicely, her slender waist pressed to his, her milky cleavage rising and falling against his chest, her plump derrière tempting him beyond reason to take all of her in his hands and hoist her over him.

And then what? Lift her skirts over her thighs and her over his ready cock? He wanted to, but he didn't always do what he wanted, despite what his kin thought. He'd wanted to kill William Buchanan a few years back when the chief had entered Ravenglade unannounced and uninvited, but he hadn't done it. He wasn't a prisoner to his heart. At least, he never had been before.

He let her go, slowly, reluctantly, stroking her face before severing his touch completely.

He didn't want to take the chance of hurting her. She liked him.

"We should head back. Harry might be lookin' fer ye."

"*Oui*, of course," she agreed, and stood to her feet. "Thank you, Malcolm."

"Fer what?" He grinned down at her.

"For stopping before I had to take my knife to you."

His smile softened at her sincerity. Let her think what

she wanted. He could have disarmed her in an instant. But he wasn't entirely a rogue.

It was the first thing that lifted his spirits since—Hell, he didn't remember. It didn't matter *when*, but *what*. A lass. A lass who was somehow finding a way to get under his skin, deeper each moment he spent with her. How far could she go? The thought of actually, finally falling in love with someone scared the hell out of him. Mostly because what he felt was never love and he'd walked away defeated and more empty than before.

"Are you smiling, Mr. . . . Malcolm?"

"I shouldna' be, but as a matter of fact, Emmaline, I am."

"You don't think I can kill you if I need to?" she challenged.

"I dinna' think ye want to kill me. Desire makes all the difference."

"We shall see," she sang, passing him.

He laughed, watching her depart in the dim light. He couldn't see much of her but it didn't matter.

Most alluring about her was the way she hadn't allowed blindness to overcome her. Hers was a difficult victory in this harsh world. But she'd learned how to let a dog lead her. She had compassion for strangers and courage in dealing with bullies. She knew as much about plants and herbs as his aunt Isobel back in Skye . . .

. . . What would Skye think of Emmaline Grey?

There it was again! Him, thinking along the lines of bringing her home! It was madness! Why would he do it? He paused his steps for an instant. Why did he allow his thoughts to travel in such unknown directions when it came to her? Why the hell was he thinking about Emma in Skye?

He wanted to shake his head to clear it. Why was he getting so worked up? He didn't feel anything for her other than deep gratitude. He was confusing it with something else.

Still, he wished he had Gascon to hold on to when the clouds passed across the moon and she slowed her steps and turned her face toward him at the same time.

"Is something wrong, Mr. Grant?"

Were her senses so keen or was he obviously uncomfortable? He felt like she could see him. Parts of him no one had looked at in many years. He wasn't certain he was ready to let her see so much.

"Just…" He laughed, feeling foolish. What would he tell her? That he thought about her often and he didn't know what it meant. He hadn't begun to care for her. It couldn't be that. It had never been that before. "'Tis nothin', Miss Grey."

"Oh, of course." Her voice fell like whispers from her lips as she turned away and gave Gascon a tug. "If that's the way you prefer it."

He barely heard her, but barely was enough. "Prefer what?" He chased after her to the brothel door.

"Our time together to be," she said, entering the dark kitchen.

"How d'ye think I prefer it to be?" He banged his foot on the leg of a heavy table but barely paused his steps after a blind lass—who hadn't stumbled—and her dog.

What the hell was happening to him?

Should he be worried?

"It seems you prefer deceit and games over…other attributes."

She was correct. Sometimes he did indeed prefer secrets and games. But not tonight. She valued truth and honesty and he wanted to give it to her. He wanted to tell her that she lived in his thoughts, night and day, more and more, and he didn't know why. But he couldn't. She would think him a fool. He already felt like one. How was it that he was learned in the bedroom but when it came to matters of his heart, he had no idea what the hell he was doing?

"Sometimes the truth is kept hidden fer a noble reason."

She tilted her chin in his direction, a smile curling the tips of her lips as they left the kitchen and approached the stairs. "What do you know of nobility, Mr. Grant?"

He smiled and lowered his gaze. "No' much."

"Ah, honesty! Better!"

He heard her sweet laughter and looked up to catch her passing him with Gascon.

"You're improving already."

Maybe he was. A little. He smiled, then laughed behind her. "Tell me, Emma. What other attributes do I lack?"

She stopped and held her index finger to her chin and tapped it. "Let's see. Humility, for one. That's large. You don't possess much of that."

"Why should I?" he asked, leaning against the banister, not offended. "Has humility ever won a battle?"

Her dark eyes settled over him, searching, listening. "There is no battle here."

Hell, if only she were correct. This, he was relatively certain, was the beginning of the biggest fight of his life. Every time he was with her, his heart beat the battle drum.

"Loyalty," she tossed at him, along with a blond curl over her shoulder.

"I'm loyal to m' kin. What else?"

"Gratitude," she fired softly, turning at the top of the stairs to face him.

Gratitude? Hell, he was grateful. How many times had he thanked her for saving him and Cailean?

Hell, none.

"I...Ehm, I..."

"*Oui*?" she prodded gently.

Satan's arse, he was fond of a lass who was unaffected by his confident dimpled grin. A lass who looked beyond the frame and expected more.

More, Malcolm Grant couldn't give her. He wished he could. In fact, if falling in love were possible for him, he wouldn't mind it being with her.

"Emma?"

"*Oui?*"

"From tonight on, I'm sleepin' in the chair."

"If you wish."

"And thank ye fer savin' m' brother's life."

She quirked a honeyed brow at him. "Not yours?"

"Mine is..." He let his words fade in the air between them and turned away. How could he tell her that there was no woman who would suffer his death too long? No lass whose life he'd deeply affected. It had hit him not long after he left Fortune's Smile four years ago. Rather than fight the dragon, he fought his physical desires and devoted his days to traveling and practicing. If he was off his horse, he was on his toes. It had done his body good, hardened him more, quickened his reflexes, and kept his thoughts from things he didn't want to face.

"I might pine for you, Mr. Grant."

He looked up to the top of the stairs. Had she whispered those words or did his own lonely heart conjure them up? How could she know what he was thinking? Feeling? And then say the one thing that could make him doubt he was deficient after all?

She said nothing else nor gave any indication that she'd said anything a moment before. He watched her return on her trek to the room they shared. Behind her, he allowed himself to wonder what losing his heart would do to him, if it were, after all, possible?

Why her? What was it about her that was beginning to keep him up at night? Hell, what wasn't it about her? It was everything. He liked her. He admired her.

Hell, he needed a drink.

Chapter Twelve

J think your brother and Emma like each other," Alison whispered above Cailean's face. "She went walking with him hours ago. Do you think he'll try to kiss her? I don't think she's ever been kissed before."

Cailean smiled and raised a hand to her cheek. His body felt warm from looking at her succulent pink mouth. If he was feverish it was because of her and not some bullet wound.

"What have I done to earn such attention?" he asked her.

Hell, he loved how that flush of pink stole across her nose before she spoke. "You speak like my attention is something to be coveted."

"D'ye think I woulda' fought four Winthers fer ye if 'twasna' so?"

She lifted her chin and shined her smile on him full force.

He wouldn't lie—he liked the look of her. She stood out to him on that first night by the way her russet hair captured every hue of the candlelight, the way she moved across the dining hall, and when, at one point, she turned, as if feeling his eyes on her, and met his gaze. He thought he'd never seen eyes so green as hers. After getting to know her a little that night, he decided she was worth the fight, worth the bullet.

"No one has ever fought for me before," she told him, her emerald eyes shining on him like dancing flames.

"Then they're fools fer m' benefit."

"Perhaps." She smiled. "But they are not lying helpless in a bed stitched up like a fine lady's embroidery."

"In yer care," he pointed out. "Helpless to yer charms."

Her laughter made him forget everything else, things that plagued him, like Sage's great head in his lap, her breath shallow, a low whine coming from her throat. She wouldn't let anyone move her away from him. Her pale gray eyes fixed on his as she breathed her last breath.

"Emma's correct, you do have sad eyes," Alison told him, taking his hand.

"Nae," he promised her, trying to stay awake. "I'm happy. When I open my eyes and see ye here, I'm happy."

He wanted to kiss her. It was all he thought about and the last thing he remembered. But he smiled at Emma instead when she returned without his brother.

Emma bent her ear to Cailean's chest and listened to his breathing pattern. She held up her finger to quiet Alison when the girl began to bid him good night. He'd slept most of the afternoon and evening, waking intermittently to smile at his breathless admirer. Alison was losing her heart to Cailean. It was clear in the way she giggled at everything Cailean said, in the wistful breaths she took when she spoke to him, or of him to Emma. Harry was being kind by letting her stay by Cailean's side for days, without working. But what would happen when her brother insisted she return?

"Has his fever come back, Emma?" Alison asked her now, her voice tense and on the verge of alarm.

"It hasn't fully left," Emma told her. Why hasn't it? Was she doing something wrong? She wasn't a physician with all medicine at her disposal. She closed her eyes because when she was little she closed them to pray. She prayed now for Cailean Grant, not because she was afraid of his family coming here to avenge him. She liked him and the honesty in his tone. His death would be difficult for her, for Alison, but mostly for Malcolm.

Keep him with us, she beseeched the Lord.

"The fever is low," she reassured Alison while she straightened. "He will be fine." She smiled to convince her though she herself was not convinced. "Now, go get some sleep. If you see Malcolm, send him to me." She had to tell Malcolm.

"Emma?"

Emma stopped and gave Alison all her attention. The poor girl needed more reassurance that Cailean would survive. Emma would do everything, everything she knew how to keep him alive.

"You care for Malcolm."

What? "No! I—"

"It's quite all right. I understand. But I would have you know that he watches you all the time. He lights up when he sees you, and when you speak to him he clings to every word. I just thought you should know that." She moved closer and before Emma knew what to do, Alison leaned in and kissed her cheek. "Good night, Emma. I'll be back at first light." She leaned down and whispered things to Cailean that Emma wished she couldn't hear.

Why would a simple peck on her cheek make her so watery? And why would knowing that Malcolm watches her all the time and lights up when he sees her make her feel so incredibly desired? Emma was glad to hear the door open before Alison thought her mad because of the foolish grin on her face.

"Oh, Mr. Grant!"

Alison's discovery on the other side of the door tore Emma's grin away. His brother wasn't doing well and she had to tell him.

"Here he is now, Emma," Alison called out from the door. "Well, good night."

His presence filled Emma's world with crackling charges that left her nerves scorched, the scents of peat, whisky... and rose. Where had he been for the last hour? When they'd returned from their walk he'd been right behind her.

"Were ye lookin' fer me?" He swept into the room and hurried to his brother's bed. "Is Cailean all right?"

She wanted to tell him *oui*, his brother was fine. But she couldn't. "His fever has returned, worse this time."

He touched his hand to Cailean's cheek and cursed under his breath. "Why?"

"I don't know," she told him truthfully. "I don't understand why this fever is lingering. 'Tis beginning to concern me."

"I thought he was stable." She could hear the worry in his voice as well.

"He is, but 'tis my herbs keeping him that way. I fear there is something I'm not seeing, something I have missed."

He was quiet for a few moments and she thought she told him too much.

"How did ye know how to treat him?" he finally asked, sounding on the verge of something.

"What do you mean?"

"Ye knew he had a pistol ball lodged in his gut. How? Did ye use yer hands?"

She shook her head. "No. Alison described it and I felt for an exit wound but there was none."

"She told ye that was the only wound?"

Emma hadn't checked! She hadn't checked for herself! There'd been too much going on. She'd never tended to men who were shot in a fight.

But she'd only heard two shots. Emma's heart fell to the ground but she managed to remain on her feet. Another wound! He'd been stabbed! No! There would have been more blood. "We need to check his body," she cried, hurrying to do so herself.

"Can we turn him over?" Malcolm asked.

She nodded and they moved him gently. From his deep sleep, Cailean groaned, and so did Emma.

"Emma."

The fear in Malcolm's voice made her breath shorten.

"There's a wound," he told her. "A slice, small in size, not deep."

"'Tis infected," she guessed. It was the only way a small cut could make him so ill.

"Aye," he confirmed.

Emma stopped breathing and counted, feeling light-headed. Fourteen. Another wound. She'd missed it. Such a small, easily treated thing and now he could die because of it. Because of her. She stepped back and almost fell over the chair leg.

Malcolm caught her. "Ye canna' give up on him now, lass. Please. Ye have to help him. Ye're the only one here who could."

He was correct. There wasn't time to feel responsible. Not now.

"I don't know if—"

"Ye can," he cut her off gently. "We can. I'll help ye, Emma. We've done it before."

She nodded. But it wasn't the same. They could lose him this time.

"Lay him on his belly."

She wouldn't tell Malcolm the high risk. She would fight to help Cailean live.

Two hours, four basins of fresh water, boiled rags, and twelve mixtures of different ointments later Emma covered Cailean's stab wound with leaves and wiped her hands.

The younger Mr. Grant lived. For now. Every hour would be crucial. When there was nothing more to do for him, Emma sat on her borrowed bed and Malcolm sat in the chair beside her.

After the way Clementine had been treated by her patients, Emma never cared who she helped or who she didn't. Why should she care? So they could burn her alive for it later? She barely trusted Malcolm not to turn her in. Would he do it after she helped his brother—or *because* she almost let Cailean die?

It was better if she never picked up another herb. She had no place learning medicine when she couldn't see her patients.

"Mr. Grant."

"Aye?"

"I want you to know how very sorry I am for not..." Oh, she didn't want to be responsible for anyone's life! Cailean was such a vital young man. The thought of his death because of her negligence broke her heart and made her do something she hadn't done in years.

"Are ye weepin', Emma?" He was out of his chair in an instant and sitting beside her on the bed the next. He put one arm around her and with his free hand lifted her chin to have a look at her. "Och, lass, dinna' weep." He sounded pained enough to almost make Emma stop.

"I should have checked him with my own hands," she cried.

He pulled her in close and held her while she gathered herself and did her best to stop crying. Being in his arms was like nothing she'd ever experienced before. No man had ever held her like this. Not even Harry. This was an embrace, all consuming, tender yet firm, a shield against the harsher things in life. She didn't ever want to move again.

"Come, lass." His voice was as deep as the shadows, caressing her, comforting her. "We willna' give up on him now."

"But I should have—"

"Hush now, Emma."

He stroked his hand down the back of her head and made her sigh against him like an untarnished innocent. But no one was untarnished.

"What's done is done," he said, moving her away so he could look at her. She could feel his gaze, his attention on her, and she was tempted to lift her hands to his face and look back at him.

"We move forward now, aye? We save m' brother."

"*Oui*," she promised, though she fought to keep her tears controlled. She wouldn't think about not being able to save Cailean. They could do it. They *would* do it. "*Oui*, we save him."

He touched his fingers to her cheek, startling her. Instinctively, she backed away, prompting him to return to his chair.

How had he so easily forgiven her for almost killing

his brother? How had he so easily pulled her back from a chasm of guilt?

"Thank you," she said softly beneath his chin. It didn't seem enough.

"What fer?" he asked. "Ye're the one who did all the work."

It was considerate of him to say so. Emma couldn't help but smile. In fact, she suddenly felt quite happy. She didn't know how he made her forget that she didn't completely trust him, but he did. "You are a mystery. One moment you prove rumors true and the next, you tempt me to stop believing what they say about you."

His lilting, liquid laughter swept over her, compelling her to tell him all. "What do they say?"

She moved out of his embrace and threw back her head to sigh at the ceiling. "That you are a master of..." She stopped before her cheeks burned and betrayed her thoughts. "That you are careless with hearts."

"Ah, but 'tis true." His voice was rich and gruff and wonderfully sensual. "Take everything ye heard to heart. I'm the devil's own."

She shook her head. "Devils don't make one feel at ease." There she went smiling like a witless milkmaid again. "Devils also have no choice but to be terrible. You know how to comfort a woman, Mr. Grant."

"Malcolm."

"If you are careless with hearts," she continued, afraid that his name on her lips might somehow touch her heart and in a single moment sentence her to a life of pining, "'tis because you choose to be."

For a few moments, only the crackling of the flames in the hearth and Cailean's breath filled her ears. Then, "Ye're verra' intuitive, Miss Grey."

"You aren't all that difficult to read if one but listens hard enough," she told him.

"Is that so?" He moved closer to her, like he meant to pull her into his arms again. Though his breath seemed a bit off, the amusement in his tone made her turn back to him.

"Tell me what ye hear then."

She shrugged her shoulders and bent her head. She was acutely aware of Cailean's deep, heavy breath. A good sign. "You're callous, but I suspect a façade. Then again, you may truly believe you don't give a damn about most things, but you cared about a dog out in the rain."

"Well done," he said, imbuing it with admiration that made her belly flip. "Ye are almost exactly right aboot me, Emma."

"What part is wrong?"

"I'm *certain* I dinna' give a damn. It's not based on whether I believe it or not. The trail of lasses I've hurt is proof enough."

"Do you regret it?"

"I…" He laughed for a moment, but he sounded uncomfortable. "I…" He tried again while he moved back, letting his laughter fade. "I regret many things."

She'd gone too far, too fast. If one didn't know the path, she would surely stumble if she raced over it. She thought the best way out was to take the light off him.

"I've described you," she said playfully. "Now describe me."

He didn't take long at all and Emma wanted to think it was because he'd been studying her more often than he let on, like Alison said.

"Ye're intelligent, brave, and determined. Verra' pleasin' qualities in a woman."

"Truly?" she asked, remembering how foolish Bess had sounded earlier. "You admire such qualities?"

"Of course, I do. All the women of Camlochlin are strong. M' sister, fer instance—Ye would like Caitrina," he continued, returning to his chair.

"Well," Emma said, lying back on the bed and closing her eyes to listen to him. "I like your brother, so that doesn't surprise me. But tell me about her."

"She was a hellion too. Now she's a pirate."

Chapter Thirteen

Malcolm didn't sleep but stayed awake until the sun rose. He spent most of the night watching Cailean and Emma sleeping. His brother woke twice and Malcolm cared for him, following Emma's instructions exactly. He didn't wake her. She'd done so much already. If his mother ever found out how close her youngest son had come to dying, Malcolm would make certain he told her how Miss Emmaline Grey saved his life, tending to him night and day.

Malcolm enjoyed watching her doing it, caring so much for a life she didn't know.

He spent the few minutes he had before Cailean drifted back off confessing to his brother that he'd told her about Caitrina and how he'd helped her convince their father that she belonged with her Captain Kidd.

He was a bit surprised when Cailean asked him his simple question, thinking his brother wasn't completely lucid.

"Why?" Cailean asked him. "Why did ye tell her?"

Aye. Why, indeed?

Malcolm wasn't completely sure why. He shrugged his shoulders and remained quiet, pensive of his reasons. "I havena' been sleepin' well. I had nothin' to do but talk." It was only half true. He could have done a number of different things. He chose to talk to her because he liked doing it.

"Remember what she's done fer us, Malcolm. Dinna' break her heart. Ferget Harry. Do it fer yer own brother. Dinna' hurt her."

There wasn't much more than that from Cailean. What more could he have said? *Dinna' hurt her.* That's what Malcolm did, wasn't it? He broke hearts. It wasn't something he boasted about or took pride over. He didn't do it to feel a certain way, to show other men up...or to break any lass's heart. He'd like more, a wife, mayhap some bairns. But what was he supposed to do, wed a lass he didn't love, mayhap he'd never love? He didn't want that—not for himself or for any lass. He wanted...Hell why was he even thinking about this? He'd tried to feel love before, the kind the other men of Camlochlin had found. He never did. He finally gave up, rejecting it as it had rejected him. But damn it to hell, it still followed him, an unfulfilling lack taunting him, tormenting him. Everyone thought they knew him, the rogue, stomping on hearts in three different countries. It was true he had no trouble leaving lasses in tears, but he never stomped on their hearts.

And he hadn't enjoyed the pleasure of a woman's body in almost four years. He thought of Emma's asking him if he regretted being a rogue. He did. He regretted all of it. Every day he regretted it more. He traveled often, almost most of the time, avoiding any kind of emotional connection always on the move, always one step ahead of the dragon.

That had changed. He'd let the dragon in. There was nowhere to run. He couldn't leave Cailean. The lad was his responsibility.

He turned his gaze from his brother and settled it, as if he had no control over his own body, on Emma. Was he mad? He liked her. He admired her and found her strong and intelligent…and good. She had a good heart fashioned with compassion and humility—when she dealt with Bess—that she wore like a mantle of grace. She challenged him to be more than just a rake. And despite her drab gowns and unpainted face, he found her more mesmerizing than any woman he'd ever met before. He had to admit there was something about her that tempted him to hurl all the principles he'd discovered over the last few years to the four winds and begin the chase.

How could he find interest in her while she lay there sleeping? But hell he did. He liked the way she looked, but more, he liked the way she sounded, the way she listened. When he'd told her about sailing upon a ship to rescue his sister, she'd leaned in and inclined her ear to his voice. She'd sat, engrossed in his tale and hearing about the men of his family with whom he'd sailed. Her subtle smiles, her worried expression when he came to a more dramatic part of the tale, and the thoughtfulness she gave to every question she asked him, all convinced him that she was there, in the story, fully immersed in every emotion.

He liked watching the different play of emotions on her face while she listened. It was better than being seen.

He didn't care that she couldn't see him, but hell, it was like stepping into unfamiliar vales. He'd always relied on his looks. Now, he had nothing but words. And he wasn't good with those. Especially when he didn't know which words to say or if he wanted to say them.

He watched the sun come up and smiled at the sleeping beauty snoring like a small bear in her bed. A little while later, he dressed himself in the clothes Harry had sent to the room, black woolen breeches and a white shirt with ruffled cuffs and some ruffles at the neckline, which Malcolm left unlaced. There was also a dark blue jacket and justacorps, but he left those alone, preferring a less formal look.

Gascon sat up and whined at Malcolm's feet.

"What?"

The beast whined again and wagged his tail.

Thanks to all the dogs in Camlochlin, Malcolm knew what this one wanted. "Come on then." He stood up and stretched. He felt quite well, besides being tired.

He and Gascon left the room quietly and headed below stairs. They went to the kitchen first, where Malcolm opened the back door and stepped outside with the eager dog. Immediately, Gascon ran for the nearest tree. So did Malcolm. The brothel did have a privy but it smelled worse than hell.

He dunked his hands into a bucket of cold, crisp rainwater. When he was done, he called for Gascon, then stepped back inside.

Voices coming from the foyer stopped him and made his blood run cold.

Pressing his back to the wall, he moved a little closer and peeked around the corner.

"I don't care if she's still asleep, Grey," said a tall blond man with pale blue eyes.

Malcolm had seen him before, the night he and Cailean had been wounded. He was one of the men who'd fought against them, one who'd gotten away. For a moment, Malcolm wanted to step forward and reveal himself. There were only three of them that he could see. He could take them down without any help. He wanted to.

But more would come and Malcolm would always be responsible.

"My lord, the baron wants the red-haired girl. The one who cost his brother Andrew his life. He wants her for one night."

Alison! Malcolm glanced toward the stairs. Cailean liked her. Malcolm liked her too. He wasn't about to let these bastards near her. He had to think of something. And he had to get past them without being recognized.

"He'll kill her," Harry said, sounding frightened but admirably determined to refuse.

"I, John Burroughs, swear to return her to you alive. Or is my word not good enough for you?" he asked in a low, threatening voice.

Harry wouldn't last much longer.

They thought Malcolm dead so they didn't give him a second look when he kept his head turned and stumbled toward the stairs like a patron who was barely sober enough to stand. He was glad he'd changed out of his plaid before he left the room.

He couldn't let Alison out of the brothel. Cailean would never forgive him. He had to do something to help keep her from Winther's men. The fever or pox was always good at scaring the hell out of folks.

As good fortune would have it, Malcolm ran straight into Bess. He told her his plan to let the Winthers know that Alison was very ill.

"Tell them Alison is verra' ill with a mysterious fever," he repeated when Bess refused.

"They'll want to see her," she argued.

"Not if ye convince them how ill she is. She could perish any moment. Tell them ye think a few of the other girls are startin' to feel under the weather, as well."

She shook her head. "What if—"

"Do this fer me, Bess," he interrupted, taking her hand. "And I'll be in yer debt."

"Take me with you when you leave."

He shook his head. That was the last thing he wanted to promise her.

"I'm no' lookin' fer a wife, lass. Nothin' has changed."

"If you want my help..."

Damn, this was going to cost him but he couldn't let Alison leave with the Winthers. She'd never make it back alive.

"All right, Bess," he gave in, needing her help. "I'll take ye with me when I leave."

"Oh, Malcolm, do you mean it?"

Aye, damn it. He just said it, didn't he?

"Now, go."

Bess did as he bid her and even coughed in the Winthers' faces, compelling them to hurry and get out before they catch death. They didn't demand to see Alison for proof. They just left.

Malcolm was so relieved he caught Bess in his arms when she raced up the stairs, back to him. But after a moment of her kissing his face, he backed away. He moved her hand away when she cupped his groin through his new breeches and told him that he looked so good in his new garb, it made her want to do all sorts of decadent things to him. When she began to describe those things, he wondered why he wasn't so much as tempted. Aye, he'd kept himself out of beds of late, but he'd been tempted. What men weren't?

Any other man would have been as hard as stone about now. But nothing. He felt nothing. It startled him. Did it have something to do with being shot? Was something damaged? Getting smashed in the skull seemed to hold a bit more weight to his sudden and utter impotence. Did it have something to do with Emma? Was it possible?

Bess moved forward and leaned up on her toes to speak against his lips. "Come, Malcolm. Let's go fu—"

"Mr. Grant?" The door to Emma's room opened up and her voice stilled the blood in Malcolm's veins. "Where is my dog?"

At the sound of her, Gascon appeared and barreled toward her. She took his huge head in her hands, and Malcolm felt his belly twist at the tender smile she offered the mongrel.

"Come," Bess urged, giving him a tug.

He didn't move.

"Forgive me." Emma's graceful voice fell like stones on him. "Am I interrupting something?"

He wanted to tell her about the Winthers returning for Alison, about what he'd done to save her, but Bess spoke first.

"Not unless Mr. Grant plans on taking me right here on the floor."

Emma turned three different shades of scarlet, then took hold of the fur between Gascon's shoulders. "Don't let me keep you," she said softly, though there was a terse edge to her tone. "Cailean is asleep. Alison arrived in your absence, so don't make haste to return."

There was a moment while Malcolm watched her and her dog walk toward the stairs that he didn't give a damn about anything other than stopping her. Beneath his breeches, his legs tightened, ready to spring forward.

What would he tell her when he stopped her? The truth. That he had no intention on bedding Bess, despite what she heard when she entered the hall.

Why did he feel the need to tell her anything? Emma didn't care if he went off with Bess. She didn't want him to hurry back to her. It stung. Like nothing ever stung before.

He didn't like it.

"Malcolm," Bess prompted. "Shall we go?"

His eyes remained on Emma's back as she descended the stairs and disappeared around the curve of the wall.

"Bess, I—"

"Why do you show interest in her?" Bess said. "She's quite plain to the eye. She's mousey if you ask me, and didn't Harry warn you about staying clear of her?"

Malcolm turned to Bess slowly; his eyes uncharacteristically hard and sharp. He didn't care about how Bess thought Emma looked, but was she making a veiled threat about Harry? Hell, he hated being threatened. Bess had been there with them when he made the promise to Harry, and now she was using it.

A younger him wouldn't have wasted a moment but tossed this wench into the nearest bed and had his way with her. Every way he wanted it.

What the hell had happened? What changed? Did he lose his interest in lasses? Nae, for he found interest in Emma Grey.

"Make trouble fer Emma and I'll see personally that ye regret it."

"Malcolm!" Bess gasped, sounding shocked at the threat.

"She's tryin' to save m' brother's life, Bess," he told her, choosing to defend Emma. "I owe her much." And he did. That didn't mean his heart was involved. She had his gratitude, nothing more.

But when he looked at Bess he still didn't want her.

"We have a bargain and I will keep it," he told her. "But I'm goin' to tend to m' brother today. I suggest ye go and do what ye're paid to do."

He didn't wait for her reaction, but walked away. This was what he was good at. Walking away. It was best if Bess knew now that she had no chance of winning him or bedding him. He'd learned that clean cuts healed the quickest. Bess would be fine. It was him who was in trouble.

He opened the door to the room and stepped inside. He smiled at Cailean and then glanced at the lass who made his brother smile again for the first time since Sage's death. Alison had no idea the fate she avoided today.

"Emma was angry with ye fer takin' her dog," Alison reported with a warm smile as Malcolm approached the bed.

"How did she know 'twas I who took him?" Malcolm asked, feeling his brother's head with the back of his hand.

"She said Gascon wouldna' go off with anyone else," Cailean told him with a wide grin.

Malcolm wished she were here right now so he could thank her for saving his brother once again. He should do something nice for her before he left Fortune's Smile and headed back home. Shouldn't he? "Ye look good, brother, and ye're cool to the touch."

"Does Emma know why his fever returned?" Alison asked them.

Ah, then she was not only oblivious to what was done on her behalf this morning, but neither Cailean nor Emma had told her that she'd failed to detect a second entry wound in Cailean's back while she had acted as Emma's eyes.

That missing it had nearly killed Cailean.

Malcolm was glad they hadn't told her. She seemed quite fond of his brother. Knowing she almost killed him would cause her anguish. "She said fevers are unpredictable."

"Mr. Grant." Emma's voice raked across his ears from where she stood at the open door. "What are you doing in here? Why aren't you wasting your time with Bess?"

He watched her enter slowly with Gascon at her right hip. Her eyes gleamed with warm hues of sable and honey but her tongue was as sharp as cool steel. And hell, her sweet nose begged to be kissed.

"Well?" she interrupted his thoughts.

Unpredictable like her—a fever that made his blood boil and his mind delirious.

Why else would he be stuck on the thought that his heart seemed to beat in rhythm with her breath?

"I would rather waste m' time with ye than with Bess." He grimaced almost as soon as he finished speaking, realizing how bad what he said sounded. "No' that our time together is wasted—"

"I know what ye meant, Mr. Grant," she stopped him. "I'd like to speak to you in the hall if you please."

She stepped back out and he followed her. He wondered on his way out the door how far he would go.

"Close the door please." She turned to him and took a step closer while he did as she asked. "Did you go to Bess's bed?"

"Nae." He breathed deeply. It was a truth he was proud to tell her. It was the first thing he felt pride in, in many years. "Nae, I havena' been near any bed but yers."

She smiled and it nearly knocked him over. His heart froze in his chest and then jolted back to beating. Over and over. He thought he might be dying. If he was, he wanted her to be the last thing his eyes ever saw.

Harry's voice interrupting them likely saved his life.

What the hell was happening to him?

Chapter Fourteen

*E*mma sat beneath the hot sun with Harry on her right and Cailean on her left. She didn't know why she was here really. Everyone had come out to the brothel's rear yard to watch Malcolm take on a rather large (according to Alison) patron. To everyone watching, it was an answer to a challenge, one issued by a boastful Highlander.

To Malcolm, it was practice.

Emma didn't like it. She didn't like the sound of metal scraping against metal. She didn't like not knowing if blood was being spilled.

"Ah, shyt, Malcolm!" Cailean shouted. "I woulda' seen that strike comin' a league away!"

Emma shook her head wondering if she'd allowed Cailean out of bed too soon.

Judging from the gasps of some of the girls watching, and his brother's taunting, Malcolm had taken a hit from his opponent. She prayed he wasn't hurt. Even if it meant keeping him here longer, she didn't want him injured.

She thought about yesterday in the hall with him.

She believed he hadn't visited Bess's bed. It made her want to fall into his arms and promise him anything. But she didn't. Part of the reason was because Harry had come upon them and asked to see Cailean. Harry seemed annoyed, but he said nothing about his mood and followed Emma into the room. Emma figured his foul temper had to do with one of the girls and didn't question him.

"Satan's arse, Malcolm," Cailean shouted again, pulling her back to the present. "Are ye blind?"

Standing somewhere to her right, Harry cursed. And then Cailean cursed, as well. Emma could feel their eyes on her, everyone's eyes, including Malcolm's.

The sound of metal smashing against metal resounded in her ears and she stood to her feet, a warning to Malcolm to take care! Fool!

She took a step forward. Gascon blocked her path—and then a pair of hands closing around her upper arms stopped her altogether. Malcolm's warm breath fell heavy on her face, the scent of sweat and fear rushed through her nostrils. He held her still and oh, but he was strong. She doubted any foe could stand against him. Still, he could get hurt. Was he hurt, bleeding? Oh, why did he need to practice anyway? No one was at war.

"I'm unharmed, lass," he reassured, his voice thick with concern and exertion. "What were ye thinkin' almost steppin' onto the field?"

She wasn't thinking. That was the problem. She was allowing her heart to rule her, almost putting her in harm's way.

"And ye, Cailean," he accused his brother, giving her an excuse not to answer. "Yer sense left ye to say something so thoughtless."

"Aye," Cailean agreed, sounding thoroughly repentant. "Fergive me, Emma. I—"

"I don't care about that!" Emma told them. Malcolm hadn't removed his fingers from around her arms. For an instant she wished Gascon wasn't between them. "I thought you were . . . why are you doing this? Do you want to die? Is that it?"

"I'm unharmed."

She wasn't listening. At least, that's what she told herself. That wasn't humor in his voice when he spoke. His fingers hadn't just moved over her arms.

The man was mad. And so was she.

"This isn't good for your brother," she continued. "I should never have agreed to it. It's too soon for both of you!"

"Here, feel me."

Before she could stop him, he snatched her hands in his and laid her palms on his chest.

"Check fer any wounds, Emma."

Her heart raced so fast she felt light-headed and feared she might have to hold on to him for balance.

What was the matter with her? She'd touched him like this before when she'd felt him with the girls. But he'd been unconscious. When she walked him about the room, she hadn't felt him, and never while he was standing over her, breathing hard.

She stood there beneath the sun for an eternal moment, in the sight of many, with her hands covering Malcolm's chest.

"Come now, lass," he tempted in a quiet voice. "I've watched ye tend to m' brother's wounds with nothin' but yer hands to guide ye."

And it had almost cost Cailean his life. Had Malcolm forgotten?

He covered her hands in his and seemed to read her thoughts. "No one else's eyes are better than seein' fer yerself—however 'tis ye see it. Aye?"

Oui. He was correct. She'd used Alison's eyes, not her own senses the night of Cailean's injury.

Malcolm hadn't forgotten. He'd seen an opportunity to help free her from her guilt and self-doubt, and he took it.

She stepped closer to him and heard the sharp intake of breath above her when she moved her palms over the span of his chest, gently, curiously down to his tight belly, then up again, slowly and with measured temperance. She moved to his sides, tracing her fingers up his shoulders while she went. Even in her darkness, his powerful form made her hands tremble. When she stepped behind him, lifting her hands to his neck, her fingertips floated across the flare of his back. The touch of his hair along her knuckles was like a sensual breath that made her knees weak.

His muscles were tight, his back, arrow straight. She didn't need to check his bottom half. If he was hurt below the waist, he wouldn't be standing so balanced before her. He was telling her the truth. He was unharmed.

What about his face? What expression did he wear? How did humor look on him? What shape was his mouth? She dropped her hands to her sides, not daring to touch him further.

"I feel nothing." She tried to sound unaffected and stepped away from him. She failed miserably. "But that doesn't mean I've changed my mind. You must cease this and Cailean must be returned to the room."

"Aye," he agreed, sounding thoroughly amused rather than repentant. "As soon as I finish this oaf."

He was already stepping away from her, disobeying her orders and returning to the field.

Involuntarily, she reached out to stop him. Prideful fool! She had a mind to mix him a refreshment that would put him to bed for another se'nnight. But then she'd have to tend to him.

With nothing else to do but wait and be ready to help him if he was injured, she returned to her seat and sat down, mumbling through her teeth as she went.

"He'll fare well," Cailean leaned in and told her. "Malcolm was trained to fight by the most skillful men in all of Scotland."

"You are as stubborn as he is," she threw at him, seething. "If I've wasted the past se'nnight keeping both of you alive for another month or less, I'll kill both of you myself."

"Emma!" Harry, who'd been silent until now, admonished. "Whatever is going on between you and Malcolm Grant—and I will find out what it is—I'll not have you threatening my guests."

Whatever was going on? Did he think—? "Harry, let me assure you, nothing is going on. I don't work here."

"That's correct, you don't," her brother snapped at her. "Remember that around him. I warn you."

He warned her? Emma's hands wound the fabric of her gown in her lap. She was happy she'd found Harry. He was all the family she had. But he wasn't her guardian. She'd taken care of herself for too many years to begin taking orders from him. Besides, what in blazes was so terrible about Malcolm Grant? The rumors may have been awful but so far he hadn't lived up to them. Of course, he was injured, so bedding a voracious prostitute was still difficult. But she'd spent enough time with him now to know that he wasn't as bad as everyone thought. And besides, wasn't Harry the one who'd insisted she stay close to the Grants?

"Harry." Bess's voice cut off Emma's as she opened her mouth to defend herself. "Be easy on her."

Emma was no fool. Bess didn't like her, so why was she taking up for her?

"'Tis difficult to remember to breathe when that pulsing beast is near,' she went on, infuriating Harry even more. "He seems to be fond of our sweet Emmaline. You cannot blame her for quivering at his touch."

Emma felt heat move over her face. She did not quiver! Did she?

"Why, just feast your eyes on the strength of his legs and the thrust of his sword. His eyes are like fire, blazing flames about to consume. Who can stand a chance against him? Don't you agree, Emmaline?"

Emma blinked, shattering the images Bess created in her mind. Images Bess had put there on purpose, knowing Emma couldn't see how good he looked fighting. Emma didn't need them. She had her imagination and it was working quite well at envisioning Malcolm thrusting and parrying. Bess was trying to anger Harry. Why? Emma needed to speak with her brother about the Malcolm she was getting to know. He needed to stop treating her like something fragile.

"Brother, I—"

"Emma, return to your room," Harry commanded.

"Harry, I'm not a child," she reminded him, giving Gascon a pat on the head when he growled at her brother. "Your friends are in my care, and 'twas you who placed them there. I'm not moved by what my eyes tell me, as Bess obviously is. I care only for the well-being of your friends' lives, and ours, if rumors of their family are true."

"They are," Cailean said, sounding only mildly interested in the conversation.

Emma let a faint smile hover over her mouth when she addressed her brother again. "I'll continue seeing to them, brother. If you wish to help, you will make your friend stop fighting."

"He has stopped," Harry told her.

"He won," Bess purred beside him.

He won. Relief flooded through Emma, forcing her to sigh. She tried to muffle it, but when she heard his voice coming toward her, she almost choked.

She liked the sound of him, all smoky and soothing, the scent of virility coming off him in waves. She wanted to kiss him and discover how he tasted.

"Why the gloomy faces?" he inquired merrily.

How could the fool make her want to smile? She didn't, knowing her brother and Bess were watching.

"I didna' injure him too severely," he informed them. "Not enough that ye would have to tend to him, Miss Grey."

"That was thoughtful, brother," Cailean complimented. "He looks—and smells—like he hasna' bathed in over a month."

Emma was grateful.

"Yes, it was thoughtful, Malcolm," Harry agreed. "And to show my appreciation, you may take Bess tonight at no charge."

It didn't matter if Emma could see or not. She knew Harry was offering Bess to keep Malcolm away from

herself. She could argue that with all the activity and...
exertion, he could have a relapse, but the air seemed to
thicken and made her gag a little. She didn't want to sit
around and listen to plans being made for Malcolm and
Bess. She was too angry with her brother to say anything without letting things she'd regret spill from her
lips. And really, it wasn't Harry's fault. He didn't know
how fond she was of Malcolm. Should she tell him?
She doubted he'd take the news well that his sister was
taken with the worst rogue in the three kingdoms. Perhaps later.

Holding on to Gascon, she rose from her seat and
walked off. When her brother called after her, she called
over her shoulder, "I need to replenish my stock of herbs,
Harry. I won't go far."

She left before he could stop her and made her way
to the edge of the woods. She tried not to think of Malcolm while she bent to her knees and felt around the sun-
warmed earth for plants and roots. She needed to forget
Malcolm. His brother was making a quick recovery now
that his infection was clearing up. Soon the Grants would
leave Fortune's Smile and she'd never see Malcolm again.
The last thing she should be doing was thinking about any
kind of future with him.

She heard footsteps. Her heart leaped, knowing the
measure of his gait. Even Gascon was happy to see him
and wagged his tail hard enough to make the rest of him
shake.

She stopped moving and inhaled his unmistakable
male scent. It went straight to her head like fine wine.

Malcolm.

His presence made her feel drunk. What about him
didn't inebriate her?

"Emma?"

Certainly the sound of him unsteadied her. His smoky, knee-melting voice behind her convinced her that trying to put him out of her mind was useless.

What was he doing here, following her, instead of taking Harry up on his offer?

"Go back," she told him. "You need your rest. I know my way around and I'll be fine."

"I know," he said softly, coming closer. "I'm no' certain I will be though."

Chapter Fifteen

"Are you hurt?" She began to rise but he stopped her with a tender touch on her shoulder and bent to his haunches beside her.

"You said you were unharmed!"

Malcolm didn't know what the hell he was. But looking at her made everything else unimportant.

"Nae, nae, I'm fine," he assured her, unable to look away.

Her hands moved out to grope and feel him. He didn't stop her. Why the hell would he? He liked how she touched him, like her fingers could see him. It made him feel slightly unstable, completely taken with her. There was something so intimate about the way she touched him, so softly, so curiously, he could barely think straight. She swept her fingers over his chest, his arms, his neck, moving closer until she was almost pressed against him. Why didn't she touch his face the way she'd touched the rest of him? Her quickened breath and worried expression so close to him tempted him to lift his hand and smooth the crease in her brow. Or pull her closer and ask her what was happening to him.

He didn't touch her. He was afraid that if he did she might shatter like a dream at dawn. He took her in, examining every inch of her face, from the gold-dusted curve of her cheekbone to the pert slope of her nose. The urge to kiss her dulcet brow made his head spin.

"I wasna' harmed, Emma." He bent and pressed his mouth to her brow.

"Then why did you startle me by saying you weren't certain if you were fine?" She pushed him away, her hands dropping back to her sides.

"Because I'm no' fine," he told her. "Many times durin' the day, I feel sick to m' stomach fer no reason."

He watched her go pale. She was thinking she'd missed something with him, like she had with Cailean. If she had, it wasn't her fault and he'd make certain she knew that.

"I understand I was struck in the head."

"You were." She nodded.

"Mayhap it has caused more damage than we suspect?"

"Are you seeing double? Odd lights?" she added when he said no. "Are you forgetting things? Do you feel unbalanced?"

"A wee bit unbalanced from time to time, but nothin' more serious than that."

"Do you remember anything specific happening when you feel this?" she asked innocently enough, her lips tempting him to abandon it all and kiss her.

"Aye, I remember what it is."

She waited, her eyes wide with concern.

" 'Tis ye, lass," he told her. "I find m'self thinkin' aboot ye and when I do, I feel ill."

That likely wasn't the right thing to say.

"Are you telling me that I make you sick?" She stood

up and glared down at him for a moment before she stormed off, into the trees.

"I'll admit it sounds worse when ye say it," he called out, and then followed her.

"No, Mr. Grant." She stopped abruptly and spun on her heel to face him. "Let me assure you, it sounds worse when *you* say it."

He stared at her and probably for too long. She looked especially beautiful swathed in a shaft of late afternoon sunlight breaking through the trees. Her curly locks fell around her shoulders capturing light and shadow. The dark circles around her eyes were gone and she looked as healthy as her two patients.

"Fergive me. Let me start over."

"All right." She waited.

He didn't want to talk. He wanted to go to her, sweep her up into his arms, and carry her off deeper into the woods. He wanted to quiet the voices in his head, the dragon at his back. He was certain that making love to her would silence everything. It always had before, but everything he'd accomplished in four years would mean nothing. He'd be right back to where he was in the beginning. A rogue who slept with women even knowing that they would never mean a thing to him. A rogue unworthy of Emmaline Grey.

"I'm not... I've never..." He looked around at the leaves on the ground. What the hell should he say? He didn't know what was wrong with him. He feared and hoped at the same time that it had something to do with her. A horrifying thought occurred to him. What if he finally found a lass that evoked more than lust in him and she didn't feel the same way?

"Emma."

"Oui?"

She stood there. A few feet away, her hands clasped behind her back. A breeze came in from the north and blew a lock of her hair across her face.

"Ye've been sleepin' in a chair. How is it that ye look so damn good?"

He'd complimented many women before. Why did he now feel like he sounded like a foolish ogre?

She smiled, which made him feel infinitely better.

"I have been sleeping better," she admitted. She didn't run or try to hit him with anything when he moved closer to her.

"I barely sleep at all."

"Why not?" she asked quietly, her eyes growing rounder as he came closer.

"I dinna' know. I was hopin' ye could help."

"Of course," she promised. "I could brew you more tea, something very mild."

He nodded. He'd take any kind of help. He had almost gotten his arse pummeled to the ground today. His reflexes were slower because he was so damn tired.

"I'll need some herbs that grow near the riverbank," she told him. "You could accompany me if you're up to it."

He laughed. "Of course I'm up to it." He might even have a rinse to wipe away the sweat of the morning.

"Tell me," he said on their way, "who taught ye aboot herbs and medicine?"

She didn't answer for so long that he stopped her and turned her to him. "Have I said something to offend ye?" He really didn't think he had.

"Why are you asking me?"

He smiled at her, but he was confused. How was commending her a bad thing? "Why can I no' ask?"

Again she didn't answer right away but when she did, it surprised him so much that for a moment he shared Emma's speechlessness.

"Do you think I'm a witch?" She didn't laugh. He waited a moment, but she didn't.

"Do I truly seem such a fool to ye?" he asked her. "Witch? Why the hell—" He stopped speaking as they came to the riverbank glimmering in the filtered light. His smile faded as it dawned on him why she asked him something so ridiculous.

"Were ye accused of it?"

"No," she said quietly, bending with him to sit at the edge. "An old woman whom I loved as my own mother was. She'd saved my life after...Harry left and then raised me as her own. One night the people she'd helped and healed came for her."

No, he hadn't meant to bring this memory to her. He tried to stop her, but she went on. "Her trial was"—she smiled but there was only sorrow in her eyes—"a charade that ended within a few hours. They couldn't wait to hang her. But that wasn't enough. They burned her after that."

Malcolm sat next to her, his elbow on one knee, his hand over his mouth. What the hell was he supposed to say to that?

"My blindness is a blessing," she continued. "I never would have wanted to see Clementine's death. Hearing it...and..." She shook her head to erase memories from it. "It has made me untrusting."

He understood why it would. "Emma, I would never bring such an accusation against ye. Ye have m' word, and nae matter what ye've heard, I keep m' word. Mostly. Besides that," he added when she didn't look convinced, "m' aunt is a healer."

"She is?"

"Aye, she is," he told her. "And if someone were to accuse her of bein' a witch, they wouldna' live long enough to draw another breath."

He watched relief fill her, dropping her shoulders from around her ears. He hated that she had such a memory to carry with her.

"I think I would have liked Clementine," he said. "If 'twas she who taught ye to be so bold."

"'Twas." She laughed and he thought how dull his life was before she came into it.

"Tell me aboot her."

Her smile went soft and meaningful. She closed her eyes, remembering. "I loved her very much."

Her breath fell warm on him, for they were sitting closer than either of them realized. Not close enough for him to kiss her, just enough to saturate himself in her.

"She was just as human as you or I. She'd had her share of sorrows, as we all do."

"What are yers?" Mayhap he shouldn't have asked, since she was talking about the woman she loved like a mother, but he wanted to know.

"You want to know about my sorrows?" she asked him faintly.

"Aye." He nodded, but he didn't think she'd tell him.

She didn't think about it. "My parents' deaths, the day Harry left, and the day Clementine died...and the ocean."

She didn't count the day she lost her sight as a sorrow but a blessing. He found it odd and quite wonderful about her. She was strong and resilient, like a Highland lass.

"Why the ocean?" he asked.

"I used to love looking out at sea when we visited my uncle. I'll never see it again."

He listened while she shared her memories of Clementine with him. He didn't understand why Harry had left his sister when she was ten and was going blind. They'd just lost their parents. Who did Harry think was going to take care of Emma after he abandoned her? It angered Malcolm and made him want to go to Harry and punch him in the mouth.

She defended her brother. "He was young. He was afraid."

"Ye could have died. Ye would have died if no' fer Clementine. Did Harry know of her?"

"None of us did. She lived deep in the woods behind my uncle's house."

"So, there's nae doubt, he left ye to die."

"He was young."

She spoke softly and angled her face away from his.

"I've gone too far." He began to move away from her, but she looped her arm through his.

"No, 'tis just that I don't care why he left. I have him back again. As much I've been angry and I don't want to be anymore."

Malcolm nodded. He liked her loyalty to her brother despite everything. Hell, he liked it very much. How was he ever going to convince her that he wasn't the callous, uncaring scoundrel that everyone said he was? He'd just suggested that she not forgive her brother! Damnation, she was right. He lacked too many attributes to win a lass like her. "Ye're correct," he said quietly, and stood up, disengaging himself from her. "Let me help ye get those herbs ye need fer m' tea. I need to sleep before I say something else and make ye hate me and want to lop off m' head."

She smiled, letting him help her to her feet. "I've wanted

to lop off your head several times since I've met you. I don't think it has anything to do with sleep. But I don't hate you. In fact, I like you."

He kept her hand in his while they walked. "That's good news." He grinned and held up her arm, then twirled her under it.

"Why is that?"

He spun her back, into his arms, her back pressed to his chest. "Because"—he closed his arms around her chest and dipped his mouth to her ear—"I like ye too."

Chapter Sixteen

*E*mma left the brothel just as the sun was beginning to come up. She needed water for the pouch of Malcolm's tea in her pocket, and the well wasn't far. She knew the path by heart and released Gascon to his own pace.

She hummed and smiled as she went, thinking about yesterday. It had turned out much better than it had begun. In his arms! Oh, in his arms! She was mad, but she didn't care! He didn't think she was a witch and he liked her!

She didn't worry about his claim of being ill. His symptoms weren't life threatening. His confession that he felt worse when he thought of her or saw her still pricked a little. He said he liked her but why in blazes then would she make him feel sick? Hadn't Alison told her that Malcolm lights up when he sees her? Emma didn't believe it when Alison told her. She thought her new friend was just trying to make her feel better. What in the world would Malcolm Grant want with her? Now he confirmed it.

And yet, damn her, her day with him was the best day she'd had in a year. She loved telling him about Clementine. She found it thoughtful and considerate that he asked about her sorrows. No one had ever asked before. His righteous anger against Harry for abandoning her was quite possibly the most knightly thing any man could ever do.

She didn't want him to be angry, but she appreciated that he was.

She would speak to Alison and ask her if falling in love felt like—

A footstep to her left and Gascon's low, deadly growl to her right stopped Emma in her tracks.

"Who's there?" She listened. Gascon's warning grew louder.

Someone was out here with her, posing a threat to her. A patron—just like the one who'd come upon Harry's wife and killed her?

Gascon's growl erupted into fangs and saliva as her dog attacked whoever was there. Gascon cried out and a hand came around Emma's face and another snaked around her waist.

She wanted to fight. She tried to, but something was smashed into her head and she began to fade away. She was dying and she couldn't stop it.

"What's going on between you and my sister?" Harry asked Malcolm in the parlor about an hour later.

Malcolm refused a seat and stood by the window. He watched his friend cross the room and pour him a drink. He thought about the right way to reply. The truth would never do; besides, he wasn't entirely sure what the truth was.

"She's been kind to me and Cailean." It wasn't untrue. "She has saved m' brother's life twice now. Should I treat her callously?"

Harry eyed him while he returned and handed Malcolm his cup. Malcolm saw the resemblance in the siblings, mostly in the way they quirked their mouths with uncertainty whenever he spoke.

"So you haven't tried to kiss her? You're not trying to win her heart?"

"Nae." Malcolm swigged his drink and clenched his teeth while the sour wine went down. He set down the cup of whatever was left of the dreadful stuff.

One thing, at least, was true. He hadn't kissed her. He was pretty damn sure that if he did, he wouldn't want to stop there. He'd woo her until he won her. And then what? Take her to his bed? Return to who he was, nothing but a rogue? It kept him awake all night. Awake in a chair to watch her while she slept. Her tea had helped, when he took it. But he'd prefer to look at her. He was mad. Why else would he let Emmaline Grey make him doubt everything he'd ever believed about himself? He'd finally fallen asleep in the last hour of darkness. He didn't sleep long and when he woke up, Emma wasn't in bed.

"You aren't right for her," Harry forged ahead, ignoring his friend's fading smile.

"I willna' hurt her."

"Whether that's true or not, no longer matters."

Malcolm eyed him narrowly. "When ye first asked me to ferget her, 'twas all that mattered. Did something change?"

Harry shook his head. "No, 'tis just that... she's a fragile creature."

Malcolm scowled for all he was worth. He didn't tell Harry that his sister was out dancing among the trees and getting her toes wet with dew. "She's far from it, Harry. Hell, ye should know that," he said, less able to forget his anger that Emma's brother had abandoned her. "Let me tell ye since ye dinna' know. She's stronger and more braw than most. She learned to survive, and not only that, she learned medicine. I understand ye want to keep her safe after Lenore. But ye underestimate her."

"No, I don't," Harry argued.

"Then ye're the blind one," Malcolm told him, turning to leave.

"Malcolm!" Harry's voice stopped him. "Stay away from Emmaline. Perhaps you should think about leaving."

Hell, what had come over Harry? Malcolm thought, leaving the parlor. Harry wanting him to leave Emma alone was one thing, throwing him out of the brothel was another. He muttered an oath and walked straight into Bess in the hall.

"Where are you off to in such a hurry, handsome?"

"To see... m' brother." He stepped around her. He wanted to see Emma. She would be back by now and likely waiting in her room for him. He wouldn't tell her about Harry and have it seem he was against her brother, when even she wasn't.

"Let me walk with you." She ran to catch up.

"Bess," he said without stopping. "Lass, I'm tired and no' in the mood to hear yer complaints aboot Emma."

She patted his arm as she took it. "I won't speak a word about her. Just walk me to my door. There's something I wish to tell you. Something very important."

Hell, he shouldn't. But what did she want to tell him that was so important? He wanted to know. So instead of refusing, he nodded, agreeing to go with her.

"I know you and Harry are friends," she said as they went. "But there's something about your friend that you should know."

About Harry? "What is it?" he demanded.

She smiled and shook her head.

"Make me sore for two days like you did the last time we were together."

"Nae."

"Make me scream and quake in your arms."

"Bess, nae. Look, here we are. Now, please, let us go our separate ways. Dinna' tell me anything."

Her eyes simmered. All four of them. He blinked and turned to go. He didn't remember falling or being aware of anything at all until he woke up sometime later, naked in Bess's bed with Bess, also naked, asleep on top of him.

What the hell? He rubbed his heavy eyes. Nae, this was a dream. He hadn't come to Bess's room— But he had. He remembered standing in front of her door. Nae, he wouldn't have. He would remember if he had...

A rap on the door dragged him from the heat of Bess's body on top of him. He left the bed and stumbled into his breeches. His belly was tied into a knot and almost made him sick. What had he done? He looked back at the bed and at Bess awake now and smiling at him.

The knock came again. Malcolm's heart raced. What if it was Emma? What would he tell her? Had he passed out? He didn't remember anything happening with Bess, but who the hell would believe him?

"Malcolm!" Harry shouted on the other side of the door. "Are you in there?"

With a thread of relief, Malcolm went to the door and opened it, then scowled at Harry's pale, panic-stricken face.

"Emma's gone. She's gone, Malcolm."

What in Satan's balls did that mean? Gone? Gone where? He couldn't think straight. Nae! He had to! He stepped into the hall and looked toward the stairs. His heart dropped to the ground at the sound of Gascon's urgent barks resonating from below.

She wouldn't leave without her dog but if she wasn't with Gascon, then she was indeed gone.

Someone took her.

He wanted to wake up now.

"We need to find her."

Malcolm agreed with Harry's lament and snatched his shirt off the floor on his way out of the room. He stopped and turned to Harry, who was looking into the room at Bess rising from the bed he just left.

"Harry!" he called out, eager to go. "How long has she been gone?"

"I don't know." His friend caught up.

"How long has Gascon been barking?"

"Just since he woke and came running back here without her a few moments ago. Gunter said that judging from the blood dripping down over his eye, he was struck and left for dead." Harry's dark eyes grew even more somber before he closed them. "Gunter left to search for her while I searched the rooms. She's gone. I fear she's been abducted."

Aye, Malcolm feared it too. Abducted by whom, and for what purpose? The thought of it clenched his guts and his jaw. Hell, he'd slaughter anyone who hurt her. If it were the Winthers who took her, his promise to Harry would wither away on the wind. He'd kill every one of them. He didn't care how long it took or how many wars it started.

"I'll find her, Harry," he said, moving quickly down the stairs.

"I'm coming with ye, Malcolm," Harry said, hurrying after him.

"Harry!" Both men turned to look back up and saw Bess leaving her room, covered now by a robe. "You cannot leave us here with no protection! If someone took Emma it could have been to lure you out and leave this place to their grimy hands."

Harry paused, considering her. Malcolm didn't.

"Malcolm!" Emma's brother called out as Malcolm made his way for the doors. "How will you find her when Gunter has not?"

"Her dog," Malcolm told him. 'Give me time to gain m' saddle, then release him from the kitchen."

He ran to the stable, letting the realization that Emma wasn't inside the brothel hit him. She was alone. Or worse, she wasn't. He fought the swell of fear that threatened to engulf him. Leaping to his saddle, he raced for the back of the brothel and whistled. Harry opened the door and released the hound.

The instant he was free, Gascon stopped barking and took off running. Malcolm kicked his horse's flanks and gave chase. They'd find her. If she were harmed, there would be blood. Who took her? What were they doing to her? His thoughts drove him mad with revenge. He'd think about why he was willing to kill for her tomorrow. Now, he needed to find her. Was he beginning to lose his heart to her? He didn't know much about it personally, but from what he'd heard, it sure as hell felt like he was. Was it possible?

Nae, it wasn't he thought, remembering waking up naked in Bess's bed. He was and would always be a heartless rogue, unable to love one woman. Och, why had he done it? he thought...He thought Emma...He shook his head in the wind battering his face If she found out what he'd been doing while she was being kidnapped, she'd never forgive him. He couldn't tell her.

He would talk to Harry about keeping it silent, and then he and Cailean would leave. His brother was well enough to go. Malcolm would find her and bring her back to safety from others and from himself.

Emma opened her eyes, then closed them again. Nothing changed. An instant of pure fear filled her to bursting when she felt the lump on her head, and a memory invaded her mind.

She'd gone outside the brothel with Gascon to fetch some water from the well.

Someone had snatched her up from behind. Just before she was knocked out, she heard a horrible sound, like a dog's cry. Had they killed Gascon?

She gathered every ounce of strength she possessed and kept her tears from flowing. The only chance she had to kill them was to keep them thinking she was still unconscious.

She pushed away the crushing pain in her chest, subdued the cries aching to escape her lips for her dearest friend. Did they enter the brothel after that and kill Malcolm or Harry or any of the others? She had to take hold of her senses and figure out where she was and with whom. How long had she been unconscious? Was it day or night?

The first and easiest thing to figure out was that she was in a saddle, propped up against a formidable chest. How many in their company? She listened to the hoofbeats around her. Three horses, including her captor's. Who were they?

"This will teach that arrogant bastard, Grey, not to refuse a Winther, and most especially not with lies about the redhead having a fever."

Alison? When had Harry lied to them about Alison?

"What does it matter?" the one behind her in the saddle said. "Oliver changed his mind and wants this one."

Oliver Winther wanted her? Why? How did he even know she existed?

She continued pretending to be unconscious. She didn't need to reach in her pocket for reassurance. She knew she carried Malcolm's sleeping tea. All she needed was water. She thought of Gascon and whoever else they may have hurt, Cailean, Alison, to keep her mind set on one thing. If the Winthers killed her dog, or anyone else she cared about, then they already started the war. She didn't care how powerful they were or how many of them there were, if she needed to kill these three, she would. The problem was she didn't know the woods. How would she find her way back to the brothel?

"Let's stop for a while," a thick voice said to her right. "I want to sample the goods before Oliver gets her. She'll be good to no one when he's done with her."

"You won't lay a hand on her," said the man sitting behind her. "Unless you want the whip."

"John, Oliver wouldn't have his own cousin whipped," the man to her right said.

"You're correct," John said. "He'd do it himself."

Emma breathed through her nose, trying to slow her pulse. She'd heard of Oliver Winther. Women described him as a golden god with beautiful pale green eyes as cold as death. The baron liked death. He liked bringing it to others, mostly innocent folks who didn't support him. His methods of killing were what invoked fear into everyone's heart at the mention of his name.

Emma was glad it was she that these men had taken, and not Alison or Brianne. They would be too afraid to do anything. Emma was afraid, but she'd been afraid before, losing her parents, her brother, her home, and her sight. She knew fear well, until she learned how to use it.

Malcolm was correct. She wasn't the frail little mouse Harry thought she was. And she wasn't about to be sampled by Oliver Winther or anyone else.

She coughed and opened her eyes. Instantly, her captor's arm tightened around her waist. She coughed again.

"Water. Please," she begged.

The brute behind her thought about it for a moment, then untied his pouch of water hanging from his saddle and handed it to her.

She uncorked it, then wiped the rim with her fingers and brought it to her mouth. She pretended to drink a sip and then coughed again.

"Do you have anything stronger?" she asked, then turned to the man on her right as if she could see him there. "I'll show you things I've learned living at Fortune's Smile."

The oaf laughed. "You look too innocent to know much. But don't fear, I'll teach you what you don't know."

She went into a fit of coughing and refused her captor's water.

"Give her your wine, Rubert," the man behind her, John, commanded. "She's choking."

Finally she was handed another pouch. When she popped the cork, the scent of stale wine assailed her senses. She pinched a thicker bunch of her special mixture between her fingers and dropped it into the pouch, as she'd done with the previous container. No one noticed. To their eyes, she didn't appear to be doing anything more serious than wiping the spout before she drank. She pretended to drink and then handed it back.

"I heard you were blind." The suspicion in Rubert's voice made her cringe. "I can't catch it from you, can I?"

"Only if you come in contact with my blood," she reassured him.

John swore behind her and loosened his grip.

Simple beasts, she thought. They were worse than ignorant, they were indifferent to their ignorance.

Now, if they'd only drink from their pouches. There was still one more brute. She'd have to figure something out. But first, she needed to know if she should kill them once they were helpless to her.

"Did you kill my dog, or anyone at the brothel?"

"You mean that ugly mongrel that came after us?" Rubert asked, then popped the cork on his pouch and guzzled his wine.

"Did you kill him?"

"Reggie there"—he paused and must have motioned to the rider on her left—"he stopped the beast with a rock. Ask him."

Emma turned her head, wishing for her sight for a moment so she could see the man's face who'd hit Gascon with a rock.

No matter, she thought when John yawned. Soon enough it would be just her and Reggie.

She was going to need a knife.

Chapter Seventeen

Malcolm didn't pause or rest his horse, but kept pace with Gascon as the dog raced around trees and crashed through shallow streams. Gascon had her scent. Malcolm had their tracks. Three riders traveling northwest, toward Newcastle. Even if they took her three or four hours ago, they still had at least six hours before they reached their destination. They couldn't be much farther in the distance.

Malcolm looked up at the darkening sky and swore under his breath. The only thing that could hinder her discovery was rain. Too much of it and tracks would be washed away, scents would be lost.

Beside him, Gascon seemed to sense their urgency and raced even harder.

Malcolm had never met a more intelligent dog. His kin would do well to breed him with Grendel's daughters.

Gascon stopped so suddenly that Malcolm had to rein up his horse on its hind legs. He said nothing, listening to the sounds of the wood creatures scurrying, the wind... He waited another moment while Gascon's low growl rumbled around him.

Or was it thunder?

He heard a sound. A distant scream, a bird overhead? Gascon took off, like a shadow of destruction, still silent, still about to take his victim by surprise.

Malcolm followed the dog until he saw what Gascon had heard. Emma! She was running from a man who chased her on foot. His head looked to be covered in blood, but he appeared quick on his feet and was almost upon her.

Malcolm and Gascon raced after him. The dog reached him an instant before Malcolm's tiring horse did. Gascon finally barked—it came out more like a guttural shout, spinning Emma on her feet—before he sank his fangs into the assailant's ankle. The man screamed in agony as his bones crunched beneath him.

Malcolm was glad she couldn't see his massive claymore swinging across the man's throat.

"Gascon!" she shouted, and reached out her arms to gather her dog into them. "Thank God you live! Thank God! Oh, you found me! Thank you, Gascon!"

Malcolm reached them and swung off his horse. He went to her, not expecting her to turn her most radiant smile on him when he spoke her name. He'd only meant to check her for injury but he took her in his arms just as he reached her. He held her there, feeling her life pounding against his chest, thankful that she was still alive. He didn't try to kiss her. Saints knew he wanted to. But she'd just been running for her life. She needed comfort, not kissing.

He needed to know the whereabouts of the other two riders. The tracks didn't lie.

"Emmaline, my dear," he said, pulling away enough to look at her, almost lose his wits right there to her. "Where are the others?"

"There are two others," she confirmed. "I fed them your tea. They've fallen into a deep sleep a short distance away. Did they harm anyone at the brothel?"

"Nae, lass." He smiled without thinking of impressing her. He smiled for no reason other than because he found her, and because looking at her, being in her company, pleased him. He wished she could see how happy she made him by surviving. He would have to find ways to tell her. She was brave and capable...

"Thank you." She graced him with a smile and then reached up, on the tips of her toes, and planted a kiss at the edge of his mouth.

The innocent gesture shook awake every emotion he'd tried to avoid. It took strength he didn't know he possessed to keep from closing his arms around her and branding her mouth with his. He wanted to hold her and kiss her. Never before had his body ached so to taste a woman, to breathe with her, to touch her so intimately with his mouth, his tongue. He bent instead to scoop her up and said nothing while he carried her to his horse. When she hooked her arms around his neck and pressed her cheek close to his chest, he nearly doubled over with a desire to protect her.

Hell, how could he have gone with Bess when the thought of days without Emma in them terrified him? When things like the quirk of her mouth, the furrow of her brow, or her delicate fingers falling over everything she needed to see haunted his every thought?

While he carried her, he looked down at the dip of her gaze, as if she were trying to hide, mayhap from her memories of Clementine. Mayhap, from him. He knew what hiding was like. It was lonely. He didn't want that for her, or for himself anymore.

"I have ye now," he whispered.

"Thank you for coming for me, Malcolm. I think that last man would have killed me in another moment or so. I could hardly keep running without injuring myself against a tree."

He closed his eyes, thinking about what would have happened to her if he weren't here.

He thought about his earlier decision, but to hell with leaving. She needed him here. He'd just have to be strong and not take anyone else to his bed, including her.

His instincts told him to move back, stay away. This was only his dragon rearing its mighty head, making him even more keenly aware of the absence of real passion in his life. But when he leaped into the saddle behind her and curled his arm around her delicate waist, he knew there was more involved than a dragon. There was something much stronger. His heart.

If it wasn't turning his whole world upside down he might have almost smiled at the irony of falling for a lass who couldn't see the face and form he'd relied on his entire life to get him what he wanted.

They hadn't gone more than a hundred feet when the skies opened up with a peal of thunder that drove Emma deeper into his arms. He wished he had his plaid to cover her. When she began to tremble, he closed his arms around her tighter and bent his head to her ear.

"Are ye afraid of the thunder, lass?"

"I try not to be," she confessed, turning slightly in the saddle to be closer to him. "But 'tis very daunting."

He caressed her to him and stroked her hair. "'Tis only a sound," he told her close to her lobe. He lingered there, then brushed his lips lightly over it. "'Tis far less dangerous than three men bent, I'm certain, on ill intent. And look what ye did to them."

She stopped his heart when she smiled up at him and then set it to pounding when she wrapped her arms around his waist.

He felt himself melting into her, stroking his fingers over her arm, wanting nothing more than to protect her—even if most of the time, she didn't need protecting.

Soon, the rain soaked through his clothes and Gascon whined, looking as lost as Malcolm knew they were. It was best to find shelter and stop and wait out the storm than try to ride through it. He could barely see, not to mention his fidgeting horse.

It wasn't safe to keep going. They had to stop. He'd be alone with her. Hell.

He found a shallow cave, which was really a rock overhang that fit him, Emma, and Gascon and kept the rain out. His horse had to wait it out under a nearby tree.

They were still cold, but at least they were less wet.

"Was Gascon hurt?" she asked him when she patted the dog's head and it whined. She crouched against the cave wall, beneath a splash of light issued from the sun trying to appear. She hugged the dog to her more gently. "They told me that the one chasing me had killed him with a rock."

Malcolm's blood still boiled but he managed a smile at Gascon, glad that the beast had gotten revenge.

"Gunter found him," he told her, happy along with her that Gascon lived. "He was knocked out fer a bit, but his determination to save ye woke him from his slumber."

"I don't know why he loves me so," she said, and kissed the top of Gascon's head.

Hell, Malcolm could have named a dozen reasons. "He's a good friend," he said. "If not fer him, I dinna' know if I woulda' found ye."

She smiled at him and nodded, stroking her dog's head. Gascon panted, then rested his head in her lap, content.

As Malcolm felt—here, under a rock roof, soaked to his skin, watching a wet lass hugging an even wetter dog.

She lifted her head to him and smiled, giving him what he was after—an invitation into her private world. His heart faltered, along with his gaze. She grew more bonny every time he looked at her, and each time, he wasn't prepared for her effect on him.

He wanted to kill the rest of the men who tried to take her. He didn't give a damn if they were Winthers or not. He'd kill them all if they dared touch her again.

"Fergive me, lass."

"What for?" she asked softly.

"They took ye right from under m' nose." He wouldn't let it happen again.

"You were asleep, Malcolm. There was nothing you could have done."

"Nae, I wasn't asleep. I was…" He couldn't tell her about Bess. "…with Harry."

He'd never be worthy of a lass like Emma. How could this be? How could he finally feel something for a lass who wanted the kind of man he could never be? It made his muscles tighten and his legs grow heavy. He'd slept with Bess. Och, nae, he just couldn't take it in. How could he forget? Had he been drugged? Had he fallen asleep and Bess undressed him? Why had she been naked too?

Damn it. What if he could lose his heart and it still wasn't enough? He didn't want to lose his heart to Emma. Not if he wasn't sure he could give his heart to her alone. She wanted more in a man than a handsome face or a charming smile. He didn't know if he was more than that.

But he wanted to be. He realized he'd wanted to be more for a long time now. Finally, he had a reason.

He almost laughed at himself. He was no knight.

But did that mean he could never become one?

"Tell me about your life in Skye," she said. Her voice rang like music across his ears. She snuggled closer to him, trying to get warm.

He was in trouble.

"And about your family. I know Cailean, and Caitrina is a pirate. Tell me of the rest, and of you."

Malcolm may not have shared his relatives' romantic natures, but he loved them all.

"I had a good childhood," he told her, astonished at the ease with which he spoke. He'd never sat with any woman and told her things about himself. He wanted to tell her, to show her more of him. "I built strong relationships with m' cousins durin' games and fights, and any bit of trouble we could come up with."

She smiled. He drew a long breath.

"Trouble seemed to follow me more than the others. Fer as long as I can remember, I was the one who stood before his faither the most times."

She breathed against him. "What's he like? Your father?"

Malcolm thought of a way to describe Connor Grant, former captain of England's Royal Guard. Highland husband to the daughter of the infamous Devil MacGregor.

"He's a happy man."

She laughed. "Is that it?"

"'Tis enough. His laughter can often be heard across the vales. His wife and children love and respect him and so do her brothers and her faither. And every woman in Camlochlin."

"Ah, 'tis him you take after then," she teased.

"I'm nothin' like him," he told her. "He has all those attributes ye're so fond of."

She sat up, moving off him, making certain he could see her face. "I think you have them too, Malcolm. You just try to keep them behind you."

He thought of waking up under Bess.

"Mayhap," he allowed, though he didn't mean it. "I'd like ye to be right, lass, but I dinna' think ye are. I would save ye the heartache I bring."

She weighed him with a grin. "What if 'tis I who bring the heartache?"

"Then I'm doomed."

She shook her head and came in closer, closing her eyes. "No," she whispered, her warm breath covering him, her plump lips tempting him beyond endurance. "I will save you."

He smiled and traced the contour of her upper lip with his thumb. He moved in, drawn to the honeyed fullness of her mouth. It wasn't safe for him to kiss her.

But he didn't give a damn.

❖ Chapter Eighteen

His heavy, uneven breath boomed through Emma's
ears and sent warm trickles down her back. His
hands on her face were hard, callused, but gentle on her
flesh. She could almost hear his blood, his desire pulsing
through his veins, as he drew her closer.

Emma had never been kissed on the mouth before. She
didn't know if she would even like it. But then Malcolm
Grant swept his soft lips over hers. It was a good thing
she was sitting, for her knees were as good as gone. It
got even better, or worse, depending on how one looked
at it, when his mouth covered hers in a masterful kiss
that tempted her to follow him to the ends of the earth.
She felt caught up, crushed against him, his mouth, hungry and possessive. She liked it. No, she loved it. She
loved how he felt all hard and demanding. She wanted to
give in to his every command, and then Emma wanted to
give some commands of her own.

Gascon shifted and moved away from her lap, giving her space to move into Malcolm, deeper into his kiss.

When his tongue flicked across her lips to part them, she gasped, then felt her face go up in flames when he withdrew.

"Fergive me."

Forgive him? He chose to be chivalrous *now*? "No! Forgive me!" She felt foolish, like a child who knew nothing about life or love. "I've never been kissed before."

"Ye do it quite well fer a novice."

She heard the smile in his voice and wanted to touch it. See it. For now, she let it comfort her. After all, that's why he said it, to relieve her embarrassment. Was it possible that everyone had been so wrong about him? Was he more than just a rogue who used women to get what he wanted?

"You're nothing like your reputation," she told him.

He laughed softly and then groaned. "I know what ye've heard…" He paused, rethinking his defense, and then apparently thinking better of it. "I earned m' reputation. Besides, I canna' go back and change m' past."

She hadn't asked him to. The idea of him going back and changing his past had never even crossed her mind. Had it crossed his? And why? Why would he care about what she thought of him? Malcolm Grant didn't trouble himself with those things.

"Would you?" she asked him now that he brought it to her attention. "Would you go back?"

She waited on bated breath for his answer, letting only one thing distract her from his reply.

His kiss. His passionate mouth taking hers over and over. Oh, if he would only do it again she would welcome his tongue.

Or should she have slapped him?

"I dinna' know if I would go back."

His answer came but it offered her no comfort. She tried not to look disappointed.

"Mayhap who I was in the past," he continued, "has shaped me into who I'm supposed to be."

"You're supposed to be a heartless rake?" she asked. It angered her that he believed it and she didn't bother to hide her fierce scowl.

"Something more than that, mayhap."

The stillness of his voice shook her to her bones. He wasn't smiling or being glib now.

The sudden touch of his fingertips on her face startled her. When he traced the pad of his thumb along the seam of her frown, she battled herself to keep from going soft all over him. What was he doing? Why had he said what he did? Why was he touching her so intimately—the way she would touch him to know how he looked?

"Ye're a bonny lass, Emmaline Grey."

Was this what it was like to be enchanted? She felt mesmerized, paralyzed, giddy with delight. This was Malcolm slaying her heart, being the charming rake he was rumored to be. He'd said Harry was correct about him, but she didn't care. Not in this moment. Whatever spell he was weaving on her, she allowed it. Helpless to do anything else.

But she did do something else. She lifted her hands to his face.

Her touch, at first, was timid, but his slowed breath emboldened her onward, that and the curved symmetry of a face crafted by a master artist bent on outdoing all past and future work. The darkness was her canvas; her fingers were the brushes that painted him. Rising up from a square jaw chiseled from stone, she traced the curve of his full lips. When he kissed her fingers, her blood sizzled in her veins. She wanted him to kiss her again, and as she took in the rest of him, she pulled him in closer.

Was this really her being so bold with a man? She couldn't stop her heart from thumping so rapidly against him. He didn't object and pressed his mouth to hers, stealing her breath and everything else inside her. She wanted to show him that she wasn't afraid and plunged her tongue into his mouth, thrilled at her own boldness.

He withdrew only enough to break their kiss and laughed softly against her lips. "Here, lass," his sensual sorcerer's voice drifted deep into her soul. "Like this."

Slipping his hand behind her nape, he tilted her head to take him at a better angle. He snatched away her breath again, covering her mouth with his in an intoxicating combination of tenderness and strength. He parted her lips gently and slid his tongue inside her.

Her nipples grew tight and hard against the confines of her gown.

Just a flick across the darkest recesses of her mouth and then gone again, over and over, devouring her until she groaned as something hot and tight twisted her innards and between her legs.

But this was no time to cower at the power he possessed. She was no mouse and followed his lead, doing what he did, matching his ardor with an unleashed passion of her own.

When his kisses fell to her throat, she tossed back her head and growled . . . No, that wasn't her.

It was Gascon.

Malcolm lifted his head from her neck, leaving her lost in the remnants of his desire. When he bolted to his feet, he woke her from the spell he'd cast.

"Someone's oot there," he said above her. "Stay here."

She heard the soft whoosh of his sword leaving its sheath as he stepped away from her. She wanted to call out when Gascon left her next. Instead, she scooted farther back into the shadows and felt around for a stick or a rock. She found a rock, about the size of her fist, and clutched it to her chest. Who was out there? Another Winther? What if he killed Malcolm? Gascon? She clutched her rock tighter.

She waited as the seconds passed into minutes, with no other sound but the rain hitting the leaves and her heart beating in her ears.

She prayed. She prayed for both her rescuer's safety, and that she wouldn't have to try to kill anyone again. She prayed to forget Malcolm Grant's kiss. It would take a miracle. His mouth was decadent, his kiss, like sin. It made her forget his reputation, her loneliness, and...

"Emma!"

"Harry?" she called out to the voice just outside the enclosure. How had her brother found them?

She smelled Gascon before he reached her and laved his tongue over her face. She held on to the beast as she rose to her feet.

They'd been rescued. She should be thankful. She wasn't.

Harry was there, almost immediately, gathering her in his arms. "Malcolm told me it was the Winthers. Are you hurt?"

"I'm well," she assured him, listening to the background sounds for any sign of Malcolm. "What are you doing here? How did you find us?"

Her brother released her, but just enough to look at her. She wished she could do the same. He sounded frightened. Like he had after their parents and uncle died. She smiled to reassure him that she was unharmed.

"When Gunter returned without you, I left him with the girls and headed out to find you myself. I stumbled upon Malcolm's horse a few meters from here. The stallion had escaped the rain by standing beneath the biggest tree in the forest. Malcolm is fetching him now. He told me most of what happened and said you'd explain the rest."

She told him what happened and how she'd drugged two of the men and Malcolm killed the last. By the time she was done, Malcolm had returned to the shallow cave.

"Malcolm," her brother said, releasing her to turn to his friend. "You have my gratitude yet ag— Behind you!"

Gascon growled then leaped away from Emma. Someone else had found them and come up behind Malcolm. She heard a scuffle and held her breath, clothes rustling together, a series of grunts and groans, and then it was over.

"Malcolm?" she couldn't stop herself from calling out. Was he harmed? He held out her arms in front of her and took a step. Gascon rushed to her side.

"I'm fine," Malcolm assured her, taking her hand as she reached him. "Thanks to Harry."

Harry remained silent. Emma could feel the force of his gaze on her, or likely on her hand.

"'Tis likely one of the men who took Emma," Malcolm continued, letting her hand go. His voice drifted across her ears like music on the wind. She was happy to hear it. "Her effects wore off."

She nodded. She hadn't been able to give them as much of her mixture as she would have liked.

"Is he dead?"

"I'd say so," Malcolm said. "His neck is broken."

And he'd broken it. The same hands that had swept gently over her features had just killed a man. She trembled in her spot and Gascon nuzzled his nose into her palm.

"The other one is probably close by. We need to go."

Harry agreed and took her arm. "I'm glad you're unharmed, Emma. I fear," he said, turning his face toward Malcolm, "the Winthers are not going to stop."

"They mentioned you refusing them Alison," Emma told her brother. "Claiming she had a fever."

"I didn't claim she had a fever. Bess did," Harry said.

Bess? Why would she deceive the Winthers for Alison's sake?

"We need to be off now." Malcolm pushed them along.

"You will ride back with me, Emma," Harry said. She was too tired to argue. After a few moments, she wished she had.

"What were you both doing in here since your escape?" Harry asked in front of her in his saddle.

She scowled. "I'm no longer a child, Harry," she told him. "I haven't been one for a very long time. The time to make decisions for me is passed. You chose to leave, so you don't get a say."

He turned a little and spoke to her over his shoulder. "Forgive me for wanting to put things right between us by protecting you and caring for your needs."

Oh, why did he have to sound so hurt? She guessed he was right a little. He was trying to catch up too fast.

"We waited," she gave in and told him. "We talked of his home and of Cailean."

"Did he tell you about Bess?"

"You mean what she did for Alison?"

"No. I mean what she did for him."

Him? Bess and Malcolm? No, he'd refused Fortune's Smile's most skilled prostitute twice now. He wouldn't—

"I found him yanking up his breeches when he answered the door earlier in Bess's room. She, on the other hand, didn't bother covering herself when she tumbled out of her bed after him."

Emma's heart stopped, as did her breath. He was with Bess, *in her bed*, before he came looking for her? No!

"Are you sure 'twas him?" She tried to stop her eyes from filling with tears, but it was no use. They came from someplace too deep. He'd deceived her, and she let him do it. How many women before her had been so skillfully seduced? He'd tried to warn her. This was as much her fault as his. She was glad her brother couldn't see her.

But, oh, Bess?

She wouldn't cry for him! He'd kissed her. He'd made her forget that he was nothing but a careless rogue, kissing one woman and then another in the next few hours! Everything he told her about his home life was part of his seduction to prey on her heart's desires. Not only was Harry correct about him, but so was she. He was nothing like the men in her mother's books.

She wanted to go home and lock herself away in her room, but his brother was there. She had to help Cailean recover soon and send them both on their way. Oh, she was a fool! A witless child gullible to the charms of a snake.

"Emma, what is it?" She heard Malcolm's voice at her right and wiped her eyes. She hadn't heard him riding up to her.

"Emma?" Harry leaned over, trying to see her in the dim light.

"I'm fine," she assured her brother. "Everything seems to be hitting me now."

"You're trembling, sister."

"Just bring me home."

"Emma?" Malcolm spoke her name again, but she didn't answer.

"Just bring me home, Harry."

Chapter Nineteen

*M*alcolm sat alone at a table in the brothel. There was no place else to go—and tonight, he wanted to be someplace else.

They'd returned from the cave last night, the cave where he'd kissed her. God help him, he'd kissed her. And it tilted his world on its axis. He knew he shouldn't have done it, but hell, how was he supposed to resist her when her mouth drove him mad with desire? He'd never had to resist before. His promise to Harry resounded in his head, and damn it to hell, Harry saved him again! He couldn't betray his friend.

But hell, she hadn't resisted. In fact, she kissed him! It was a wee bit chaste and raw, but her innocence just sealed her deeper in him. He thought of her soft throat and the scent of her when he kissed her skin. Her eagerness for him scalded his blood.

What the hell happened then?

He was sure she'd been weeping in the saddle with Harry. She had denied anything was amiss, but she hadn't spoken a word to him since they'd returned. The instant she'd entered the brothel, she grabbed hold of Gascon's fur and hurried to her room. He tried to follow, but she denied him, asking him to stay away.

He did as she asked.

"Whisky?"

He looked up and groaned to himself when he saw Bess standing over him. The last thing he wanted was her company.

"I've already had two cups." He declined her offering.

Why the hell he did it, he didn't know. He should have a dozen more cups. He'd need that many cups of this watered-down shyt to restore his old self. And why not do it? He wasn't born to this "two hearts, one love" lifestyle. Why was he fighting it? A couple of nights without sleep and he wasn't strong enough to deny Bess, of all people.

"Has the rogue turned into a priest?" Bess bent over him, dangling her bosoms just beneath his chin.

"Was I a priest yesterday too?" He prayed she answered aye. He still couldn't remember a damn thing.

She tossed him a wicked smile.

He felt off balance, a wee bit dizzy. He reached up with one hand and snatched the cup from Bess's hand. He gave her wrist a tug and pulled her into the nearest chair with the other.

"Or did you put something in my . . ." No, Bess hadn't given him a drink. Harry had.

"I don't know what's more insulting. That you think I would need to drug you to get you to bed, or that you don't remember." Bess tugged his arm. "Bring me upstairs and I'll remind you."

"Mayhap later." He deflected her hands and began to turn away.

He found Mary's gaze and aimed his most welcoming smile her way, ignoring Bess's departure.

He looked around at all the bonny faces. For a price, he had his pick of the bunch. Hell, when he all but signaled for another drink, five of them came running.

This was who he used to be. It seemed, who he would always be. The scoundrel who only gave little bits of himself because giving more was impossible.

No, mayhap not impossible.

Hell, this wasn't who he wanted to be. He'd given up long ago wanting more. He'd put away those desires of having what his kin had. But Emma made him want it again.

He looked up the stairs and tapped his boot under the table. He wanted to go up there to her room and talk to her.

"There ye are, brother."

Malcolm grinned at his brother descending the stairs with Alison at his side, offering aid he didn't appear to need. He looked strong and fit again, the Cailean who Malcolm had taken from Camlochlin. Only better. His younger brother was happy again. He sure as hell looked happy with his eyes peeled to Alison while they reached the table and she separated her arm from his.

"How are ye fairin', Cailean?" Malcolm asked, standing at their arrival. "Are ye strong enough fer a drink?"

Cailean pushed his curious hands away when Malcolm tried to feel for a fever. "Ye sound like Emma. Leave off me, then."

Malcolm glanced up the stairs and looked for her. "Is Emma joinin' us?"

"I doubt it," Cailean said, holding out a seat for Alison first and then taking one beside her. "Since 'twas she who asked us to give her a few hours alone."

Malcolm looked up the stairs again. This time, purposefully forgetting, soon—and frighteningly—enough, who he thought he was and all the fair maidens ready to wait on him. He may have been that man once, but he wasn't anymore. He didn't want any of these women.

"Alone," Cailean repeated, reading his brother's thoughts.

"Of course," Malcolm reined in with a gracious smile that took everything he possessed to maintain. "She suffered an ordeal yesterday."

"But thanks to you, she's returned safe and sound," Bess quipped, returning to the table, sitting, this time, near Alison.

Was Bess a danger to Emma? Should he be watching her more closely? He didn't want to watch her, or be with her, and he hated himself for doing it. He may as well admit it, he thought, calling for more whisky. He wanted to be with Emma.

When Harry took a break from counting his coin and joined them for even more drinks, Malcolm settled back into his chair and remained there, none any wiser that he'd been moments away from springing to his feet and making a fool of himself.

No. She wished to be alone. Alone she would be. He pushed her out of his thoughts and enjoyed the next hour with those present at his table, along with Gunter and Brianne, who joined them a bit later.

They laughed over how much Cailean owed Harry for Alison's time. But Malcolm could see more in his brother's eyes than a mere dalliance, and when Cailean spoke next, Malcolm knew he was correct. "I plan on takin' her from ye, Harry."

"Not without getting me a replacement."

"Ah, but what ye ask is impossible," Cailean drawled. "No one can replace her."

"Well then," Harry told him, stretching out his hand

for his third cup. "You won't be taking her anywhere. Isn't that correct, Malcolm?"

Cailean's and Alison's eyes fell on him, waiting for his answer.

Malcolm nodded, wondering what the hell he was going to do about taking Bess. He'd given his word to get her out of the brothel. He sure as hell couldn't take her to Camlochlin. His mother and every other woman there would go after him with anything that wasn't tied down.

"Ye canna' take a part of a man's business," he said, "and leave him without a sufficient source to keep his establishment runnin'."

Cailean's eyes opened wider, like vast, indigo skies. "Where the hell am I supposed to find a prostitute who doesna' already work here?"

Malcolm shrugged and went back to his drink. "Try a different brothel."

Cailean argued something but Malcolm didn't hear. He spotted Emma at the top of the stairs with her enormous gray hound at her side. Her head was tilted slightly in his direction like she was searching for him—or for Harry.

For a moment, Malcolm simply sat there, taking in the sight of her. Mayhap he was deeper into his cups than he thought because he couldn't move. He could barely breathe at the vision of her perched above them all, her long waves falling like a golden veil over her shoulders, her huge, soulful eyes piercing him like arrows. His gaze fell to the delicacy of her fingers clutching the railing. Och, what was happening to him? He flicked his gaze to Cailean. Should he talk to his brother about what he was feeling? Could he describe it accurately? Cailean would never believe that Malcolm might be falling in love with

Emma. Hell! He couldn't believe it either and it was happening to him! Alison caught his eye instead and smiled like she could hear his thoughts.

Emma began her descent with a small booted foot the same moment Bess burst into laughter.

Malcolm watched in horror as Emma's step descended too late. She was going to fall! He sprang from his seat and pushed it out of his way just as she righted herself and continued gracefully down.

Seeing his sister—and undoubtedly Malcolm's reaction to seeing her—Harry rose and left the table. He turned before reaching Emma and cast Malcolm a knowing scowl.

Malcolm cursed under his breath and returned to his chair. Was his friend hurrying off to warn her some more about what a devil he was? And hell, he was! Hadn't he decided, this very night, that being a rogue was better than pining over a lass?

And yet, the thought of her had kept him from wanting anyone else. The mere sight of her made him want to rush to her feet. If he wasn't the right man for her, he wanted to try to become the right man.

Harry was leaving, stumbling up the stairs to his room!

At last, Malcolm could speak to her alone, but she was leaving too, letting Gascon lead her toward the kitchen.

He rose from his chair again, ignoring his brother's warning look and his own warnings to himself, and took off after her. He didn't care if she favored him or not, he would no longer continue to let her be angry with him unless she told him why.

"Emma, wait," he called out. She didn't stop. He had a feeling she wouldn't.

Picking up his steps, he moved in front of her and

Gascon and blocked their path. "If ye're sufferin' memories of the attack, I can help ye."

He thought it torturous enough to have to stare down the soft slope of her nose before she spoke. But it was harder to resist her when she lifted her face, giving him a full-on view of her dark expressive eyes and the plump cut of her mouth. "The memories that haunt me," she told him softly, "have nothing to do with the attack. Now step aside please."

"'Tis me ye're angry with then," he said, not budging. "I suspected as much. Tell me, what have I done?"

He caught the slight, wry crook of her mouth and let the sight of it warm his spine and thighs.

"You proved the tales about you to be true, Mr. Grant," she said, sounding impassive about the whole thing.

What was she talking about? Did she know about Bess?

"I never claimed them to be false, lass."

"*Oui*, you even warned me that every word was true."

"And more," he agreed. "But then I..."

She tilted her chin up to him and let him feel the anger in her glimmering gaze. "And then you kissed me."

"Ye had nae objection, Emma."

She looked like she wanted to hit him. And she might have done it too, seeming to sense the full, indulgent grin he finally allowed to shine on her, if Alison hadn't stepped up to her and hooked her arm through Emma's.

"Emma, dear, come join us at the table," she said, saving him from a possible punch.

"Thank you, Alison, but I couldn't."

"Why no'?" Malcolm asked.

"Yes, why not?" Alison echoed. "You have never sat with us. Now, you have no excuse. If any of the patrons bothers you, Malcolm, here, will see to them. Isn't that correct, Malcolm?"

He nodded, happy that he'd saved her from the Winthers, even if it meant vowing something to Bess he never intended on fulfilling. And she was good for his brother. "Aye, 'tis correct."

"No, I—"

"Bess is gone," Alison informed her, interrupting her again. "Please, Emma, come sit with your friends."

Malcolm watched Emma's resolve to remain detached falter. He guessed it had to do with her never sitting with any of them before. She wasn't one of them. She was nothing like any of them. She didn't belong here.

"For a moment, perhaps," Emma relented, and turned her back on him.

Watching her departure, Malcolm let his smile deepen on more than just the sway of her hips. Hell, if the back of her captivated him the same way the front of her did, it was already too late for him.

When she was about to sit, he hurried forward, took her hand, and pulled out her chair, causing Cailean to choke on his whisky.

"Are you feeling unwell?" Emma asked him right away, taking the seat Malcolm offered her.

Malcolm tossed his brother a murderous glare.

Ignoring it, Cailean continued. "The sight of m' brother doin' something chivalrous caught me by surprise."

Malcolm mouthed a gruesome end to his brother's life, which Cailean also ignored.

"In that case," Emma said, joining his brother in pretending he wasn't there, "I'm surprised the shock of it didn't bring back the fever and render you unconscious."

"Gunter," Malcolm said as he turned to the hefty

guard. "Has she been this disagreeable since she came here?"

He heard her sharp intake of breath and was glad to gain her attention.

"Cailean." She turned to his brother fully. "Does he do anything in Skye besides wreak havoc on poor, trusting maidens?"

"Aye," Cailean replied, finally looking at him.

Hell, was that all Cailean saw in him? Was that all he was? A rogue?

"He builds houses," his brother continued, surprising him. "Good, sturdy homes fer our kin."

Emma turned back to him, not seeing the meaningful look he cast Cailean.

"You build homes?" she asked him, the cold edge gone from her voice and replaced by curiosity ... and something else that made him ache to build her something grand.

But hell, he'd given her a kiss and she hated him because of it. What would she do if he told her he feared he was losing his heart to her?

Chapter Twenty

For another hour, Emma sat at the table with people she barely knew. She learned, after months of living with her, that Alison had a twin sister living in Newcastle, and Gunter, her escort since she'd arrived here, was once wed and lost his wife in a fire. But the most shocking thing she learned was that Malcolm built houses. She wished she could see them. Were they massive structures or cozy cottages, where children's laughter permeated the air?

Thankfully, conversation and laughter helped keep her mind off such useless longings. But soon she grew tired. Whatever little sleep time was left, she needed. So, after another round of drinks, she told them she was retiring to bed.

She heard Malcolm leave his chair. "Let me walk ye back."

"There's no need," she said, still angry with him but not remembering why. "I have Gascon."

Blast him for not giving a damn. He stepped to her side and lifted her hand to the crook of his arm.

Too sleepy to fight him, she let him lead her up the stairs.

"I enjoyed yer company tonight."

The wine helped her forget everything. She enjoyed his company, as well—along with the sound of his rich laughter...the sensual cadence of his voice.

"I'd like to hear more about these houses you build," she said, hoping to compel him into talking.

He needed no further prompting as they climbed the stairs together. "I helped m' faither build our home when I was two." He laughed softly, making her question why she wasn't in his arms. "I was more like a pain in his arse, I'd imagine. But he taught me what he knew, which was quite a lot. Ye should see the house he built fer m' mother in England. 'Tis Cailean's now."

While they walked to her door, he told her about Ravenglade, his inheritance in Perth, and though she enjoyed his descriptions, she found herself envious of him.

"Will you live in Ravenglade or Camlochlin when you marry?" she asked when they reached her room. Would he sleep inside tonight?

"I dinna' think marriage is in m' future."

Oh yes, he was a rogue. He didn't...

Bess. She remembered! She was angry and she remembered why now. She was also a little drunk and extremely exhausted.

"Find someplace else to sleep tonight."

"I will," he answered shortly. "But first ye will tell me why ye're angry with me."

"Very well." She folded her arms across her chest in defense of wanting to throw herself into his arms. She wouldn't do it. Ever again. He was correct. He was even worse than the rumors about him. "Harry told me he found you and Bess naked in her room when he was searching for me."

He went utterly still and remained quiet for so long,

she repeated her question to him, demanding an answer. "Was my brother lying to me?"

"Nae, but I—"

She would hear no more. He was a silver-tongued Highland rake who was likely quite good with deceit and denial. Why should she believe a word he said?

His fingers locking around her wrist stopped her departure. "Please, dinna' go. Let me explain."

"Explain how you could sleep with a woman one hour and kiss another with such passion in the next. Truly, your heart belongs to no one."

What more was there to say? She could think of nothing. And to think, she'd believed she gave her heart to him. She could have laughed, but she was holding back a flood of tears.

How could she have not known this was coming? She stumbled over the leg of a stool left in the middle of the hall. She didn't fall but he was there in an instant, his arm steadying her.

"I'm fine." She righted herself and stepped away. It was a hard thing to do, too. His voice, his embrace was so comforting, she never wanted to move again.

"Good night." She opened the door when she reached it and stepped inside, alone, with only Gascon at her side.

She lay in her borrowed bed and hoped Malcolm wouldn't knock. She was too sleepy to speak to him. She thought about never speaking to him again.

She closed her eyes. He didn't knock.

She was awakened a short while later when Cailean returned to the room.

"Fergive me fer wakin' ye, Emma," he whispered, petting Gascon. "Now that ye're awake, I'm well enough to give ye back yer bed."

She shook her head. "I'm not moving. I'll take it back tomorrow."

She listened to the sounds of his garments being tossed aside and him changing in a nightshirt. There was a scent to Cailean that he shared with his brother. She couldn't place it. It was like a heathery-peaty-misty smell. Very distinct. Cailean's was much stronger. Emma guessed it was the fragrance of their home and Cailean was there more often.

"Did you see your brother?" What did she care? She pounded the mattress and turned over, trying to get comfortable. She didn't care where he slept. Was he with Bess? Why did it make her feel like grabbing a broom and sweeping up the pieces of heart off the damn floor?

"Aye, I saw him," Cailean answered, getting into his own bed. "He seemed quite miserable. He didna' return to our table but brooded alone in the parlor."

"Brooded?" Emma opened her eyes. "Alone?"

"Aye. I tried to talk with him but he barely spoke. He said things like, 'I'm a fool. I canna' change.'"

"He speaks the truth. He cannot."

Cailean sat up and turned to her. "But that's just it. He *has* changed. Ye dinna' know him. Whatever ye've heard of him is in the past. He is nae longer that Malcolm Grant, but another. He thinks many of us in Camlochlin dinna' know, and he's right. But a few of us know the truth."

"What truth?" Emma asked, sitting up now, as well.

"That he's been celibate for a few years now, abandoning his rakish ways to preserve his life."

Emma was dreaming. She wasn't sitting here listening to Cailean tell her that Malcolm had given up his carefree lifestyle...to preserve his life..."How?"

"When ye go so long without carin', without feelin', it

makes ye harder and emptier. He has a good heart despite what others say."

She knew he did, but why would he have sex with Bess and return to a lifestyle that sounded miserable? Was Bess that good?

"His reputation follows him nae matter what he does to repair it."

Emma nodded, lost in his words and her thoughts. Mostly memories of Malcolm earlier trying to talk to her. Did she assume he was lying because of the rumors about him? Should she give him a chance to explain? Oh, but Harry had seen them! She couldn't get past it; visions of him and...

"He saved Alison."

"What?" Emma breathed.

"The Winthers had come and were demanding Alison in payment of their brother who was killed here. Malcolm told me that he'd enlisted Bess's help to tell the Winthers that Alison was ill and to save her from them."

It was Malcolm who'd saved Alison? Why hadn't he told her?

"He has a good heart," she agreed. "But he's still a rogue."

"Nae, I—"

"Harry found him lacing up his breeches and Bess naked in her bed behind him."

"All right, I agree that isna' good. But I'm sure there's a good explanation."

Emma quirked her lips at him. "You are so quick not to doubt him?"

"Ye spoke to him aboot this?" Cailean asked, sounding more interested in her answer than in her question.

"Oui."

"It explains why he's brooding. Hell. He has changed. Alison suggested it but, knowin' m' brother, I laughed it off."

"What did you laugh off?" Emma asked him, her heart pumping hard. She didn't know where the conversation was going, but the air felt charged with something vital.

"There's only one thing that could change a man like him. I've seen it at work with m' own eyes. Fickle hearts transformed into loyal, possessive ones. M' cousin Darach, who was as reckless with hearts as m' brother is, found it in a stable. M' uncle Tristan, I'm told, was once one of the biggest cads in the three kingdoms, until he fell to it in an English garden. But m' grandsire, Graham Grant, was the worst. The tales our bards like to tell is that he never spared honor, especially a lass's honor, a thought, until he surrendered all in the Highland mist. Love changed them into noble men."

"Love?" she uttered. Her blood rushed through her veins, making her head spin. What did she know of it? Could he have taken Bess to bed if he loved her?

"I know," he said at her stunned silence. "He's convinced that he's incapable of fallin' in love. But hell, love is a powerful thing. Even at its stirrings, it makes the heart rethink everything it knows. It makes men give up their wars and the beds of other women. It makes women give up kingdoms."

Goodness, it sounded terrifying to lose yourself so much in another person, Emma thought. Did she feel that way about Malcolm? Love was new to her but apparently Malcolm believed he couldn't fall. How awful for him.

And Cailean thought Malcolm was in love with her? It was all so ridiculous! Foolish fancies aside, why would a man, who every girl in the brothel agreed was a god among men with a heart of stone when it came to women, want her for anything permanent? If he believed he couldn't love, why did Cailean think Malcolm loved her?

"I must assume, judgin' by m' brother's foul mood, that ye expressed anger aboot this thing with him and Bess."

"I was slightly angry." She nodded in the dark. Did she want to tell Cailean too much?

"Ye care fer him then?"

Had she given so much away? She began to deny it, but then decided why bother? Apparently, she was enough to read. "I...It's not that I..." Why was the truth so difficult? Was she so afraid or unfamiliar with love that she let it keep her in the shadows? Was it the same for Malcolm? Was he afraid for his own reasons? "I find him in my thoughts often."

"In yer thoughts," he began, "d'ye want him to stay?"

Oui. Oh, *oui.* She never wanted him to leave. He brought light into her dark world. Excitement where there had been gloomy boredom. But she knew he would go. He'd told her so in the cave before Harry found them. She couldn't admit to being such a fool.

She nodded and then went back to sleep.

Malcolm leaned his head against her door and closed his eyes. He was used to the hard ground beneath his arse from sleeping outdoors in the past. He didn't mind sleeping sitting up either. He wasn't leaving the door. He didn't care about Harry's prepared room. He wasn't leaving. The Winthers had taken her once. If they came back they'd have to go through him.

He'd kill every last one. He didn't care how many of them there were.

He quit thinking about what his feelings meant and decided to simply protect her. He heard her muffled whispers to Cailean inside. He pressed his ear to the door like some stricken wretch, trying to hear what his brother was telling her.

He couldn't so he leaned back on the door and thought about how he ended up in Bess's bed, naked. Missing pieces haunted him. How could he not remember? Even if he fell asleep from exhaustion, Bess couldn't have done anything without waking him. He wasn't that light of a sleeper. It seemed more likely that he'd been drugged. But if he had been, Harry was the only one who could have done it. Malcolm remembered the sour wine searing his throat as it went down. Why would Harry do it? He had to be wrong.

He'd find out the truth. He closed his eyes and yawned. But first, he had to convince Emma that he hadn't slept with Bess. He knew she liked those ideals his kin revered of knights long past. Could he ever be one? He ignored the voices in his head screaming that he was a fool and tried to remember some of the things his cousins did for the women they loved.

Hell, this wasn't going to be easy.

Chapter Twenty-One

Malcolm came awake abruptly when the door behind him opened and he spilled backward inside Emma's room. He looked up in time to close his eyes again as Gascon's tongue descended on his face.

"Malcolm, did you sleep outside the door all night?"

Emma's voice was a welcome addition to his morning greeting. He pushed the dog off and sat up. "I was..." He stopped and blinked to clear his thoughts of his dreams.

She was real, standing over him, bonnier than any image his memory could conjure. She wore a yellow mantua with lace stitched over the snug-fitting bodice, and a petticoat, which he wanted to help her remove. He hated the cumbersome things.

"Emma!" he said, bolting to his feet. "I didna' sleep with Bess."

He looked toward his brother waking and returned his smile. Cailean believed him. It was good to know.

"I dinna' know how I came to be in her room. I give ye m' word aboot that. I was talkin' to her ootside her door one moment and wakin' up in her bed the next."

"Sounds like someone drugged ye," Cailean suggested, leaving the bed.

"Aye," Malcolm agreed. But he didn't mention Harry in front of Emma.

He looked down at the top of her head and the thin ribbon she'd woven through an upswept braided masterpiece of art. Who had done it? No one had gone into the room while he slept. Any movement would have woken him. Who had plaited her hair so precisely? Cailean sure as hell hadn't done it. He glanced at her fingers, drawn to her sides. Fingers that prepared life-saving medicine and dug holes in men. Fingers that touched him like they were teaching her things about him even he didn't know yet. He was beginning to understand just how capable Emma truly was, not only despite her loss of vision, but because of it. She would fit in nicely with the strong, independent women of Camlochlin, if he ever brought her home.

As if seeing the smile he helplessly offered her, she returned her own to him.

Did she believe him about Bess then?

"Malcolm," his brother called out, interrupting them. "Leave me to dress. We'll meet below stairs to discuss who drugged ye."

"Aye," Malcolm agreed, and took her arm to lead her out the door with Gascon keeping careful pace on the opposite side of her, free of her hand.

"So, you think Bess drugged you?" she asked him when he closed the door behind them.

"I know it sounds like nonsense I'd use to get oot of this. But I speak the truth, Emma. Nothin' feels right aboot it."

"Perhaps she did put something in your..." She wrinkled her brow. "You said you were standing outside her door and then woke up in her bed. What were you doing before coming to her door? Were you drinking anything with her?"

Harry. He drank with Harry.

"I was with Harry. The wine tasted sour. She could have drugged it or m' cup before I got to the parlor."

Emma nodded. "Sour?" She stopped as they came to the stairs. "What else? How did the cup smell?"

He shook his head. "I dinna' remember."

"You would remember if you took her to bed, Malcolm."

"Aye, I know. That's why I tell ye that I didna' take her to bed. 'Twas ye who was on m' mind, ye I was headin' up the stairs to see."

She smiled like she wanted to believe him. "I don't know what I think," she said honestly.

He could fix it. She gave him hope. The more he thought about it the more he wanted to do it.

"Ye look bonny this morn." Was this him speaking, sounding like he was fighting for breath? Madness! He'd told lasses they were bonny all the time, never once afflicted like this.

"Did I look so dreadful before then?"

He was about to curse his inability to compliment a lass properly when he saw that her smile remained, softened as she teased him.

"Nae," he told her, unaware of the thickening cadence of his voice, or the way it caressed her ears. "'Tis just that a golden crown suits ye well."

"Ah, you speak sweetly, Mr. Grant," she said. "How do I know you're telling the truth?"

"Because lyin' is one of the flaws that I left behind a few years back."

"Ah, *oui*, Cailean mentioned that last night."

Malcolm scowled. What had Cailean told her? His brother didn't know he was celibate, did he? Was that the slightest trace of a smile he saw on her face? "What did he talk aboot?"

"Your family, the men, mostly."

He heard the humor in her airy voice, but what she said next hit him in the guts before he could stop it. "There was one in particular whom I'd be most interested in meeting someday. But there were so many names, his escapes me."

He felt his belly drop to his boots. "Adam?"

"*Oui*! That's him. How did you know?"

"He's the most handsome," he muttered.

She let her smile widen into a grin he found impossible to ignore. "Do you mean you are not the most irresistible man in Scotland? I find it hard to believe that you don't think so."

He stared at her, glad she couldn't see his fierce scowl. She was having sport with him. He was all for playful teasing. At least, he always had been before. Before the teasing was about Emmaline Grey being interested in one of his cousins. Still, he would thrash Cailean into the nearest wall for telling her about Adam MacGregor.

"Ye wouldna' like him," he told her, wondering at the truth of his words. "Adam lacks even more of those attributes ye care so much fer."

"Is that so?"

"'Tis," he replied a bit stiffly, escorting her down the stairs. "Even the proscription of his name canna' sway him from a fine arse. Whereas I fought against the realm because of it."

She paused at the bottom and turned to him, her enormous eyes curious with a hint of mischief. "Because of a fine arse?"

He blinked at her, then gave in and smiled. She didn't give a damn about Adam. She was trying to rattle him, most likely because of Bess. It was working. Things rarely rattled him. How had this wee wisp of a thing gained so much power over him? And if the sweet grin on her face told the truth, she was thoroughly enjoying his discomfort. Ah, but he'd let himself fall into the trap. He decided, without much thought to the matter, that he didn't mind. "Nae, lass, because of the proscription. Before there was yers, nae arse I'd ever come across was fine enough to fight fer."

Her eyes opened even wider and for an instant Malcolm basked in the humor that filled them.

"Emmaline," Harry called out, glaring at Malcolm. "Where are you off in your finest dress?" He reached them and let his gaze sweep over her from head to foot. "Is there a ball I don't know about?"

Lifting her hand to her pinned tresses, her merriment faded, though her smile remained intact. "Though I cannot see, I wish to be seen."

"I've no doubt about that," Harry said. "If the Winthers see you looking like this, they might mistake you for one of the girls—"

"Harry!" Malcolm cut him off, seeing the effects of his words on Emma. He didn't tell her she looked lovely. He told her she looked like a whore. Why would he insult his sister so?

"If the Winthers come," Malcolm assured him, "they willna' live long enough to touch her."

"Haven't you done enough, Malcolm?" Harry accused him in a quiet voice. "I never had any trouble with the Winthers before. Now, they tried to kidnap my sister. Will you kill more of them until you bring all of them here? You can't fight a hundred of them."

Harry was right, the trouble he was having with the Winthers was his fault. If Cailean hadn't rescued Alison from Andrew Winther that first night they wouldn't have gotten shot and would have been long gone by now. He wouldn't have known Emma. These maddening contradictions wouldn't be making him question everything he knew.

Before he said anything else, Emma turned on her heel, reaching for Gascon's fur.

"He's correct," she said so softly Malcolm would not have heard her if he wasn't standing so close. "'Tis best if the Winthers don't see me."

When Malcolm would have followed her, Harry's hand on his arm stopped him. "Do you think it's wise to go chasing after her?"

Malcolm's eyes flicked to Harry's and he stared at him as if he was seeing him in an entirely new light. "Mayhap no'," he said truthfully. "But since ye are no' moving yer arse to chase after her, I decided it should be me." Malcolm owed Harry his life, and now he owed him for Cailean's as well. But it didn't mean he'd stand by and let him hurt Emma.

"Ye insulted her, Harry. Ye had an opportunity to tell her that though she lives in darkness, she shines brighter than the North Star. Instead, ye told her she looks like a whore."

He held up his palm to silence Harry when her brother began to defend himself.

"Ye tell me ye want the best fer her." He turned to see her paused at the top of the stairs, her head slightly tilted, listening. The sight of her moved him in places he'd insisted didn't exist. "And yet ye keep her hidden away upstairs, more lonely than any princess in any of m' grandmother's books." He took a step toward her when she smiled, and then he turned again to Harry. "I'm takin' her oot today. I'll protect her. Ye have m' word. I'll have her back by nightfall."

"Malcolm, I—" Harry tried to stop him.

"She's been locked away long enough, old friend. Give her a day of freedom in the sun. I'm leavin' in a few days—fer yer sake and because of what I owe ye. When I go, she'll return to her tower. But today"—he moved closer to Harry and stared him in the eyes—"I'm takin' her oot."

He remained in his spot for a moment or two longer, but Harry said nothing more. Without further ado, Malcolm pivoted on his heel and headed for the stairs. He looked up, hesitantly at first, at her waiting there, afraid he might see a look of disapproval on her face. She was still smiling, though a hint of sadness shadowed her gaze while he climbed the stairs.

"Does the prospect of spendin' the day with me cause ye dismay?" he asked, coming toward her.

She shook her head and looked at the floor between them. But he saw it, a gossamer tint of crimson across the bridge of her nose.

"I willna' seduce ye, if that's what ye're afraid of, Emma."

Finally, she returned her gaze to him. Smoking warm and inviting. "I'm not afraid of that."

She fired his blood to molten lava. He didn't think she'd be afraid. Curious, cautious, eager, playful, but not afraid. He knew what she wanted, what she deserved, but hell, he wasn't sure he was prepared to be gallant and honorable.

"Besides," she went on speaking, "you've tried to seduce me before and it didn't work."

He laughed. "What? When have I tried? Ye suffer delusions, Miss Grey."

She ignored his teasing and called down to her brother. "I will be safe, Harry."

"Malcolm."

Malcolm turned to greet Cailean on the stairs. His brother looked fit and well enough to go home.

"Change of plans, brother. I'm takin' Emma on an outing and we're leavin' now. We'll talk of the mystery later, aye?"

"Aye," Cailean said, already forgetting him when he spotted Alison serving a patron breakfast.

Seeing that he'd lost his brother's attention, he took Emma by the hand and led her down the stairs. "Let's get some food and be on our way, aye?"

"Where are we going?"

"Ye'll see," he said, hurrying her along. He didn't want to give Harry a chance to change his mind. He wanted to be alone with her. For more days than just this one. Many thoughts like these vied for his attention, so he didn't realize what he'd said to her.

He also didn't see her smile deepen into something more joyous than anything, even her brother, had seen on her before.

Chapter Twenty-Two

Emma had only been on a horse a few times in her life. She didn't like it. Sitting with both legs slung over one side made her feel unbalanced and tense. A few breaths in and her bottom was killing her from bouncing between Malcolm's thighs, not to mention her teeth clacking together until she was sure they would break and fall out of her head. It was a good thing Gascon was long-legged and big enough to keep up with their swift pace as they left the brothel. She would not have left her friend behind.

When they were far enough away, Malcolm slowed the beast and gave her and Gascon some respite from their arduous outing.

Resting in the crook of his arm, she let herself relax a little more. Not too much though. He was leaving in a few days and that made her feel more unbalanced than riding on the damn horse.

She should have been prepared for this. She'd known from the beginning that he was going back home. He never made any promise to the contrary. He'd been honest.

What else had he done to make her care? He'd saved her dog. He'd saved Harry before she met him. Of course that mattered. But after that, he'd gone out of his way to prove the rumors about him were true.

He'd almost succeeded a time or two. But as of late, it was like he was removing his shield and proving the opposite. Did chivalry lurk somewhere in Malcolm Grant? He was being noble by promising not to seduce her, kind when he comforted her...

She suspected he might be everything she wanted in a man, after all. She wanted to believe he hadn't slept with Bess, or at least hadn't gone to her bed willingly. And it did make sense that Bess would do anything to sleep with him. Besides the attributes he apparently *hadn't* ignored when honor was being taught at Camlochlin, besides that—he didn't treat her like a helpless, unfortunate waif. For that alone, she could love him.

Was Cailean's suspicion correct? Was Malcolm falling in love with her? He slept on the hard floor in front of her door, refusing the bed Harry had prepared for him. And all to tell her first thing in the morn that he was innocent. Was Cailean sincere when he spoke of Malcolm's celibacy? Good heavens! She never would have suspected that! But as far as she knew, he hadn't slept with any of the girls since he came here, and he could have. All of them, save Alison and Brianne, threw themselves at him whenever they visited the room. If Malcolm was celibate, he was to be admired for the control he possessed. She would ask him about it later.

She didn't feel guilty for teasing him about Adam MacGregor. What was it Cailean had told her? Love made men possessive. Emma had decided to test that theory by showing interest in Malcolm's cousin. The handsome one.

She hadn't needed to see Malcolm's face to know he didn't find the topic a pleasant one. Was he jealous? Possessive of her the way Cailean had described some of his relatives after they lost their hearts to their women?

It was hard to tell.

But what did it matter? He was leaving in a few days. She didn't want him to, but how could she get him to stay?

She closed her eyes to think about it as a warm breeze lifted a few loose tendrils of her hair away from her neck. The sun felt delightful on her face, and the fresh aromas of trees and soil made her thankful to be alive. Already she hardly remembered what Harry had said about her appearance. She did, however, remember what Malcolm had said. She remembered everything. He called her a lonely princess. The memory of the way his voice dipped with emotion made her radiant. She could feel her face glowing with the force overtaking her heart.

What would she do if he left?

"Ah, I see ye're rememberin' our last kiss."

She laughed, liking his sometimes insufferable arrogance—and the warmth in his voice. "In truth," she told him, "I was recalling the way you tumbled into my room this morn. 'Twas very ungainly for such a stealthy warrior. It makes me wonder if it wasn't your clumsy footing that cost Scotland her independence when your cousins tried to stop the Act of Union."

"Ye dinna' look like the kind of lass who hides such a viperous tongue behind those bonny lips."

He sounded amused rather than angry. Another thing to like about him; he laughed often. He made her want to laugh with him.

"Besides," he continued, "we didna' succeed in our mission because m' cousins were distracted by love."

"And that is something that would never happen to you, correct?"

"Correct."

"You're afraid."

He laughed, a starkly male, arrogant laugh that made her glad she knew the truth about him. His arrogance was a mask. He was as unsure and unsteady about life and love as she was.

"Afraid of what?"

"Love, of course."

He laughed even harder, but before he spoke again, she did. "'Tis nothing to be ashamed of. I'm afraid of it too. I . . . What is that scent?" She knew it was water, a great body of it. She'd smelled it before when she sailed to France and again when she returned. She was quiet and listened to the sound of distant waves rolling toward the shore.

She sat up and drew in a deeper breath. The aromas of trees and soil disappeared and were replaced by a fresh, briny scent of sea and sand.

"Are we going to the sea?"

"Aye, lass."

Was he going to bring her to Camlochlin today? What about Cailean? What about Harry? Could she leave her brother after just finding him? Harry might not be the best sibling, but he was her family. All she had left.

"Why are you taking me to the sea?"

"Because it reminds me of ye," he said with a tenderness in his voice that made her go soft against him. "'Tis wild and yet contained. But every now and then, it breaks free of the tide's confines and floods the earth around it, bringing disaster and restoration."

For some incredibly foolish reason, she felt like weeping.

How did he know? How did he know that she wanted to break free of her confines and run, unhindered, unafraid?

"Do you think I'd cause disaster?"

"Aye, Emma. And restoration. 'Tis what I feel ye'er doin' to me."

What was he saying? She wasn't sure, but she liked how he sounded saying it. She wanted to touch him so bad her hands burned in her lap. "What is it you mean?"

He thought about it for a moment, remaining quiet, and then he sighed, bending to her ear. "I dinna' know the right words to tell of it, Emma. So I'm taking ye to a place that will help ye understand."

"How will it help me?" she asked softly. Part of her wanted to run for her life before another moment passed and she could no longer deny her heart. The rest of her wanted to believe that she'd won the heart of the infamous rogue.

"Come."

He slowed his horse and Emma could hear Gascon barking at a screeching bird overhead. The sound of rolling waves was closer and the different scents of sand, salt, and fish assailed her senses. She felt Malcolm separate from her and his horse but instead of helping her out of the saddle right away, he pulled off her boots, and her stockings next.

She already felt exhilarated, away from the brothel and Harry's doting attention, away from the smell of medicine and sickness, and the fear of losing one of her patients.

She wiggled her bare toes and tossed back her head with laughter when he fit his hands around her waist and lowered her feet to the sand.

"Can we go in the water?" She knew she was asking much, but she'd never been to the coast for adventure or rest. She wanted to do all so that she could have something wonderful to remember it in the days ahead.

He hadn't answered her. "Malcolm?" Only then did she feel his full attention on her, searing through her flesh, her bones, until he arrived in her heart.

He took her in his arms and held her tight against him. His breath was warm, sweeping over her, caressing her. His voice seared her nerve endings and set her on fire.

"D'ye know how fine ye are to me, Emma?"

She shook her head and suddenly the sea and everything of concern was forgotten. Her? Fine? Even Clementine had told her that she was plain. Nothing fancy. Did he mean it?

"Ye're more bonny than any lass I've ever laid m' poor eyes on. I canna' breathe when ye smile."

She reached up and coiled her arms around his neck. Was it true then? Did he love her? Did the man who hadn't given his heart to anyone lose it to her? The thought of it made her want more of him, all of him.

"And I cannot think straight when your lips are so close."

He dragged her deeper, closer, pressed her against him while he bent to kiss her.

His mouth covered hers like fire, consuming her from the inside out, laying claim to her heart. His tongue, a flame scalding the inside of her mouth with languorous delight until she wanted him to eat her alive. What was he doing to her? What had he done? She felt wild and wanton and dangerous, and it still wasn't enough.

She felt him begin to withdraw, but she pulled him back, not understanding the power she possessed.

She groaned like a beast she didn't recognize, then gripped handfuls of his shirt when he cupped her buttocks in his large hands and dragged her hips over his. She felt him through his breeches, growing hard for her. If they didn't stop soon, it would be too late. Oh, but he was delectable. She didn't want to stop. She wanted to . . . to rub herself over him until he had to have her and took her right there where they stood. She wanted to tear her way out of her dress and offer him to take his fill of her breasts. Her heart banged with primitive desires she had no idea how to stop. She wanted him to take her. She was a virgin, but her body ached for his. She wanted to strip him and then herself, and then she wanted to climb up on him and nestle him between her legs.

She gasped and quaked in his embrace.

No. She wasn't like the other girls at the brothel. She wanted a man who loved her. Only her. And she wasn't sure Malcolm loved her. Cailean said he might be falling in love. Emma hoped he was. Oh, how she hoped. She certainly was falling in love with him.

She severed their kiss slowly, reluctantly, short of breath. He didn't force her back. "You didn't answer my question," she accused with a teasing smile replacing her dreamy one. "Can I go in the water?"

"If ye like," he answered easily, and took her hand.

It was a simple gesture, nothing extravagant like kissing the curls out of her hair. His hand around hers meant nothing, and yet, it was so strangely comforting and intimate, Emma found her breath short once again and her blood scalding her veins.

She inhaled a deep breath, hoping to cleanse kissing him and other things from her thoughts. But when the fresh, raw air filled her lungs, she felt more alive than ever before. The urge to abandon all to him tempted her to madness.

Thank goodness there were other wonderful things to occupy her attention.

She loved how the sand felt between her toes, yielding and warm. But soon, it changed, becoming wetter and harder under her feet.

He led her to the shoreline, where the waves washed the hard sand away and almost made her lose her balance. She wasn't prepared for the icy water cascading over her ankles and squealed, then laughed, jumping in place to avoid it.

The sound of a faraway horn coming in on the tide stopped her. She tilted her head to listen and imagine who was on that boat and where they were heading. Gascon's barking drew her to her left. She smiled, hearing the excitement in his bark.

"Is he running?"

"Aye," Malcolm told her softly.

"Are there trees?"

"Nae, lass. There's nothin' but sand and sea."

"I want to run too." She returned her attention to directly in front of her and breathed deeply, closing her eyes. "But not yet."

He was silent for a while, letting her take in what was around her.

"What d'ye think of it, Emma?" he asked, closer to her than he was before.

"'Tis powerful, able to kill a thousand men in a single instant. 'Tis breathtakingly vast and all perfectly balanced. I feel quite small standing before it." She'd wanted to see the ocean again. She thought once she went blind, she never would. But today, she could almost see it. "Describe it to me."

He did, giving her clear images of dazzling light dappling the surface of what looked to be endless water.

Instead of overtaking them in a flood, waves rolled forward with impotent savagery and licked at their feet. The vast sky, a cool color blue, was filled with large scavenger birds that teased her dog, soaring in close enough to end up in a set of fangs, but escaping just in time.

"Ye crossed the water before, aye, lass?"

"*Oui*, to and from France."

He asked her about her childhood, giving her memories, both good and bad, the weight they deserved. When she finished telling him, she felt weightless and picked up her skirts to follow the sound of her barking dog.

"Can I run?" she called to Malcolm over her shoulder.

"Aye, lass, ye can run."

Chapter Twenty-Three

I'm finding it difficult to subdue the urge I have to stand up and slash my dagger across your throat." Oliver Winther, Baron of Newcastle, met his commander's gaze steadily, studying him. "I don't do it because your wife would look to me to help raise your brats. I show you mercy for your Hebburn blunder because you are not entirely to blame for being a whimpering idiot, what with Janice as your wife."

John Burroughs's jaw twitched and grew taut. Oliver wanted to demand that his commander challenge him on it. When no challenge came, he sighed and looked around the hall. Thankfully, half the candles had burned down during supper, bathing the hall in a dim, golden light. With the curtains drawn, no outside light could get through, saving his sensitive eyes from the pain of the bright world. One physician from London, and one seer all the way from his father's homeland of Norway, and neither could help Oliver. They told him what he already knew.

"My lord has my gratitude," John said, bowing his head like a supplicant servant instead of the leader of Oliver's army.

"What are you kissing his arse for now, Burroughs?" Garbed in black and the quick, slight twist of his grin, Sebastian Winther, youngest of the Winthers, dead and alive, slipped into the chair beside John's.

Oliver had rested his eyes this morn and could see Sebastian clearly. He watched him the way a bird of prey might size up a mouse—but with more amusement. Everyone surrendered to Oliver's power. No one resisted him, save his brother. Sebastian was no mouse.

"Sebastian," Oliver said in a low, sinuous voice that sought the shadows once expelled, "why weren't you a part of the endeavor to bring me Harry Grey's sister?"

"Because you needed me to quell the uprisings against you in Westerhope."

Oliver eyed him and held up his hand for a refill on his drink at the same time. "Mmm, I remember now. How did it go?"

If kitchen gossip was to be believed, different fathers may have sired them, but Sebastian's eyes were the same as Oliver's. Deadly. The brothers were like twin falcons, one dark and the other light.

"There are no more uprisings, Oliver. That's how it went."

Oliver should have known. He'd sent Sebastian to Westerhope to quiet the people, in whatever ways he saw fit. He knew Sebastian. He'd seen his eyes, as black and cold as coal while he'd ended lives. Instead of apologizing, Oliver turned his attention to... "Burroughs the dolt allowed a blind girl to singlehandedly take down three of my men." He stopped and closed his eyes and his fists. He clenched his jaw to keep from shouting for John's head!

"A blind girl, Sebastian," he emphasized. "And the most mortifying part isn't that she's blind, but that the entire kidnapping was arranged. Nothing should have gone wrong. Burroughs lost her. Just as he lost our brother Andrew at that cursed brothel in Hebburn, the bodies of the two Highlanders who'd patronized there and killed Andrew, and two of his own teeth! Tell us again, John, how you managed to kill two men who, according to you, killed eight of my men that night."

John said nothing. Oliver wished he wasn't his commander so he could kill him.

"I told you," Sebastian said. "I'll get the names of the murderers when you let me go to Hebburn." The edge of Sebastian's mouth slanted curiously. "But why were you kidnapping the girl?"

"Because she's Grey's sister," Oliver indulged him. "She's the only way he'll talk and tell us the truth about the Highlanders. Also, if I'm to believe John again, she escaped two men without lifting a weapon against them. I find that quite curious."

That was all his brother needed to know. He didn't have to tell him that he wanted her because he wanted to learn how she lives being unable to see. He wanted… no, he needed to learn how to defend himself if he lost his vision.

Sebastian turned to John for clarification. "What happened?"

"She drugged us," John told him.

"There was no one else there with her?"

"Not when I was awake."

Sebastian showed his dissatisfaction by turning away and not sparing John another glance while he spoke. "Where are the other two?" He asked Oliver, his feathers unruffled.

"Answer him, John!" Oliver roared, and slammed his fist down on the table.

"We haven't found Rubert yet."

"But I would think," Oliver drawled, "that if he were alive, he'd have returned by now."

"Unless shame stops him," Sebastian interjected. "If he is alive, then she was most likely alone and is a clever one."

"We found Reggie's body and his head a short distance away," John told him while Oliver glowered at him to tell the rest.

"Well then," said Sebastian, "that proves she wasn't alone. It's not easy to remove a head. It takes great strength."

"You let a girl poison you, John."

"She's an odd one," Burroughs defended. "It's like she can see without her eyes."

Yes, Oliver had been told of her.

"It could have happened to anyone, Oliver."

"Don't defend him, Sebastian," Oliver warned, cursing mercy under his breath. He decided to have a little fun with his brother. Better that than send him and John to the gallows. He saw one of his servants and snatched her wrist.

Sebastian glared at him when he pulled her into his lap. Oliver smiled behind her neck. What if he put a choice before Sebastian? Damn, but he was a master fighter and a ruthless warrior. Oliver didn't want him to have a weakness, even if it was the opposite sex.

When Sebastian turned away, Oliver wanted to cry foul. Instead, he hunched over the girl and bit her throat. When she struggled a little to be free of him, he closed his hands over her breasts and squeezed.

"Oliver, is that necessary?"

The fish was caught. Now to reel him in. Pale green

eyes, large and menacing, glanced at Sebastian from around her neck.

Oliver laved his tongue over where he'd bitten her. "Yes, Sebastian, it is necessary when it comes to keeping my hands from John's neck. Sinking my cock into a woman will soothe me." He pushed the girl to her feet and held her still in front of him with one hand while he unfastened his breeches with the other.

"Which will it be, Sebastian, John's life or this wench's *honor*?" He smiled, then bent her over the table and pulled her skirts slowly up her thighs.

Sebastian watched, deadly silent as Oliver prepared to have his way with her here in the Great Hall.

Which would he choose?

The table separating them and hosting the handmaiden flew across the hall, providing the answer. Oliver stood in his place, in front of his chair, holding the wench. He released her and sent her off running away.

"Your loyalty is misplaced, little brother."

"Don't make me choose, Olie," Sebastian said, sheathing his sword. "I won't stand around while you push your weight around."

Oliver waved away his brother's concerns and warnings and shouted for a new table. He also ordered John to get the hell out of his sight. When they were alone he motioned for Sebastian to return to his seat.

"I won't continue to let you demean my authority in front of others." Oliver's voice dripped with acid, but his smile remained intact. "Even if your defiance is feigned, you sometimes go too far."

Sebastian tunneled his fingers through his mane, pushing it away from his face. But it only fell over his eyes again when he let it go. Eclipsed behind strands of obsidian hair,

Oliver could see the arch of Sebastian's raven brow. But he couldn't tell if it rose with jest or menace.

"My defiance isn't feigned."

Unlike his brother, Oliver didn't hide behind a stoic frown. He sat back in his chair and tossed his ankles on the table and his chuckle across Sebastian's ears. "That's why I'm sending you away. I thought a pair of weeks away killing in Westerhope would have been enough to quell this unwarranted anger you feel toward me. You need more fighting to divert all the gloominess that surrounds you before you force me to kill you."

"Where am I going?"

"Where you've wanted to go from the beginning."

Hope fanned an ember glow in Sebastian's gaze. "Hebburn."

Oliver nodded, his smile fading. "Instead of sending the army, I showed them mercy by sending only for the red-haired girl whose fault it is that our brother is dead. I was refused her." He lowered his ankles from the table and sat up. "Refused!" he repeated, then smiled. "Thankfully for everyone in the place, I was promised someone so much better."

"I thought this was about finding who Andrew's killers are … or were. Not about kidnapping blind women."

Oliver tossed his brother a murderous smirk, which Sebastian ignored. "She was promised to be delivered to my hands."

"By who?" Sebastian asked, boldly provoking Oliver.

"You don't need to know anything else. Just bring her to me. If you don't do it, I'll go to Hebburn myself and slaughter everyone in that accursed brothel. I should have done it as soon as word came about Andrew."

"And the names of our brother's killers?"

Oliver glanced around the hall and beckoned another servant to him. "Do what you must," he said, waiting for her. "Bring the names back to me and we'll ride together to the Highlands and kill their families."

Oliver watched his brother leave. He should have sent him to Hebburn right from the beginning. He'd have answers and possibly a new blind handmaiden by now.

Speaking of handmaidens, he stood up and took the hand of the girl coming to him and led her to his room.

Sebastian sat up in his bed long into the night, an array of nautical maps strewn across his lap. He studied them by the light of two candles until the wicks burned down. Pity, he didn't have to cross the sea to get to Hebburn. Or Westerhope. Oliver was wrong. He didn't need more fighting to escape the gloom. He needed a ship. First he needed to learn how to sail, but he could do it. He *would* do it. Someday. Tomorrow, he had to avenge Andrew.

He'd insisted on going to Fortune's Smile the day they found out about Andrew, but his brother had refused. When Sebastian had asked him why he couldn't go, Oliver admitted that it was a feeling in his belly. Something telling him that his youngest brother wouldn't return to him.

Sebastian laughed it off. He didn't give a damn about superstitions. But he also didn't want to push Oliver too far. He wasn't afraid of anything his brother would do to him. But when Oliver's mood went foul, everyone around him suffered. The baron enjoyed killing, and Sebastian didn't doubt that he'd reign down terror on the people of Fortune's Smile.

Someday he'd get his ship and sail away from Newcastle and everywhere Oliver ruled, but first, he had to find out who killed his brother.

Chapter Twenty-Four

*E*mma knew night had fallen by the different sounds and scents in the air, like the sweet fragrance of partly closed honeysuckle blossoms and the sweetly seductive scent of jasmine carried on the night breeze. The hoot of an owl, the scurry of a mouse, and the squeak of bats and their small flapping wings overhead all told her when it was.

She'd never been out, enjoying a night, before. Her knowledge of its scents and sounds was learned every night for the month or more she had watched over Gascon from the brothel window.

Nestled now in the crook of Malcolm's arm on their way back to the brothel, Emma grew thoughtful about all that had changed since he had arrived and brought a flash of light into her dark days. She had so much to thank him for. So many reasons to love him—and many of them had to do with those attributes she didn't think he valued. But where would it all lead? They'd been out all day running, swimming, laughing, and he hadn't brought up taking her and Gascon home with him. He hadn't tried to lay with her either. She wasn't sure how she felt about his celibacy now that it involved her. Was he truly just going to leave Fortune's Smile and her? What would she do? She wanted a taste of what the others had with Malcolm. But what if he left her with child? How in damnation was she going to let him leave without falling apart at his feet?

"D'ye understand aboot restoration now, lass?"

She loved the pitch of his voice when he lowered his mouth to her ear. How was it possible that every woman he came in contact with didn't love him, whether they shared his bed, or not? She hadn't slept with him and she was dreadfully sure she was falling in love with him. She could be wrong, but what else could make her heart leap in her chest the way it did when she heard his voice? What else could make her willing to give up anything in her life? Hadn't Cailean mentioned giving up kingdoms for love?

"I think so," she replied softly. "I could hear the power of the wind upon the waves, swirling monsters to life. I understand the sheer, raw strength of nature and the damage it can inflict." She thought of her afternoon chasing Gascon, of how it had taken a few moments or so for her to trust the feeling of being alone, with no guard and no dog. At first, she'd held her arms out in front of her, but soon she let go of caution and spread her arms wide.

It was the most magical day of her life.

She saw the sea again and then she flew.

"But with the end of disaster comes restoration. Things are reborn, better than before."

"Aye, that's aboot right."

"And you say I have restored you this way?"

"Aye."

"What will this rebirth of yours mean for me?" she

asked him, her heart clanging like a cymbal against her ribs. Would she go with him if he asked her? How could she leave Harry so soon after their reunion? How could she not?

"I dinna' know, love, but we'll have to discuss it later. We've arrived home."

This wasn't her home.

He dismounted first, then lifted her out of the saddle and set her feet firmly on the ground. Gascon arrived almost instantly and waited for her to move.

"Go," Malcolm said. "I'll see ye inside after I tend to m' horse."

She would go, in a moment.

Rising on the tips of her toes, she whispered close against Malcolm's neck, "Thank you for the perfect day." Whatever happened, whatever decision he made, she would never forget the day he gave her.

She felt his body go tight, his breath grow short. He reached for her but she stepped away. "I'll see you inside."

Without waiting for his reply, she took off at a brisk pace, still exhilarated by running. She didn't trip, thanks to careful Gascon. She smiled at absolutely nothing—or a dozen things—and entered the brothel through the kitchen.

"Ah, perfect," said a male voice as smooth as honey and as deep as the ocean she just left. "Are you the cook?" he asked, blocking her path.

Gascon growled low in his throat and Emma turned her face toward the door behind her, hoping Malcolm would get here soon. It wasn't because she was afraid— and she was. She didn't know if the stranger was holding a knife. She should excuse herself and move around him. Chances were he meant her no harm. Besides, Harry didn't let her speak to the customers.

"Forgive me," the man amended quickly, sensing her anxiety. "I didn't mean to frighten you. I'm Sebastian Fletcher—a guest at this fine establishment while I journey to Newcastle to trade some goods. I arrived a short while ago from Durham, seeking some food and a place to rest my head."

The pitch of his voice was deep and honey thick, and well practiced in the art of attraction. He sounded like a man built for seduction, not violence. Emma sighed. Another handsome face who believed his charm worked on every woman.

"After a delicious meal served by a lovely maiden called Brianne, I had the desire for something sweet. A scone, perhaps?" He shoved his hand into the saddlebag hanging at his side. "I can trade you a small pot, or perhaps a book?"

She could hear the smile in his voice and gave in to the urge to smile back.

"Do you know if there are any scones in here?"

She nodded. Best to help him be on his way. Harry wouldn't like a patron in the kitchen. She held on to Gascon with one hand and reached out before her with the other, moving toward a shadowy alcove. She felt around for what she was looking for and smiled when she found it. A basket of butter scones, freshly made this morning. Harry's guest would be pleased.

"You cannot see," he observed when she turned back to him with the basket.

"That's what they tell me."

"That's a curious thing to say." The timbre of his voice softened, as if he were smiling. "Can you see or can't you?"

"I can, just not with my eyes."

He didn't respond right away and in the silence a chill swept down her spine.

"I've heard of you," he said quietly. "People around here say you were recently abducted and escaped. Is it true?"

Her eyes opened wider. "People around here speak of me?" Her belly felt like it was falling to the ground. What were they saying?

"Come, now." He laughed softly. "Is it so far-fetched that they would?"

She nodded, not sure why she was still standing here talking to him. She wanted to ask him if they were calling her a witch.

"Escaping an abduction is an extraordinary thing worthy of whispers around a kitchen fire. It must have been terrifying." His voice dipped with sympathy. "How did you do it?"

The door opened and Malcolm entered with the wind at his back. His footsteps were swift and heavy, bringing him to her side. He stood at least two heads taller than her, rock hard and ready to pounce if there was trouble. She fought the urge to slip her arm through his and let it proclaim to everyone in the dining hall that she was Malcolm Grant's and Malcolm Grant was hers.

She kept her arms at her sides as Sebastian introduced himself to Malcolm, his voice every bit as friendly as it had been to her.

"And you are, sir?"

"Malcolm Grant of Perth."

Perth? Emma struggled to keep from yawning. What about Skye…and Camlochlin? She shrugged, too tired to really care. She hadn't slept well in over eight months since Clementine's death. But lately, especially tonight after being in the sun and the water all day, she could barely keep her eyes open. She had Malcolm to thank. He'd brought laughter to her, and passion. Whether she was kissing him or arguing with him, he scalded her blood and made her want to remain in his life. Oh, what would she do without him? She had to find a way to make him stay.

"I'm a trader," Sebastian Fletcher was saying. "I can get you anything you need."

"I dinna' need anything," Malcolm replied.

Emma hated that he believed what he said.

"Where d'ye keep yer goods?"

"In Durham," Mr. Fletcher told him, and then patted his bag. "Among other places."

"And how did ye come to find yerself in the kitchen?"

Emma listened to Mr. Fletcher explain his scone tale and then she tugged Gascon's fur. "If you will excuse me, I will retire. Enjoy your stay, Mr. Fletcher. Good night."

"Miss..."

"Grey," she provided.

She might have let her gaze swing to Malcolm's for an instant or two. She wanted him to follow her and she hoped he saw it in her gaze. Without another sound, she curled her fingers into her friend's fur and let Gascon lead her away.

She'd almost made it to the stairs when Harry spotted her from the parlor and hurried after her.

"Cailean Grant is well enough and I've moved him to his own room."

"Good news, Harry, *oui*?" Was that all he wanted to tell her? A relief. She smiled, patted his arm, and continued on. She'd miss sharing her room with Cailean but she also missed her privacy.

"Emmaline. I think they should be leaving tomorrow, the next day the latest."

She paused and said a silent prayer for patience. She should have known there was more on his mind. He didn't allow her to spend the entire day away without a few words. She was too tired for this.

"I'll examine Cailean tomorrow and see if he's strong enough to leave us." She started up again.

"You were gone all day." His voice shook with restraint.

"*Oui*, I was."

"Where did you go?" he asked, trying unsuccessfully to sound mildly interested. "What did you do?"

"We can speak of it tomorrow, Harry. I need sleep."

"I think we should speak of it now. I—"

"But I just finished answering a host of questions to the patron in the kitchen."

"The kitchen?" he demanded. "There was a patron in the kitchen? Where is he now?"

"Still there, I assume. His name is Sebastian Fletcher and he claimed to be looking for a scone."

"And you believed him?" her brother shouted at her while he raced away toward the kitchens.

Emma smiled, thankful for escaping a confrontation with Harry. It was easy when his kitchen was involved.

Malcolm waited in the shadows. When Harry disappeared into the kitchen, he took off for the stairs. On the way, he caught sight of his brother in the dining hall, holding a scone to his mouth. Harry wouldn't find Fletcher in the kitchen because he was already at Cailean's table surrounded by Mary and Jane, and thankfully, even Bess.

Deciding to look in on his brother later, Malcolm took the stairs three at a time and hurried silently down the hall to Emma's room. He'd caught her reckless glance before she left the kitchen. An invitation he couldn't refuse.

Before he knocked, the door creaked open to let him in.

He rushed in and met Emma on the other side. He wanted to gather her into his arms. He wanted to slip one hand around her nape and tilt her mouth to his.

She stepped away while he hesitated and let that moment pass.

He resisted tossing back his head in frustration with himself and ran his hand down his face instead. She tempted him beyond endurance. He could easily bolt the door, undress her, and kiss every inch of her delectable body. Could he stop there? He didn't think so, not if the thought of her beneath him, pushing her hips against his in a rhythm of drumbeats and blood flow, didn't drive him mad with desire for her.

"I must go, fer yer sake."

"My sake?" she asked him quietly, quizzically, bathed in soft, golden light.

"Aye, lass, I'm no' sure I can keep m' mouth, or m' hands, off ye."

"Oh," she said quietly. "And what is so bad about that?" She lowered her chin to hide her burning cheeks from him. When had she become so wanton?

"I dinna' want to do anything to ye that ye might one day regret."

She moved closer to him and put her hands on his chest. "Like loving you?"

"Aye," he answered just as quietly.

"Because you believe you cannot love me back."

"What?" He covered her hands with his. "Where did ye hear that?"

"From Cailean," she told him. "He also told me you're celibate, but I must admit I don't get what one thing has to do with the other in your case."

What? Cailean knew? And he told Emma? Hell, Malcolm was going to kill him.

"Well?" She blinked her glorious eyes at him and waited.

He didn't want to be talking about this with her. He remembered his encounter with the trader from Durham and shoved his hand in his pocket.

"I got this fer ye," he said, placing a leather-bound book in her hands.

She smiled and brought it to her nose. "Where did you get it?"

"From the trader, Mr. Fletcher."

"Malcolm," she barely whispered, pulling him in closer to hear her. "What is the title?"

"'Tis *Le Morte d' Arthur*."

He regretted trading one of his daggers for the book when her tears fell on the old leather.

"'Twas one of my favorite tales when I was a child," she told him.

"Aye, m' grandmother's too," he shared. Then, more gently. "Why are ye weepin', lass?"

"I miss the tale desperately but I cannot read, Malcolm."

He smiled at her. "I know ye canna' read." He walked her to her chair and sat her in it, then came around her and sat on her mattress, facing her. "But I can."

Chapter Twenty-Five

Malcolm read her three chapters and then they talked about each one in between. He loved watching her listen. She did it so intently and seemed to hear so much more than he did.

Hell, if Cailean or his cousins found out he'd read Mallory to a lass in her bedroom, they'd likely toss him over a cliff believing he was an impostor who'd murdered the real Malcolm Grant.

It got worse.

"Love does elude me, Emma," Malcolm found himself answering her earlier question of what celibacy and being incapable of falling in love had to do with each other before he could stop. "Withoot it, m' life was verra' empty and meaningless. I tried to ferget it existed by indulgin' m' physical whims. But I stopped wantin' one withoot the other."

She looked like she was about to say something but stopped herself and then began again. "Are you trying to bring honor home to your father?"

He smiled. "Mayhap. Who knows?" He didn't. And it didn't matter now. Only she mattered.

"Tell me what turned you into a rake."

He laughed, and then he shook his head at himself. He'd always been so charming before, never awkward or exposed with any lass. Why did Emma and her questions shake him up so? What turned him into a rake? How the hell was he supposed to answer that?

"Lasses never denied me anything. I learned how to get what I wanted with no' much more than a smile. It made me lazy. I didna' realize there was somethin' different between me and m' cousins when they used to talk aboot the lasses they thought they loved. Even as lads, they were always fallin' fer this lass or that. But no' me."

Was this him speaking? Sharing things he never shared with another soul? He stared, enchanted by the subtle grace of her beauty while she leaned her head against the chair and blinked slowly, heavily.

"Do you truly believe you cannot fall in love?"

Did he? Still? He didn't know. He didn't know if he was falling in love with Emma. He hated that it frightened him, but that was the truth of it. Even worse was that it wasn't just love, it was loving *her* when he wasn't sure if he was worthy of her.

The problem was that just looking at her made him forget everything else. He wanted more time with her, mayhap even all the time he had left on this earth with her.

"I want somethin' that I stopped believin' I needed," he confessed. His smile lingered over her closed eyes. Was she sleeping? She'd had an adventurous, tiring day. He knew she was exhausted.

He got up and scooped her into his arms.

"*Oui*," she said quietly, coming awake for a moment. She didn't open her eyes but smiled when he laid her in her bed and covered her with her blanket. "I want that too."

He leaned over her and spoke close in her ear. "Even with a rake, lass?"

"A reformed rake, *oui*," she whispered back groggily.

He kissed her forehead, and then her temple, before he stepped away. It took every ounce of strength he possessed to leave her room. He wanted to climb into bed beside her and hold her close to him. He wanted to throw caution to the four winds and tell her how important she was becoming to him, but he'd wait until she was awake and alert enough to understand. He didn't fully understand it either.

His muscles were wound tight. What he needed was a drink. He patted Gascon's head and left the room. Reaching the bottom of the stairs, he spotted Harry sitting at one of the tables in the tavern with Cailean and Alison, and surprisingly, Mr. Fletcher was still with them. Curious about Fortune's Smile's new patron, he headed in their direction.

He thought of the woman he just left asleep in her bed. Was he a fool to go? Nae, he wanted to be a better kind of man for Emma. A man she deserved. Malcolm the Rake was fast becoming Malcolm the Considerate, the Honorable, the Gentleman.

He'd seen it before—this…affliction plaguing the men of Camlochlin. There was no more question.

He was falling in love.

'Twas possible after all!

Satan's bloody balls!

Sebastian studied Malcolm Grant as he approached the dining hall from the stairs. He knew as soon as he first laid eyes on the strapping Scot, that he was the one who attacked John's small troupe when they abducted Miss Grey. Grant was big enough to swipe off a man's head.

Even dressed in civil garb, Grant had the look of a Highlander, untamed and unruly, a bit less refined than the younger Grant at the table. They could be the two Highlanders John had spoken of. Or not. According to some of the girls he spoke to, several traveling Highlanders had passed through in the last fortnight.

Sebastian didn't think the Grants were the alleged dead Highlanders though, because John Burroughs wouldn't recognize a Northman dressed like an Englishman and would not have described Andrew's killers as Highlanders.

Still, he'd find out who the Grants were. If they were guilty, he'd make certain their deaths were drawn out and painful.

"I hope I didn't frighten Miss Grey too much," he said to Malcolm when the Highlander came near. "I came upon her in the kitchen," he explained when Harry questioned him.

"She was well when I last saw her, Fletcher," Grant told him. "She does no' frighten easily."

Aye, Sebastian remembered.

"She's pleasing to the eye." He slipped his eyes to her brother. "Are you certain you will accept no offer for her?"

"I'm certain, Fletcher," Grey stammered.

Sebastian laughed and shrugged his shoulders, turning back to Grant. He expected some kind of reaction from the Scot. But he wasn't sure he could call what he got a reaction. It was more like a stare with the cold promise of death in its glacial depths. No boast that she was his. No words at all, but a blaring warning nonetheless.

Grant and the proprietor's sister cared for each other. Sebastian had thought so, but he had to be certain. Now he was. How long were the Grants here for the brothers to have formed relationships with the women? Perhaps they were here for the fight.

The best way to get men to talk was to get them drunk. He brought another round and laughed with the others when Harry, retiring for the night, stumbled up the stairs.

"I think I'll be goin' to bed as well." Grant stood up. He turned to his brother. "Comin'?"

"Aye," Cailean advised with a slight smile. "But I'll be sleepin' in Alison's room tonight."

Malcolm smiled, then looked a little worried. "Dinna' overdo—I mean—take care to—Hell, nothin' at all. Good night."

"Was he ill, wounded?"

"What?" Malcolm turned and saw Fletcher behind him.

"Your concern," Fletcher explained. "Is he recovering from something?"

Sebastian was tempted to look away from the power in Grant's sea-foam eyes. He seemed to be searching through Sebastian's thoughts, trying to pull him into the light to find the truth. No, he didn't suspect anything. Sebastian almost smiled to himself. He couldn't panic. He wouldn't.

"He's a virgin," Malcolm finally said.

Sebastian grinned. "In that case, I envy him."

Malcolm eyed him. "Ye look quite young to envy such a thing."

"I was introduced about a year ago and have been practicing often."

Malcolm laughed and picked up his steps.

"I'll walk with you, if you don't mind." Sebastian hurried after him. "I paid for a room but I'm not sure which way to go."

Grant nodded, accepting his company.

"By the way, I didn't mean to step on your boots,"

Sebastian told him as they continued their way up the stairs. "I didn't know you fancied Miss Grey."

Grant cut him a shrewd glance, his half smile tainted with doubt and embellished with a deep dimple. He didn't say anything though he suspected Sebastian wasn't telling him the truth.

A perceptive enemy was the most dangerous kind.

Sebastian would have to use a bit more caution around this one in the future.

For now though, should he continue this deception and risk losing Grant's trust, or go another way—a way less expected?

He remained silent for three more stairs, then threw up his hands. "All right, I confess the notion that you cared for her passed across my head. But I didn't know if it involved your heart or just what's in your breeches. As a man of honor, I'll not go after another man's woman. Rather than ask and perhaps embarrass her, I knew a degrading offer for her would surely offend a man who cares for her. You were easy to read."

Grant's smile faded. "Was I?" His shoulders, broad as a damn mountain, straightened a bit more.

This wasn't so difficult, Sebastian mused, maintaining his expression of sympathy. Grant was hiding his affection from Harry Grey or Cailean Grant. He had no reason to keep it from his brother, so Sebastian determined that Malcolm was keeping Harry in the dark. Sebastian didn't need to know why.

"Known her long?"

"Long enough."

Sebastian smiled and nodded. Perhaps not so easy. No matter, tomorrow was another day. He didn't want to push too much. Just one more thing he wanted to know.

"There are whispers about her," he said, moving closer and lowering his voice. "They claim she escaped her abduction. Seeing she's a slight woman, and blind no less, I think it was you who rescued her. Am I correct?"

Honesty disarmed the enemy every time. Sebastian could see the effect it had on this Scot. It created trust—small doses they might be, but trust nonetheless.

"Aye," Grant admitted, turning to him, his voice a low drum, his gaze defiant and proud, like an unmovable mountain when he told Sebastian what he'd done to her attackers.

"I would have done the same," Sebastian told him honestly. What the hell was wrong with Oliver to kidnap a blind girl? Her abductors deserved what they got. "But I'd heard there were three men."

"Yer curiosity is starting to rub me wrong," the Scot said in a low warning voice that didn't rub Sebastian too well either.

No. Sebastian had to back up. He'd gone too far. "In truth," he said, breathing out a self-deprecating laugh, "I have a wager on whether or not she fought on her own or had help." He grinned. "You just earned me a hundred pounds."

He was relieved to see Grant's hard expression soften. Perhaps Sebastian's new friend even smiled before he turned for the dimmer lit western hall.

Sebastian went in the opposite direction. He walked about fifteen feet when something soft stepped into his path.

"Ah, a beautiful lost boy." Her low, decadent voice was like pure sin to his ears. Bess. "Let me help you find your way."

He couldn't help but smile. Out of all the girls at Fortune's Smile, Bess was the most useful. At least, he hoped so.

"Lead the way." He offered her a path to take. "But I should warn you. I'm a man, not a boy."

Alison lay in her bed gazing into Cailean's eyes. She never expected to fall in love with a patron, but here she was, ready to give her heart, besides her body, to a man. She giggled at the sounds of Bess's passion seeping through the walls. It emboldened her to climb atop him and begin removing his clothes. He didn't speak, but stared at her in the candlelight while she took in the sight of him. She knew he was a virgin; she didn't know that he was a virile piece of artwork crafted to make her lose her mind.

"You have nae mercy fer m' wound."

She leaned down and kissed a trail down his bare chest, stopping at his scars. "If I harm you, I'll just mend you back together again."

He grew serious while he unlaced her gown and slipped it off her shoulders. "I knew ye'd be mine the first night I laid eyes on ye."

"Here I am," she whispered against his lips.

"Here ye are," he said, kissing her once, and then again. "Restorin' life back to me."

"And you bring hope to me."

She lifted the rest of her skirts over her head, freeing their bodies from the last restraint of clothes. She knew what she was doing even if he didn't, and she did it well. He learned quickly though and soon drew himself on top of her and took her like he was master of her body.

Guarding the entrance to Emma's room with his body, Malcolm leaned his head against the cool wood frame of her door and closed his eyes. He'd already decided after the abduction that he would guard her door. He waited until he couldn't keep them closed anymore and cursed the night when they opened again. How the hell was anyone supposed to get any sleep with all this moaning and groaning haunting the corridors? Why were the damn walls so thin anyway? Were they like this when he was here four years ago? He didn't remember. The sounds hadn't tortured him like they did now.

A long, satisfied cry assaulted his ears from somewhere down the hall. He swore an oath and ground his jaw when the memory of her untried, hungry mouth rushed across his thoughts. She fired his blood like no one before her ever could. And yet, here he was allowing a slab of wood to stop him from ravishing her. He'd gone mad.

But she was different from the others. She wanted more from a man. At first, he thought that man would never be him. Then he thought he didn't have what it took to be that man. Now—

Another long, masculine moan, then the tinkle of feminine laughter.

He'd denied himself in the past. This was harder, almost impossible. He'd never wanted any woman the way he wanted Emma. He drew his palm down his face and calmed the deep thumping of his heart.

He groaned along with the rest of the voices seeping through the halls. He restrained himself, as frustrating as it was, because he wanted to be a different man for her.

Even if it killed him.

Chapter Twenty-Six

There were two things Emma thought about just before dawn broke when she opened the door to her room and Malcolm spilled across her boots for the second day in a row. This time he was awake with a half-eaten apple in his fist.

First, she probably should have held Gascon back—but he loved Malcolm and was as happy to have him there as she was. Second, he brought joy...and the sea to her, and she loved him for it.

She listened to him greet her dog, and Gascon's subsequent crunching on Malcolm's apple. Her guardian groaned a little and muttered something about his back.

"Fool!" She laughed, abandoning the shadows. "What have I told you about sleeping at my door?"

She tossed back her head and squealed with laughter when he closed his hands around her calves and pulled her down. She held her breath when he gathered her in his arms and kicked her door shut.

"I'm nae longer yer patient." His throaty whisper fell

over her bottom lip as he rolled her to her back, still holding her close.

"Indeed," she agreed, running her fingertips over his bicep. "Your strength has returned."

He covered her mouth with his, drawing a shuddering breath from her. He consumed her in a lick of fire, his tongue sweeping over the roof of her mouth, then deeper, burning her nerves, boiling her blood until he ignited something somewhere deep within her center. Oh, it was only a day or two ago that she'd pitied anyone who completely lost their heart to another. It was happening to her. It terrified her. What if she surrendered all only to watch him get on his horse and ride out of her life? How would she get over him? He had her heart. She wanted his in return. It was the only way he wouldn't abandon her. He consumed her in a raging fire that heated the crux between her legs. He wouldn't be celibate with her. She knew it, sensed it in his quickened breath, his deepening kisses. He'd take her here on her bedroom floor. She was sure of it when she felt him stiff within the confines of his breeches. Dare she release him? He wanted more. And so did she.

But she'd have his heart with it or not at all.

She stopped, withdrawing slowly, her breath short and shallow.

"Fergive me," he said, sounding terribly repentant while he lifted her off him.

Forgive him? She almost laughed. For what? For making her feel alive? She wanted to live and die in his arms and then beat him over the head for making her fall so hard.

She'd stopped kissing him because she was afraid of what she wanted him to do to her.

"Of course." She granted his request while he rose from the floor.

"Goin' somewhere, lass?" he asked, taking her hand and pulling her to her feet. He pulled her close to him but kept his arm at his side.

"*Oui*, I'm going for my morning walk."

"May I accompany ye?"

She smiled and he moved to her side, taking the heat with him, and slipped her arm through his.

"You can sleep in a proper bed, Malcolm," she told him in the hall. "I lock my door, and my windows, as you requested, lest you forget. And I have Gascon with me. I'm safe. I don't need you snoring at my door."

"We shall see, lass."

She rolled her eyes and then thought about kissing him again as he led her down the stairs and out of the brothel.

Emma stepped outside and smiled at the chilly air blowing in from the north. She took a deep breath and gathered in the scents that carried on the wind—the scent of the man standing next to her. Even without sight, she knew he oozed virility.

"You must stop kissing me whenever the mood strikes, Mr. Grant."

"I canna' give ye m' word on it, Miss Grey. I find ye irresistible."

She laughed again, softer this time and led him through the woods.

They stopped, hidden within the trees, when Malcolm gathered her in his arms. "D'ye know that when ye laugh"—he moved closer and bent to speak low in her ear, his voice a hypnotic blend of silk and velvet—"yer nose wrinkles just enough to set m' heart to racin'?"

Her color deepened as she reached her fingers up to

her nose, as if to feel what he saw. "Are you trying to seduce my heart?" she asked him, tilting her lips closer to his while she spoke.

"I would like to," he admitted softly, his smile evident in his light voice.

"What stops you?"

He grew more serious. "A promise I made to yer brother, and the one I made to m'self."

Ah, yes, he didn't want to make love without feeling love. Wasn't that what he'd told her? That didn't bode well for her. Her stomach tied into a tight knot. Perhaps Cailean was wrong. Perhaps Malcolm wasn't in love with her.

She called out to Gascon and somehow she held back tears that threatened to form and spill down her cheeks. Truly, love made one foolish. And a promise to Harry?

"What did you promise my brother?"

"To leave ye alone. I owe him much," he added when she began to protest. Then, "But despite m' debt to him, despite everything Emma, 'tis almost impossible to keep m' word around ye."

"Poor dear. Let me help." She spun on her heel and went back to the brothel. Alone.

She didn't stay that way long, however. Inside Harry's kitchen once again, Mr. Fletcher stood in her path; this time Cailean and Alison were with him.

"You're not a man of your word then, Mr. Fletcher?" she coaxed.

"Ah, Miss Grey," he said with a bow. "I'm at your mercy not to inform your brother of my transgression."

"That depends on what the three of you are doing today. She listened for the sound of Malcolm marching back, alone and angry. He was about to get a lot angrier.

"We're headin' oot to catch some fish fer breakfast," Cailean told her. "Where's m' brother?"

"He's just outside. Please, let me come with you," she pleaded. "There are herbs and fragrances along the bank for..." Damn, she forgot Mr. Fletcher was there with them. Before he thought her a witch for knowing medicine, she backtracked carefully. "...things like lavender and daffodil that would blend perfectly with my stuffed bass."

There was no lavender at the riverbank, but none of her companions would know it.

They agreed to let her go, and on the way out the group laughed at something Mr. Fletcher said.

Emma didn't know that Malcolm was watching her traipse off to the riverbank. But she hoped he was.

Emma was grateful for Mr. Fletcher's company over the next two days. He followed her about most of the time, doing or saying things to make her smile, much to Malcolm's frustration, since she didn't smile with him. Mr. Flet...Sebastian didn't mind her using him to make Malcolm jealous. He even agreed that she was doing the right thing.

"If there's something real here for Malcolm, he should be put to the test. If his heart is true, it won't fail him."

She agreed. If Malcolm truly cared for her, he needed to fight whatever stopped him, and win her. Time was running out until he left.

"But," Sebastian went on, "what makes you think you've won what other women could not?"

"Cailean thinks so, but," she confessed with a smile, "for me 'tis wishful thinking, I admit."

She wasn't sure why she shared so much with a man

she'd only known for a few days. Sebastian was easy to talk to. She showed him what Cailean meant when he told him she saw with her ears. He didn't seem to mind her chattering at all, and he even told her about his nights with Bess and what he'd learned. Malcolm, for instance, had spent his night alone, refusing Bess's company, and every other girl's.

"She has no softness for you," he said of Bess.

Emma sighed. What could she do about it? "She doesn't matter right now."

"He does. I know, Emma."

Cailean got in on it too, claiming that if anything could make a man see the light, it was jealousy.

She didn't know about seeing the light, but if it meant tempting Malcolm to punch Sebastian through a wall a time or two, then it was working. He hadn't done it yet. But it was coming. Emma didn't want Sebastian to be hit. Something, somewhere, would get broken. It was childish anyway, wasn't it? To make a man jealous?

Sebastian swore he could take a hit, especially for her, and insisted on continuing.

Though only a few days had passed she'd grown fond of Sebastian. She thought at first that he wanted to win her, but he'd discovered soon enough that her heart was lost to someone else. He didn't try to go near her room, not that he could have with Malcolm sleeping in front of her door. He just wanted to be her friend. And right now she needed the help of one.

"He was very fidgety at the table this morning," Sebastian informed her on their second afternoon together. He walked her to a nearby tree and waited while she sat beneath it. "He did speak to me though."

"Oh?" she asked, surprised. "What did he say?"

He sat beside her in the grass. "He said he spoke to you yesterday and you asked him not to harm me. It was the only reason I still had any teeth."

Emma covered her mouth to hide her shock, but Sebastian saw it and laughed.

After a moment, he leaned in to her. "He's coming over."

Emma's heart pounded in her chest. Was Sebastian correct when he said that if Malcolm was so ready to leave without her, what was he still doing here?

"Emma." He reached them in a few long strides and stood over them. Gascon whined for his attention.

She didn't know if he gave it; her heart thumped in her ears too loudly.

"I wish to have a word alone with ye."

Should she go? Sebastian remained silent. No one else was there to stop her.

She didn't want to refuse him. She wanted to touch him, run her palms down his strong arms and over his muscular chest. She missed spending hours with him. Sebastian was wonderful, but she wanted Malcolm.

She remained sitting and bent her head. "I don't know if I shou—"

He swooped down and without a word to either her or to Sebastian, plucked her from the grass and hefted her over his shoulder.

Gascon barked, then whined, then grew silent when Malcolm made a sound with his mouth. If she screamed, she'd alert Harry, and he and Malcolm would likely fight. Harry would lose, of course, and she'd be out on the street, begging for food.

But if he thought she'd go without a fight, he was sadly mistaken.

She straightened her body, balanced enough to provide the right amount of force when she bent her arm and jammed her boney elbow into his collarbone.

He yelped and set her feet on the ground. The instant she was down, she held her hand to him, measuring the distance between them, making sure she didn't miss when she hauled back her hand and slapped him as hard as she could across the cheek. Gascon barked again, then ran forward and then back to them again, like he was eager to go.

"How dare you manhandle me?" she demanded.

The problem was that she couldn't see her captor bending for her again. When he tossed her over his shoulder a second time, Sebastian finally intervened, calling as he caught up to them.

"Grant, wait, there's something you should know."

What? What was he going to say? Emma lifted her head where it dangled against her captor's back. She shook it, hoping Sebastian saw her. Hoping he heeded and didn't mortify her!

"If ye're goin' to tell me ye care fer her," Malcolm warned without stopping, without turning, "dinna' waste yer time. It willna' change anything."

Emma hoped Sebastian remained quiet.

"This was a ruse."

Oh no! No! "Sebastian, don't bore him with foolish drivel." But she should have expected this. Sebastian's bare honesty was what she liked most about him.

Malcolm stopped and turned, leaving Emma's face toward the brothel. "A ruse?" he asked while she pounded on his back.

"To make you jea—"

"Malcolm!" Emma cut Sebastian off before she fainted

from embarrassment. "Put me down or I will never forgive you!" she finally demanded. He obeyed and set her down. She felt around with her foot, found what she wanted, and bent to pick it up.

Sebastian saw the rock coming and moved away in plenty of time to escape it.

"Don't be angry with her," he said even as she turned her scarlet face away from him. "It was my idea. Not hers."

He left, passing them to stride to the brothel and disappear inside, leaving her to her own defense after he betrayed her friendship.

"What exactly was his idea?" Malcolm's breath stole across her face, deep and dark while he moved closer to her and stood above her.

She would never admit to him that she'd used Sebastian the rat to rouse Malcolm's heart into action. The rat, it appeared had been correct though. Malcolm was roused.

"Toss me over you like a sack of grain again," she warned, hoping to divert his thoughts in another direction, "and you'd best sleep with one eye open."

"I'll risk it if ye dinna' accompany me to m' horse on yer own."

Oh, he couldn't be sincere. Would he truly toss her over his shoulder for a third time like some...some...

"Lass."

The thread of warning in his voice convinced her that he would do as he said.

She wasn't afraid of him and she would tell him so later. For now though, to keep Harry from more endless questions, she sank her fingers into Gascon's fur and picked up her steps beside Malcolm of her own will.

"What is it you want to speak to me about? And why

can't we speak here?" she asked him as they came to the stable.

"I want to speak to ye alone. We're no' alone here."

"Where are we going?" She did want to go to the coast. Could she trust herself there with Malcolm? It was difficult to keep her hands off him the first time. Now it would be impossible. No matter how angry she was at him.

"Quit askin' questions," he commanded. "I'm verra' angry with ye and I—"

"Ha!" She laughed and beside her, Gascon gave a soft whine as they entered the stable. "I'm calling on the last of my resolve to keep from clawing out your eyes!"

"Is that so?" he demanded, stopping them in a beam of light that filtered through the wooden walls. Emma could feel the heat of it on her face. "Fer what, then? Because I refused to deceive ye and told ye how I feel? Aye, remind me never to do *that* again, lass."

He sounded so repulsed; Emma felt the urge to laugh. But he was too serious. She imagined he shared his heart with very few.

Still, he deserved this for tossing her about. "*Oui*, I shall remind you," she promised. "'Twill save other women from learning that they mean very little to you, and worse, that you mean even less to yourself." She cast him a bland expression. "I promise you 'tis not attractive."

Was that his laughter filling the stagnant air with fragrance? Goodness, how was it possible that he didn't consider himself up to her standard when he thought he was a prince? She'd never met anyone like him.

They said Oliver Winther was the most arrogant man in England. Rumor was that he believed he was an eagle, the most majestic of predators. He wore a golden eagle feather tied to his waist and took down his prey without mercy.

Was Malcolm as bad as that? "Listen, Malcolm," she said, wanting to fall into his arms but stepping away from him instead. "Nothing more needs to be spoken between us. If you're leaving Hebburn, then go. You don't owe me any explanations, and in honesty, I don't want any. I just don't wish to drag this out any longer."

His fingers closing around her wrist stopped her departure. "Emma, d'ye care fer Fletcher? Tell me and I'll no' bother ye again."

"No. I don't. But I could if I had no one else."

"Ye do have someone else," he said softly into her curls.

She knew being alone with him was dangerous. She didn't care. She lifted her hands to his face and traced his mouth while he told her how beautiful she was to him. Her breath grew short when she felt him lean in. She ached to kiss him and sighed into his mouth as he crushed her up against him.

She opened to his tongue. She felt him against her teeth, sensual, probing. Her blood rushed through her veins, forging a sizzling path to her groin. She burned in his arms and the intensity of it frightened her. She'd never been with a man, never even kissed one before Malcolm, but she lived in a brothel. She knew about sex. The walls were thin and the talk was crude, at best.

Curling her arms around his neck, she pulled herself up his body, just enough to feel the steel between his thighs. Instinct made her lift her leg and try to wrap it around him.

He groaned like a wounded animal and cupped his hands around her buttocks, covering them.

She felt like biting him, eating him alive. She told him and he laughed before returning to her mouth, hungrier than before. Soon though, he withdrew, his breath hard.

"Come." He growled the demand and she let him lead her to his horse.

Chapter Twenty-Seven

$\mathcal{M}$ alcolm couldn't tell which was harder to contain, his heart from bursting through his chest while he lay beneath Emma, taking in every beautiful contour of her face, or his unyielding cock from his English breeches.

He'd taken her to the sea, to a small cove nestled between the cliffs. The sand was warm and soft beneath him. The sound of crashing waves filled his ears... unless what he heard was his blood moving through him.

She did this to him. This wisp of a woman shackling his wrists over his head and straddling him, her skirts pulled up over her supple thighs.

He hadn't guarded his heart against her because he'd convinced himself that he couldn't experience love, that he was somehow deficient. That belief hit him hard and took much from him. But Emma brought it all back.

"Tell the truth," she said, wearing a playful smile behind a soft yellow tendril. She tempted him to obey her every command. "Were you jealous?"

Hell, he was. Fletcher was fortunate to still be breathing. He laughed. "Was that the plan?"

When she gave him a smile and lowered her chin to hide the blush stealing across her nose, he realized with a jolt of something hot that went deeper than any chasm the human mind can conjure, that he'd been wrong all these years.

She let go of his wrists to trace the contours of his face, his nose, his dimples, his lips, pausing while he kissed her curious fingers.

"What plan?" she teased, leaning down to plant a kiss on his mouth. "I have no idea what you're talking about."

"Mmm." Her distraction was working. He didn't care about plans or a ruse or whose idea it was to make him jealous. It had worked.

"Aye," he whispered against her lips, and drew his hands over her soft, bare thighs. "I was jealous, crazed with it." He grew even harder against her when she gasped at the feel of his hands on her buttocks. He was hard enough to take her, and by the way she was rubbing her sweet body against him, she was getting ready to be taken. "I thought of a dozen ways to kill him. Another day and I might have done it."

She licked the seam of his mouth, then drew her tongue over it. "I don't belong to you, Mr. Grant."

His control nearly snapped. It would be easy to slip out of his breeches—in fact, he was nearly there now—and teach her how to ride him like the wind rides the surf. *Then* she would belong to him and no one else.

But he wanted to be different with her. Pride and logic were the next to go. He'd miss them.

"Tell me what I must do to win ye then."

"Do you want to win me?"

"Aye, lass, I do."

She laughed, tossing back her head and exposing her throat to his hungry mouth.

"The man worthy of winning my heart," she half-panted, half-purred while he bit her neck with tender urgency, "must not care that I cannot see."

"But ye can see, m' love. Ye see what the eyes miss."

Her breath came quicker as she worked his shirt loose from his breeches and pulled it over his shoulders. "His own eye would never roam once he won my heart."

"Why would he ever look anywhere else again once he'd won yer heart?"

She sat up straight on him and with her hair tumbling down around her face, began untying the laces of her gown. "And most important of all, he must build me a home."

He raised an eyebrow at her. "What about those attributes ye talked aboot? Honor? Humility?"

She shrugged and slipped her shoulder out of her gown. "I'd rather have an imperfect man than a knight."

"Imperfect?" He pinched her rump and she shrieked.

His head shouted warnings at him even as he laughed with her and sat up to meet her and claim her mouth. There was Emma's future to consider, as well as his word to Harry.

He closed his arms around her and rolled her gently on her back in the sand. They would keep their feelings hidden from Harry until Malcolm could figure out what to do. For now, nothing mattered in the world but kissing her.

He took his fill, tasting the deepest corners of her mouth, breathing her, consuming and being consumed by her. When she tugged on his breeches, pushing them over his hips, he nearly groaned at his freedom. He ached and pulsed for her, but he waited and released her breasts from the laces of her gown.

He should stop. She was innocent, untried, and he was...

The tips of her breasts were like ripe, coral berries. He wanted to bask in their sweetness and lose himself in every inch of her. Was this what the other men in Camlochlin felt? Was this what called them to battle themselves and become better men?

He watched her flesh tighten as he ran his fingers over her nipple. When he dipped his mouth to drink from her, she groaned and relaxed her thighs beneath him.

"I want... I want..." she gasped, not knowing.

He knew. He wanted it as well.

He pushed the front of her skirts above her thighs, exposing her to his ready cock. He paused, his muscles twitching with impatience to have her. He'd done this before and he'd never stopped himself just before. This was different. He never let himself think of the consequences of his actions, or in what terrible state a lass could leave his heart.

He never expected her to coil her legs around his waist and pull him down between her thighs. She took his lower lip between her teeth and bit down gently. He groaned and pushed his hard tip to her entrance.

Her sharp intake of breath cautioned him to continue slowly. She was a virgin—another honor she offered him. A virgin with a sweetly wanton appetite.

The caress of her legs around him tortured him, as did the sight of her spread beneath him. He pressed his hips against her and moved with languid ease over her crux. She grew warmer, wetter, moaning softly with need. How was he supposed to resist her? He couldn't. So instead of trying, he bent to kiss her and tell her how she made him feel. When she tossed back her head, he raked his teeth over her warm throat and sank halfway into her.

Her sheath was tight, licking fire down his shaft. Her short gasps fueled the flames. On the verge of bursting, he pulled out, drawing a long, languid groan for her. He pushed against her again, entering deeper this time. She tried to close her legs but he held them open with the strength of his thighs and dipped his hungry mouth to her nipple. Suckling her made her moan and drip around him. When she wiggled under him, he answered with an even deeper plunge.

"I would have ye, Emma," he said thickly, close to her mouth, his eyes locked on her.

She grew slicker. He thrust harder.

"It pains me," she said, pushing her face into the crook of his neck.

"I shall stop then." He moved to withdraw, but she held him tight and pushed him back to his original position, beneath her.

She squeezed her eyes shut and sucked in a great breath when she straddled him, taking him whole, from tip to base. He watched her fling back her golden curls and wriggle her tight body atop him. The eruption came quick. He cupped her hips and drew her off him while his seed shot upward from his body.

She must have thought they were done because she broke free of his embrace and leaped up on her feet. She took off toward the waves while he recovered.

"Emma!"

He heard her laughter on the wind before it lifted her gown off the sand, where she left it, and set it over his face.

He sat up and turned around to see her running, wearing only a thin chemise, her tresses flowing out behind her. He laughed when she spread her arms wide.

Rising, he pulled his breeches off his ankles then took

off after her. He caught her moments after her feet hit the water. Their laughter echoed off the high cliff walls as they fell into the shallow waves.

She shivered in his arms and he held her tighter, kissing her while the surf rolled over them and the sea reclaimed the sand underneath.

Emma closed her eyes as a violent jolt of pleasure shook her in her skin. Her flesh cooled by frothy waves and heated by Malcolm's tongue trickling down her belly to her inner thigh. Her senses came alive like never before. The sound of his breath, hard and heavy, rushed through her ears like the whitecaps rolling in over them. His wet fingers tickled her skin and made her giggle and gasp at the same time. She'd heard the girls talking about this kind of play—when a man put his mouth...there. She'd wondered what it might feel like but never...never imagined it would feel this good. She felt consumed by heat, engulfed in flames as he laved his tongue over her sensitive nub and then kissed it. Instinctively, she spread wider and arched her back. He licked her so indecently, she felt the urge to push him away, but she didn't. She couldn't. She never wanted him to move from where he was.

The world shook around her. Sand washed away beneath her with the pulling of the tide, and she felt herself being carried away toward the crest of oblivion—pure, pleasurable oblivion. Before she knew what she was doing, she pushed herself upward, pressing deeper, moaning at the cascading bliss sparking light all around her. She bit her lip and cried out, bucking her body involuntarily beneath him. Pleasure exploded into something she never experienced before and she reached down and grabbed his face in her hands, guiding him to drink of her deeper.

She cried out his name and tossed her head from side to side as passion overtook her, turned her world upside down, and then drained her.

She lay sprawled in the sand like one overcome by a sea monster, her breath short, fast and hard, her muscles trembling.

"What did you do to me?" she asked him, winded.

"Something I hope to do more often if ye let me." He lay beside her on the wet sand.

"I wouldn't dream of stopping you." She smiled, then blushed at her boldness.

She wanted to ask him how he intended on pleasuring her again when he was leaving. She wanted to ask him once and for all if he planned on taking her with him to Camlochlin or if he still believed he couldn't make her happy.

But her courage left her.

She loved him too much to feign bravery if he told her he was leaving without her.

So she didn't ask.

Chapter Twenty-Eight

$\mathcal{M}$alcolm and Emma lay dressed in the dry sand, warming beside a small fire Malcolm had made with a flint rock and some shavings from inside a piece of driftwood. He never wanted to go back to the brothel. She didn't belong there.

"D'ye remember how the moon looks?"

Snuggled close in the crook of his arm, her cheek pressed to his bare chest, she nodded and gazed up at the night sky. "I think so."

"'Tis full and bright tonight," Malcolm told her, looking at it reflecting in her eyes. "It shines upon ye like ye're a newly formed goddess, pure and resplendent. I canna' take m' eyes off ye."

"Close them."

"What?"

"Close your eyes, Malcolm."

"All right." He agreed with a short laugh to do it.

"Are they closed?" She laughed with him and lifted her fingertips to his eyes. Her touch was so light it almost halted his breath. When she was satisfied that he was telling the truth, her fingers traced the contour of his cheekbones, his nose, the ridge of his upper lip.

"Now." She lowered her hand to clasp his and then lifted his fingers to her face. "Tell me what you see."

His hands were nowhere near as soft or light as hers were, but he moved gingerly as he could over her features, the way she'd done to him.

Her face was beautiful. Anyone with a pair of eyes in his head saw it. That's why Harry kept her hidden. With men like the Winthers around...

"I see a heart more courageous than the hearts of some men I know. M'self included. I see an intuitive, intelligent, infuriating woman who enjoys renderin' me helpless with sleep, or with her smile."

"On those several occasions when I made you sleep," she defended, touching his dimples, "'twas for your own good."

"Several occasions? Exactly how many were there?"

"I don't remember. I didn't count. And I wouldn't have had to do it if you weren't so insufferable at times."

"Ah, so 'tis m' own fault then."

"Most of the time, *oui*."

She smiled, touching his laughter, slamming his heart hard against his ribs.

"Why me?" she asked him softly when his amusement softened into a smile.

He was looking at her again, drinking in the soft curve of her nose, the thick spray of lashes resting on her round cheeks. "Ye give me a reason to start over, a deeper desire to change who I was. Ye examined the man I thought I wanted to be and made me examine him next."

"I'm the fortunate one," Emma told him, pressed close to his chest. "Never having the experience of losing my heart to anyone, I'm glad 'tis you."

He looked at her, wondering if she remembered loving her parents, her brother. He wasn't sure if she was the fortunate one. Not so long ago he wasn't sure that love was even real. Much had changed.

"Malcolm." She leaned up on one elbow. "You are returning to Camlochlin, are you not?"

"Aye, I am—"

"Hell! There ye both are!" Cailean's voice from far above put an end to the remainder of their conversation.

Malcolm glared at the top of the ridge where his brother appeared and then disappeared. "If he lectures me aboot bein' with ye," he growled, sitting up and stretching, "I'll knock oot his teeth."

"No you won't." Emma smiled, restoring his good mood. "You love him."

"Only when he's unconscious."

He rubbed his arm when she pinched him and tossed her a dark look, which she didn't see and likely would have ignored anyway.

"He's coming," Emma informed him, tilting her head to hear the hoofbeats of Cailean's approaching horse. "How do you think he found us?"

"I dinna' know, but I'm sure Harry sent him to find us. He likely has Gunter searchin' fer us too."

Emma covered her mouth with her hand. "Oh my, I completely forgot about Harry!"

Gascon began barking as Cailean's horse rounded the sheer rock wall separating the cove from the rest of the shore.

Malcolm rose to his feet when his brother came into view in the moonlight. He wasn't alone. Another horse followed behind his. Malcolm squinted, trying to make out who it was. Harry?

No. Sebastian Fletcher.

Malcolm stepped around Emma, blocking her from the handsome young trader from Durham. He wasn't still jealous. He knew Emma was his. He wanted Fletcher to know it too.

"How did ye find us?" he asked his brother.

Cailean dismounted and walked to him. "'Twas his idea to look." He pointed to Fletcher dismounting behind him.

"Miss Grey mentioned that you had taken her here once before. 'Twas one of the best days of her life."

"Mr. Fletcher," Emma said through tight lips behind him. "Do you intend to tell him everything we've ever discussed?"

"No, Miss Grey, only what will benefit you."

"Speakin' of that," Malcolm brought up, turning to his brother, who'd taken a seat in the sand beside Emma. "Were ye in on their 'ruse'?"

"Of course," Cailean admitted effortlessly. "Ye dinna' know a good thing. Ye needed help to open yer eyes."

Malcolm stood there staring at him. At first, he thought to answer the insult, but once he thought about it for longer than a moment, he knew Cailean was right.

"So ye knew where to find us," he said to them. He almost reached out his hand to stop Fletcher from sitting.

He'd come here to be alone with—

Was that cheese and bread, dried meat, and wine Fletcher was unpacking?

"You've been gone all day," the thoughtful trader said from over the flames. "I imagined you were both hungry."

Malcolm rubbed his belly. Aye, he was hungry. He hadn't thought about it until now. He caught the apple Fletcher tossed him and bit into it.

"I was hoping to speak to Miss Grey."

"Speak to her aboot what?" Malcolm asked, sitting on the other side of Emma.

"I don't need Malcolm's permission to speak to you. I am just not certain I want to."

"What did ye do, Fletcher?" Cailean asked, tearing off a chunk of bread.

"He told Malcolm about the plan to make him jealous." Emma advised him, then blushed when she realized she admitted there was a plan after all, making Malcolm smile. He didn't care if she schemed to make him jealous. She cared for him, and for that, he was happy.

"I told him because he seemed very angry with you," Sebastian told her.

"What did ye think I'd do, Fletcher?" Malcolm grumbled while he poured Emma a cup of wine.

"I didn't know what you meant to do after you hoisted her over your shoulder and stormed off."

"I'd never harm her," Malcolm said.

The trader wasn't listening to him but looking at Emma. "I didn't mean to betray your confidence. 'Twas hard for me, but I thought you might be in harm."

Malcolm examined him over the firelight and was thankful Emma couldn't see the smooth-speaking stranger. Shadows etched in obsidian covered his jaw and touched lightly above his upper lip, defining his features in soft brushstrokes. He spoke well and comprehended much for one his age, which appeared to be close to Cailean's. His eyes were as large as a puppy's and fastened on Emma.

"I beg your pardon, Miss Grey." The pup sealed what he was after. Malcolm didn't know whether to punch him in the mouth or applaud his cleverness.

"Of course, Mr. Fletcher," Emma said, granting his

request. "I understand how it looked with me flung over Malcolm's shoulder."

They all laughed, except for Malcolm. He soaked in the sight of her bathed in moonlight and firelight, lost in the sweet wrinkle of her nose, the glorious curl of her lips. He wanted to spend the rest of his life looking at her. Or die now, with her being the last thing he saw.

"I want to bring Alison home to Camlochlin," Cailean told Malcolm while they ate.

"I suspected that," Malcolm replied. He raised his cup. "She's a good lass."

"She's very fortunate."

Malcolm didn't have to be blind to hear the change in Emma's voice when she spoke. She sounded needful, envious. Would she leave Harry and go home with him?

They all spoke of marriage and wounds, which, of the two, Malcolm always thought the latter was preferable.

"What d'ye plan on doin' aboot Harry?" Cailean asked him when supper was over and they sat around the fire for one last cup of wine. "We left him quite angry with ye for takin' Emma oot."

"What is he afraid will happen between you and her?"

Malcolm slid his gaze to Fletcher. "He's afraid I'll break her heart."

"I will speak with him," Emma promised. "He'll listen to me."

"What will ye tell him?"

She took Malcolm's hand and after entwining her fingers with his, she brought them to her lips and kissed them.

"I will tell him that I could never love you enough to let you break my heart." She smiled up at him and brought his fingers to her lips. "I shall lie."

Chapter Twenty-Nine

He's too barbaric for my taste."

"Well, I'm relieved to hear it." Harry nodded and continued eating.

"So stop becoming so anxious when I am with him. Your worries make it seem like you believe I'd let him whisk me off to the ocean and lay waste to my virginity."

Harry nearly choked on his supper, and it would have been a shame too, for Cailean was in the kitchen today and he'd prepared a delicious meal of rich celery soup made with parsnips, wine and nutmeg, fresh brown bread with sweet butter, and savory slices of goose covered in blackberry sauce.

Emma gave him a smack on the back. "Better?"

He nodded, then coughed softly into his hand. "I'd prefer it if you ate upstairs in your room, Emmaline. There are patrons looking at you."

"So, let them look. I don't want to go upstairs," she told him, gathering her strength. "I don't care who looks at me."

"You're odd, Emmaline. Odd to see with those hands

always touching everything. You attract scum. It's not safe for you down here."

She sighed at Harry's caution. Part of her wished she hadn't left France. She was tired of life at Fortune's Smile, tired of needing an escort. She wanted something more.

"She doesn't listen to what I tell her." Her brother turned to Gunter and Brianne sitting next to him at the table. "Sometimes I think she's deaf as well as blind."

"Harry." Malcolm's voice as he approached them was clipped with warning. "Have a care how ye speak to her, old friend."

"Do you threaten me, Malcolm?"

Malcolm shrugged and sat in the chair beside Emma. "If ye wish to take it that way."

"Harry"—Emma slammed her hand on the table, startling him—"that's enough."

"Is it wrong for me to want you to be safe, sister?" he asked her more tenderly. "I just got you back, Emmaline. I don't want to lose you again."

Emma remained quiet, listening to Malcolm's breath, wanting to touch him, take him by the hand and pull him outside...She didn't want to live in obscurity anymore. She wanted to come and go as she pleased. She wanted to know what Malcolm felt for her. Good or bad. She loved him, but he hadn't told her he shared her feelings. Oh, why did she have to fall for a man who believed he was incapable of loving someone?

"I'm thinking of going back to France," she said, more for Malcolm's reaction than for her brother's. "I want to live in a cottage, in the woods, like I used to."

"How will you live?" Harry asked, stunned.

"Why d'ye have to go to France to live in a cottage in

the damn woods?" Malcolm asked her. "What's wrong with England or . . . Scotland?"

"And what do you care either way, Malcolm?" she demanded.

Instead of answering her, he bolted up out of his chair, bent to seize her hand, and then proceeded to drag her out of the brothel.

"Malcolm!" Harry shouted after them. "What do you think you're doing?"

"I wish to have a word with yer sister, Harry," Malcolm called back. "Follow and ye'll insult me and m' clan name."

Clever, Emma thought, to use Harry's self-proclaimed fear to keep him at heel. She didn't ask where they were going when he led her to the stable and his horse. She wasn't angry with him, not truly. One couldn't force another to fall in love. Although he did seem quite bothered by France. She was thrilled. She'd clear everything up with Harry later.

When he was done saddling the beast, he lifted Emma on first, then leaped up behind her and they took off.

Here was what she loved, what she needed. The outdoors, where the air was laced with pine and honeysuckle, amid vast sounds and scents that awakened her senses— sweet, spicy, minty with a hint of dandelion mixed together. Clean, fresh air washed through her lungs, leaving her clothed in an earthy fragrance.

Horses were a bit uncomfortable, even with Malcolm's thighs to cushion her from the saddle. But his arms around her, holding her steady, were worth every aching bounce. Sunlight warmed her skin. Malcolm's arms warmed her bones.

Wherever they were going was fine with her.

They rode for a quarter of an hour without speaking. She didn't mind. The forest was filled with sounds Emma enjoyed and missed. She knew she was doomed to love him forever when he laughed before she did at two larks conversing from the trees. She loved him for listening with her. She loved him for knowing that's what she was doing.

"Emma?"

"*Oui*?" Her heart thumped wildly. Was he going to tell her that he loved her now? She held her breath.

"D'ye truly want to go back to France?"

Of course she didn't want to go back to France. Not unless he was going. She wanted to be with him. "Stop the horse."

He did as she asked and didn't stop her when she slipped from his lap and walked on her own.

"You suggested I stay in England or go to Scotland." She paused, folded her hands across her chest, and tilted her head up to him. "May I ask why you care? Would you visit me?"

He leaped down and blocked her path. "Aye, I'd visit ye. Every night when I came to bed."

"And you think I'd just let you in?" When he stepped closer and closed his arms around her, she knew she would.

He dipped his head to hers and whispered against the seam of her mouth. "Would ye turn me away, then, lass?"

"*Oui, oui*," she insisted weakly as he pressed his mouth to hers. "I would."

He laughed, pulling back for a torturous instant. "Nae ye wouldn't," he teased, angling his head to her again. "Ye'd welcome me into yer arms. Yer bed." He captured her breath in a deep, titillating kiss.

She made a little eager yet contented sound she hardly recognized with her own ears and placed her hands on his hips. His tongue flicked across the darkest recesses of her mouth. He consumed her in his size, dominant, hard, possessive.

She wanted more. She wanted to feel him. All of him. She wanted a really good look at who was about to turn her bones to liquid. She hadn't examined him enough the first time they were intimate. Now she wanted to take her fill.

Her touch was light across the span of his chest, up the dips and curves along the expanse of his shoulders. His muscles trembled under her fingers. She ran her hands down his tight, sinewy arms, back to his hips.

Boldly, she touched the wool of his breeches. She discovered they fit snugly. The wool stretched across the front of him. Her heart pounded in her ears. Her blood burned. Dare she be so bold?

He groaned when she spread her fingers over the hard mound. Goodness, had she truly taken all of him? She closed her fingers and squeezed and kneaded him through the wool. She wanted to bite his neck and blush at the same time.

He claimed her mouth over and over in deep, ruthlessly sensual kisses that drew the breath from her body. He was ready to take her. But she wasn't ready to be taken.

She wanted more.

She broke away from their passionate embrace. "I would," she repeated, breathless but triumphant and turned to go to the other way.

He laughed, scalding her blood. An eagle called out high above the forest canopy and Malcolm moved up behind her, stopping her with one hand curling around her waist and the other scooping her hair from her nape.

"Are ye sure aboot that, Emma?" he groaned against her ear, his erection pushing up against her rump.

Without giving her time to think about her answer, he tilted her head, exposing more of her neck to his hungry mouth, and drove her even madder when he dipped his other hand from her belly to her skirts and began pulling them up.

She had no defense against him. She didn't want any. She wanted him inside her and she told him, begged him.

His hand disappeared under the folds of her skirts and fell to the crux between her legs. She opened wider to his probing fingers and lifted her arms behind her and around his neck.

She didn't know whether to smile with relief or tense up her body in anticipation for the force of his cock when she felt him freeing himself from his confines. Somewhere in the back of her mind, she told herself to demand more, a promise. But when he turned her around to face him and lifted her with one arm, she coiled her legs around his waist and held on.

Malcolm held her up around him, his breath hard against her throat. Perched upon the tip of his cock, her moist heat tempted him to impale her as deeply as he could go. The primal need to satisfy his desire almost overwhelmed him. But he held her up, a hairsbreadth above him and hard enough to hurt.

"Why do you hesitate, Malcolm?" she asked him, touching his face. She sounded disheartened and out of breath.

She wanted him. It meant more than ever before. It meant everything. He looked at her and fit her in the palms of his hands. "Tell me why yer eyes are misty," he commanded gently, brushing her up the length of his shaft. His body shook, along with his heart.

"Emma," he told her. "I've never loved before..."

Her tears fell freely now between them.

"...I dinna' know what ye've done to me, lass. M' whole life I felt...unfinished, empty."

"And now?" she asked, slipping down him.

"I..." He stopped and clenched his jaw to keep from releasing himself when she swallowed up the tip of him in her fiery cavern. "Now." He spread her a little more and pushed, knowing she was still new to this. "Now, I feel filled to bursting."

He stretched her farther and set her down with his hands. She was tight and hot around him. He lifted her up and down, slowly, taking more of her each time. Another thrust and he lifted her completely off and shot his seed over her opening. Wet enough to take him farther, he buried himself in her and tossed back his head with the urge to let loose some victorious roar. He watched her through hooded, passionate eyes as she took him again and again, draining him of his strength and all logic. He pushed her back up against the nearest tree, bent his knees, and drove himself into her until she grew slicker and tighter.

He wanted to tell her what she meant to him. He wanted to promise to be faithful to her till the end of his days. He'd bring her to Camlochlin, if she'd go. Harry could come too. Malcolm didn't care; as long as Emma stayed with him, he'd be happy.

But when he opened his mouth to tell her, only a tight moan escaped him. He thrust harder, faster, making her grunt when she breathed. She reached for his face and spread her fingers over his clenched jaw and beguiling dimple when he smiled at her.

"I didn't know 'twould feel so good," she told him, and then took a succession of short shallow breaths and quaked in his arms. Her body caressed him, lit him on fire. He watched her climax, tightening his grip on her rump and slowing his movements while she came on him. He followed shortly after, filling her with himself while she covered his face with her fingers and watched.

Afterward, they rested for a little while, laying in each other's arms in the grass beneath the trees.

"I like making love to you in the woods," Emma told him softly, finally sitting up.

"Then I shall make certain to bring ye there often when we get home."

Did he...? Did she hear him right...? She turned on her rump and threw herself on him. "Are you asking me to go home with you?"

"Aye." He laughed when she squealed in his ear. Once. Twice. "Will ye come?"

"*Oui*!" She kissed his face over and over. "*Oui*, I will."

※

Chapter Thirty

*B*ess's teeth along his shaft enticed Sebastian to release himself in her hot mouth, but how the hell was he going to get Emma away from Malcolm? He had to bring her to Oliver as ordered or else his brother would come to Hebburn himself and kill anyone who came against him.

Bess's tongue licked its way down his shaft like a velvet flame.

One for the sake of many. And if he found out that the Grants were responsible for Andrew's death, he'd kill them. With his duty to his dead brother done, he'd leave Newcastle and go find his boat.

Why was he thinking of sailing away when a beautiful woman was snuggling deeper between his thighs and sucking him harder? He closed his eyes and groaned with sheer delight. Bess was an experienced whore who knew how to please a man. She was good at it because it pleased her too. He enjoyed her and even paid more for longer hours with her.

She used her tongue to lick and revel in the taste of him, her lips to caress him, and her teeth to drive him to the edge of oblivion. He promised while he pulled her up over his wet cock, straddled her legs around him, and impaled her to the hilt to be a loyal customer, seeking her out first when he visited and wanted a woman who could match his fervor.

She liked hearing that and drove herself up and down on him, tossing back her head, her full, round breasts poised just above his hungry mouth.

He came. Hard and full—then continued, relishing the searing flame of her claws down his back when he flipped her over and took her from on top. The hellcat didn't like his dominant position and gave him some fight, which made him full to bursting once again.

She'd been with many men and didn't peak often. Sebastian was here to change that.

Oliver would have laughed at him and his concerns about a woman's pleasure, but there were many things Oliver didn't know about him. Sebastian liked it that way. It was safer for all concerned.

He dipped his head and drank from her swollen breasts until she bucked like a mare beneath him. He withdrew and reclaimed in long, smooth strides, closing his arms around her waist, his hands over her silky buttocks to drive her to him closer.

"Tell me, Bess, my scintillating seductress, what do you think of Malcolm Grant?"

"He's going to take me with him when he leaves Fortune's Smile."

"Ah, and what will he do with you and Emma both? You don't think he's leaving without her, do you?"

He hated to use Emma in his schemes to get information, but Bess knew things that she didn't tell him because of some fancy that Grant might actually care for her.

"Does your heart still beat for him?"

She opened her sapphire eyes and looked him straight in his. "Who told you that it does?"

"Your eyes told me."

Her luscious mouth hooked into a smile. "Then I'd rather you didn't see my face."

He kissed her mouth dangling below his, then sat up and turned her over on her belly.

He gripped Bess's hips and in one fluid motion he hauled her rump up in the air and sank deep inside her.

"I'll take you with me, Bess," he promised, kissing the back of her neck.

"Who cares about the heart?" She turned to look over her shoulder at him. "It's the body you want to possess, and you, dirty boy, possess mine well."

He wanted to possess every inch of her and make all her fantasies come to life. He moved his fingers over her tight, round arse and smiled behind her while she convulsed around his thickness, at the pinnacle of her pleasure.

Slipping both hands around her, he rose up on his knees, their bodies still attached. She groaned and wilted against him when he ran his fingers across her swollen nub in front of him. He rubbed again while he took her from behind, kneading her between his fingers until her cries grew more urgent.

In the perfect position to whisper in her ear, he told her that he was about to fill her again and asked her if she could take it.

When she began to pant, he laughed, scraped her hair off her nape, and sucked on her neck. He brought her to climax and went there with her, muffling her cries with his hand. When it was over, they rested. For a little while.

• • •

Malcolm woke before the sun rose the next day and went to his window to look out. He knew Emma would be there, traipsing about in the pre-dawn light. He smiled when he saw her, lost to the sublime beauty of her. What had she done to him? How had she done it? Emmaline Grey loved him. She wasn't the first to say it, but she was the one who mattered because Malcolm believed her when she told him. He wanted to be a better man for her, a man like his father. Hell, he wanted to pick flowers for her the way he'd seen his father and his uncles do for the women they loved.

He dressed quickly and left the brothel to begin his task. How does one go about picking flowers? Which flowers would do? He saw something that resembled heather growing along the side of the brothel. When he tried to pull it from the ground, he ended up yanking all the tiny petals off the stem. He tried again, with another stalk. Same result. He looked around and saw another type of pink blossoms, but they were covered in bugs. Next, he found a patch of little yellow flowers with green centers. They weren't as pretty but they seemed sturdy enough when he pulled them from the earth. Hell, he should have paid more attention to the bouquets the men of Camlochlin handed out. Theirs always looked so well thought out; especially the bonny bunches his uncle Jamie picked for his aunt Maggie.

When he gathered enough to make a small bouquet, he set off to find Emma. He walked behind the brothel to the woods and found her asleep in a bed of bluebells. In the pale filtered light, he felt something stir in his chest at the sight of her. He felt a tether to her that they were both different and somehow deficient. But he was wrong. He wasn't deficient and there was nothing lacking about Emma. She was perfect in every way.

He gave Gascon a pat on the head and leaned down next to Emma in her flowery bed. He smoothed a strand of her hair away from her cheek and whispered her name, once, twice.

She smiled and then opened her eyes. "Good morn, Malcolm."

His heart swelled. "Why are ye sleepin' in bluebells, lass?"

She stretched. "Because they smell good."

"Ah, and I thought that allurin' fragrance was ye." He leaned down and kissed her. He loved kissing her. He wanted to kiss her for the rest of his life.

"What's this?"

He looked at her and saw his pathetic bouquet in her fingers. Her free hand explored the surface of the blooms and then each petal and a light touch across the center.

"Dandelions." She smiled and held them up. "From you?"

"Aye, but they're more like weeds compared to what ye found to sleep in. Why are ye smilin' at me like that, Emma?"

"Because they *are* weeds and I think I shall die from how sweet it is."

"Hell," he groaned. "What do I know of flowers? And worse, I've never been called sweet before. I'm not certain I like it."

She laughed and pulled him to her.

They were too close to the brothel to make love in the bluebells so they rose up and went back.

"Malcolm?" Emma said, tugging his sleeve as they strolled back. "Thank you for the flowers."

He smiled. "'Twas nothin' lass. I'll learn how to pick better ones."

"You will?"

Aye she was worth hours, days, learning how to pick delicate heather.

"Aye, lass, what's yer favorite?"

She looked up and smiled, slaying his heart as they entered the brothel. "All of them."

"Malcolm," Harry called out when he saw Malcolm entering the dining hall with his sister. "Your brother wants to take Alison from me. He is costing me much and now, with all the ingredients he uses to cook—"

Malcolm raised his palm to quiet him. Harry was loyal and true but he was also a stingy bastard. He was serious when he complained about losing Alison. Cailean was going to have to replace her before they left. "Aye, Harry, everything will be taken care of, 'tis why we're still here. I know ye seek recompense."

Hell, Malcolm needed to speak with him. Now that Emma had told her brother she didn't love Malcolm, the task of telling him the truth about his feelings for Emma was going to be more difficult. He'd already waited too long, done too much to the lass he'd promised not to touch. Each day it grew more difficult to talk to her brother about her. His feelings for Emma would mean little to Harry, especially when Malcolm wasn't completely sure how deep his feelings were. Of course, Malcolm could, and likely would, remind Harry that he'd abandoned her— while she was going blind! Malcolm didn't give a damn about Harry's need to make things right if it meant staying apart from Emma.

He'd also have to tell him—and Emma—that he'd promised to take Bess away from this life. He wouldn't take her to Camlochlin, but he'd help her start her life somewhere else.

The doors opened, spilling cool, damp air into the brothel. Malcolm continued to eat while watching three men enter the brothel. He didn't recognize any faces from the Winther fight so he stayed in his seat.

"Who is the proprietor here?" one of the men called out.

"I am." Harry rose from his seat and stepped around the table to go to them. "Welcome to Fortune's Smile. What can I do for you?"

"We want some food," one replied.

"And some women," said another.

Harry nodded and pulled out a seat at the nearest table. "As fortune would have it"—he smiled and offered them the seat—"you've come to the right place…Ehm, my good man…" Harry reached out to grab the patron's sleeve when the man started moving toward his sister's table. But he missed.

Malcolm watched his approach, noting the customer's stumbling gait. These men were already drunk and looking for trouble. Malcolm knew their type well. Usually no amount of logic could talk them out of their purpose.

"Who is this pretty little thing?"

Gascon growled and Malcolm stood up. "Cut that curiosity aboot her from ye like 'twas a disease that will kill ye."

At first the patron looked terrified—Malcolm was at least two heads taller—but then his drunkenness took over and he challenged him.

"This is a brothel. That is a whore. If I want to pay for—"

His words were cut off abruptly when Malcolm's fist shot out and cracked the patron's nose in two places. Blood spurted everywhere as the man sank to his knees.

His friends moved instantly, brandishing knives and

promising Malcolm that they'd enjoy cutting him to pieces and feeding him to the rabid mongrel growling beside him. That must have been why the first one to reach the table didn't go for the pistol tucked in his belt.

Malcolm took possession of it a moment later when he snatched the assailant's wrist and twisted his arm back until he heard the break and pulled the pistol from the screaming man's belt.

It was over before anything really began—with Malcolm aiming the pistol at the third man, who surrendered without further ado.

He turned to see Emma, and found her crouching down and running her hands down the man's broken arm.

"I'll fix you something for the pain," she promised the stranger. "And then I'll fix you. But if you or your friends try anything else, I'll let him kill you. Do you understand?"

Malcolm glared at him, proving that she spoke the truth.

"I understand," the man said, sobering quickly.

Malcolm didn't like the fact that she would be tending to these men, but this was who she was, a lass full of compassion and concern—and, he reasoned, she'd likely smash a wooden bowl over his head and kill him dead. It wouldn't be the first time she did it. He never told her that she'd killed a man with Gascon's supper that first night Malcolm had arrived. She didn't need to know. She'd never forgive herself.

He watched her enlist Harry's and Gunter's aid in helping the men sit at the table, and then he turned to the staircase, feeling another set of eyes on him.

Sebastian Fletcher looked like he just stumbled out of bed—which he likely did—and continued down the steps a moment or two after Malcolm met his steady gaze.

"I've seen very few men as quick with their hands as you. I'm quite impressed with your reflexes and skill."

Malcolm shrugged. He knew he was a good fighter. He didn't need flattery.

"Cailean's in the kitchen," he advised, and returned to his food.

"Who were they?" Fletcher asked him, raising his hand to a server.

"Just trouble seekers."

"Seems they found it."

"They usually do."

Fletcher laughed and then beckoned again. "I remember talk of a brawl here a se'nnight or two ago. A Winther was killed, if I'm not mistaken. Were you and Cailean here for that as well?"

Everyone at the table froze.

"Nae," Malcolm told him. "We were no' here."

"Too bad, eh?" Fletcher asked with a wink. "I'm sure you would enjoy smashing a few Winther heads."

"I've never heard of them before this moment."

Fletcher smiled. "Oliver Winther deserves the misfortune that will one day come upon him. Hell, I'm hungry."

Malcolm shook his head. When the hell had he become so suspicious of everyone? Fletcher was as innocent as all the rest of the honor-bound lads he knew.

"Why are you so late to dine?" Emma asked him, reaching into a pocket of her skirts and pulling out two vials.

Forgetting the Winthers, Malcolm watched her slip the herbs into a cup and feed it to the man whose arm he broke. She did it so effortlessly, the patron didn't see; neither did his friend.

"I was occupied." Fletcher told her, winking and doing his best to ignore Malcolm's hard stare.

When Bess appeared on the stairs, looking as unkempt as Fletcher, dressed in her robes, the trader smiled and called to her. "Venus has awakened! Come, goddess, sit with your lover."

Malcolm was stunned to hear Bess giggle. She looked happy, satisfied. She even tossed Emma a brief smile, before her warm gaze fell back to Sebastian.

"I'd rather be—"

He kissed her and withdrew smiling. "Say good morn to Malcolm."

"Good morn, Malcolm," she drawled, and reclined in her seat without so much as a glance in Malcolm's direction.

Impressed with the man sitting next to him, Malcolm winked at Fletcher and patted him on the back. "Ye've won her."

Sebastian turned his smile on Bess and lifted his cup. "She's won me."

Chapter Thirty-One

*E*mma continued wrapping the patron's broken arm, with one ear on the customer and the other on Malcolm and Sebastian laughing together at the other end of the table. She knew they'd end up becoming friends. She was glad. She liked Sebastian and his honesty.

The wounded man was beginning to doze off, thanks to her herbs. They'd have to sit him in a chair with arms once he fell asleep or he'd end up sprawled out on the floor. There was nothing she could do for the man with the broken nose except slow the bleeding. If his nose was straight before, it wasn't going to be in the future.

She wasn't angry with Malcolm for hurting them. He was protecting her and she liked it. There was a sort of freedom and comfort in knowing that she was safe, away from the brothel.

"This is precisely why you don't belong down here in the middle of my business. It's too dangerous for you."

"Aye," Malcolm joined in, "'tis. That's why I want to bring her home with me, Harry."

"No!" Harry smashed his cup down on the table so

firmly it bounced off and hit the floor hard. It had its desired effect though; all attention fell on him. "She cannot go with you!"

"Harry," Malcolm said, sounding repentant. Emma was certain he hadn't wanted her brother to find out like this. "I wanted to speak—"

"I asked you to forget her, Malcolm," Harry cut him off. "You assured me ... I trusted you."

"I know," he said gently, "but I fear I can never forget her."

"No!" Harry shouted. "You cannot take her to Skye! I forbid it!" He went to Emma and took her by the hand. "He'll get you killed, and even if he doesn't, we likely would never see each other again."

She'd just found him. Did she want to give her brother up so quickly? No. But she wasn't sure she could survive another day if Malcolm left.

"He won't get me killed, brother. He's kept me safe from harm, and Gascon too since the first night he came here. He's not the snake you think he is. He may have been before but not now."

Harry laughed. "That's what you all want to tell yourselves about a handsome man who doesn't give a damn about any skirt he's ever sampled."

"Harry." Malcolm left his place near Sebastian and Bess and came forward.

"His appearance means nothing to me, Harry," Emma told him. A slight tremble in her voice proved she wasn't feeling as confident as she tried to sound. "He will be loyal to me."

"No one could change him but you, is that right, sister?"

"That's correct, Harry," Malcolm answered in her place. "No one but her."

"I want you to leave, Malcolm," his old friend demanded.

"No, Harry!" Emma insisted.

"I'll be takin' her when I go," Malcolm informed him. "Let's go talk about it, aye? We can work oot yer concerns."

"I should have refused to serve you that first night, after your brother picked a fight with Andrew Winther."

"Harry," Malcolm tried again. "Let's go talk aboot it. Hear what I would say."

"I don't want to hear anything. Not now." Harry pushed her hands away when Emma reached for him. He stormed away, out of the brothel.

"We need to get this man into a sturdier chair," Alison said, breaking everyone's silence. "He can barely keep up his head."

Emma agreed and followed Malcolm silently while he dragged his victim, not too gently, to a different table and a heavier chair.

"Are you certain about this?"

"He willna' fall, lass."

"I mean about taking me to Camlochlin? I don't want you to lose your friend, and am I correct? Will you be loyal to me?"

He took her in his arms and pressed her to him right there in the dining hall. "Aye, I'm sure. Ye captured m' heart, ye and no one else. There will never be anyone but ye."

She sighed dreamily and traced his smile with her fingertips. What would he do once he got her to Camlochlin? Would he make her his wife? He loved her, didn't he? He told her he'd never loved before. Now he told her she had his heart. He hadn't told her outright that he loves her, but she assumed...

"And you," she said, reaching her fingers to his face, "you have captured my heart, as well. Ye and no one else,

Malcolm. There will never be anyone but you for me. The gossip about you was false. Truly, you're not that bad."

He threw back his head and laughed and she lavished in the sound of it, the feel of his wide, open smile and deep, beguiling dimples against her fingertips. Emma wasn't sure why Malcolm had chosen her, but he had and she was happy. Really, finally, happy. Soon though, her smile faded. What would they do about Harry?

"I'll speak to him," Malcolm assured her when she asked him. He set her arm into the crook of his elbow and walked her back toward their table. "He can visit whenever he wants. He'll always be welcome."

Emma would thank him for his generosity later tonight. She let him go, knowing that if she didn't and she had to breathe in his virile scent one more instant, she might pull him away now.

"When are we leaving?" she whispered to Malcolm as they reached the table.

"As soon as ye wish."

"Speak to Harry first, and I shall also. I don't want to leave him with bad feelings between us."

"Emma," he said as he stopped her. "Bess is comin'."

She laughed. Was he mad? "Bess?"

"Aye," he insisted steadily. "I promised I'd help her in exchange fer helpin' me keep Alison from the Winthers."

"Of course," she said softly. She wouldn't ask him to go back on his word, but she wouldn't hesitate to beg him to drop Bess off at the next town, if she had to.

She left him with a short, no less hot, kiss to get ready for her journey with Alison on her arm.

Malcolm stepped outside, unsheathed his sword, and swung. Hell, he needed practice. He turned and was surprised to see Sebastian standing close, watching him. His eyes were too dark, too deep to ignore. He was angry. In fact, he stared at Malcolm like he wanted to kill him.

"Where is home exactly?" Fletcher asked. "You said you came from Perth but Grey mentioned Skye. Which is it?"

Malcolm eyed him. Why was this important suddenly? "D'ye care fer her then?"

"Who?"

"Emma?"

Fletcher smiled and Malcolm wondered how he managed to look so wide-eyed and innocent one moment and as dark as a wraith the next.

"What do your untruths have to do with Emma?" he asked.

"What untruths?" Malcolm asked him, and then held up his hand. "I have to go find Harry first. We'll talk later."

He found his old friend in the parlor sipping brandy with Bess. When Harry saw him, he turned away. Bess rose to leave, apparently knowing what happened and giving them privacy to speak together.

Or at least for Harry to do all the talking. Malcolm sat down and took every insult Harry slung at him. They were true. He *was* a wolf that cared only for his own survival, a serpent, a heretic preying on the unsuspecting. He didn't know how many lasses he'd left brokenhearted over him. Harry was right; he hadn't cared.

He didn't try to tell Harry that his skirt-chasing days had come to an end years ago. Or that Emma was his reward for giving up his selfish lifestyle. Harry didn't see the inner strength or outer glory of his sister—who was a stranger to him. He wouldn't understand why Malcolm was willing to give up his heart for her.

"Regardless of what ye think of me," he told Harry after a while, "she doesna' belong in a brothel."

"Is that it?" Harry mocked. "Very well then, you have my guarantee that she won't remain in one."

"What will ye do, Harry, buy her a house? And what happens when she wants to leave it?" Malcolm challenged. "To go fer a walk with her dog?"

"She is blind!" Harry shouted at him. "She could walk off a cliff!"

Malcolm shook his head at him. He truly didn't know his sister.

"She's coming with me."

"Why? Why her?" Harry pleaded. "Is this your way of repaying her for saving your life? Is it guilt that because of you, she must live in fear of the Winthers?"

But she wasn't afraid.

Malcolm rose. Speaking to him now was a waste of time. Harry was understandably angry. "Ye can visit her whenever ye wish. The door will always be open to ye."

"And how will I get there, Malcolm?" Harry shouted again, furious. "Who will watch over the girls? You're a selfish bastard and you will never change! You'll take her away and then leave her where you set her, in the middle of people she doesn't know, who will be afraid of her disease and banish her to live in a cave, branded a witch."

"Ye describe yerself well, Harry. Is that no' almost exactly what ye did to her as a child? Ye dinna' know her."

"And she doesn't know me. Now get out."

Sebastian left his bed. He didn't wake Bess. It was still daylight. There was still time to kill his enemies. He dressed, slipping two daggers in his boots and a set of pistols in his belt. When he tried to talk to Malcolm, the

Highlander hadn't realized what Harry Grey had said while they were fighting.

He looked at the beautiful blonde asleep in his bed. He'd done much to her for the information she gave him. He already knew that she was working with someone else in the brothel for his brother, Oliver.

Working for Oliver. Damn it to hell, Sebastian thought. He liked Bess. He thought they had something genuine.

Harry had said the Grants picked a fight with Andrew. It was them. They lied about being here, about living in Perth, about everything.

After another night of making Bess reach her climax, she told him that Malcolm and Cailean Grant had fought the Winthers in the brawl that cost Andrew his life. Gunter had been protecting Emma, so he wasn't there. The Grants were the only two Highlanders who fought and the only two capable of killing so many men against the two of them.

Oh, Sebastian agreed. He'd seen Malcolm subdue three drunken troublemakers in the space of a few breaths. He was skilled and so most likely, was his brother.

According to Bess, they were kin to the MacGregors. That explained why no one talked when John had come. Sebastian had heard of the outlawed clan. They had a violent history, and a reputation for taking on an entire generation before giving up their revenge.

Sebastian hated having to cross them and bring them down on the Winthers, but they killed Andrew. They had to pay. Didn't they? And Oliver didn't really give a damn. He just wanted Emma.

He didn't find Cailean in the kitchen as he'd hoped. Slicing his throat wouldn't alert anyone and he still could have possibly taken Malcolm by surprise. Did he truly want to do this after what happened in Dunston?

"Looking for scones again?"

He spun around and felt his heart falter at the sight of Emma. Gascon's incessant barking from the other side of the door would alert the dead.

"Better let him in."

She turned from him and held out a hand in front of her while she went to the door.

"Are you feeling better?"

He didn't know if she was speaking to him or the dog.

"Alison said you looked pale earlier."

He shook his head. He didn't want to tell her who he was. He wasn't prepared for the shock of *that* revelation. Her friends killed Andrew and yet Oliver wanted her. Sebastian wouldn't bring her. He didn't want Emma to know he was the brother of a monster. She'd know if Oliver ever got his hands on her.

"I'm well. Where are Malcolm and Cailean?"

"Outside."

When he moved to pass her and leave the brothel, she stepped in front of him, almost onto his boots.

"Sebastian," she said, her lovely face tilted up at him. "Tell me we will always be friends."

"Always."

She crinkled her nose and threw her arms around him. "You are one of my very first friends." She stood on her toes to whisper in his ear.

Someone opened the door and stood in the doorway, blocking the light.

"There ye are," Malcolm called out. "I was lookin' fer ye earlier."

Sebastian wanted to pull out his pistol and aim it at him. It wasn't because Andrew was his favored brother. Sebastian didn't have a favorite. They were all selfish, prideful fools and one was already dead before the age of thirty years. But Andrew was his brother and his death would be avenged.

There might be hordes of Winthers in Newcastle, but when their mother died and their father left them shortly after that, no one came to the aid but the people of Dunston. They took the three brothers in and tried to raise them. Oliver wouldn't "be raised with the savages" and got them away quickly. Oliver taught them that all they had was each other. And as terrible as his brothers could be, he still lived by that code.

Would he shoot Andrew's killer right here in front of Emma? What if it was Cailean? It didn't matter. If Sebastian killed one, he'd have to kill them both if he wanted to get out of here alive.

"I was with Bess." His voice sounded empty and thick and he wondered if it would give him away.

"Well," Grant said, leaving the entrance and moving toward him. "I found myself concerned aboot ye."

Sebastian laughed. "About me? Why?" Grant should be concerned for himself.

"I'll be outside," Emma said, excusing herself quietly. "Come, Gascon."

Sebastian watched her leave and thought about the fastest way to kill Malcolm. Emma would hate him for doing it. He might even hate himself some afterward. You weren't supposed to like the man who killed your brother.

"Ye seemed verra' upset yesterday. I know there was something on yer mind and we didna' get to talk aboot it. Mayhap we can speak of it now."

"Now?"

"Aye. I want ye to trust me."

"After all the lying?"

"What have I lied aboot?"

"You pretended ignorance about the brawl. You were here for it. Harry admitted it. Bess told me things too. You and Cailean were injured and recovered here."

"That's right," Grant confirmed. "I lied because we suspected the Winthers would return yet again and Harry didn't want them knowing he'd lied to them. So we told no one."

"Emma thinks you can keep her safe, but how can you do that when you are the one who killed a Winther? Have you never heard of the Winthers? They won't let you live."

"They think I'm dead."

Sebastian should have shot him. Oliver would do it. He'd kill Harry too and Cailean, and possibly Alison. They'd all lied and conspired to save Malcolm and Cailean. Emma had lied too.

"I know I put Harry and Emma in danger, but there was no other option that night."

"What happened?" Sebastian asked. He wanted to know how his brother died and why.

"Andrew manhandled Alison. He and Cailean fought."

"How did he manhandle her?"

"He flung her over a table."

Hell, Sebastian thought, that sounded like something Andrew would do.

"It wasn't enough to lose the fight, Andrew returned later that night with more men. He meant to kill us, so I killed him first."

"How?"

"I shot him." Grant stopped and studied him with narrowed eyes. "Why all this interest in Andrew Winther?"

Grant was lying again. They'd recovered Andrew's body. He wasn't shot. No one knew what killed Andrew but him, Oliver, and Andrew's killer. Was Grant protecting his brother? Had Cailean killed Andrew for mistreating Alison?

Sebastian wanted the truth and he wouldn't get it by killing Grant. Why the hell did Andrew—and Oliver—have to be so damn violent all the time? If they were any other men, Sebastian would have killed him himself. "My interest is because I've come to like you, Grant. I fear what the Winthers will do if they find out you live."

"How will they find out?"

Sebastian shrugged. Malcolm was an untrusting soul. The slightest thing could make him suspect Sebastian. Right now, Sebastian had the upper hand. He didn't want to lose it. He wanted more information before he made decisions. He wanted to know more about Malcolm Grant and he wanted the truth about Andrew's death. First, he wanted a cup of wine.

"Tell me there is wine outside with Emma. I'm in need of a cup."

They went outside and met with Emma, Cailean, and the others. Sebastian accepted a cup of wine from Cailean. The youngest Grant reminded Sebastian of himself. Measured up against their brothers, theirs were the more considerate hearts.

He cared for Oliver, probably less than Cailean cared for Malcolm, but there were times when he just wanted to take his brother down. He couldn't disguise the defiance in his gaze, his tone. Oliver knew it; that was why he sent Sebastian to Dunston. He thought that if Sebastian killed a few dozen people, he wouldn't be so eager to fight his dense older brother. Oliver was wrong—about many things.

He sat in the grass with them, between Gascon and Cailean.

"When are you leaving?" he asked Malcolm when the Highlander sat beside Emma.

"As soon as Harry understands that I must go," Emma answered for him. "I don't want to fight with him."

"Of course not," Sebastian agreed. "He's fortunate to have such a considerate sister."

She dipped her chin in modesty and smiled.

She was pretty; the more he looked at her with her long golden tresses, wide haunting eyes, and just a tint of blush across her nose, the more becoming she grew. She was no dormouse though. Oliver was going to like her. He wouldn't care that she'd lied to protect her lover.

"Do you have a sister, Mr. Fletcher?" Alison asked him.

He smiled at her. "A brother. I had two, but one was killed."

They all offered their condolences, which he accepted with a nod.

Malcolm stretched his arm out and gave him a pat on the back. "I almost lost Cailean recently. I canna' fathom the pain of losing a brother."

"Aye," said Cailean. "Ye shoulda' told us sooner. We would have lent an ear if ye needed it."

Damn it. Sebastian liked the Grants. He didn't want to kill them. He thought of Dunston and Oliver and sighed.

Chapter Thirty-Two

$\mathcal{E}$mma left her room with Gascon at her side, her fingers buried in his fur. It was a new day, a new chance to change Harry's mind. If he didn't give his blessing soon, she would have to leave without it. She was optimistic though. Harry loved her. He wanted the best for her. And the best was Malcolm.

She smiled, heading for the stairs, thinking about how Malcolm left her at her door last night, jaw clenched, his slow, languid tone proof of his desire for her. He hadn't wanted to leave her, but he didn't want to take her right under her brother's nose. But soon, he promised, soon they'd be away from here.

Damn it. She loved chivalry. She was the one who had complained to him that he ignored such values, and now that he was trying to prove to her that they mattered to him, she wished they didn't. Just for now. Just while he kissed her and claimed her.

He wasn't in front of her door this morning. Good thing too because if he spilled into her room again, she would have locked the door and kept him in there.

"How long do you think he'll stay with you?"

Emma stopped and tilted her chin in Bess's direction. "None of us knows the future, Bess."

"You're very innocent, are you not?" Bess moved closer to her and circled her like a cat. "It must be pleasant to be a fool enough to ignore everything he is and still blindly trust him."

"You seem to have been at it longer than I have, Bess. Why don't you tell me?"

She could feel Bess's anger infusing the air. She stepped away from the stairs. "Why can't you just be happy with Sebastian? I understand from Mary and the others that he's quite striking and he seems to—"

"Leave Sebastian out of this!" She grew angry immediately and then sneered again. "He is going to take care of everything," Bess told her, ignoring Gascon's low growl. "Malcolm promised to take me away but then he fell for you. I'm not a fool like you, Emma. I know he won't keep his word. But Sebastian will. He's leaving soon and he's taking me with him. He won't drop me at the next brothel. He'll keep me with him and . . ."

"That's wonderful, Bess. I hope you're both happy together. If you'll excuse me."

Without waiting for Bess's reply, Emma clasped Gascon's fur and turned for the stairs. She turned around and glared in Bess's direction one last time, just to let her know that if Bess had any intention of pushing her down, Emma was ready and would retaliate. She was blind, but she was no mouse.

"Come, Gascon." When she reached the bottom landing, she gave the air a slight sniff and then smiled.

"How long have you been there, Malcolm—and you too, Sebastian?"

"Long enough.' Malcolm pushed off the old wooden banister and moved closer to her.

"We heard everything," Sebastian told her. "Don't spare it another thought. I'll take care of things with Bess."

"M' cousin Kyle wouldna' like yer keen senses of hearin' and smellin'" Malcolm told her. "He likes sneakin' up on folks."

"Isn't he the one who sails the seas with your sister, Caitrina, and her husband, the pirate?" she asked, curling her arm around his elbow.

"Your cousin is a pirate?" Distracted by the topic, Sebastian forgot about Bess and hurried after Malcolm.

"Aye, he has become a pirate, along with m' sister."

Sebastian sounded rather dumbfounded for the first time since Emma met him.

"With a ship?"

Malcolm smiled. "Aye, pirates live on them."

"I know. I've always wanted... Why didn't you tell me? What kind of ship do they sail? Schooner, sloop?"

"Brig," Malcolm told him, and then laughed.

Emma guessed Sebastian had a pleasant reaction to that bit of news. She was glad. He seemed so sullen since yesterday.

"A brig. Hell, I'd like to see it."

"Mayhap, I can arrange it next time Captain Kidd drops anchor in Scotland. I'll check with Cailean but I believe they'll be returnin' from the West Indies next month. If ye're free, come to Skye. Leave a message with the ferryman in Kylerhea and he'll get the message to me. I'll come get ye."

"Tell me where to find you and I'll save you the journey."

"Nae," Malcolm told him, growing only slightly more serious. "Ye'll either be shot with arrows or cannons before ye reach me. If no' that than the landscape will kill ye."

"How will I fare against the landscape?" Emma asked with a hint of worry in her voice.

"I'll be with ye, lass. Ye'll do fine." Malcolm closed his arm around her, filling her senses with sheer, rock-hard strength, the off-timing of his breath when he touched her, and the subtle fragrance of the sea. Was he at the coast while she slept? She wanted to go there, to be alone with him.

"Do you think this Captain Kidd would let me sail with him?" Sebastian asked, pulling her attention back to him.

"I'll do m' best to get ye aboard," Malcolm promised. Then, perhaps sensing her eagerness to be alone with him, he clapped Sebastian on the back. "We'll talk more aboot it later, aye?"

They parted ways with Emma thinking how fortunate she was to be leaving the brothel, even if it meant leaving Harry.

"Should we find Harry first?" she asked on their way toward the front door.

"Nae," he whispered close to her ear. "He isn't goin' anywhere. Let's go swimmin'."

It was easy to forget her brother, the brothel, or anything else when she was in Malcolm's arms. And in the sea. Was this real? Could she have truly won the heart of this man, whom her mother would have agreed was doing his best to step from the pages of her books? Not a knight, but a treacherous rogue, whom no heart should trust. But that wasn't Malcolm Grant anymore.

She didn't care if she was a fool like Bess said. She had tried, but how could she not fall in love with a man who brought the light back to her life?

The water was cold and a bit choppy but he kept her warm, pressed close to his body. They laughed together in the waves while Gascon barked at them from the shore.

"What's Camlochlin like?" she asked against his neck, then gave him gentle kisses where her breath lingered.

She felt him getting harder, despite the cold. It made her blood burn. She wanted him inside her, the ultimate, most intimate touch. Buoyant, she pressed in close and rubbed her body against him like a lusty siren. She gasped a tight little gasp when his hands closed tight around her buttocks.

"'Tis beautiful." His heart raced against her and his pitch was low, almost pained. It made her smile that she could do this to him. He continued, kissing her wet lips, taking her mouth like a hungry lion until he broke free and burned a path of kisses down her throat. "The kind of beauty that makes a man forget his own existence..." He lifted her easily in the waves and suckled at each of her breasts poised above him like delectable berries offered for his pleasure. "...and makes him want to become a part of what he sees instead." He pulled her legs around his waist and lowered her onto his erection.

The water took away her slickness so it took a bit of coaxing to let him inside. Like gyrating on his tip, and hearing him swear in his deep, guttural voice. His hands on her thrilled her and when he covered her buttocks and began to guide her movements, she received him, his full length making her writhe with ecstasy in his embrace. The more he retreated and entered again, the slicker she became. But there was still enough resistance to drive her mad with desire. She slowed to keep from erupting and keeping him from doing to the same.

It made him more wild for her. When he squeezed her rump, she squeezed him back, taking every inch, dragging groans from his tight, trembling body. She took her pleasure in his big, hard, willing body and pulled every drop of passion from them both.

Chapter Thirty-Three

I'll never give my blessing to this," Harry promised Malcolm, then turned to glare at Emma. "How could you let this rake convince you to go with him?"

"He has changed, Harry!" Emma argued with him. This was her last chance to speak to him. Malcolm wanted to leave tonight. She didn't want to leave the brother she'd just found knowing he hated her now. "Harry, I—"

"I don't want to hear anything else!" He cut her off, but she wouldn't have it.

"You will hear me, Harry!" she shouted back. He paused for a moment, but that was all she needed. "You left me when I was ten years old; our parents had just died and I was losing my sight! You left me and didn't come back! I forgave you, Harry. All these years, I forgave you. I also survived just fine on my own without you. After they murdered Clementine I left France and came looking for you, but this isn't the life for me, Harry. I thought I could pretend to make you happy that I was here, but I cannot. I want to go with Malcolm. I *am* going. Please, don't let there be bad blood between us."

Her brother went to her and took her face in his hands. "Oh, Emmaline, don't you understand? I cannot let you go? I need you."

Poor Harry. She was grateful to Malcolm for staying quiet and letting her handle it.

"I do love you, brother, but I'm going with Malcolm." When he finally gave in, Emma could feel his nod; she leaped into his arms and hugged him. She had it! She had his blessing to leave. It was a bittersweet moment for her.

"All I ask, Emmaline, is another day or two. Just stay with me another day or two, I beg you."

She went to Malcolm and sensed his nod and smile as he caught her up in his arms.

When Harry asked her for a few moments alone with Malcolm, she happily agreed and ran off with Alison to pack.

She didn't have much: a few gowns, mostly her medicines and jars. She wanted to bring it all. She was happy Alison was coming too. They were friends. Dear God, was this truly happening? Was she leaving Harry and the brothel? Was she really going to hop on a horse with a Highlander and let him bring her to his home in the mountains? She had to be mad, but she couldn't stop smiling!

It didn't take her long to finish packing. She left her room with Gascon in search of Malcolm and found him preparing to go find a replacement for Alison—Sebastian would now be responsible for finding a replacement for Bess. Malcolm would ride to The Thieving Prince at the southern tip of Hebburn and be back in a few hours. Cailean wanted to go with him, but Malcolm refused. He'd get back sooner if he was alone. Cailean agreed to stay at Fortune's Smile and cook a feast.

Emma agreed to it all. She would have agreed with anything.

She stayed with Harry in the parlor. Cailean, Sebastian, and the girls joined them for a bit. Bess sat with them but remained silent and close to Sebastian.

"Ye know, Harry," Cailean said, "ye're always welcome to come to Camlochlin. We'll find a place fer ye there."

"You think I'd be able to find your home when armies have failed?"

Emma thought of Camlochlin, a sanctuary cloaked in obscurity, strewn across the clouds. A home for many, a life source for a few. How would her mind's eye see it? Beautiful, but cold? Or brutally isolated at the edge of the world where even armies cannot find you, and warm?

Like Malcolm had done earlier, Cailean told him how to reach Skye and about leaving a message for the MacGregors with the ferryman in Kylerhea.

"We'll come get ye," Cailean promised him, making her love Malcolm's younger brother all the more.

"You'll come when you're ready, Harry." Emma reached for her brother's hand. "We don't have to remain apart. We can catch up on all the years we've missed together. You'll come."

"Perhaps," he said, smiling a bit stiffly. "I will, when I'm—"

Gascon got up and went to the front door, growling on the way. Emma sat up straighter in her chair at the sound of horses in the front of the brothel. Sebastian leaped from his chair and ran to the window. When he turned back to Emma and the rest, his voice was almost unrecognizable.

"Cailean! If you want to live, hide!" Sebastian shouted.

Cailean stood up. "What's going on?"

"Hide now and don't show yourself!" Sebastian warned urgently. "Oliver Winther is here, about to enter this place. With him is his commander John Burroughs, who saw you the night Andrew was killed! Go!"

Cailean stood there for a moment, stunned and confused. "How d'ye know all this?"

Emma listened, heart pounding, to Alison begging him to go and his refusal unless she and Emma came with him.

"No." Sebastian rushed toward them. "He knows Emma's here. He'll demand to see her and kill anyone who stands in his way."

"Sebastian!" Emma exclaimed. "What's going on and how do you know the baron and his commander? And why the hell does he want me?"

"Emma, please trust me," Sebastian told her. "Cailean," he said, turning back to him, "if you don't run, you'll die the instant John identifies you. Please. Go. I will explain everything later."

Emma heard Cailean curse as he pulled Alison away. "I'll be close by, Emma," he promised, and then was gone.

She was afraid, but she turned to Sebastian and squared her shoulders. "How do you know what the Baron of Newcastle knows?"

"He's my brother."

Emma's heart resonated in her breast. She took a step back and almost stepped on Gascon's paw. "You're a Winther?"

"Emma..." he said, but nothing else. What more could he possibly say?

"You lied to me," she accused very softly. Too softly for most to hear.

Sebastian heard her. "I'm sorry."

How could he do this? How could he bring his brother here? Her throat stung and her eyes burned. She'd liked Sebastian. She'd credited him with being raw and genuine.

"Why does he know about me?" she demanded.

"Be meek, Emma," he warned hastily. "He doesn't like it. Weep and he will not give you attention."

Weep. Over him? Was he mad? She wanted to tell him to go to hell, but when she heard the voice that chilled her blood coming from the opened doorway, she reconsidered.

"Well." He jeered. "Isn't this cozy?"

If Sebastian Fletcher was really Sebastian Winther, then he likely knew what he was talking about. If she had to be meek to live through this visit, she would be. She knew how to stay in the shadow even in plain sight.

Gascon's low growl caught the baron's attention.

"Kill that mongrel," he ordered, sweeping inside the brothel like a plague. More men followed him in.

All fear and willingness to submit vanished, leaving Emma with rage. Did he just order someone to kill Gascon? She stepped in front of her dog, blocking him from another man who'd taken the order. "Touch him," she warned through clenched teeth, "and I'll feed your blood with my foulest poison. You'll be dead before the night is over and your death will be most unpleasant."

"Step away from her, John," the man, whom she assumed was Oliver Winther, drawled in a deep, dangerous tone and moved closer to her. "It's clear she terrifies you. Slightly understandable since she poisoned you once already, proving she's capable."

She'd poisoned him before. Ah, *oui*, John, one of her

kidnappers. It seemed he'd escaped Malcolm with his life that night.

Gascon whined and sat on his haunches, eager to do more but obedient to Emma's touch.

"Oliver Winther, my dear." He took her hand and brought her knuckles to his lips for a kiss. "Baron of—"

"I know who you are. Stay away from my dog."

She knew he bent in front of her to look into her eyes by the way his breath now touched her face. It wasn't altogether unpleasant but sweet, with a hint of mint from a leaf he likely had been chewing sometime earlier.

"And if I don't stay away from your dog?"

She could hear the indulgence in his voice. He was mocking her. She should be afraid but she was too busy wanting to scratch out his eyes.

"Do you think I cannot inflict harm on you, my lord?" she asked him in her most innocent voice.

"What harm could a delightful wisp of a woman inflict on me?"

And the rumors about his arrogance were true.

"I could have laced my knuckles with a berry taken from the Nightshade plant. Are you familiar with it?" she asked him. "'Tis poisonous. Or perhaps I prefer arsenic. 'Tis used to treat syphilis and some other conditions, but I know a perfect mixture that will eat away at a pair of lips quicker than fire melts butter."

He remained quiet for so long, she began to grow fearful again. What if her boldness got her killed, or worse, got Gascon or Harry killed? He seemed to be waiting for a reaction to any kind of poison. When it didn't come, he laughed, and quite loudly too. It was a merciless sound but it brought Mary rushing to his side next.

"May the Lord have mercy on me here and now," Mary

fawned, reaching the baron's side. She sounded breathless and mystified. "What brought you in here, honey? You look like you fell from a bolt of lightning."

"I didn't fall, my dear," the arrogant baron replied. "I jumped and captured the bolt and keep it here."

"Oh my!" Mary giggled and Emma rolled her eyes.

"Miss Grey," the baron called out, catching her disgust. "You're a fire cat all neatly stacked in that fine, lithe body."

"Oliver," Sebastian interrupted. "I wish to have a word with you."

The baron let go of Mary and looked at his brother. "Now?"

"Yes."

"If it's about her, no."

Emma's heart thumped hard in her chest, but she managed not to sound too anxious when she spoke. "What do you want with me?"

"Everything," the baron told her. "I want everything, beginning with you."

"Oliver," Sebastian warned in a low, threatening voice. "Leave her out of this."

Emma listened to him. He didn't sound like the Sebastian she knew and liked. He sounded detached and void of anything but anger toward the man he faced. She remembered his warning to her about being meek and weepy. The baron didn't like it.

"You care for her, is that it, Bastian? That's why you didn't bring her to me."

"Am I hearing this right?" The female equivalent of the baron's frigid indifference sounded in Emma's ears.

Bess.

"Tell him you don't care for her," she told her favored lover.

"Bastian, who is this whore, and why does she tell you what to say to me?"

Bess stepped forward despite Sebastian's low spoken warning to return to him. "My lord." She ran her hand down his arm and practically purred against him. "I've been a valuable help to your brother."

"Is that so?"

"Yes, and I can be an even bigger help to you."

They both laughed and Emma angled her head toward Sebastian. It had to be difficult for him to watch Bess flirt with his own brother.

"Sebastian," Bess said, "tell him about Malcolm Grant."

Emma had had enough of this and made a sound much like a snort. It drew the baron's attention.

"Do you know a Malcolm Grant, Miss Grey?"

She breathed. At her sides, hidden in the folds of her skirts, her fingers trembled. Saying no was the obvious answer. She had a feeling the baron was expecting the obvious. "*Oui*, I do know him. He's a frequent patron here who thinks he fancies me but is only curious about bedding a blind girl."

"He killed Andrew Winther," Bess told the baron next.

Emma laughed. "That's absurd; Grant is never sober. He couldn't shoot the trunk of a tree if he was sitting under it. This is absurd. Bess will say anything to find favor with a man and procure for herself a new and better life than the one at Fortune's Smile. I wouldn't trust her '*help*' were I you. Tell him, Harry." Her brother had remained ominously quiet since the baron arrived. He remained so now.

She could almost hear the baron thinking over what she just said. Finally, he spoke. "Sebastian, is this true?"

Nothing for a moment or two, then, "Yes, 'tis true."

Emma was surprised and relieved that he lied for her.

Bess spat an oath at him. Sebastian's brother made a low sound in his throat.

"Bastian," he snarled, "twice she told you what to say to me and now she curses you and you do nothing. How many times did you take her to your bed?"

"Oliver. Cease this."

"You care for her." Oliver Winther laughed, a vacant sound void of mirth or mercy. "When will your heart stop bleeding for these needy bitches, brother?"

Emma heard the sound of a dagger leaving its sheath. She knew immediately what was happening. And it was her fault! "No!" she cried out as the baron jammed the blade deep into Bess.

Sebastian's shout boomed through the halls and Emma's head, almost bringing her to her knees.

Finally Bess's body hit the ground. She was dead.

"How the hell could you trust a whore, Bastian?" he said to Sebastian while his younger brother knelt over Bess's body. "And what's more, to think that I'd trust her as well. One day you will learn."

Chapter Thirty-Four

Cailean watched the new guests of Fortune's Smile from the shadows. So, this was Oliver Winther, the man Harry was so terrified of. It explained why Grey hid in the shadows now. Cailean had to admit: the baron bore resemblance to something unholy. He was tall and broad shouldered, with long elegant limbs and a slow, determined gait. He wore a coat, fashioned masterfully in animal hide, the hem reaching his dusty boots, the collar lined with ermine and stiff about his shoulders and neck. His hair was shaved close to his scalp, like pale gold dust. Pale, pitiless eyes surveyed the dining hall and the entryway to the parlor, his mouth curved into a sinuous smirk mostly aimed at Emma.

Twice Cailean moved to go to them but Alison pulled him back. John Burroughs would identify him. So what? He could take them all on. He shouldn't be hiding in the shadows like some frightened lad.

His eyes flicked to Fletcher. What the hell was he doing with the Baron of Newcastle? Cailean would find out, and then kill him.

How was he going to warn Malcolm?

Mary joined them and Newcastle laughed like a self-made god chuckling at the mere humans around him.

While Narcissus gloated in himself, Cailean looked to Emma. Och, how his feet ached to go to her, for his brother's sake and for his good, and for his own, as well.

He owed Emma much. So did Malcolm and their kin when they saw the happy man Malcolm had finally become. If the baron meant to stop any of that, Cailean would kill him. He wouldn't hide in the damn corners!

"Cailean, please, my beloved." Alison clung to him when the tension in his muscles was about to burst. "Please don't go," she cried softly. "Don't leave me in this world without you."

He remembered the first night he saw her bathed in russet firelight. A flame brushing across him and stirring emotions he hadn't thought capable of feeling again. Emma may have saved his life, but Alison brought him back from the dead. "I willna' go, lass. Dinna' cry. I willna' leave ye."

He kissed her head and watched Bess step up to the baron. Did he just hear someone say brother? Was Bess telling him about Malcolm? When he heard her tell Winther that Malcolm killed Andrew, Cailean swore and wiped his brow.

When Emma lied about Malcolm the drunken patron, Cailean could only admire her control and strength. She'd do nicely in Camlochlin.

Cailean didn't breathe when the baron turned icy on Bess. He didn't expect Winther to stab her. He quieted Alison and held her close as Bess's body hit the floor.

Cailean should have expected Emma to try to help. She took a step forward, her hands held out before her.

Cailean didn't know what she might do, or if the murdering bastard would try to kill her next.

Alison didn't have time to stop him. Before he had time to think or remember the words he'd spoken to her a few moments ago, he ran from the shadows and from Alison's side and flung his own dagger at the baron. His blade missed its target when John Burroughs, seeing what Cailean meant to do, leaped in front of his lord and took the dagger in the guts. His body slammed into the baron's, and both men went down.

Cailean swooped in and dragged his sword from its sheath. He raised it high and brought it down in a blow that would rid the land of a monster.

Another blade smashed into his, stopping its full descent. Cailean looked up from his hilt and into Sebastian Fletcher's eyes.

"Cailean, cease this now before you kill another one of my brothers. Although, I must admit, I'd like to kill him myself right now."

"What?" Cailean asked utterly confused while one of the men beneath him moved. "Yer brother?"

Something hit his head hard: the hilt of a sword, the handle of a pistol? He fell to the ground and felt his consciousness fade. He held on. He saw a figure standing over him; his face was blurry but his eyes weren't.

Oliver Winther leaned over him and may have smiled. "You just ended your own life and it's a true pity. You're courageous."

Cailean didn't remember anything after the man kicked him in the guts, except mayhap, Emma's scream.

"Don't kill him, my lord!"

Emma knew she was taking an enormous risk to reach

out her hand—covered in Bess's blood—and touch the baron's sleeve to stop him, especially since he'd just murdered Bess where she stood. But Emma would have done anything to stop him from killing Cailean.

"Spare him! I beg you," she pleaded.

"You beg for his life?" the baron asked her, stilling his hand against Cailean a third time. "Why? Who is he?"

She paused, not wanting to give his real name and not knowing what else to say.

"Cailean Fletcher." Sebastian spoke for her while he hurried to John's side.

Oh, she was so angry with him. He'd betrayed them all. He'd come to the brothel to get information about his brother's death. He'd gotten what he needed and then sent for his murderous brother. But he'd lied for her. Twice now. Why?

"He travels alone," Sebastian lied. "Oliver, John needs attention. Let Miss Grey have a look at him."

Oliver chuckled. "Bastian, Miss Grey is blind."

Emma didn't want to help John. She didn't want to practice her medicine on anyone who would likely turn on her later and burn her alive. But if she didn't help John, she couldn't help Cailean. "I may be able to do something," Emma offered, desperate. "Don't kill Mr. Fletcher and I will do what I can for your commander."

"You ask much of me," the baron said to her.

"I offer much in return," she replied. "Unless you want him to die."

He laughed and still didn't move to see about the man who'd saved his life. She didn't think he'd go for the deal.

"Come then." He finally stepped away from Cailean and held his arm out to her. She didn't want to take it. "Save John and save this Cailean Fletcher of yours."

With a sigh of relief, she accepted his offering and

took his arm. He was taller than she expected, with barely an ounce of fat on his arm. He led her to his commander in silence.

The instant he released her, she went to her knees and examined John Burroughs's wound. She'd rather be tending to Cailean. How bad were his injuries?

"Is Cailean awake?" she whispered to Sebastian.

"No."

She needed to get to him.

"How could you do this to us, Sebastian? I thought you a friend."

"I am," he assured her quietly while the baron made his way across the hall. "I didn't send for him, Emma. Someone else did."

"Who?" she asked. Who would betray them all like this?

"Harry Grey!" the baron called out. "Come out of the shadows. We have unfinished business to discuss!"

No. "No," Emma breathed. "Not my brother." She swiped a tear from her eye. "Not Harry."

"I'm sorry," Sebastian whispered.

She shook her head and rose to her feet. "Harry?" she called out. "Harry! Answer me!"

"Emmaline," her brother's shaky voice scratched across her ears. "I had to. He threatened to kill us all and burn the brothel if I didn't do as he said. If I didn't . . ."

John Burroughs groaned.

"Emma." Sebastian stood and leaned in to speak in her ear. "Will John recognize Cailean when he awakens?"

Oui, he would. Cailean would be the next to die in this hall. She had to put Harry's betrayal out of her mind and concentrate on keeping John asleep.

She reached for the vials of herbs she kept hidden in her skirts but the baron's cool voice stopped her.

"What do you think you're doing, Miss Grey?"

"Making certain he has less pain and sleeps through my ministrations."

"He doesn't need to sleep," Winther insisted. "He needs to be on a horse and ready to leave in—"

"Harry, you bastard." She couldn't contain her anger, her heartbreak. "You've always been a selfish son of a—"

"Your brother told me you are a lady, Miss Grey," Oliver Winther said. "Are you not?"

"Why?" she asked. "Does being a whore make one less of a woman? Someone easier to kill?"

"No, one is easy to kill when they attempt to use my brother for her own gain. You said yourself I shouldn't trust her."

"I didn't tell you to kill her," Emma retorted. "But feel free to do what you wish to Harry."

She refused to think of her brother ever again. She wouldn't shed another tear over him. But even as she vowed it, she knew it wasn't true.

Where was Alison? Emma wondered, pushing her brother from her thoughts. And Gunter and Brianne? She prayed they were together, somewhere outside waiting to warn Malcolm.

She did what she could for John, dressing his wound and stitching him up on the floor of Fortune's Smile. She fed him enough roots and herbs to make him sleep for a full twenty-four hours. After she saw to John, she went to Cailean. His temple was swollen and she prayed he didn't suffer any permanent damage. His pulse was strong and his flesh felt warm. He didn't wake up after another half hour, or when Oliver ordered Sebastian and the rest of his men to help John to a horse.

Sebastian pulled his brother out of earshot, even for Emma, and asked him what the plan was.

"We're taking Miss Grey and Mr. Fletcher with us."

"No, Oliver," Sebastian insisted. "We don't need—"

"I do," his brother interrupted. "She belongs to me now."

"What the hell does that mean?" Sebastian demanded.

"Her brother gave her to me in exchange for my leniency after Andrew died in his establishment."

"She's not a servant, Oliver."

"I know, but I need her to help me with something and am I not being more than merciful and understanding by allowing that Fletcher fellow to live?"

"What is it?" Sebastian demanded. "What do you need with her?"

"What it is, is none of your concern."

"No," Sebastian countered, just as menacingly, "what it should be is your greatest concern. For if you harm her in any way, I'll leave your presence forever. You will have no choice but to consider me dead because you will never see me alive again."

Oliver laughed. "Do you think that threat means anything to me at all?"

"Yes, I do," Sebastian said.

The brothers were quiet for a moment or two, with Oliver giving in first. "Fine. If it means that much to you, I will not touch her, take her to my bed, or harm her in any way. You have my word. But I won't let you stop me from keeping her. She is vital to the future of Newcastle. I need her help and if I need to kill everyone here to get it, I will."

"You don't have to," Emma said, coming up behind him. "I'll come with you and help you, my lord," she announced, silencing everyone. She wasn't about to let any more of her friends get hurt. "But first, you will tell me what I'm to help you with."

He moved closer to her and growled back at Gascon. But when he spoke to her, his voice was like a deep, melancholy sigh. "Very well, Miss Grey." His face dipped, as did his tone, low enough so no one else but she could hear him.

"I'm going blind I need you to help me see without my eyes."

Chapter Thirty-Five

$\mathcal{M}$alcolm hated having to drag a woman through the rain, on a horse, with barely any light to guide their way. This one didn't complain, but rather, kept him smiling the entire way. Her name was Leslie and he didn't find her at The Thieving Prince. The proprietor wouldn't let any of his girls go for anything less than robbing him. Hence the damn name of the place.

He'd had to travel leagues away, to a small brothel in South Hetton, to get Leslie.

She didn't put up any kind of resistance when she was informed that she was leaving Hudson House with him. If Fortune's Smile's patrons looked like him, she was happy to go.

"Ye're certain ye won't be staying there a bit longer?"

He shook his head and smiled. "I wish to go home."

"With Emmaline Grey, lucky gel."

They had to talk about something on the trek back, didn't they? He told Leslie about Emma and Gascon and everyone at the brothel.

"Why couldn't ye stop at Hudson House that night,

instead Fortune's Smile? Ah well," she said with a long, regretful sigh, "perhaps I too will meet my Prince Perfect there."

He laughed. "I'm no' perfect. Och nowhere near it."

"And humble too."

"Ye're good fer m' pride, Leslie."

"I could be good for more than that, my lord."

Leslie was quite bonny with stark black hair and soft blue eyes, sweet, humorous, but he wasn't the least bit interested. He'd been celibate, not disinterested. Emma was the reason. Ah, how good it was to finally understand the tales of love from bards like Finn Grant, his uncle. To know what had made the others give all for the women they loved.

"Here we are." He stopped his horse and turned to watch Leslie do the same. He'd paid handsomely for the horse, even though they all knew the old mare wasn't worth much.

Leslie dismounted without any help from him and looked up at the place where she now lived. The rain had finally stopped and the moon cast its pale light on the double row of windows. She saw something and stepped back.

Following her gaze, Malcolm saw the man's face at the window just before whoever he was moved out of vision.

"Why did ye bring me here? How could ye?"

"What?" Malcolm reached for her but she pulled away, looking afraid.

"Ye knew he was here and ye didn't tell me."

"Who is he? D'ye know him?" Was she mad? Is that why Will Burnet gave her up so easily?

"Oliver Winther. The Baron of—"

Malcolm's heart accelerated rapidly. No! She was

mistaken. A trick of the light. "That was Oliver Winther in the window?" he asked again to be sure.

"Aye, 'twas him fer certain."

He freed his sword in one hand and a pistol in the other. The terror rushing through his veins was almost paralyzing. Was the infamous madman inside with Emma? Cailean? Had he hurt them?

"Ye don't ferget when ye've slept with the devil."

Hell! It was Oliver Winther. He'd come and Malcolm wasn't here. "I didna' bring ye here to him," Malcolm vowed to her. "He's inside with…" He didn't finish. "I must save them. Take m' horse and go."

"Yer friends are likely already dead. Ye should come with—"

He left her there with his horse and hers, and disappeared around the house. She could have been wrong. It was dark, with only the light of the moon to capture a glimpse of the devil himself.

He came around to the kitchen door and tried to open it. Locked. Thankfully, his mother, Mairi MacGregor, had taught him how to pick locks.

The inside was quiet. Too quiet. It made the beats of his heart boom through his head like battle drums reaching a crescendo. There were no sounds of lovemaking coming from any of the rooms upstairs. No patrons. It was possible, but improbable. Where was Cailean? Harry? Gunter?

He moved through the kitchen and the dining hall cautiously, making certain there were no other Winthers hiding in the shadows.

He moved toward the parlor but his boot kicked something soft. The ground opened up and yanked at his stomach until he felt sick. He looked down at the body, his breath suspended by the terror that it was Emma.

Bess. He felt little relief in her death because anyone else could appear, just as cold, around any corner. He kneeled at her side and felt her skin. She'd been dead for a few hours now.

He didn't want to find the woman he loved or his brother dead. He didn't think he would recover from that.

But this was battle. No opponent would ever find him running from a fight. If he found his loved ones dead, he would do what needed to be done.

Emma's was the first room he checked. He found it empty, though deep down he'd suspected that condition.

Giving away his position never crossed his mind as her name erupted from his mouth.

"Emma!"

Before leaving her room, he peered around the entry to make sure the hall was clear of any enemies. It was, but Newcastle was here. Malcolm could only hope that the others escaped before the baron had arrived.

"Show yerself, coward!" Malcolm challenged. "Come meet the man who will end yer life."

Mary's door, three down, clicked open and Mary stepped out. Someone was behind her, leading her which way to go. Malcolm knew who it was before he spotted the flash of silver from the dagger aimed at her throat.

"Ye hide behind women, Newcastle?" He laughed. "I'd heard ye were fearless and ferocious. Against children, mayhap."

"I use women," the baron corrected. "Watch." He leaned down over Mary and traced the tip of his blade across her face, from ear to ear. "Tell me this man's name or else I will skin you alive, from that sumptuous inside, out."

"M' name's Malcolm Grant. Let her go."

"His name, woman!" He pressed his dagger closer to her flesh.

"Malcolm Grant!" Mary cried out.

Newcastle smiled and convinced Malcolm of what kind of soul he was dealing with.

"Strange," Newcastle snarled. "You don't seem like a drunk to me. Tell me, Mary, which of the girls is he here to see?"

The baron heard the click of Malcolm's pistol lock and looked up, away from Mary.

"Let her go or I'll move ye m'self and then kill ye."

The baron didn't appear to sound too worried. "You sound like one of those Highlanders, Mr. Grant," he said, holding Mary closer. "But that would mean my brother lied to me about everything."

What brother? What the hell was he talking about?

"Perhaps you have the courage to tell me the truth. Are you simply curious about Miss Grey's blindness? Or do your feelings run deeper?"

"What does Emma have to do with anything? Where is she? Where are the others?" he demanded.

"Harry Grey is asleep in his room, I suspect. Miss Grey is on her way to Newcastle where she will become my wife—"

Malcolm's smile was a promise of utter destruction. "She can't wed a corpse."

Newcastle grinned and continued. "And a young man she seems quite fond of—a Mr. Fletcher—"

"Sebastian Fletcher?" Malcolm breathed.

The baron gave him a pointed, curious look. "My brother, Sebastian *Winther*," he corrected. "*Cailean* Fletcher. As I was saying…"

Satan's scorched balls, he had Cailean too! Malcolm

would get them back if he had to kill every Winther in England—including Sebastian. Hell, Fletcher was the baron's brother. He'd been sent here to spy. It was all too much to take in. For now, he had to focus on Emma and Cailean.

"I'm goin' to kill ye," Malcolm promised him.

The baron smiled. It did nothing to soften his features but rather, it made him look even more dangerous. "Like you killed Andrew? Tell me, was it you and that Fletcher lad who did it?"

"I've killed many. Andrew Winther doesna' stand oot in m' head."

The baron's slow, sinuous smile was chilling. "I *will* find out."

"Unfortunately fer ye," Malcolm corrected, "ye'll be dead soon and there will be nothin' ye can do aboot it."

"We shall see." Newcastle pushed Mary forward and took off back into her room.

Malcolm caught her, made sure she wasn't hurt, and then disappeared into the room next.

The baron was gone. The shutters pushed open on the window proved his cowardice. Malcolm spread his gaze over the front yard but saw no movement. Rushing back out, he discovered from Mary that Gunter, Brianne, Alison, and some others had escaped. She didn't know where they were.

Malcolm swore on his dash down the stairs. He'd told Sebastian Winther that he killed Andrew. He told him about Skye. He was going to kill him. He had to. No enemy could ever know how to find Camlochlin. The MacGregor name was outlawed. There were none left on the mainland and sympathizers were hung along with their stubborn brothers at arms.

Malcolm had put his kin in danger. He had to fix it. But first he had to get Emma and Cailean back.

He left the brothel, listening to the sounds of the night. He'd find the baron here or on the way to Newcastle. It didn't matter. He had to get to him before the baron got to Emma and Cailean.

He thought about killing the Winther brothers. But something didn't sit right with him. If Sebastian was sent to spy, why didn't Oliver Winther know anything, like him and Cailean were brothers, for instance?

Movement to his left. He swung around and pointed his pistol into the gray, muted light of the moon. Until the clouds passed, he couldn't see a thing. He closed his eyes. The blood of ancient warriors flowed through his veins. When the elders made the lads and lasses of Camlochlin learn to fight blindfolded, none of them complained. Not if you wanted to live in a fight—and Highlanders liked to fight.

"Ye reveal yer fear of me, Winther," Malcolm whispered.

The baron's heavy breath made it easy to find his position. Malcolm lifted his blade and blocked a strike to his head. That one being the last to threaten his vitals, Malcolm overpowered him and delivered a blow to the face that sounded like his nose was cracked.

Malcolm prepared for the next round but Winther was gone.

"Is this yours?"

Malcolm turned to the voice and found the moon clear of clouds and spilling an ominous glow over the small meadow behind the brothel. For a moment, he saw no movement, but then he spotted her. A woman running toward him. Her hair was dark. Alison? No, darker.

Leslie.

He broke free of the shadows of the brothel and took off toward her. What the hell was she still doing here?

A shot rang out!

Leslie's body jerked, then began to go down. Behind her, the baron stood a few feet away, smoking pistol in hand.

No! Malcolm ran harder, his sword held over his head. He didn't stop when Newcastle held up another pistol and fired into the upper left side of Malcolm's chest. Pain lanced throughout his entire body and kicked him back... and almost down. He didn't know how, but he kept running. Emma and Cailean counted on him not to give up. Once they arrived at The Castle Keep it would be harder to save them.

Instead of stopping to check on Leslie like the baron expected, Malcolm kept going and leaped into the air. He brought his sword down with him as his knees hit the ground, slicing a clean twelve-inch deep line down the baron's face, chest, and belly.

Was it deep enough? How much time would it buy him? Hell, he thought, watching the baron rise up, strong enough to take a step toward him, unsteady or not. It wouldn't buy him much.

"You've impressed me, Grant," the baron said, holding his blade against Malcolm's throat while blood soaked the front of his clothes. "Most men don't. I'm surrounded by submission, fear, surrender, all of it, all the time. But there are a few who aren't afraid. You are one of them. No, you are more! You fought me in the dark! Will you teach me how to do that?"

"Winther." Malcolm pulled himself up. He wasn't sure how much damage he could inflict while losing so much blood. A little lower and the pistol ball would have gone through his heart. But it didn't. He was alive and he was planning on staying that way. "I want ye to understand this. I dinna' give a rat's unholy arse what ye're surrounded by, or who's afraid of ye. I'm not, and if ye weren't afraid of me, ye'd leave me alive to fight another day."

"I fear nothing," the baron confirmed.

"Prove it."

Chapter Thirty-Six

*Y*ou're going to have to speak to me sooner or later."

Emma kept her eyes straight ahead while Sebastian trotted his horse beside hers, leading her by her mare's reins. "Later, would be just fine," she said. "Never would be better."

"I lied to him for you," Sebastian reminded her, his voice too kind and sweet to belong to a Winther. "He has a terrible temper and could have hanged me."

"But he didn't hang you, Sebastian! He stayed behind at the brothel, demanding the attention of Mary and Jane. He will very likely meet up with Malcolm. What do you think Malcolm will do when he finds his brother and I have been taken to Newcastle?"

"It'll likely be bloodier than either of ye realize."

Emma spun around on her horse at the sound of Cailean's voice. He'd awakened, thank God. When they'd left Hebburn, he was tossed, unconscious, over a saddle, limp and lifeless. She was so happy to listen to him maneuver himself around until he straddled the saddle properly.

"Is Alison with us?" was his first question to her.

"No. She remained hidden, I'm assuming with Gunter and Brianne."

Relief flowed from the breath he exhaled.

"How do you feel?" she asked, waiting for him to lead his mount to her.

"No' too bad considerin' I canna' feel m' head or face."

She turned back to Sebastian and vowed that if he refused her she would never forgive him. "Perhaps we could stop somewhere? I could prepare something to ease Cailean's pain."

"Ah, the traitor rides with us," Cailean accused Sebastian. "I assume we're going to Newcastle then, prisoners of his mad brother."

"I warned you to hide, did I not?" Sebastian countered.

"Enough!" Emma held up her hands. "Cailean, do you truly want to fight someone who will likely punch you in the face?"

"I wouldn't fight him in his condition, Emma," Sebastian corrected her. "I'm not a barbarian." He sounded insulted, genuinely cut to the quick.

Though Malcolm filled her thoughts, Emma felt like smiling, just for a moment. "I'm relieved to hear that, Sebastian."

"Is an hour enough time?" he asked.

"No, but I won't refuse it."

They stopped at the next town they came to and got a room at an inn. Emma helped Cailean to a chair and turned to Sebastian. "I need opium preparations."

He laughed. "Where am I supposed to find a merchant who sells opium preparations?"

"Ask around," she told him. "You're a Winther. Push your weight around a little."

She was surprised when he did as she asked with nothing more than a muffled oath.

"Emma?"

She turned to Cailean's voice, then hurried to his side. His face needed to be cleaned and prepared for some bandaging.

"Why were ye smilin' at that traitor?"

"He's done everything in his power to protect us from his brother. I don't think he's a traitor. I think he's genuinely sorry that his brother found us."

"Then why does he no' let us go? His brother isna' here."

"Where will we go? You cannot protect me with your eyes half sealed shut. Even if we stay here at this inn, the instant anyone knows I'm blind and I have little protection…"

"All right, I understand," Cailean stopped her. "I can still fight."

"Of course you can," she assured him indulgently.

She cleaned his face and the wounds that covered it and told him everything that had happened since he was knocked out. She told him her fears that Malcolm had returned to the brothel and found the baron there.

"Malcolm will kill him and come to us, lass."

Oui, that was what was going to happen. He was correct. His brother knew him better than anyone else, didn't he?

She'd never touched Cailean's face before. She did now, liking his resemblance to Malcolm, though his forehead was higher, his eyes wider apart, and the deep, permanent dimple in his chin gave him a beautifully innocent face, while there was nothing innocent about his brother.

When she raised her hand to his cheek and felt him smiling, she pulled away.

Sebastian returned less than a quarter of an hour later with a small satchel and a little brown bottle. She didn't ask questions but set about working on the right mixture. While she prepared Cailean's painkiller, she listened to his conversation with Sebastian.

"Ye claim to want to help," Cailean was saying. "Is that why ye told yer brother that I was a Fletcher?"

"Yes, John told Oliver that two Highlanders traveling together killed Andrew. Two Highlander brothers were most likely traveling together. Do you agree?"

Cailean nodded. Sebastian was clever and did what he did to save them.

"Why?" she asked him.

"What?"

"Why do you protect them if you believe they killed your brother?"

"I don't know who killed Andrew. But it wasn't Malcolm."

"How do you know?" Cailean asked him.

"Because he claims to have shot my brother. But Andrew wasn't shot."

"How did he die then?" Cailean put to him. "Blade?"

"I can't say. It's the only way we'll know if we have the true killer."

"Then tell your brother that!" she demanded. "Tell him 'twasn't Malcolm and demand that he let us go!"

"And if it was Cailean who killed Andrew?"

"It doesn't stop you from helping him now, Sebastian. So I ask again, why?"

"I like them," he admitted.

"How can we trust ye?" Cailean asked.

Sebastian was quiet for a bit. Emma heard him shifting in his seat. "I will tell you both something that will get many killed if Oliver finds out. That's how you will know you can trust me."

"What is it?" Emma asked while she prepared Cailean's tea.

"Dunston."

"In Gateshead?" Cailean asked.

Sebastian nodded. He told them how the people of Dunston tried to help raise him and his brothers after their mother died and their father left them. "Oliver sent me there recently to quell a small uprising. He thinks I stopped it by killing the instigators."

"And did you?" Emma asked him quietly.

"No, I did not. My family lives in Dunston."

"Yer family?" Cailean asked him, taking his tea and sipping it. "There are Winthers in Dunston too?"

Sebastian shook his head. When he spoke again, his voice went softer, lower. "Fletchers. My true father, Samuel Fletcher. He was my mother's lover twenty-one years ago. I have two half brothers who are nothing like Oliver."

"Does the baron know?"

"No, Emma, he does not. I don't speak of them. Ever. If he knew..." He paused and drew out a long, worried sigh. "Hell, there are so many reasons he'd want them dead. And when Oliver wants you dead, you usually end up that way. He thinks I'm a savage like him. He takes pride in it. So there you are. I'm telling you this so you'll trust me. Sam Fletcher is a good man and he taught me to recognize other good people when I meet them. That's why I didn't kill Malcolm or Cailean when Bess told me they killed Andrew. Andrew wasn't a good man."

"Ye have m' word that I shall never tell... Whatever ye fed me is... quite amazing. The pain is gone and I feel rather good."

"Good enough to ride?" Sebastian asked from the doorway. He was eager to get back on the road.

She helped Cailean to his feet and waited until he was steady.

"I'm good enough to go," he murmured with a quirk of his mouth.

"I trust you, Sebastian." Emma stopped him at the door. "And I'm grateful to you for not..." Her eyes filled with tears. "Forgive me," she said quietly, head low. "I worry about Malcolm. My heart is so lost to him I fear I could not go on without him. If the baron has hurt him... if Malcolm is...and Harry, my own brother." She shook her head and squeezed her eyes shut to stop from crying.

Sebastian took her hand. "I'll do everything I can to protect all of you."

Would Sebastian keep his word? He'd come to the brothel as a spy for his deranged brother, who tried to kidnap her! He'd had them all fooled by being pleasant, seemingly honest, and very likable. But he hadn't told Oliver anything or Cailean would be dead now.

Which he was almost about to be again.

Cailean hadn't taken five steps through the inn, half his head bandaged and a smile on his face, when six men tried to rob him.

Sebastian decided to stop them and disappeared from her side. In an instant he was gone, leaving her with the sound of a scuffle, the clash of blades, and bodies hitting the floor.

She took Gascon by his scruffy neck and started toward Cailean to make certain he was all right.

"Stay there!" Sebastian called to her. "I'll come and get you."

She ignored him and let Gascon maneuver her around the bodies.

When she reached Cailean, he assured her he was untouched. "He had all six doun in half a breath fer each," he told her, verifying what she suspected. "Ye're fast," he said when Sebastian came near to escort them the rest of the way out.

"Oliver Winther is my brother. I learned early how to fight to stay alive."

They stepped out of the inn and Emma reached her hand out to Sebastian, stopping him. "I'm sorry for the loss of your brother, Andrew."

"You have my thanks." He lifted her hand from his arm and held it to his lips. "You're the only person who has said it, though I understand why others have not. And Emma?"

"Oui?"

"I'm sorry about Harry."

Chapter Thirty-Seven

*M*alcolm tried to open his eyes but his eyelids hurt like hell. He groaned and tried to turn over in his bed but the pain in his sides was too great.

His bed?

He was in the brothel? How did he get here? He opened his eyes and looked around. He was in Emma's room. A lass was crying. Emma! He spoke her name, not recognizing the gruff, weak voice meeting his ears. He tried to get out of bed, but the pain lanced through his body like a hundred swords. Someone pushed him back down gently.

"You mustn't try to get up." It was Alison's voice. Not Emma's.

Emma was taken.

"Your body isn't fully healed."

"Emma."

At the mention of her name, Alison began to cry again. "Oh, Malcolm. He took her. He took them both. Gunter wouldn't let me go to him. He held me still in the shadows while the baron ordered them to be taken away. They are likely dead by now! You've been so ill. I didn't know how to treat your broken bone—"

His rib. He remembered Oliver kicking him after he hit him over the head with…hell, he didn't know what the baron had struck him with. He was shot. He knew that much. And his face hurt.

"I tried to remember the things Emma had done for you and Cailean, but I don't think I did very well."

"Ye did just fine, lass," he reassured her.

"You've been in and out of delirium for almost four days and I—"

"What?" He fought a wave of pain and nausea to sit up. "Four days? Winther has had Emma and Cailean for four days?" Terror gripped him. No! He had to get up now! He had to get to Newcastle before he was too late. His stomach turned and twisted into a knot. Was it already too late?

"Where's Harry?" He squeezed his aching eyes when pain assailed him, but he sat up and moved his legs over the side of the bed. The more he moved the stronger he felt.

"He's exactly where he deserves to be. Secured to his bed," Alison told him. "'Twas him who betrayed his sister, Malcolm. Seems he made a deal with the devil after Andrew Winther was killed and gave up his sister to save his own arse." She wiped her nose with a small cloth and stared at him with clear, green eyes. "Gunter tied him to his bed. We didn't know what else to do with him."

Harry? Aye, it made sense! Harry pretended not to want his sister with Malcolm because he didn't believe Malcolm was good enough for her. But the baron was? Harry never gave a damn about Emma. The bastard! Malcolm would see to him. Made a deal with the devil, did he? Hell, he didn't know the devil. Yet.

"Oh, Malcolm. You're their only hope."

"I know," he told Alison, trying to sit up again. This time, he did it. Nothing was going to stop him. He knew he was the only one who could stop the baron. This time, he wouldn't get shot. "I'll get them back," he promised.

She nodded, going for the door. His voice stopped her. "There was a lass with me, yer replacement at the brothel..."

Alison pointed to Emma's bed. Leslie lay in it. She smiled at him when he looked at her.

"I'm glad to see that bastard didn't kill ye," she said when he swung his legs over the side of his bed and stood up.

"How are ye, lass?" He grimaced from the pain in his side.

"Well, he shot me too, but I think his hand was shaking. He got me in the leg. Alison tells me I need the healing hands of Emmaline Grey to relieve me of the pistol ball. So I'm waiting for her until you bring her back."

Malcolm smiled at her and she blushed.

"Gunter wants to help," Alison told him, reaching the door. "I'll get him."

"Alison." He stopped her again. "Where's m' plaid? I'm done with this English garb. Newcastle is about to face a Highlander."

Alone with Leslie, he let the enormity of what happened sink in. Either he or Cailean had caused Andrew Winther's death and these happenings were the effects of it. Bess was dead and buried. Leslie was shot. He felt his skin crawl at the thought of Emma, his wee angel—Nae. Emma was no delicate flower. He almost smiled wanting to imagine her feeding the baron some of her teas.

Gunter burst into the room with Alison, Brianne, and the rest of the girls.

"We all want to help."

"Have any of ye killed a man before?" Only Gunter raised his hand. "The rest of ye will help by remainin' here. Please," he said gently, "let m' head be filled with thoughts of only Emma and Cailean, not the rest of ye."

"You don't look well enough to fight that cold beast," Brianne offered, taking Gunter's hand. "Give us one more day to find some remedies you can bring with you."

"Nae, I'll be off in a moment's time. Gunter," he said as he turned to Emma's guard. Now he must ask Gunter to be the same for him. "Ye'll ride with me to Newcastle as m'—"

"What's this?" Alison asked, stepping forward. "You think I'm staying behind when that Winther bastard has Cailean?" She folded her arms over her long russet braid. "Whether you like it or not, I'm coming with you."

He didn't argue. There wasn't time.

Malcolm folded his plaid around his waist and secured it at his shoulder. This is who he was. A Highlander, ready for war no matter how bad he felt. It wasn't his body that pained him though.

He left his room and checked in on Leslie, who'd been moved. She was still in good spirits and he promised to return soon with Emma. He was leaving her in good hands with some of the other girls. He reached Harry's room next and stepped inside.

Harry looked like hell.

"Malcolm," he immediately began to beg. "You must believe me I didn't want to betray her. I—"

"Have ye eaten?"

Harry shook his head. "No! Gunter gave orders that I should only receive water."

Malcolm nodded. "Good. Ye deserve nothin' more fer betrayin' yer sister." Without another word, he turned and walked out, closing the door behind him, and ignored the calls and curses from inside.

He stepped outside and looked at the others waiting by their horses. He didn't need to ask anyone what it was he felt. Only love could make blood rush, heart palpitate, hands sweat, thoughts scatter, desires heighten. He was in love with Emma and it came bursting forth from every pore, over and over, in waves as he'd dressed. She restored him of any deficiencies he thought he had. She regarded him in a way no one else had ever bothered to try. And after seeing what lay deeper, she still fell in love with him.

"Ah…God." He sorrowed. If this was love, he hated it. He was afraid. No, he was terrified of losing her. He shook with the fear of it. The thought of Oliver Winther's hands on her made his guts knot up and his heart rage until he feared nothing would satisfy it but the death of every Winther who crossed his path. If the only way of saving her was to die for her, he'd gladly take a sword to the heart.

"We'll get them back."

What? Gunter. Malcolm turned to him and nodded. "Aye, we will. But we cannot just go riding into the castle. There's too many of them. We need a plan. We'll discuss it with the others before we continue on."

Gunter nodded. "You're a fortunate man to have won Miss Grey's affection."

"Aye," Malcolm agreed again, so much so that he wasn't sure if he could take another breath. "I am."

Och, to hell with love! Malcolm had the urge to run. His heart banged against his chest. He was better off when he couldn't feel, when there was only a dragon on his arse.

"That's why I canna' lose her, Gunter."

"You won't, Grant," the beefy guard promised. "We'll see to it."

"You've done what I ordered and brought them here," Oliver told his youngest brother while having his wounds tended to by his new healer.

He'd reached The Castle Keep an hour after Sebastian arrived and had Emma Grey brought to him at once. Mary from the brothel had told him all about how Emma had saved the two Highlanders who were wounded the same night as Andrew's death.

And there it was, so simple. He had the names of Andrew's killers and the bodies themselves, not dead, but alive! He was too curious to kill everyone outright. So, he waited, patient, as he was known to be. When playing with his prey.

"You saved me from having to kill you, Bastian," he said. "Don't think I didn't want to. I don't know this deceitful side of you. I don't think I appreciate it."

"I really don't care."

Oliver lifted his hand high, then brought his fist down on the table beside him. "You had better begin caring! I could have you flogged!" He looked at Emma Grey. "I could have—" He stopped when Sebastian held up his hand.

"All right," he drawled. "You win. I care."

Oliver threw back his head and laughed. "Of course, you do."

Sebastian smiled with him. It always struck him oddly how Oliver was a merciless monster to most but a thoughtful, sometimes kind brother to him. Could he use his brother's affection to get Emma and Cailean out of Newcastle safely?

"Now will you tell me who inflicted such a wound on you?"

"It's heinous, is it not?" Oliver looked down at his bare torso and shook his head at the long line of stitches traveling down to his hips. "A few inches lower and he would have sliced my cock clean off."

He glared at Emma when she pierced him too deep with her threaded needle.

"Who?"

"Malcolm Grant . . . Aw, hell, woman, have a care!" He cringed at her sharp little needle and cursed it for ruining his reveal to Sebastian. "I'm beginning to think you mean me harm, and Burroughs too. Why isn't he awake yet?"

"Infection," she told him.

"He's weak," the baron informed her, then returned his attention to his brother. "By the way, didn't you tell me you killed Grant outside the town?"

His smile remained on Sebastian while his brother shifted very slightly in his chair. "Imagine my shock when he showed up resurrected at the brothel with a pistol pointing at me."

"Did you kill him?"

"Ah! You do care about something!"

"Yes." Sebastian smirked. "I care about the people who live here, including you. The Grants are kin to the MacGregors."

"There are no MacGregors," Oliver said, watching Emma's reaction to their conversation. She stopped working on him and turned away. "The name is outlawed."

"The ones that Malcolm Grant lives with don't give a damn about laws, Oliver. I chose not to kill him and unleash a hoard of lawless Highlanders on Newcastle."

No. Not Sebastian. "You're afraid."

His dark brother hooked his mouth into a confident grin. "You know better than that. I won't waste time fearing the inevitable. If I live or die, it doesn't matter to me. But the days, and the way I spend them, do."

He didn't care about living or dying. It agitated Oliver to hear him speak like this. His brother was young and pleasing to the eye; rich, and skilled with every weapon, taught to fight at the end of his brothers' swords. The world lay open at his fingers and he didn't care if he lived to enjoy it? But this was what made Sebastian fearless in the face of a monster.

"The outlaws will come here, Oliver. They'll kill everyone. It will be a war and even if we win it, we will have lost much. It's rumored that they have the queen's favor thanks to her dear friend the Earl of Darlington's marriage to the MacGregor chief's daughter, Abigail. I think of Newcastle and wonder how quickly the queen would hand it over to her friend, the earl."

What a clever brother he had! Always thinking things through, so focused and determined. Sebastian was an intelligent hunter, not a savage one—unless he had to be. Pity, he didn't know he was the prey.

"Do you think he had anything to do with Andrew's murder? The truth now, brother. You know how I value it."

Sebastian didn't hesitate. "No, Oliver. Nothing at all."

"Did you kill him?"

Emma's heart paused after she asked but she continued wrapping her new patient in bandages. If he said yes, she would poison him tonight. She had the concoction already prepared.

"Sebastian already asked me that question before I dismissed him."

"And you didn't answer him."

"I'll answer you if you answer me first."

"No, you first," she insisted, much to his humor. "And I heard you tell Sebastian that you value the truth, so please show me you meant that and I'll be sure to give you the truth. Did you kill him?" she asked again when he nodded his agreement to her terms.

"No, I did not kill him. I could have; I tell myself every hour that I should have. I believe he killed Andrew."

"No," Emma insisted. "Sebastian said that Malcolm admitted to shooting him, but—"

"Andrew wasn't shot," he finished for Emma.

She nodded and tied off his bandage at his waist. "Why didn't you kill him if you thought he killed your brother?"

"Because he was an extraordinary fighter, striking damn good blows in the dark, with his eyes closed. Did you teach him that?"

"No." She was so filled with sheer relief that she felt light-headed and giddy. Malcolm wasn't dead. He lived. She believed the baron. She didn't know why, but she did.

"We fought and he challenged me not to kill him but let him live another day to fight me. I would have refused anyone else, but he wasn't at all afraid. He came at me like a lion, determined to reach me and succeeded in scarring me for life. I want to fight him again and give him the death he deserves, so I let him live."

Oh, she wanted to tell him not to come. What if the baron killed him? He said they would fight again.

"My turn now," the baron said. "Do you know why my brother answers my every question with deceit?"

Emma finished wrapping him and sat in the chair next

to him. How much could she tell him without him getting angry? She had to tell him the truth. It was the deal.

"I haven't spoken to him about it but I believe it's because you and he are so different. He believes that whatever he tells you, you will disagree with, whatever he asks you will be denied. He makes his own decisions based on what he believes. He may seem to take things lightly, but he wouldn't risk your wrath frivolously. He is passionate about things."

"Do you know what I'm passionate about, Miss Grey?"

She shook her head. What would she do if he tried to have his way with her? She'd have to kill him.

"I'm passionate about the truth. If Malcolm Grant didn't kill Andrew, then that leaves Cailean Fletcher. Did he kill my brother?"

He wanted the truth but he apparently knew more about what happened that fateful night than he let on. She told him what she knew.

"I don't know, my lord," she told him honestly. "I didn't see anything."

She also didn't see him grinning while he watched her leave.

Chapter Thirty-Eight

"What is it that makes you so gloomy?" the Baron of Newcastle asked Emma. "You've been pouting for a few days now."

"My lord, I don't pout."

"Scowl then," he corrected. "I haven't killed your Mr. Fletcher, even though my commander still sleeps."

"True, but Mr. Fletcher is a prisoner here, locked away in his room—"

"What would you have me do with him? He'll escape if I let him roam free. I spare him for you. You know I think he's responsible for Andrew's death. Some of my relatives will not be so merciful if they run into him. He is safest where he is."

She shrugged her shoulder and dressed one of the last herb-resistant spots along the twelve-inch-long wound running down the front of him. "Perhaps you're right."

"Of course I am. Now, tell me, what brings about these sour moods? Is it your hero, Malcolm Grant? Are you so melancholy because he hasn't yet arrived here to fight for you?"

"Unless you lied to me and killed him."

"That stings," he purred to her. "We had a bargain."

If Malcolm wasn't dead, then where was he?

"You said you didn't harm him. Was that true?"

"You know, my dear, Sebastian is quite fond of you, as am I. I think it might be time to forget about Grant and come to a Winther bed."

"No, thank you, my lord." She tied the small knot in his bandage and bit it off.

"Why not?" He pounded his fist on the table.

"Because I don't love you."

She listened to his frustration. He asked her almost every night to forget Malcolm and give him or, and in some instances "and," his brother a chance instead.

"Why don't you?" he demanded. "Have I not been kind and generous to you all these days you've been my prisoner?"

Goodness, like Narcissus, he was so focused on himself, he couldn't think in any other expressions but of "me." He was like a spoiled, selfish child always wanting his own way.

For some odd reason, he seemed to like Emma, though she'd done nothing to warrant it.

"What stops me from taking what I want?"

"Some sense of integrity in your bloodline, I suspect."

He laughed, a brisk, sharp sound. What made Oliver Winther so dangerous was how quickly his mood could change, and how drastically. Emma already knew the trick was to remain unfazed. Make him no more important than a fly on the wall.

"Is it integrity you're looking for?" he asked. "Sebastian is your man then. Insulting me is one thing; don't insult my brother by refusing him."

"I can't refuse him if he hasn't asked anything of me."

"He will. Soon," the baron informed her.

"I will not marry him."

"You'll do what I tell you if you want your friend, Mr. Fletcher, to live."

"You would have your brother bound in marriage to a woman who doesn't love him?"

He moved closer to her and gripped her upper arms. "There you go insulting him when I just told you not to."

"I cannot help how my heart feels."

"Then tell me instead what you're doing to mine."

"Oliver, let her go."

Emma was never so happy to hear any voice as she was to hear Sebastian's. Oliver listened to his youngest brother. True, it was usually after some bodily threats, but he made a point of trying to be more agreeable. When his efforts paid off and Sebastian fought less with him, he thanked Emma.

"I'm not going to marry Miss Grey and neither are you."

He picked fights with Oliver less often, not completely.

"You won't tell me who I can or cannot sleep with." The challenge in the baron's voice was unmistakable. "I please the eye, Bastian, and sooner or later, they all give in to the beast," he said with arrogance, besting his anger as he cupped his groin.

"Miss Grey will be no exception."

Emma turned away from him, rather than laugh directly in his face.

"They all want a bit of me when they see me naked," he continued his defense to his brother. "But if a bit is more than their weak souls can handle, and they run weeping from my room, that is no fault of mine."

"Mine," said Emma, without turning back to him, "is no weak soul."

"Yes, I know," he said, somehow making it sound like a promise.

Or a threat.

Emma didn't give a rat's flea-bitten arse how pleasing to the eye he was! She didn't care if he was feared from Newcastle to Durham. If he had even a smidgen of a thought of winning her favor—or not—and taking her to his bed, she needed to vanquish it now.

She turned, boldly, to face him. She wouldn't blush now. "I know what you want in your bed, my lord. You want a wildcat who will give as good as she gets. Well, that will never be me. I will lie as if dead the entire time, just to spite you."

She called softly to Gascon and began to leave the room.

"Tomorrow, Miss Grey," the baron called out, slowing her pace. "Show me how your dog leads you so you don't stumble."

Her blood ran cold. What if he wanted Gascon? What if he took him? Oh, she had too many reasons to poison him! It was beginning to look more and more like she was going to have to do it. Where was Malcolm? She prayed he wasn't dead. Why hadn't he come?

"There's no one like you, Emma."

She stopped and turned on her heel at the sound of Sebastian's voice.

"That's how you've won the hearts of men who didn't know they had them, Malcolm; my brother. You must stop being so different, at least, while you are here. You don't anger Oliver, not even when you threaten him. If I hadn't seen it with my own eyes, I'd never believe it. But it will continue to make him want you more."

She knew he was trying to protect her. He was correct

in what he said, and she certainly didn't want to make the baron want her more. But she didn't have a choice.

"I'm keeping Cailean and me alive, Sebastian. As long as he's interested, he'll keep me around until Malcolm gets here."

He remained quiet for a little while and then agreed. She was thankful that he didn't try to tell her Malcolm wasn't coming. "I'll do my best to be submissive and weepy."

"He won't believe it."

"He will if I tell him my emotions are due to my shattered heart that Malcolm has forgotten me."

"I don't believe that's true," he told her, kind to her to the end. He could have said anything to make Malcolm out to be the worst kind of coward.

"Neither do I," she told him. "That's why I'm going to kill your brother."

"I can't let you."

A whiff of something caught her attention and nagged at her memory.

"Then you'll have to kill me," she told him.

She knew the scent. It was familiar. It made her stomach bundle into a knot, and the sound of the baron's voice calling out to them from down the hall didn't help.

"Ah, Eleanor with my basil, finally!" The baron let out a gusty sigh. "And enough for a month! For this, your family will eat well this month!"

"Are the headaches worse?" Sebastian asked his brother.

Basil.

Her mouth went dry. No. No, it couldn't be.

"You chew basil to ease a headache," she said, trying to sound impressed rather than terrified. "How clever. Where did you learn to do it?"

"There was an apothecary living in the town for many years," the baron told her, taking up a place beside her, his breath fragranced with the sweet herb. "He first gave it to us in dried form for our tea. But Andrew discovered that chewing the raw leaves offered more comfort. His headaches were always worse and he ended up rubbing it in his scalp."

Emma felt sick. She had to be away from them.

"When the apothecary ran out of the herb, Andrew killed him."

She excused herself and turned to go but Sebastian followed her. "What is it?" he asked when they were far away from his brother.

"How did Andrew die, Sebastian?"

"I told you I can't—"

"He wasn't shot. You said so yourself. I suspect he wasn't stabbed either since it's not a strange enough way to die that only the killer would know."

"Emma." He tried to stop her but she kept going down the stairs. "Please tell me what is wrong?"

Cailean was kept in a room on the lowest landing, held captive but unharmed. She had to talk to him and tell him what she planned to do, since his life was at stake.

"Sebastian, you must let me in to Cailean's room. I have to speak with him." She finally stopped and wiped tears from her eyes.

"About what, Emma? What is it that upsets you so?"

She closed her eyes and said in a soft voice, "I think I killed Andrew."

Malcolm rode at the head of his small group. The sun rose three hours ago, at about the same time as they'd rested the horses. If they needed to get away fast, the horses couldn't be too tired to run. If they stopped now to rest the horses, they'd arrive in Newcastle in one hour. If he didn't stop, they'd likely end up stranded in Newcastle for a day or two while the horses recuperated. The longer he was there, the more fights he'd have, and he was in no condition for a lot of fighting. His side still hurt like hell and he felt like someone was sticking a hot poker in his chest from the pistol ball wound.

"What's the plan, Grant?" Gunter asked, riding at his flank and slowing with him.

"It hasn't changed," Malcolm replied. "Kill whoever is in the way. First though, give the horses a quarter of an hour before we head out again. They're goin' to need to be strong."

Gunter nodded and rode back to the others, leaving him alone with Alison.

Malcolm turned to her and noted her red, swollen eyes. She looked almost as bad as he did. He let her catch up.

"He's alive. I know it. I'll bring him back," he promised her again. "Cease yer cryin', lass. All will be well."

It had to be. He couldn't have met the woman who fought her way under his skin and emerged victorious with his heart as the prize, only to lose her.

No, he pled with God; he would rather lose himself. Let him fall into forever with Emmaline Grey in his arms. No one but her. Let him surrender all for her, *to* her, his most cherished wife. He was humbled, torn asunder at the power of what he felt for her. Let him tell her. She made him dig deeper than his veneer and find the man he could be, if he chose to.

He chose to.

"Cailean is with Emma," he reminded Alison, loving her as a sister because of how she loved his brother.

Cailean would do well marrying her. "If he's badly injured as ye say he appeared to be when they took him, there is no one I'd rather him be with then Emma."

Alison nodded. "I agree."

Finally a smile.

"She's more resilient than she looks."

"Aye." He smiled back. "She is."

"I . . . I just can't stop the thought of him . . ." Tears filled her eyes once again. When he tried to offer her words of encouragement, she held up her palm. "I haven't been at this business long, but I've been at it. I never thought a man like him would ever love me. I wasn't prepared."

He nodded his head. "Neither was I."

Chapter Thirty-Nine

$\mathcal{U}$nlike Gascon and Cailean, Emma didn't make a sound of protest when Sebastian pulled open Cailean's door and pushed her inside.

"What are ye doin', Sebastian?" Cailean asked him, coming to her aid should she need it. "What's goin' on?"

"Tell him," Sebastian told her as she fell against the wall after he shut the door.

That's what she came here to do. "I think I killed Andrew Winther," she told Malcolm's brother.

"No." He voice was firm, dancing at the edge with fear. "No, Emma. Pistol balls, daggers, chairs, arrow, every damn thing was flyin' that night. Ye were no' even there, but locked away in yer room."

"I was there, stranded in the middle of a violent fight, with no dog or no escort to see me back to my room. I carried no weapon in my hands but a wooden bowl of food for Gascon."

"I'm not hearing this."

Sebastian's voice echoed in her ears. She couldn't stop now. This was the only way to find out if she'd done it.

Was Andrew Winther killed by a blow to the head? Was she proving her innocence or her guilt to Sebastian? She needed to know.

"A man came at me, and not willing to die or worse, I smashed the bowl over his head. He fell at my feet."

"That means nothin', lass." Cailean came to her defense. "With nae dishonor to ye, ye dinna' know what Andrew even looked like."

"No," she agreed. "But I know what he smelled like. Basil. He was covered in the scent of it."

"Emma." Sebastian drew in a ragged breath. "It was you all this time."

"Winther, nae!" Cailean pulled her away. "'Twasn't her."

"It was," Sebastian lamented.

A wave of dizziness came over her. It was her. The blow to his head had killed him, not a pistol ball or knife. The baron was going to kill her. Perhaps Sebastian would do it. What would become of Gascon? Would Malcolm care?

"I cannot offer you anything but my deepest regret concerning your brother," she told him. "But he left me no other choice. I didn't know I killed him, nor did I know he was your brother."

She could hear him breathing. Short, shallow breaths. She'd killed his brother. He hated her and she didn't blame him.

"Sebastian, I'm—"

The door opened. The baron stood on the other side and looked in. "Bastian, we have company."

Emma's heart leaped. Malcolm? Had he come? Her joy and relief quickly turned into dread. What if the baron killed him? What if Sebastian told his brother who really killed Andrew? Her heart thrashed and her mouth grew dry. Panic engulfed her so swiftly she grasped Gascon to keep her on her feet.

"Stay here," Sebastian demanded quietly.

His brother had other plans. "No, she comes with us. Both of them do."

It was Malcolm! It had to be! He came for her! She wouldn't let him die. She followed the sound of the baron's voice and let Gascon lead her to him. It was better if she came along. She could help Malcolm.

"Is it Grant?" Sebastian voiced what Emma was anxious to know for certain.

"No, it's a man and a woman seeking directions to Sandgate Street. Come, Bastian, and tell me if they're from Fortune's Smile." He smiled at his brother and crooked his finger at him. "I smell rats."

A man and a woman? Who were they? Why would the baron suspect Malcolm because of their arrival? She was about to find out as she walked into the large castle front room, led by Gascon, with the Winther brothers in front and Cailean flanked at her side.

"As I told you, my lord."

It was Gunter! Emma calmed herself to keep from reacting. More than likely Malcolm was somewhere close. She thought she could hear Cailean's short, erratic breath, but it may have been her own. There was a plan under way and hers and Cailean's behavior could save or destroy it. She slowed the pace of her heart. If there was one thing Emma knew how to do, it was survive. Cailean's breath evened out with his next step. They wouldn't fail.

Sebastian slowed his steps and caused Gascon to stop her. "Stay here."

It wasn't her or Cailean she worried about.

"My wife, Brianne, and I arrived from Sunderland about an hour ago and soon realized we were lost."

Brianne. Breathe.

"What brings you from your safe home to Sandgate Street?" the baron asked Gunter.

"Pigs, my lord. I'm in need and was told of an excellent merchant here in Newcastle."

"Pigs." The baron turned the direction of his voice and laughed. "Is there anything you would like to ask, Sebastian?"

Emma stilled her shaking fingers but crossed her wrists behind her in case they moved again.

"Hmm, let me think." Sebastian moved away from her and toward the couple. When he reached them, he turned back to his brother.

Or had he turned even farther right, to her? It was hard to tell.

Was he about to give them all up because of her? She bit her tongue to stop the burn of tears from stinging her eyes.

"You dragged me away from what I was doing because these two are from Sunderland, or because of pigs?" Before the baron could reply, Sebastian called for someone named Roger to escort these nice folks to Sandgate Street, and then he went to his brother. "He isn't coming, Oliver. He felt the strength of your arm, and knowing you, the unabashed disregard you hold for body, mind, and spirit. And everyone who isn't you," he added, playfully.

"You know me well, brother." The baron laughed with him.

"Perhaps. Perhaps not, Oliver. I only know what I see."

"Then more's the pity that you didn't have Miss Grey teach you how to see without your eyes while you spent all that time with her in Hebburn."

Sebastian was silent. Emma had the feeling he was looking down the hall at her.

Then, "You're right about that, brother. I'd like to see what she sees. But regardless of all that, Grant doesn't ever want to face you again. Like your many other enemies, he wouldn't dare come against you a second time."

"He wouldn't live."

"Why would a fool deserve to live?"

The baron laughed. "This is one of the many reasons I favor you, Bastian. That streak of violence and malice comes from our mother. Sadly, you've also inherited her disloyalty."

Sebastian stopped. "What?"

"I know you betrayed me. I know it was Malcolm Grant and his brother, Cailean, who killed Andrew. I know they made Miss Grey tend to them until they were well. I know you met them and you knew they were brothers. You knew, and not only did you do nothing, you lied to me about them all this time, helping them just now by sending my best warrior, Roger, alone with the couple. You put your sword through my back, so now I must do the same to you."

"Nae," Cailean said, next to her. "Baron, dinna'—" He took off toward them.

Before Emma could think about what was happening between Sebastian and his brother, the foyer echoed with the sound of another rap on one of the front doors. The baron cursed through clenched teeth.

"Open it," he ordered one of the guards on Sebastian. "And if it's that couple again, kill them."

Emma wanted to shout and give warning to whoever was on the other side. She kept silent, her attention torn between the door and the direction of Sebastian.

The door succeeded in winning her attention when the

guard pulled it open and a booted foot kicked it the rest of the way, almost off its metal hinges.

Realizing what was going on, Cailean hurried her on her way down the hall to hide. She hated having to go, but she was no fool. She wouldn't last long enough to succumb to fatigue.

She would be reunited with Malcolm upon his victory.

Malcolm didn't see his brother escorting Emma down the hall. He knew, thanks to Gunter and Brianne, that she was here with Cailean. They were both safe and unharmed. This knowledge gave him renewed hope and vigor. He'd find her after he killed the baron. He hacked away with his sword, taking down two men, then another, as his eyes caught sight of Cailean dragging the younger, injured Winther down the hall and out of the way of the melee.

Gunter slashed his giant blade across two men at once. Cailean returned and attacked the baron, going at him with strength and passion, but the baron was ready for each strike.

Finally, after finishing his game, he grasped Cailean to him and brought the tip of his blade to Cailean's throat. "Grant!" he called to Malcolm, who was finishing the last of Winther's personal guardsmen. More were coming. "This is for killing my brother."

"No!" Emma's voice rang out from the shadows just before she appeared with Gascon, her hands covered in blood.

The sight of her filled Malcolm with both joy and dread. She was safely away! What was she doing running back into the fray? Running straight for Winther!

"He didn't kill Andrew," she cried out, staying his hand.

"Emma, nae!" Cailean yelled, but she continued.

"I killed Andrew!" she shouted, hurrying to them. "I can prove it! I hit him over the head with a wooden bowl. Spare Cailean, my lord! He did nothing!"

Malcolm, like everyone else still alive in the front hall, went quiet, stunned by Emma's confession. What? How? He remembered the man at her feet in the dining hall at Fortune's Smile the night Andrew was killed. Killed by a wooden bowl.

Winther didn't let Cailean go. He didn't kill him either. "You?" he asked her, stunned disbelief and fury vying for dominance over his features.

"I'm sorry, my lord," Emma cried. "But Sebastian... He still lives. He—"

"Sebastian betrayed me for you," he said softly, years of regret and weariness weighing down his voice. "I cannot say I blame him, Miss Grey." He grew quiet again when he heard the click of Malcolm's and Gunter's pistols, both aimed at him.

Silence resounded off the wall, and then Winther shoved Cailean toward Malcolm and ran. He disappeared down the hall and through a long corridor of shadows. Malcolm let him go and ran to Emma.

"My love, my love." He could say little else as he gathered her in his arms and kissed her face, her cheeks, her head, her lips. "We must hurry. More men are comin'. We must go."

"No!" She shook her head. "Not without Sebastian. Malcolm, he'll die here left alone. He didn't betray me to his brother."

Malcolm wasn't about to refuse her anything. He would have given her his life.

Cailean was eager to get to Alison, who was waiting,

hidden in the stable with Brianne and the others, but he led Malcolm to Sebastian first. Emma had wrapped his wound tightly to stop the bleeding. He was still conscious and when he saw Malcolm, he asked if Oliver still lived.

Reassured, he allowed Malcolm to help him to his feet and then under his arm to aid him with moving forward.

With Sebastian's feet just hitting the ground and the force in his command to the rest of Castle Keep's men, warning them not to attack, Malcolm and the others hurried toward the stable to gather the other and ready their horses.

They made it about halfway when Alison, seeing Cailean safe and sound, ran from the structure, ready to leap into his arms.

No one was prepared for the shot that rang out. They all startled in their skin and hit the ground. Malcolm shouted orders to Cailean and Gunter, but the former had fallen to his knees with Alison limp in his arms.

"M' love, och, m' love, please hold on."

Alison closed her eyes. "I'm sorry, Cailean," she whispered before she took her last breath.

Standing to his feet, despite the danger of getting shot next, Malcolm watched in horror as sweet Alison left them.

"Someone had to pay for Andrew, Grant!" The baron's voice called out from about fifty yards away. "The redhead started it all!"

Malcolm didn't reply but sprang forward and sprinted, sword drawn, to Winther.

Seeing such fury come at him, the baron tried to load his pistol in time, but finally gave up and threw it to the side. He unsheathed his sword just in time to slide and screech against Malcolm's.

They fought for a time, with Winther once again proving his skill, but this time, Malcolm bested his every move. He parried and jabbed, sliced and slashed at the man who killed Alison and Bess. Malcolm thought of their faces as he fought, and they gave him new strength, superior skill. The baron blocked many of his attacks but the edge of Malcolm's blade caught him about the face and body a few times, spilling his blood, making him weary. He heard a terrible sound behind him, like a growl rolling in thunder. He turned to see Cailean running toward them and managed to step aside just in time to avoid being cut in half by his brother's blade.

Oliver Winther wasn't so fortunate.

Chapter Forty

She'll sleep for a few hours," Emma told Malcolm when she stepped out of the room Sam Fletcher's wife, Constance, had prepared for Leslie. "The wound is closing nicely."

Malcolm drew her under his arm and kissed her head. "That's good news, m' love. And Sebastian?"

Young Fletcher had received a nasty wound from his brother's sword in the halls of Castle Keep. But happily, he too was on the mend.

"I dinna' think Cailean is comin' home with us," Malcolm told her. "He mentioned stayin' behind with Sebastian for a few months and then returnin' with him fer Hogmanay. So we can be on our way whenever ye wish."

"Tomorrow?" she offered.

He nodded and led her downstairs. It was a cool, clear night, good for walking.

They passed Constance Fletcher in her kitchen and waved. "We'll be back shortly, my lady," Malcolm let her know. Constance adored Malcolm and Emma adored Constance, but she wanted to go home.

"You'll have to tell him when we get back that we're leaving tomorrow."

They stepped into the brisk night air and he slipped his fingers through hers. "The nights in Camlochlin will be much colder than this."

She stopped and turned to him. "Do you still want me to go with you? So much has happened. I am a lot of trouble. I understand if you've changed your mind."

His finger softly pressed to her lips quieted her. "Changed m' mind? Lass." He pulled her into his embrace. "I dinna' want to live anywhere withoot ye. I wanted another chance to tell ye things and to show ye who ye have awakened in me. But now that I have ye here in m' arms, I want a lifetime not just days or even weeks. I want ye and ye alone at m' side and in m' bed. I love ye, Emma, with all of me, so much, that at times I dinna' like it."

She giggled softly and he kissed her laughter from her mouth.

"Marry me, lass. Grant me this and I'll build ye a house crafted the way ye like and a bed big enough for us to play in it."

"*Oui*," she kissed his mouth. "I grant it. I will marry you."

His lips were like hot brands or honey-coated cakes, enticing her beyond reason. He swept his tongue over hers in one possessive move and then ended their kiss with a series of short kisses.

"Thank you for coming for me," she whispered against him. She loved the way he breathed, the sound of him, the feel of him so tight and tense in her arms, her hands.

"I would have come sooner."

"I know."

"Bring me back to the house and take me to bed."

Malcolm promised he would, but first there was something he had to do.

He led her back to the house and went directly to Sam. "Are ye ordained?"

"Sixteen years now."

Malcolm turned to her. "D'ye want to do it now, lass?" The excitement and happiness in his voice wore off on her.

She nodded, beaming like a fool.

"Marry us," Malcolm said, returning to Sam.

Later, after Malcolm Grant vowed to love her and honor her until death, he took her down the road to an inn and carried her to bed. It was the first bed they'd been in together, and as he undressed her, he told her what she meant to him.

When she lay with him naked and blushing, he didn't say anything else but touched her, learning her with his fingers, as she taught him to do.

His callused hands felt exhilarating on her breasts, rough and yet tender. His hungry mouth made her toes curl and sparked a fire deep within her belly.

She was his wife. His wife! Oh, how had she done it?

"Ye're lookin' verra' triumphant, wife." He lay poised above her; his voice was light yet thick. "Are ye relishin' in yer victory?"

She laughed and coiled her arms around his neck. "What victory is that?"

"That ye tamed Malcolm Grant."

She smiled and then sighed with utter pleasure when he nestled his hot, hard body between her legs.

"*Oui*, 'tis sweet."

He kissed her and spread her legs wide with his, then whispered along her mouth. "And I vow to ye, m' one true love, 'tis goin' to get even sweeter."

Epilogue

"I think I found some Saint-John's-wort," Emma called out to the beautiful redhead a few feet away.

The redhead lifted something in her hands and held it against her chest. "Look what I found, Emma! An abandoned baby bird. Poor thing. I should bring it back to Skye."

"No, Mailie." Emma shook her head. "Your mother said no more animals, and 'tis still her house."

Mailie stopped and stared at her. "Emma, are ye ill?"

"No, why do you ask?"

"Because ye're speaking nonsense. Ye know I'm taking it. 'Twill die oot here on its own."

Emma smiled. Out of all the visitors from Camlochlin, Emma liked Mailie MacGregor best. Mailie's mother, Isobel, knew much about herbal medicine and she and Emma spent most of Emma's first month as Malcolm's wife teaching the other what they knew.

They remained in Camlochlin for a little over a month and then came here to Ravenglade three months ago. Emma loved Perth but everything about Skye had won her over, the bracing winds across the vale, the jagged mountain ranges, the seclusion, the quiet, and most of all, the Grants and the MacGregors.

She was happy that Malcolm's family visited Perth so often. There were plenty of rooms for everyone and they all kept her company during the day when she didn't see Malcolm at all.

He assured her that he was busy working on their home, building it for her. But he never let her visit. She'd been to his cousins' homes in Camlochlin, whimsical manor houses of different shapes and sizes, strewn across the vale. Some closer to the main castle than others.

Why was Malcolm building their home here on the mainland? She knew deep down that she didn't care where she lived—Camlochlin, Perth, or anywhere else as long as it was with him.

She touched her swollen belly, content to know that she carried her husband with her, even though she missed him terribly during the day.

She trusted his fidelity with every shred of her being, for no man could come home to her each night rock hard and hungry, if he was eating elsewhere.

No. Her man was hers. If she could only enjoy her husband at night, while he built her a home in the day, she would do it, happily.

Besides, living in a castle had its advantages. It kept her busy learning every hall, every curve, every room. It gave her an opportunity to spend time with Malcolm's entire family at one time or another. Someone always wanted to escort her, which gave Gascon more time to become sire to so many puppies.

She loved Malcolm's "kin," as he called them. Abby was so ambitious and inspiring, Emma began riding a horse on her own. She almost had one trained—a particular russet mare—to follow Gascon and trust that she wouldn't run them off a cliff.

"Pardon me, lasses."

His voice pulsed through her, moved her to step closer to him. "My love," she said, reaching a hand toward him. He caught it in his and brought it to his lips. "'Tis early in the day. I didn't expect you until much later."

"Come with me," he beckoned. "Excuse us, Mailie," he called out, then noticed his cousins' wives, Amelia, Sarah, and Janet, in the grass, lounging in the sun. He smiled. "Ladies." He didn't wait for a response but took Emma and lifted her into his saddle.

"Where are we going?" she asked when he mounted behind her.

He buried his face in her neck and reveled in the scent of her. "Home."

They rode away from Ravenglade and into the woodlands. Malcolm felt her inhaling deeply in front of him. Pine, oak, birch. The damp, leaf-carpeted ground beneath them. The birds overhead, the gnats in the shafts of pale late summer sunshine before them, squirrels chattering as they chased one another through the maze of branches above. Emma knew where they were.

"Malcolm," she said on an uneven breath. "Did you build me a house in the woods?"

"Aye," he affirmed, helping her out of the saddle. "I didna' know what Clementine's looked like so I just went with m' guts. This one is yers."

He walked her to it, leaving her at the front door of the home he built her, with some help from his kin, to explore and see what she thought.

She stepped away, hands before her, and stopped when she came to the door. He'd carved some of the wood, but his father had done all the intricate vine carvings. Malcolm could see all the delicate flowers worked into the wood, but Emma's fingers could see them better. She took in every inch, standing on her tiptoes to follow the length of a certain vine marked with butterflies Malcolm hadn't even noticed. She smiled the entire time, finally moving on to the outer walls made of boulders and mortar. She was careful not to trample the flowers growing around the house, touching them as she touched the walls. Her fingers danced over all of it, walking around the entire perimeter.

It wasn't overly massive but large enough to house the both of them and a few bairns.

She hadn't yet gone inside, but she stopped when she returned to the door. He saw her tears and moved to go to her. But she ran and leaped into his arms, capturing him in her arms and legs and careful of her wee belly.

"No matter what I say, 'twill never be enough to thank you." She ran her fingers over his face. "So come, carry me into our new home and take me to our bed." She quirked her mouth and tilted her face up to him. "Do we have a bed?"

He hefted her up higher on his waist and said hoarsely, eager to get her there and strip her before him. "Let's go find oot."

Sinfully sexy romance and
wild adventure continue in
Paula Quinn's new MacGregors:
Highland Heirs novel featuring
Malcolm's brother—Cailean
Grant!

Please see the next page for
a special preview.

*G*len Lyon Castle sat perched atop Carm Gorm, one of the four Munros surrounding the hamlet, so the ride down in the vale wasn't long. A crisp chill in the air produced puffs of white from the horses' noses as they descended the mountain. From here Cailean Grant could see a procession of lights moving in the darkness. Where were the people of the hamlet going? His cousin Patrick MacGregor was fighting for his life because of someone who lived in Invervar. Cailean was tired of waiting. He wanted recompense and was glad they were finally on their way to get it.

He thought of his family on the way down. He'd been thinking of them often lately. He'd left Camlochlin four months ago with Patrick. He hadn't seen anyone else from Camlochlin since. He missed them, but he couldn't go back. He wasn't ready, he thought while he and the others tied black kerchiefs around their faces and pulled up their hoods. He wasn't sure he would ever be.

When they reached the bottom of the glen, he looked around. There was nothing to see but darkness and only the small cluster of fires and lanterns to the west. He hadn't been here before, having arrived at Lyon's Ridge a se'nnight after the harvest. But he believed the people were in the fields.

The Black Riders proceeded with more caution entering the hamlet, unseen, like a plague on the midnight gales.

The first thing to rake across Cailean's ears was the laughter. It filled the air before voices, young and old, rose in song.

They were celebrating—Christmas most likely, Cailean suspected, surveying them from the shadows, ignoring their joy and looking for weapons. His gaze flicked over the inhabitants and settled on the lass from the market-place. Did she live here? Was she traveling back with the man who shot his cousin? The tall man standing beside her mayhap? Cailean wanted to reveal himself and question them. But before he could stop them, his eyes returned to the lass, her face tilted toward the moon-lit heavens, elation lighting her smile as she sang about the mountains and the King who made them all. Her joy was radiant, all-consuming. Crippling to his senses. He couldn't remember when he'd been so joyful.

He looked away from her.

Never again. Never again.

"Seth Menzie!" Duncan called out.

Duncan had told him about the leader of Invervar before they left. He had a daughter and a passion to defy the laird he'd sworn fealty to.

A few of the women gasped and cried when the Black Riders came closer to the fires and into view. Cailean looked around at the fear in their faces. He would make certain none of them were hurt as soon as they handed over the man who shot Patrick.

"Duncan Murdoch," the tall man called back, stepping forward. "Welcome to Invervar. I—"

"I don't need your welcome upon land owned by my father."

"Of course," Menzie agreed.

An old woman wearing a patch over one eye glared at them with it and stepped closer to Menzie.

Cailean's eyes returned to the lass who'd been singing moments ago. The joy in her expression was replaced with fear and anger while she too raked her eyes over them.

For a moment, Cailean felt ashamed and glad no one, including her, could see his face.

"I meant no disrespect," Menzie continued, sounding repentant but not looking away or lowering his gaze. "What can I do for you?"

"To begin," Duncan sneered from atop his mount, "you can tell me what you're celebrating tonight."

Cailean knew perfectly well what they were celebrating. The same thing his own kin were likely celebrating this sixth night. So what? Murdoch sure as hell didn't enforce the law on Christmas. They'd come here to find out who shot Patrick.

"The birth of our Lord," the leader stated, his feet firmly planted in the land he worked. "Christmas is a se'nnight away."

"Then you're breaking the law," Duncan advised him coolly.

"Who gives a damn aboot that, Murdoch?" Cailean kept his voice low so that only the closest men to him could hear.

Duncan ignored him.

"I see it in your eyes," he said, setting his merciless smile on the leader. "What you want to do to me is quite clear. You want to shoot me, just like you shot this man's relative today."

"I was in Kenmore," Menzie replied, his voice seemingly calm but an octave more raspy. "I shot no one." Suddenly he was looking at Cailean, his eyes piercing Cailean's skin, trying to see him beneath his hood. "I did not shoot your relative. You have my word to do all I can to find out who did."

Hell, he sounded sincere. Did Cailean believe him?

"I could drag you back to Lyon's Ridge and have you hanged."

"No!" Two women said at the same time.

"Or," Duncan went on, "you could offer me your daughter for the night."

"Duncan," Cailean warned. Avenging Patrick was one thing. He wouldn't stand around while a lass was being raped. "Ye're makin' a mockery of what happened today. He's agreed to help us."

"Leave her alone," the leader warned.

Cailean hated Duncan for laughing just then. He was a spoiled, spineless child. It made him dangerous.

"We don't want trouble with you," Menzie said, sounding no more compliant than he had before. "Leave us alone."

"Is that a threat, Menzie?" Duncan's agitated voice set his mount's nerve and the beast pranced in place, eager to run. Despite the leader's negative response, he motioned for Cutty to dismount and take hold of the leader.

There was a reason Cutty was given that name. The flash of his dagger glinted in the moonlight. He was going to kill Seth Menzie. It had nothing to do with Patrick, and everything to do with Duncan hating the leader's defiance.

"Wait!" Cailean leaped from his saddle and held out his hand to stop this. He realized now, possibly too late, that this was a bad idea. He didn't know if Seth Menzie was guilty or not. He didn't think he was. He had to stop Cutty. But the hired killer from the high north stepped behind the leader and swiped his hand across Menzie's throat.

It was so quick Cailean's mind didn't finish taking it in when Menzie began to fall. Menzie landed at the feet of his small family.

His daughter's soul-wrenching scream went up toward the heavens, then came down like an arrow straight into Cailean's chest. Whatever shards were left of his heart were completely shattered. Time slowed as he watched her fall to her knees and drag her father into her arms, where he drew his last breath.

Dear God! What had they done? Cailean couldn't breathe. He didn't want to see any more but he couldn't look away. He knew the pain that contorted her face and made her shriek from someplace so deep, even she seemed not to recognize it coming from her.

"No! No!" she cried, "Please, Papa, no!"

He did this to her. To Seth Menzie's family.

Time sped up again and he mounted his horse and moved to stand in front of Duncan, blocking his path to the family.

"Yer faither will hear of this!" Cailean promised. "Unless we leave them alone. Get oot now. We've done enough. We were wrong to come here."

Duncan gave in, realizing what he'd done. If these people didn't farm, his father would lose an enormous amount of coin at the marketplace. Edward Murdoch wouldn't be pleased, and Duncan didn't want to be the cause of that.

Heads would roll. Perhaps even his. He called to the men and immediately they turned for the mountain. Cailean lingered in the shadows watching the two women weeping over Menzie's body. The rest of the villagers either wept or tried to help. Nobody could.

Fall in Love with Forever Romance

A BAD BOY
FOR CHRISTMAS
by Jessica Lemmon

Connor McClain knows what he wants, but getting Faith Garrett into his arms this holiday is going to require more than mistletoe...

SNOWBOUND
AT CHRISTMAS
by Debbie Mason

Grayson Alexander never thought being snowbound in Christmas, Colorado, for the holiday would get so hot. But between working with sexy, tough Cat O'Connor and keeping his real reason for being there under wraps, he's definitely feeling the heat. And if there's one thing they'll learn as they bring out the mistletoe, it's that in this town, true love is always in season...

Fall in Love with Forever Romance

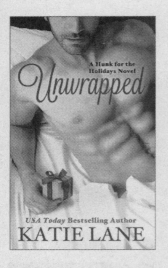

UNWRAPPED
by Katie Lane

Contractor Patrick McPherson is deeply committed to his bachelor lifestyle. But as the Christmas season approaches, he still can't quite forget his curvalicious one-night stand. Then Jacqueline shows up unexpectedly, and all holiday hell breaks loose. Because this year, Patrick is getting the biggest Christmas surprise of his life...

PLAYING DIRTY
by Tiffany Snow

In the second book in Tiffany Snow's Risky Business series, Sage Reece must choose between bad-boy detective Dean Ryker and sexy power-player Parker Anderson. Caught between a mobster out for revenge and two men who were once best friends, Sage must play to win—even if it means getting dirty...

Fall in Love with Forever Romance

THE TAMING OF MALCOLM GRANT
by Paula Quinn

The beautiful and blind Emmaline Grey risks everything to nurse the mysterious Malcolm Grant back to health. But can she heal his broken heart too? Fans of Lynsay Sands, Karen Hawkins, and Monica McCarty will love the next book in Paula Quinn's sinfully sexy Scottish Highlander series.